BENEATH
THE
SURFACE

J. E. Mullane

By: J. E. Mullane

White Dog Publishing

Beneath the Surface
by J. E. Mullane

Published in the United States by White Dog Publishing,
New York.

ISBN: Softcover 978-1-7334455-0-4
Ebook 978-1-7334455-1-1

1. Serial killer—Mystery & detective—Fiction.
2. Murders—Fiction. 3. New Jersey—Fiction.
4. Racial strife—Fiction. 5. 1960s—Fiction.
6. Vietnam War—Fiction. 7. Mutilations—Fiction.

Printed in the United States of America

For Manon
whose love and support make all things possible.

At the sound of the approaching car Rosaria stepped out of the street light's halo, into the shadows. She hurried off the still-baking sidewalk and onto the weed and gravel-strewn path leading to the water. Sliding her purse off her shoulder, she dropped it in the dirt and crouched, waiting for the sound of the car to pass.

Using the existing light she bent, searching through her purse, sweat sliding off her nose and wrists into the bag. After a moment she gave up and squinted into the gloom before stepping onto the dark, weed-choked path that led to the bay. She almost tip-toed down the path toward the sound of the lapping water. Thinking of the day, Rosaria couldn't help but smile, spent with her two favorite men, Marcus, the love of her life, and Alfonso, the sweetest little brother on earth. At Roseland, riding the rollercoaster, Rosaria on one side, Marcus on the other, and Alfonso sandwiched between them, arms raised high, screaming as they dropped, dropped, until they were swept up and away again. She wished the day could have lasted forever. But all too soon she came face to face with Mama. Rosaria's pulling Alonso from school for the outing had made Mama mad. The two of them spending the day with Marcus had made her furious.

Most of her anger was aimed dead on at Marcus. If only she'd give him a chance…but that would never happen. Rosaria's father had stayed in the picture just long enough to see her born before he left. It took Mama about eight years to trust another man, then bang and adios! He left about six months before Alfonso arrived. Ever since, to Mama, the opposite sex was close to toxic and simply not to be trusted.

But Marcus was Rosaria's lifeline. She would be lost without him. If he ever got drafted into that damn war she'd steal a car and drive him all the way to Canada. They could live together there, safe and away from Mama. Rosaria had no idea if they had any Puerto Ricans up in Canada, if not, she and Marcus could start making some!

The thought made her smile, but it quickly faded. Thoughts of the war brought memories of the boys from her class at Hoffman High, boys that got sent over there and never made it back. R.J., Luis, and Benny. They got killed so fast! It seemed one month they were messing around in the school cafeteria and then, before you could blink, their parents were getting a knock on the door. Christ. Every night on the news it's 'this number of good guys dead, but it's okay because we killed this bigger number of bad guys'. Rosaria hated Walter Cronkite's voice. To her, his was the voice of death. And there was no way in hell that voice would ever be including Marcus in its roll call.

Rosaria reached the water's edge and headed north toward a small jetty that stretched into the bay toward the muted lights of Staten Island. Again she rummaged in her bag, this time finding what she wanted, more by sense of touch than anything else. Plus, something extra.

"Yes!" She snatched the transistor radio out, unwound the white ear plug from the radio and pushed it into her ear. Radio reception was always best down by the water with nothing obstructing the airwaves between her and the city, but even here the oppressive heaviness of the air made it difficult to pick up a clear signal on her transistor. The radio had been a present from Marcus, and it was her most prized possession. Marcus knew how much she loved her music and needed to escape for a little while each day on the notes that flowed into her head. She clicked on the power dial and turned it up loud. It took a minute to find WABC. The tuning dial must have slipped off the station while being jostled in her bag. Ooh, the Beatles.

Rosaria stepped around a large clump of seaweed, bright shiny green by day, now dull gray in the murky night. Her toe caught on a barely visible beer can half buried in the sand causing her to stumble and the dial to again slip off the station. Thumbing it back, she heard the final 'Yeah, yeah, yeahs' of "She Loves You". Damn.

What was that? She turned to look over her shoulder and nearly pulled out the earpiece. She quickly faced forward again and tightened the plug in her ear before twisting her whole body to check behind her. Pretty dark, but nothing there.

At the water she sat on a large stone block at the base of the jetty. Rosaria closed her eyes, nearly oblivious to all around as she swayed to Mick Jagger singing "Ruby Tuesday". That reminded her of the little bonus she'd found in her purse, a cherry-red push-up popsicle. Liquid, of course, she'd forgotten she tossed one in her purse before putting the rest of the box in the freezer. She just loved the super-sweet popsicle juice.

Rosaria set the radio on the rock next to her, careful not to pull the plug from her ear. She fished out the plastic-sealed popsicle from her purse and tried to gently tear one end open with her teeth. She immediately felt a stream of warm juice run down her chin and…shit. She pulled the leaking plastic from her mouth, wiped her chin, and inspected the damage. A large red stain was blossoming almost dead center on her pale yellow halter top, the one that looked so good against her dark skin.

She'd definitely have to soak it when she got home, especially since it was Marcus's favorite. She wanted to keep him happy now that they were, well...you'd have to say living together, right? It had just started today, but it was the truth, they were. Rosaria was dizzy with happiness. It all felt so adult. She wished Marcus felt the same. He said he did, it was his idea after all, but there had been a little hesitation. She'd seen it, she was sure. I guess I'll just have to make him the happiest, most satisfied guy in Pendale, she thought, and smiled.

Rosaria sucked the remaining juice from the plastic before tossing it away. She licked her fingers and thought about the beautiful day. Ah, neat! "Downtown" by that English girl with the flower name, Tulip or Petunia. You can go...Downtown, da da da da dum...Downtown.

Over the strands of the music she heard a rock skitter nearby. Ugh, those nasty rats! Down here at the water they were everywhere, like the litter. People could be such pigs.

Her golden shoulders had just begun to move again with the music when Rosaria felt the sky collide with her head, sending her crashing to the ground. Gravel, dirt, and shards of broken glass bit the skin of her forearms. Her dark hair hanging on either side of her face, like curtains, obscured her vision. Sweat and blood flowed from her hairline into her eyes, stinging and blinding her even more. The coarse ground seemed to fade in and out before her. She saw the heel of her left hand pressing down on a used condom and her brain registered disgust just as a blow to the back of her head sent her elbows from beneath her and drove her chin into a half buried stone. The impact forced her bottom front teeth up and through her lower lip, simultaneously breaking her jaw.

Rosaria fell onto her side gasping, and peered up at her assailant through sweat, blood, and caked filth now sticking to her face. It was this movement that dislodged the plug from her ear. Still attached to the transistor, it dropped in front of Rosaria, its tinny melody a backdrop to the final seconds of her life.

Rosaria saw her attacker's arm rise and her last thought in life was not of her love Marcus, nor of her mother, but of her brother, Alfonso, and his cries of delight as the roller coaster lifted them high into the sky.

The killer's arm rose and fell again and again. The strangled exhalations almost in sync with the muffled tolling of a buoy in the gloomy bay, its slow, flashing beacon marking the distant darkness. There was a quiet lapping of the tide against the jagged rocks of the breakwater. A dislodged stone gave away the presence of a rat disturbed from its rocky lair.

The killer gasped over the wet, muted sound of Rosaria's broken skull being pummeled, again and again.

Far beyond the buoy came the sound of a boat's engine. A single fishing boat returning very late from a day's catch in the Atlantic. Too far to be seen from the shore, even with its running lights on, the sound traveling a great distance over the dark, rolling waves of the bay. It seemed to break through to the attacker.

The killer stopped, looked down at the carnage wrought, and then to the bloody club in hand. The murderer moaned, dropped the club, and knelt on the gravelly shore.

Gasps beginning to subside, the murderer began at last to take some notice of the surroundings. The thick, dark, heavy night air had hidden the violent act from all others. Not that there would be much in the way of bystanders on this deserted stretch of waterfront at this time of night. The humid air seemed to swallow any sounds of the attack, those made by the victim as well as the killer's, and the thick smell of decay and rotting fish was an assurance that this piece of shoreline would offer any privacy necessary. No, the dead, bloated bodies of fish along the polluted waterline, together with the decaying shells of horseshoe crabs every dozen yards or so, were certain to keep away the curious.

In the baking sun of the afternoon the dead marine life would be roiling with hot white maggots beneath the screams of hungry, diving gulls, but not now. Not in the lonely darkness of night. Now, just two vague forms occupied the rocky beach. One on its knees, the other a flattened mass on the ground. The only sounds were of the water against the shore, the tolling buoy in the distance, and the now controlled breathing of the killer. The rat hid quietly.

The killer grunted, picked up the club, stood over the body, and then laughed. Grasping the left wrist of the corpse, the killer leaned away and slowly dragged the dead weight over the baked earth of the waterfront to a place of concealment where still more work was to be done, the most important work of all. Left behind was a bloody wake among the fish-smelling, seaweed-stained stones.

A short while later, the hungry rat carefully followed that wake, as would others, while from the waterline at the jetty, the barely audible, swampy voice of John Fogerty sang to his beloved Suzie Q.

❖ 2 ❖

Eddie walked, swinging his stick in wide arcs, eyes scanning the ground before him. Swish, swish, swish, the Z of Zorro hung in the air, leaving his mark on all who did him wrong. Like the TV guy, on his horse, and dressed all in black.

Eddie pushed over a rotten piece of driftwood. Nope, nothing there.

He was on the lookout for snapping turtles. Last weekend Tommy Gilcrest caught one that was at least a foot long. He carried it back from the marsh, its mouth clamped onto a stick over his shoulder, like a hobo carrying his bindle. Once its mouth bit on the stick you could swing it around like a baseball bat and it still hung on. That's why you better not let one grab your finger because if it did, brother, that'd be all she wrote, Tommy'd said. You'd be picking your nose with your knuckle.

Eddie wished he could've seen the turtle himself. Problem was, Eddie had been called inside for bed. His bedtime was *so* early. And the other kids sure let him know it. Most days he even missed the Mr. Softee truck. There was nothing worse than hearing the ice cream truck from your open bedroom window and knowing your buddies were all lining up for Fudgsicles and Nutty Buddies.

Too bad Eddie'd missed the turtle, but it ran away later that night.

"It ran away?" Eddie asked. "I didn't know turtles could run."

"Well, this one did," Tommy replied. "It was so big it could."

Eddie tried to get a picture in his head. "They never let go of the stick once they clamp down, right?"

"Well, yeah."

"If it still had the stick wouldn't it be really hard for it to walk? Wouldn't it be dragging along the ground, making it go in a kind of circle or something?"

"Um, no, it was a real strong turtle."

"Wow," Eddie said trying to envision a turtle loping along the ground, a three foot stick jutting out the side of its mouth like a giant stogie. "Did it maybe walk backwards and drag the stick along the ground?"

"Don't be a retard, turtles don't walk backwards. You ever see a snapper walk backwards?"

"I guess not," Eddie said. Truth was, he'd never seen a snapper at all, walking forwards, backwards, or sideways.

"Too bad you missed it. Mommy had to put you to bed. You'll probably never see one like it again, ever."

"Yeah," Eddie said. How could he have missed this once in a lifetime event?

But now Eddie was out to find a giant snapper of his own. He poked and pushed away pieces of trash and empty bottles and cans. Once he saw something furry scurry out of one of the cans, but it moved too fast and he barely caught it in the corner of his eye. There sure wasn't much in the way of turtles around.

Eddie sighed, it wasn't the adventure he'd thought it would be. He stepped over a spray of shattered glass and around dried up crab shells, steadily working his way toward the water. His arm was getting tired. Where were the stupid snappers?

He thwacked his stick in the late afternoon heat, working his way to the pebbly area near the shoreline. Ten more minutes and then back home for supper. Mom got really ticked when

Eddie kept them waiting for meals, and Eddie had forgotten the watch he'd gotten as a First Communion gift from his grandma two years ago, so he had no idea of the exact time. He could tell by the sun though, it was starting to get on toward dinner. But it was still pretty hot. It sure was causing all the dead fish and crabs to stink. Eddie couldn't remember the waterfront ever smelling so bad. He pulled the bottom of his tee shirt up to cover his mouth and nose and headed toward where the shore met the tufts of crabgrass. Up ahead to his right he could see the old concrete beach bunker.

Constructed over twenty years ago during World War II, it used to house a huge gun aimed out into the bay ready to blast away at any German subs that came to attack New Jersey. But not even Hitler was dumb enough to try to take Jersey on its home turf. Still, the bunker had been ready, just in case. The gun long since dismantled and carted away to some armory, the bunker itself served as a shelter for beachcombers during bad weather or in recent years, yet another spot for teens to hang out, drink, and well...you know.

Eddie had been inside the bunker once. It had been cooler in there, out of the sun. He thought he'd step inside now, but the smell seemed to get worse as he got closer to it. Gagging, he turned away and gulped to keep his stomach down. He was ready to call it quits when he heard something from inside. It was a kind of ticking or clicking noise. He stood absolutely still. There was no pattern to it like a ticking watch, it was more like hearing little twigs breaking or pebbles tumbling against each other. Eddie took a step toward the entrance and the noises stopped. He waited, holding his breath to hear better, as well as to avoid the smell, and the clicking began again. His sense of curiosity overwhelming his sense of smell, he squinted into the darkness of the bunker and tentatively stepped through the entry.

Eddie couldn't see a thing. Darkness aside, it was as though the stench of the bunker hit him in the face, obliterating all other senses. Even the scraping and clicking sounds ceased to exist for a moment. The smell seemed to enter his body at every opening and pore. He could taste it; he could feel it in his ears and hair. It got into his eyes. But even with this assault on his entire body he moved forward, something within him needing to know the cause of the noise.

With his shirt still over his mouth and nose, the smell entering his belly button, he stepped forward again, now totally engulfed by the interior shadows. He squinted and then blinked into the darkness.

The coarse concrete blocks were covered with over two decades of graffiti, salt, and pollution. He saw a candy bar wrapper (Clarke Bar-his favorite), also a pile of rusted beer cans with two triangular holes poked in opposite sides of each can's top.

In the far right corner of the bunker he saw something move in the darkness. Something was stirring on a small mound of earth there. He inched forward and realized it was not a rise in the ground. It seemed to be a bag of trash or bundle of rags. Moving closer he saw stained denim and a solitary leather sandal. Something snapped beneath his foot. Startled, he looked down and saw his sneaker atop a thin piece of driftwood, its salt-stained gray color just visible in the gloom.

A sharp crackling brought his attention to the bundle before him. Its surface seemed to be shifting back and forth as he strained to see. It wasn't until Eddie was able to make out a shiny claw silhouetted against the gray concrete that he realized what he was seeing and hearing.

There was quite a banquet in progress. Scores of land crabs were crawling over the mound. It was their continuous motion Eddie first saw in the dimness. Their claws tore at the meal and at one another. They tumbled over themselves, their shells scraping against small stones on the ground, as well as each other. One crab emerged from beneath a tangle of dark hair. Added to this was an occasional ripping sound as a rat tore a shred from the feast. They too were present.

Eddie stumbled backwards into the daylight, his shirt still pressed up over his mouth and nose. Blinded by the sudden brightness, Eddie fell to his knees and vomited. Most of it caught in his shirt and splashed back against his face before he realized what was happening. His mind, though, barely registered this. It was on that bleached piece of driftwood he'd stepped on in the bunker. The driftwood that was wearing a wristwatch and was being gnawed on by…. Eddie puked again, this time pulling his shirt away. As tears streamed down his face he thought, at least now I can tell Tommy I saw a snapper. A big one.

⤎ 3 ⤏

ather Josh Ryan leaned back, eyes closed, in the darkness of
the confessional in St. Margaret's Catholic Church. As the
adolescent droned on behind the sliding screened window
to his right, the priest's mind wandered as it had so often of
late, and he thought again about the sacrament of penance in
which he was now supposedly playing such an important role.
Divine forgiveness from a just and loving deity? Or absolute
bullshit giving the penitent an excuse to go forth and sin
again? He sighed.

Either way he sure could use a cigarette. He snuck a peek
at his watch. Christ. Forty-five more minutes. I'm certainly
paying for my sins, Ryan thought.

"Ah, Father?" the young voice on the far side of the screen
asked.

"Um, yes, my son, is there more you wish to confess?"

"No, well, maybe…I guess…it's just…you know, sometimes,
um…"

"Yes, my son?"

"I ah, think about some girls at school and well…I kind of
play with, ah…"

Father Ryan sighed. Not a week went by…. "You know it's
wrong to treat what God the Father has given you like some
sort of plaything, don't you?" asked Father Ryan.

"Yeah," came the meek answer.

"Your body is not a toy, it houses your soul, that which is valued most by the Lord. What do you think God would say if he chose to speak to you about what you are doing?"

There was silence as the boy envisioned a discussion with God about the evils of jerking off. "I guess he'd tell me to keep my hands off my thing, huh Father?"

"I guess he would," said Father Ryan, rolling his eyes in the darkness wondering for the ten thousandth time at the banality of it all. "Now, for your penance say ten Our Fathers and ten Hail Marys. Go and sin no more."

"Thanks, Father."

Father Ryan heard the boy rise from his knees on the other side of the screen. Just as he was about to turn to listen to the confession behind the screen to his left, he heard a frantic whisper, "Father!" from the boy and the sound of the kneeler being depressed again.

"Yes, my son?" the priest asked, genuinely curious.

"What if I got to pee?"

"I don't understand."

"What if I got to pee? Can I touch my thing if I got to pee? Will God get sore if I fish it out of my pants to pee?"

"Ah, I see."

"I mean, I got to grab it to aim, right? Oh, Jeez, God don't want me to pee sitting down like a girl, does he?"

"No, that's–"

"Sometimes walking home from school I got to go so bad I take a leak under the Union Street Bridge. How can I do that if God wants me to pee sitting? No way I can just drop my pants and squat there with my butt hanging out. Oh, Father, I'll have an accident in my pants and my old man will beat the crap out of me."

"Listen to me. God has no problem with you touching yourself when you need to urinate," Father Ryan shook his head again in the darkness.

"Thanks, Father." Pause. "Um, Father? If I have to, I can always come here again, right? I mean, if no matter how hard I try to not touch myself and I accidentally do it, I can come and get forgiven again, right?"

"Yes, confession is always here and God will always forgive a sinner who truly desires forgiveness."

"Great, thanks again, Father," relief in his voice. "See ya."

Hearing the boy rise again, Father Ryan said, "Son, don't forget your penance."

"Huh? Oh yeah, bye, Father."

The priest sighed, wishing for a smoke. He turned to his left, slid the screen, and leaned to listen.

The thirty-year-old Josh Ryan had been the junior priest at Saint Margaret's in Pendale, New Jersey for just a few years. It wasn't his first parish placement. That had been an inner city church in Trenton, St. Lucy's. A tough place for a new priest to begin no thanks to the senior priest who ruled his parish with an old testament, iron-fisted vehemence. Father Alfred had taken just one look at Ryan and knew there was no way in heaven or hell the young priest would ever make a home at St. Lucy's. And he made sure of it. Ryan was removed by the bishop and reassigned to St. Margaret's inside of a year.

Ryan often wondered what exactly Father Alfred had said to get him reassigned so quickly. He'd heard the word 'distractions' mentioned on several occasions. Apparently his presence at several Civil Rights and anti-Vietnam rallies had been noted and frowned upon.

Jesus, thought Ryan, if that's the case then Father Alfred, the bishop–they could both go to hell. He never felt so alive, so sure of himself, as when he was marching arm in arm with all those other young people, in fervent support of a single cause. The stimulation of the camaraderie generated from these beliefs moved him even more than his faith in his vows. What he had never stated aloud was the extent to which he began to question that faith. Whether Father Alfred saw this in him was moot. Not long after, Father Ryan found himself at Saint Margaret's.

After the initial humiliation, Father Ryan found some contentment. The senior priest, Father Dwayne, was about a hundred and twenty years old and decades ago he had discovered if he simply looked on, kept his nose out of things, and left subordinates and church volunteers on their own, then the middle-class, Irish-Polish neighborhood parish ran pretty well without his having to do too much. The church itself may have been a bit shabby, it never would have cut the mustard with Father Alfred in Trenton, but that was fine with this congregation. They didn't put on airs and distrusted those who did. They were working class and that's what they expected to see reflected in their church. The choir's robes worn by one generation were fine for the next generation and possibly the next. A green lawn beside the church? Hell, the majority of parishioners didn't even have lawns. Crabgrass? Who cares? The Church didn't exist to be in Better Homes and Gardens. It was where you went to pray, get baptized, receive communion, confirmation, confession, get married and eulogized at. A lawn? Please. Furnace a bit balky? When the joint's packed with sinners, no one notices. Besides, the chill is nothing compared to those drafty churches back in the old country. Grandma said you could practically see your breath in there year round. And remember, boyo, the Lord doesn't want you to get too comfortable. You need to remember we were put here on earth to suffer for Eve's sin of tricking Adam to take a bite of the apple. The house of God isn't meant to be cushy.

No, the parishioners of Saint Margaret's wanted to see themselves in their church. They wanted to see their history. A little worn, a bit frayed around the edges, a stain here and there. That slightly darker patch on the blue carpet just in front of the altar where Eileen Sakolish threw up during first communion rehearsal back in '58. The jagged chunk taken out of the bottom granite step in front of the church. A reminder of Sean O'Neil piloting the town's only snowplow while dead drunk during a rare blizzard in 1963. Sean got married on those very steps a year later to Mary Wisnewski.

Yes, St. Margaret's was the sum of its people.

Father Dwayne had presided over these people and the major events in their lives for the majority of his priestly tenure, and by the time Father Ryan arrived, he was tired. All Father Dwayne asked was he be allowed to preach the later Sunday mass, he felt he had earned the right to sleep in, and say Christmas and Easter services. Father Ryan could handle the rest.

After initially believing that he'd landed in the urban equivalent of Hooterville, Ryan found himself settling into the parish and life around it. He particularly enjoyed working with the youth choir and a Young Christian Men for God group he'd initiated. He made a conscious effort to avoid the endless chaos of the evening news and just immerse himself in his job. He even tried to avoid the radio, but found too much temptation there. Like Adam, he thought, I just can't resist. The Beatles, The Supremes, Cream, those evil Rolling Stones. Ah, at least one could pray for salvation from it all, Father Ryan thought, with a grin. I am, after all, simply a sinner like everybody else.

He walked through the side entrance toward the center communion rail, near where Eileen Sakolish made her mark almost a decade ago. He genuflected and strode through the door off the altar into the sacristy. Opening the scarred closet door he checked the condition of the priests' robes and the altar boy's surplices. He decided they were fine for the time being and in no need of laundering. A quick glance at the level in the bottle of sacramental wine told him he would need to have a stern talk with the altar boys soon. He was inventorying the sealed packets of communion wafers when he heard sirens and glanced out the narrow leaded window at the black and white police car screaming down the street in the direction of the waterfront. He said a quick prayer and returned to the counting and the communion packets, softly singing about how he can't get no satisfaction, without realizing he was making a sound.

❖ 4 ❖

Vern Wilson had lived on Augusta Street his entire life.
Except for basic training and the months he'd been overseas,
he'd never spent more than a night away from home. He
remembered sitting in the front room as a kid listening to the
big Philco. The Shadow, Suspense, Gunsmoke, barely able to
wait until he got old enough to get his first gun. Watch out all
you bad guys, Vern's coming and he's going to shoot your asses
off. As the 50s progressed Vern cared less and less about getting
the bad guys. In fact, the bad guys started to look pretty damn
cool. He saw them at the Palace Theater downtown, roaring
into some one-horse town on their motorcycles, raising hell,
kicking ass, and taking whatever the hell they pleased. That
usually included some sexy, big-titted blonde perched on the
seat behind the gang leader as they peeled out of town leaving a
wake of destruction and frustrated grownups wondering what
was the matter with those damn kids.

Vern looked around the living room. In the old radio's
place stood a portable black and white TV sitting on a bent
aluminum stand that leaned precariously to one side. Tin foil
wrapped around the rabbit ears to pick up a clearer signal never
seemed to work for shit. Faded rose petal wallpaper that had
adorned the walls forever hung in water-stained strips due
to faulty upstairs plumbing. The discolored ceiling bulged

downward as well, under the weight of years of ignored leaks. The worn linoleum floor was littered with newspapers, empty beer cans, cigarette butts and the remnants of last night's supper. And several suppers prior to that.

Nora don't do a damn thing around here, he thought. Place looks like hell. I give her a roof to live under and she pisses all over it.

He scuffed into the kitchen to see what there was to eat. Stupid bitch probably didn't leave him anything for lunch. Man, it was hot. Sweat rolled down his temples. Vern squinted into the refrigerator then closed his eyes, letting the cool hit him in the bare chest. He had no idea how long he stood before the open door. It wasn't until a sharp shiver shook him that he opened his eyes and was aware his torso was covered in goose bumps.

Hell. Everything in the fridge was now covered in condensation. Nothing worth eating anyway. He poked at a plate of dried meat loaf leftovers and some hot dogs going green. Fuck it. He grabbed a beer and slammed the door shut. He yanked open a drawer searching for the can opener. Where the hell did she put it now? He opened and slammed close drawers in growing anger until he found a screwdriver in one of them. Vern stabbed the top of the beer can twice and threw the screwdriver back in the gaping drawer. Beer foamed over his hand and down his forearm to his elbow as he sucked it into his mouth through the small punctures. He held the cool can to his brow to quell some of the fire there.

Goddamn, it's like being back in the jungle, he thought. Except it wasn't, and Vern knew it. There were no bugs the size of your fist trying to suck you dry, no razor sharp palm leaves slicing you open, your sweat sliding into the wound and stinging like nothing you've ever felt before, no commanders in your face screaming at you for fucking up, no gooks slipping through the trees quiet as death, either.

That quiet was the worst.

He could handle sounds of the gunfire, explosions, that nigger-music they all played over there, even the screaming platoon leaders. But that quiet, Jesus. That was the sound death made right before it grabbed you by the balls. And it had grabbed a lot of them. It seemed Vern's platoon shrank almost daily. Whenever he found a guy that wasn't a complete asshole, someone he could see eye to eye with, the guy got himself blown up or shot. He got to feel like he was a target on a shooting range sitting in the bull's eye while all the guys in the circles around him got picked off. The shooters getting closer and closer to Vern at the center. He kept it all together for as long as he could, but in the end, it all flew apart.

He was on night watch and it was so fucking hot. Usually it cooled off when the sun set, not that you could ever see the horizon with so many damn trees everywhere, but not that night. If anything, it seemed to get hotter. Standing at the perimeter of the camp he peered into the trees. It was black. You couldn't see nothing. And it was still, not a single palm rustled. But that meant zilch, because fucking Charlie could float through the jungle like smoke. No, it was most dangerous when it was quiet.

Vern stared hard at the darkness, not daring to blink. Frozen, he stared for what felt like hours, knowing the bastards were there, just beyond the outer range of his vision, just waiting for him to relax for a second, for him to turn his head away, to blink. Vern wouldn't allow that. He would be vigilant, alert, ready.

He'd been screaming for what seemed like days when they finally broke through to him. His rifle, now empty, hugged to his chest, three platoon members on him, pinning him to the ground, his sergeant leaning over him from above punching him in the face, screaming his name.

"Wilson! Wilson! You asshole, what the fuck did you do?"

As Vern's head cleared, he looked up at the crazed eyes of the sergeant. Sweat poured off the man, dripping onto Vern's frantic face beneath him. He tried to blink it away and shook his head. "What, what?"

"You goddamn fuckup, what did you do? What the hell's the matter with you?" Tears joined the sweat rolling down the sergeant's frenzied face. "You fucking fragged Washington!"

"What? No! They were here! I heard them! They got around us somehow. They're so fucking quiet! They got around us, but I heard them. I caught one trying to sneak behind me. I got him, and I'll get the rest! I'll get them, Sarge!"

Vern looked into the horrified and disgusted faces of the men around him. As the sergeant rolled off him, Vern saw the body of Washington, his eyes staring blindly into the night sky, a bloody cavity where his chest used to be. Vern hadn't had much to do with Washington, the black soldier preferring to be with his own kind. What Vern did remember was Washington grinning to his buddies, talking about those lovely Supremes and that yummy little Diana Ross. How when he got back stateside he was going to head out to Mo'town on some 'Supreme business'. Not now. Not ever.

Not long after that Vern was hospitalized and eventually discharged, then shipped home. No longer considered stable enough to inhabit the least stable place on the damn planet. Back to Augusta Street, two mandatory visits a week to the VA for psychiatric treatment, twice daily medication, and his veteran's benefits which stated he wasn't fit to hold a job either. Shit.

Where the hell was Nora? He was starving. No wonder, she worked in the kitchen at the children's hospital and everyone knew hospital food was the worst. Vern wondered how he was able to choke down any of the crap she fixed. He allowed his lazy little sister to live here at a low-ass rent and all she had to do was a little cooking and cleaning. Christ, the fridge was empty and the place looked like a dump. He drained the can and threw it into the corner behind the overstuffed easy chair his old man had sat in for so many years before his lard-filled heart exploded. The empty can clanged against its many mates there.

Talk about eating, that guy could put away a platter of pork chops and a mixing bowl of fries while killing a six pack at dinner. The old man wouldn't have stood for anything less than meat and potatoes six nights a week, with a fish fry on Friday. Maybe, if it was summer, a big dish of ice cream on the porch afterwards. Yeah, that was eating. But Dad was gone now and so was Mom. She went soon after he did. Lung cancer, could you believe it? Women don't die from lung cancer. They're saying now that smoking can cause it. Christ, pretty soon there won't be anything left to enjoy. Mom sure loved her Camels, two, three packs a day. Maybe there was something to this cancer stuff.

Now it was just him and Nora. At least the house was all paid for. Somehow, after thirty-five years at the shitty job driving the town street sweeper, Dad had made enough to pay it off while keeping himself in chops and beer. About the only decent thing he ever did for Vern was leave the house in his name, not in Nora's or even Mom's. Women have no heads for business he told Vern one night on the porch while polishing off a post-dinner six pack and listening to the Dodgers on the portable radio. It's a man's responsibility, he said, before belching, leaning back in his aging porch chair and swearing how the fucking spics and niggers were ruining the national pastime.

Time for another beer. Vern walked back to the kitchen, dug out the screwdriver, stabbed twice and headed back to the living room licking the foam from his hand. He grabbed his smokes from the coffee table and kicked open the screen door leading to the front porch. Maybe there was a breeze outside.

He sat, gulped some more beer, and fired up a smoke. Screw the cancer. He scowled into the street, immobile, until from the east, down by the waterworks, he heard the sound of sirens. He stared in that direction, thankful for the sound.

⤞ 5 ⤝

Minna Copper dragged a large bag of wood chips from the detached garage toward the front of her house. She planned to cover the exposed areas of the flower bed under her salon window. She always referred to it as her salon. In reality it was an expanded front porch which her late husband, Arnie, had enclosed and added heating to back in 1940.

That had been such a lovely time. Life in Pendale was just fine. The pace was leisurely, prices were low (or so they seemed in hindsight), people were friendly, crime was almost nonexistent. The Young people were polite and the coloreds and Spanish knew they weren't wanted here. Arnie managed Green's Haberdashery downtown while Minna stayed home and hoped to raise a family. Children hadn't worked out for them, however God obviously had other plans for Minna and Arnie.

Minna had always cut Arnie's hair and the hair of her friends and family, so it shouldn't have been such a shock when one cold January day in 1940 Arnie said, "Min, how about I do some handiwork on the porch and make you a little place where you can open up a beauty shop? It'll keep you out of trouble and off the streets," he added with a grin.

She knew he wanted to keep her from obsessing over the fact they could never have children of their own. Arnie was such a caring man, his love for her was truly boundless. They had briefly discussed adoption, but really, it could never be like actually having a family of your own. And you never knew what those children's real parents were like. They said the apple never fell far from the tree and Minna believed it.

No, a career, a career in business, Minna thought with a giggle, that's what the Lord must have in store for her. The rest of that winter and spring was taken up with choosing wallpaper, searching for second hand hair dryers, a sink, buying plumbing fixtures, and working on a list of clientele. At first, when Minna's friends and family heard she was going into business they were pleased for her. Then the realization hit that they would now be paying for what was once free, and they became less than enthusiastic. A happy medium was reached when Minna promised them discount service because they were, after all, the impetus for her starting up the business. Also, a free manicure or haircut for every new customer they steered her way. So, despite the disappointment of not being able to have children, life went on for the Cooper's, and barring a few bumps in the road, it went well for many years.

I shouldn't complain, thought Minna, as she shoveled woodchips from the bag into the flowerbed. My life has been a blessing. True, she didn't do the business she did after the war and then in the fifties, but that was by choice. It wasn't so easy being on your feet for hours once you passed the half century mark. No, it was easier just handling one or two old customers a day. That way if there were inquiries from people she'd rather not have to deal with, she could simply smile and say that she wasn't taking new customers. And it was no lie.

She looked up at the gold leaf letters painted on the window and thought it might be time for a cleaning. It had been so hot this spring the dust and grime from the street was just everywhere. She would see if she could get the neighbor boy,

Eddie, to do her windows. He was a bit small, but he'd done them last fall and hadn't done a bad job. It was so hard now finding young people willing to do a little work, even with the promise of pay. They were too busy getting drunk or smoking drugs or listening to that awful noise they called music. It hadn't been like that before, no sir. Then there was music you could dance to, not throw fits to. You could understand the words, and there were orchestras, too. Thank goodness New Jersey's Frank Sinatra was still singing. *That* was music. Minna picked up the empty wood chip bag, shovel and gardening gloves and walked around the side of the house humming in agreement with Sinatra; those old days certainly had been very good years.

✣ 6 ✣

Will and Lynn McConnell walked softly down the stairs after tucking in their only son. Will had insisted on giving Eddie a mashed up sleeping tablet dissolved in a glass of warm milk. After a short, frantic drive to the Pendale Police Station, they found their son uncommunicative, sitting in a pale gray interview room strewn with coffee mugs, his face covered in tears and dried vomit. Lynn ran to her son and clutched him to her chest. She demanded of the officer sitting in the room accompanying Eddie, "Is he sick? What did you do to him?"

"No, ma'am, he was like this when we picked him up. He didn't throw up here or in the squad car," answered the officer, his young face was covered in acne, a name tag stated, 'MacDougall'.

"Why didn't you clean him up? You just let him sit like this covered in his own vomit?"

"Um, we thought we better call you first thing." Officer MacDougall's face blushed, his acne becoming almost purple. "We asked him about what happened and why he was down there by the water and then we called you right-"

"You questioned my son without us here?" snapped Lynn. "You questioned my son about some...dead person he was unfortunate enough to discover, while he's sick, probably in shock? You did this while he was alone, without his parents present? What kind of man are you? Did you at least call for a doctor?"

"Er...well...," stammered MacDougall, his acne becoming even more pronounced, "The coroner's on his way, but the body's dead alright. Can't be any doubt about that."

"Not for the corpse, you idiot, for my son!" shouted Lynn.

"Lynn, please, this isn't helping Eddie," said Will. "Officer," he glared at MacDougall, "please call Dr. Silverman, our pediatrician, he's listed in the book, and explain to him exactly what happened, and ask if he could drive over to help. And maybe then you'd be kind enough to tell us, this boy's parents, exactly what happened?"

MacDougall hurried out of the room looking as though someone had shoved a sharp stick up his butt. Will turned to Lynn and Eddie, his son's eyes staring across her arm at the bare, gray wall.

"Hey, big guy," Will said softly, stroking Eddie's hair, "Quite a day, huh?"

Eddie nodded mutely, eyes not leaving the wall.

"Feel like talking about it?" His eyes met his wife's over Eddie's head.

"Not really," Eddie whispered.

"Well, when you do, Mom and I are right here with you to hear it all, okay, Bud?"

"Yeah," Eddie turned his face to Lynn's shoulder and began to quake silently. Will motioned to Lynn he was leaving the room.

Will strode out of the room. He followed the sound of a voice which seemed to be speaking on the phone. He entered what appeared to be a squad room. Four desks, each with its own black telephone. A small table next to each desk, on which sat a typewriter. Several of the desks had blotters, corners of which were jammed with various bits of paper, notes and in one case a stained menu from a pizza shop the McConnell's often frequented. MacDougall sat at the far desk, near the pebbled glass window that read 'Pendale Police Department' in reverse and backward. Now that the sun was lower in the west, the Venetian blinds were louvered open. An oscillating fan mounted on the wall above the doorway through which Will had just entered stirred the humid air. With each pass of the fan a corner of the menu on the desk rose and fell. The officer's eye caught Will's and he said into the receiver, "Yes, that's right doctor. He's here and he's okay. Just looks like he lost his lunch, that's all." He listened. "Oh, yes, right. Absolutely. I understand. Well, we'll be waiting. Yes, okay. Bye." He hung up the phone and turned to Will. "That was Dr. Silverman. He said he'd be right out after he finishes with his current patient. Said to keep the boy quiet and warm. Give him a drink of water, maybe. Shouldn't be too hard keeping him warm in this weather, huh?" he said attempting a smile.

"I didn't know you had a medical degree as well as your police training, officer," Will said.

"What? No, I'm just a policeman, a cop, you know. I don't mind being called a cop, it's a lot better than what some of those kids are calling us. Can you believe it? Where's the respect?" MacDougall asked, his smile still uncertain.

"I asked that because you seem to have no problem diagnosing my son as 'okay' despite the fact he apparently stumbled over a rotting corpse. An event I'm certain, though I don't have your medical expertise, would plunge most people into shock. As for 'where's the respect?' respect is something that's usually earned. Now how about making an attempt at showing my family some by telling me what the hell happened to my son!"

"Yessir, alright," MacDougall said quickly, reaching to the surface of his desk for a sweaty pocket spiral notebook. He fumbled through the first half dozen pages or so before finding what he was looking for. "At exactly 5:40, the station received a call from Mr. Joseph Alenciwitz, of 4222 Bridge Street. It seems your son, ah..."

"Eddie."

"Yes, Edward McConnell," he emphasized the first name, "stumbled to his front door saying something about a dead person. By that time he'd already soiled his shirt." He added quickly, "It didn't happen here." He continued, "Mr. Alenciwitz is a retired fisherman who is familiar with the waterfront. He proceeded to the location your son described. It was the abandoned World War II bunker that used to house–"

"I know the bunker, officer," Will interrupted, "You don't need to give me a history briefing."

"You asked for the details Mr. McConnell, I'm simply–"

"Just go on!"

Looking back to his notebook Officer MacDougall continued, "Anyway, as Mr. Alenciwitz neared the bunker he was struck by a strong smell. Being a retired fisherman, he knew it wasn't just rotten fish. Also, he's a veteran, he fought in France. He immediately recognized the smell for what it was. He returned to his home with your son, phoned us, and waited. When we arrived at the scene we proceeded to the bunker and discovered the body. It appeared to have been in that location for–"

"Where was my son at the time?"

"He was with us, safe, he showed us where–"

"You took him back there? You took a nine-year-old boy who just received the shock of a lifetime back to where that shock occurred?"

Blushing again, Officer MacDougall said, "We needed him to point out exactly–"

"You *know* where the bunker is! Every person over the age of five in this town knows where the damn bunker is! You didn't have to take him back there. What kind of fool are you, officer? Are you *trying* to lose your badge? Does this department *want* a lawsuit brought against it?"

"Mr. McConnell," the officer stammered, "that's no way to speak to me. We did what we felt was necessary and handled it as best we could," MacDougall said, turning redder still. "Now," he said gathering himself, "We'll need to speak more with Edward after Dr. Silverman is through with him."

"You're through speaking with him today. If you want to talk with him more, you'll speak with either me or my wife," Will turned to leave the room and return to his family. He looked back in disgust, "How long has he been with you? Half an hour? An hour? And you didn't even clean his face."

Dr. Silverman gave Eddie a brief examination at the police station. The doctor told Will and Lynn to get him home to bed and keep an eye on him. If there were problems during the night, phone his service. He gently cupped Eddie's now-clean face between his large, gentle hands and assured him he'd been exceedingly brave and now was the time to get his strength back. If Eddie had trouble dropping off to sleep, don't be afraid to give him something to make him drowsy, maybe warm milk.

"Now," he said with determination, "I'm going to give that officer a piece of my mind. That's no way to handle a child in distress. The idiot." He nodded to Will and Lynn and left in search of the unfortunate Officer MacDougall.

Lynn was sitting at the edge of the sofa when Will came downstairs from checking on Eddie. "Sound asleep," he said. "Dead to the world."

"God, Will, don't say that," Lynn grimaced.

"Sorry, wasn't thinking, anyway, he's sleeping and it doesn't look as though he's having any bad dreams."

"Thank God for that. Can you believe this, Will? Can you believe something like this could happen to our little boy? I mean, this isn't New York or some other big city, this is Pendale. How could this happen here?"

"Hon, we don't know what *did* happen. For all we know, the heat gave some poor beachcomber a heart attack at the old bunker and they were unlucky enough not to be discovered right away."

"Until our poor Eddie found them."

"Yeah, until Eddie found them. What was he doing down at the waterfront alone? That's not some new hangout for him and his friends, is it?"

"No, when I put him to bed he told me he was looking for snapping turtles because Tommy Gilcrest told him he'd caught a big one a while ago. Will, I don't like that boy. His drunken parents are always screaming at each other and when he was here last week I heard him bragging to Eddie about filching some of the wine at church."

"I'm sure he was just blowing smoke about the wine, trying to impress Eddie."

"Whatever he was doing, I don't like him."

"I know, Lynn. We'll just have to be extra vigilant keeping an eye on Eddie to see how he handles this thing. Can you get some time off at the nursing home to be here in the afternoons?"

"I can try," she said, running a hand through her close-cropped, black hair, "but it won't be easy. They're short of help as it is."

He grunted.

"Will, not now. Don't insinuate that I'm a negligent mother because I have a job, and it's not like we don't need the money. And the past six months, you've been spending more time than ever at work. Thank God you were home today. It seems the only time we see you is when you're getting ready to walk off to

34

meet the train. When was the last time you had a game of catch with Eddie?"

"Now who's doing the insinuating? What do you want me to say, Lynn, that I'm sorry? Okay, I'm sorry, but I have no control over it. If I'm going to get anywhere I'm going to have to put in the time. You think I enjoy an hour and a half on a damn train every day?"

They heard Eddie turn over and grunt lightly.

"I'm sorry, Will," Lynn whispered. "I know you work hard. I think this, this thing, has me shaken. Let's just both do what we can to be here for Eddie. Okay?"

"Yeah, fine," Will looked away, walking to the front window and staring out into the dark.

"What do you think happened down at the water, Will?"

Looking out, his back to his wife, Will said, "Damned if I know."

✦ *7* ✦

Nora winced and ducked. The plate hit the kitchen wall by the phone, splattering spaghetti and tomato sauce over the receiver, the worn wallpaper, as well as the outdated calendar marking the month December, 1965. Norman Rockwell's Santa caught a chunk of meatball right in his chubby groin.

She ran to the living room. A fork flew over her shoulder, but the glass smashed against the back of her head. Lukewarm cola dripped down her collar creating a sticky stream between her shoulder blades and down her back. The cut itself stung with the carbonation.

"You're a fucking hour late with dinner, it's hotter than hell, and you fucking bring home fucking take out spaghetti! You fucking stupid bitch! Who the fuck eats spaghetti when it's a hundred fucking degrees out?"

Nora had been kept late at the hospital because of a problem with one of the refrigerators. Because she was low man, or woman, in seniority, the age of most of the other employee's kids, she was told to wait for the repair guy. When he finally showed up, stoned off his ass she guessed, he took a quick look at the unit's motor and said, "Broke. You need a new one."

Well, great, she thought. It really pays to wait for the expert. She considered calling home to tell Vern she'd be late, but rejected the idea knowing he'd just explode at her over the phone, and then again when she got home. With any luck he'd have drunk himself into a stupor and wouldn't even be aware of the time. She'd stopped at Jo Jo's on the way home to pick up some take-out. The counter girl was buzzing about the cop cars that had raced down the street earlier. Probably some kind of gang thing she said. The Puerto Ricans were at it again.

Nora tuned her out and sat at one of the tables near the window while she waited for the food. She lit a cigarette and gazed in the direction of the waterfront, wondering how long she could continue this way. She couldn't remember a day of her childhood without her father's voice telling her how slow she was, how dumb she was, how ugly she was. 'Christ, why the hell a damn girl? With a face like that she'll be with us forever. The only silver lining is we'll never have to pay for a wedding. Jesus, get in the kitchen and help your mother get dinner together.'

Her mother wasn't much better. She took refuge in cooking, hiding behind pots and pans, finding solace and contentment in being the consummate wife. But she seemed to become less of a person herself. She came to blend into the walls of her refuge. As Nora's father grew and grew to well over three hundred pounds with her mother's cooking, Mom became less and less, until shortly after his death she seemed to vanish completely in a cloud of cigarette smoke. Now it was just Nora and Vern.

Him, half crazy with whatever the hell happened over in 'Nam, not that he'd ever been exactly stable before, and her, tied to him by bonds of responsibility. Tied to a house she'd hated living in every day of her life, tied to a job doing the same thing her dead mother had done for her dead father, and tied to a town which defined her entire past. That in itself was enough for her to hate Pendale. It was enough for her to almost put an end to it all. Get her hands on some pills and just drift off in a quiet sleep. She'd been planning it. What was it The Beatles said about turning it all off and floating downstream? Yeah, she'd been ready.

But not now.

No, now she had a reason to live. She had something no one else knew about. A secret. One she wanted so much to share, but with who? There was no one else, and that was *so* hard. This secret made her special, it gave her purpose, made going home to Vern bearable for another day. She could face herself in the mirror and know there was a reason for her existence.

Nora paid for the food and carried the hot, greasy bags to her car, smiling. The smile faded as she heard the sirens issuing from down by the waterfront.

Arriving home she dumped the contents of the cardboard containers onto plates and pulled knives and forks out of the gaping kitchen drawers. The refrigerator door was ajar and most of the beer she remembered seeing that morning was gone. She reached for a barely chilled bottle of cola, grabbed the opener from the top of the fridge where Vern usually left it, and poured the soda down the side of a glass, trying to keep the foam down. She carried the dinner into the dining room. It truly was a dining room in that they sometimes ate there, but normally it was cluttered with laundry, an open ironing board, and once, for about four months, a leaky lawn mower engine her father had gotten into his fat head to fix during one long winter.

Vern glowered at her from his side of the table, his fork stirring the spaghetti round and round his plate. Despite his complaints of hunger, he didn't eat. Instead, he drank beer in long steady gulps, looked every few seconds toward the front windows, and continued stirring the pasta, sauce dripping over the edges of the plate, the fork tines scraping. As the sound of a passing car reached their ears through the open window he stiffened for a second before returning to the stirring.

"So big brother, anything exciting happen today? No? We had a refrigerator break down at the hospital. Probably end up having hundreds of dollars of food spoiled. I had to wait for a repair guy to show up. It took forever. I thought man, it's a good thing my big brother isn't here waiting. He'd rip this guy a new one, making him wait so long. Teach him a little respect. Like the song, right? 'R-E-S-P-E-C-T, sock it–'"

At that moment Vern erupted and sent the dinner flying at her.

"Christ!" Nora flew through the screen door to the front porch holding the back of her bleeding head. Just a while longer, just a while longer, she thought, he forearms wrapped tight to the sides of her head to drown out her brother's screams of rage. A little longer and Vern will just be a distant, unpleasant memory, never seen again. She prayed to a seemingly indifferent God to give her strength.

8

"There was no identification on the body?"

"No, Captain, nothing yet." MacDougall shifted the receiver as he reached across his desk to grab the file he was looking for. "It was pretty bad. We do know it's a young woman, by the skin tone and hair color, in all likelihood Puerto Rican—"

"Or maybe just a dark haired white girl with a tan," Captain Clarke's voice interrupted.

"Yeah, that could be." MacDougall rolled his eyes.

"Don't make assumptions."

"Right, I know, sorry. Anyway, there was no identification on the body, but we're scouring the surrounding area. Maybe we'll find something. There's no way to identify the face with the condition it's in, but we might get lucky with a fingerprint match. They may be on file somewhere, you never know with these people."

He heard Clarke sigh on the other end of the line and wasn't sure whether the Captain was going to jump in. Nothing. He continued, "The victim was wearing dungarees, leather sandals, and she'd been wearing a halter top. It was pretty badly stained and laying about three feet from the body."

"Torn off? Is there evidence of sexual molestation?"

Ready for the question, MacDougall said, "Well, yes and no."

"What the hell does that mean?"

MacDougall went on slowly, "It doesn't appear that she was raped, or just had sex, but...,"

"But what? Come on, MacDougall, I'm not a mind reader."

"Her...her breasts were gone."

There was silence in MacDougall's ear. Then, "Explain what you mean."

"The victim's breasts were cut off."

"Jesus," Clarke breathed through the line.

"Yeah," agreed MacDougall. "They weren't around anywhere. It looks like whoever did this took them with him. It was...it was...,"

"It's okay, Kevin," Clarke said to his young officer. "I can only imagine what it looked like. Whatever you're feeling, it's okay."

The two men were quiet for a moment.

"You said there was no evidence of sexual molestation."

"Right." MacDougall rallied. "The pants were zipped and buttoned up. Though I guess the killer could have put them back on her and done them all up after the attack, but what's the point? It's not like he was trying to hide what happened or leave a tidy crime scene. And the pants were really tight, almost painted on. You know how the kids wear them now."

Middle-aged Chief Timothy Clarke almost smiled listening to twenty-five-year-old Kevin MacDougall talk about 'the kids'.

"It'd be nearly impossible to get them on a limp body, all that dead weight," MacDougall went on, oblivious to what came out of his mouth.

"Anything else?"

"The halter is stained with blood-obviously, brain matter, dirt and debris consistent with what's found at the waterfront, and something else."

"Don't leave me hanging, Kevin."

"Not sure, but it looks like cherry Kool Aid."

"Kool Aid?"

"Yeah, right in the middle, here," he said, tapping his sternum before remembering that the Captain couldn't see him. "At the, ah, breastbone. A big stain. And a little more off to the side."

"Kool Aid?" Clarke asked again.

"Yeah, it's a kid's drink, comes in lots of flavors, you add sugar and mix it in water. The commercials on TV have a big dancing pitcher."

"I *know* what Kool Aid is." Jesus. "I'm trying to make sense of it."

"It's wild alright."

Wild, yeah. "Have you checked yet for reports of any young women missing?"

"That's the very first thing I did," MacDougall sounded hurt. "None. I even checked a twenty mile radius. Nothing."

"Okay. Good job." He could almost hear MacDougall grin through the receiver. "I should be back in town in about two hours. Anything else you need to fill me in on?"

"Uh, not really. We might want to talk about the boy who found the body. And his parents, but it can wait," he added quickly.

"You sure?"

"Oh, yeah, no big thing."

"Okay, see you in a bit. Keep searching the area for something to identify that young woman."

"Sure will, I bet it won't be long."

Surprisingly, MacDougall was right.

Two hours later, sitting at his cluttered desk, Clarke glanced down at the itemized list before him. A small fan mounted above his office door slowly swung right to left and back again. A weighted pencil can kept the paper from blowing to the floor. The perks of captaincy, he thought grimly, a private broom closet-sized office and your own fan. The typed page flapped as the fan breezed by. To its right was a large denim purse with a long shoulder strap. The inventory listed its contents: makeup pouch with lipstick, eyebrow pencil, blush (no surprises there, thought Clarke), a very feminine-looking folded handkerchief (white), half a roll of peppermint Lifesavers, a set of three keys on a brass key ring with a heart ornament, (none of the keys appeared to be for an automobile), and a red plastic snap style wallet.

Clarke searched through the bag and drew out the wallet. Inside were four dollar bills, seventeen cents in change, and a torn movie ticket to a recent return showing of 'Doctor Zhivago' at the Palace downtown.

Most important, tucked behind a little plastic window, was a social security card issued in the name of Rosaria Regina Donez. There was also a library card in the same name and a picture of a dark, attractive girl, maybe in her late teens, with a younger boy, perhaps seven or eight, who looked similar enough to be a brother.

Damn, Clarke thought staring down at the picture he'd placed on his desk blotter. Way too young.

The fan blew the small picture to the floor. "Shit." Reaching under the desk to retrieve it, Clarke whacked his head on a protruding drawer.

"Shit!"

He straightened, rubbing his forehead.

MacDougall stuck his head into the office, "You okay, Captain?"

"Yes! Hit my head, dammit."

"I do that all the time."

"Don't go anywhere. I'll want to talk with you in about half an hour. I just got off the phone with the father of the kid who found the body."

"Okay," was the meek response as MacDougall's head vanished from the doorway.

He looked at the picture again, this time holding it securely between his thumb and forefinger. The girl could almost be described as beautiful. Dammit, dammit.

He tucked the photo back into the wallet. In doing so his index finger felt something else deep in the slot which held it. Clarke pulled the photo back out and dug further with his finger. He felt stiff paper, maybe cardboard. He gently coaxed it out of the crevice until he could hook his forefinger behind it. It was a twice folded over strip of pictures. The type taken in those photo booths on the boardwalk. You got three pictures on the strip for a quarter. Could be he was dating himself, maybe it was more like fifty cents now.

Each picture was of the same two people, the girl from the other picture, and a young man. He appeared to be about the same age as the girl. He too appeared to be of Hispanic descent. In each picture they were hugging and smiling at the camera. Carefree, brilliant smiles of two people very happy to be with each other. They made a very attractive couple. He was as handsome as she was alluring. Hell, *he* was almost pretty.

The first two pictures were very similar, perhaps a slight change in the angle of their heads being the only noticeable difference. The last picture showed each of them still smiling, but there was something a bit different to it. Clarke pulled his reading glasses from his top desk drawer and slid them on the end of his nose. He found the right distance to hold the picture from himself and examined it closely, starting with the girl. Her smile was a bit wider and her eyebrows looked different, raised slightly. As though she was surprised or about to break into a laugh. There wasn't any discernible change in the boy's face. Clarke continued inspecting the tiny photo. Finally, he found the reason for the girl's reaction. The left arm of the boy was around her back as it was in the other two photos, but in the final photo his hand was just visible on the side of the girl's left breast. He appeared to be giving it a slight squeeze through her blouse.

Clarke slid off his glasses and sat back in his chair. That's why she had the photo strip tucked into the back of her wallet. Modest enough not to want anybody seeing it, especially not a nosy parent, but sentimental enough to want to keep it with her, to take out when no one's around. No one except maybe her photo partner.

A girl with hidden pictures of herself and her boyfriend in a moment of playfulness. A girl who likes a romantic movie and love story. A girl who loves her little brother. A girl who should not have died as she did. Clarke peered at the three picture photo strip, squinting at the face of the young man.

"MacDougall!"

"Captain?"

"You boys missed something. It appears we may have a suspect."

9

She thought she was dead. Her eyes wouldn't open. There was a dull, static hum in her ears. Inside of her mouth was a cactus strewn desert. Her body was numb, as though wrapped tightly in cotton, almost cocooned. There was no feeling at all in her extremities. Okay, she thought sluggishly, that covers sight, sound, taste, touch…what was the other sense? Jeez! There may not be any feeling in her fingers, but man, her head was coming to life fast. It was ready to split with all this deep thinking about her senses! Oh, yeah, smell. What did she smell? Deep inhale… Something wasn't right. Almost no air was coming in and what did smelled like wool. Old wool. Dirty, old, stinky wool. Maybe a call for help was in order. Filling her lungs the best she could, she let out a yell. The result was a soft grunt and the pain of an anvil dropping on her skull like in those Roadrunner cartoons. Goddamn. No way she'd try *that* again. The cocoon was way less painful. A few seconds, or maybe hours later, she made a tentative effort to turn her head. Shocked, she felt her body move. This was evident by the sensation of something rough moving across her face. Whatever was happening, it seemed to restore her sight, partially, anyway. Something was coming into focus in her left eye, the right one was still blind. A source of light emanated from the far left. Directly in her sight line was a shapeless red object set in a brown background. This background looked rough with smaller dull, colored specks strewn throughout it. The red shape shone in the light coming from the left. Whatever its property, it reflected light more than the brown behind it. There were black markings on the red. It seemed twisted and torn in areas, enough to show bits of its interior. This was gray and shiny as well, a bit like...*oh shit. Not again.* A bit like, a lot like, exactly like...foil. Because what Nikki was looking at was a torn condom wrapper tossed on the dirty brown carpet next to her bed. Half her face peered over the edge of a filthy quilt lying on an equally filthy mattress. She was staring at her bedroom floor. Okay, familiar territory. Not great territory, but at least she knew what was what. Kind of.

After a few careful breaths she gingerly pushed herself up on an elbow. The feeling was gradually returning to her limbs and feeling was *definitely* present in her head. If she didn't find some aspirin fast, it might roll off her shoulders and join the wrapper on the floor. No, this wasn't anything new, but it sure as hell wasn't pleasant.

She took a deep breath and turned to look to the other side of the bed. Empty. She slowly leaned and looked warily over the far edge of the mattress. Nope, nobody down there. Just the used condom itself. Lovely. Her guest had apparently come and gone. Ha, Ha, oh, ouch, damn head, funny girl, Nikki. At least she avoided that awkward moment of shame and dismay that sometimes occurred at 'discovery time' the morning after, having to guess the the identity of the comatose guy next to her. And hey, he'd used a rubber: a real gentleman. Chivalrous. Either that or concerned with self-preservation. Smart, too.

Nikki slowly sat up and looked down at herself. She was not at all surprised to see she was naked and...well, the condom pretty much said it all.

There were empty beer cans on the nightstand, an overturned ashtray with its contents spilled on the floor, her clothes strewn about. Some clothes anyway, where the hell were her jeans and underwear? She saw them just outside the bedroom entry in a tangle on the floor. Wow, she thought, did we start out there? Yup, there was another red wrapper on hall floor. The condom was sure to turn up soon. A Casanova as well as a gentleman. Bet I had a great time. Lucky girl, Nikki.

Cautiously, she stood, and using her hands to feel along the wall, inched to the bathroom. Consciously avoiding looking in the mirror, she opened the medicine cabinet and poured herself several aspirin. She let the water run for a while before filling the glass and gulping down the pills and water. The glass had a residual taste of bourbon. Oh, man. That, too? No wonder she felt like hell. She gingerly bent over, her head almost to the level of the sink and began gently splashing water on her face. The cold water made her gasp as it ran down her face, off her chin to her chest, before dripping off her nipples onto her bare toes. At any other time sure to be an arousing sensation, this morning, or whatever time of day it was, excruciating.

She braced herself on the sink with both hands and raised her face to look in the mirror. Not great. But not as bad as she feared. Not as bad as some occasions. Her pale ginger hair was a tangle that any rat would have been glad to call home, but at least she'd avoided last week's disgrace of puking in her sleep and waking with it dried to her head. What a way to greet the morning. Her eyes were red as raw beef and the heavy kohl makeup around them had smeared across both cheeks and the bridge of her nose. That's what I get for trying to look like Twiggy, she thought. There were slight bags beneath the makeup, but that was the extent of the damage.

Nikki dragged the blue Noxema jar from the shelf and began to slather it on. "When are you going to smarten up, Nik?" she asked the mirror. How many more nights like last night? More important, how many more mornings like this one? A raging head, dry mouth, shaky hands, and absolutely zero memory of what happened after going to the Bottle Top. She reached for some cotton balls to remove the Noxema and then remembered she was out. Had been for a while. She unwound a fistful of toilet paper from the roll, getting dizzy with the effort, and rubbed it across her face. After washing off the last of the makeup remover, she chanced another look at herself. The smattering of freckles across her cheeks and nose stood out against her colorless skin. Her eyes were indeed bloodshot, but the green irises stared back at her as if admonishing her yet again. "Bleah!" Nikki said to her reflection.

She pushed away from the sink and sat on the toilet. When through, she looked in the bowl before flushing. No blood. Good. There was that time after a similar lost night a couple months ago. She'd bled for almost a week. God knows what the guy had done to her, she sure didn't. But she'd been scared. More scared then she'd ever been. It actually got her to cut out the drinking for awhile. Then the bleeding stopped, she started feeling good, healthy, even a little in control. Made her feel maybe, this time she'd put a stop to all this nonsense for good... well, not yet. Once you forget how lousy you felt, you think, hey, what the hell, it's not a huge deal...and here we are again. Back on the merry-go-round. Trying to remember who you fucked last night. Or fucked you. She thought of the condom wrappers. Twice.

Nikki flushed, turned, and tottered back into her room. She knew even though she felt like death, she'd better try to get some food down. History told her she rarely ate when out on the town. Nor when she was feeling hung over. Even on the best of days Nikki barely broke the ninety pound mark. And just because there was no puke in her hair, didn't mean it hadn't happened. In fact, she ran her tongue over her teeth and gums. Yuck. Returning to the bathroom she squeezed the last of the Pepsodent on her toothbrush.

Afterwards she felt almost human. Maybe Mrs. Gorman has some dry toast, she thought. Nikki scooped her underwear and jeans off the hall floor, sniffed, and gave them the once over. No embarrassing stains, but damn, the stray condom was stuck to the cuff of her jeans. Nikki carried them to the bathroom and peeled the condom off using toilet paper. She then picked up the other one on the floor by the bed and tossed it away with its mate. Looking at the stain on the jeans she hesitated....aw, fuck it, she thought, and pulled them on before fishing her Mets T-shirt out of a drawer. Like I haven't dealt with worse than *that*. Sliding the shirt over her bare shoulders she noticed her prominent ribs. Yeah, definitely some toast. And if that doesn't kill me, maybe an egg. She knew Mrs. G. was usually more than willing to feed her.

Nikki Greene lived in a small apartment in the rear of the Gorman's house. An in-law apartment as it was advertised in The Pendale Citizen two years ago when Nikki'd first seen it. She'd just graduated from high school. Her father had passed away a year earlier, a stroke. Way too early, and she'd been living with an aunt. Mom had taken off long before she could remember. The year with the aunt had been about eleven months too long, and she was ready to bolt and begin the next chapter in life. New life, new town. Why'd she choose Pendale? Why the fuck not?

Nikki met Donald Thompson at Stewart's Drive-In, parked next to each other, waiting for the ditzy carhop to figure out the dinner orders she'd totally screwed up. They rolled their eyes at each other as the girl tried to remember who had what. Soon, nature as they say, took its course.

Donald had seen the ad first and pointed it out to her. They visited the apartment together and met Mr. and Mrs. Gorman.

The apartment was private, had its own entrance, and was behind the kitchen of the main house. Mr. Gorman had converted the two rear rooms into a separate residence. Nikki later wondered if the couple knew Mr. Gorman would be gone less than six months after she moved in. Maybe he was setting up his future widow with some financial security. That fucking lung cancer. It was everywhere.

"We knew the minute we saw you, you'd be perfect for the apartment," Mr. Gorman said, lighting a Lucky Strike. "This was all to make Rose feel comfortable," he said, referring to a short list of questions scribbled on a telephone message pad and placing his hand over his wife's.

"Oh, don't you lie, you," Mrs. Gorman argued. Looking at Nikki and Donald she said, "When I told him a young girl called, he was worried you were a hippy or a communist. That's why the questions. But you two, you look like fine young people. And also," she leaned forward, her large bosom resting on the table top, "you look very much in love."

They nodded and laughed as they laughed about almost everything the entire time they were together.

When Donald went off to school though, being apart was tough. Lafayette College wasn't too far away, but it wasn't convenient either. Once Nikki had somehow wrangled time off from the Rexall Drug Store where she worked to visit Donald for a weekend. The bus ride through the winding Pennsylvania back roads was as harrowing as the scenery was beautiful. It was Homecoming Weekend and the campus was ablaze in color and activity. Nikki was amazed at the number of students there, as well as awed by the college atmosphere itself. It was another world from what she knew in Pendale. Students lectured to handfuls of supporters on some cause in one corner of the school quad, while dissenting opinions were expressed in the far corner. Everyone seemed to know each other and students that Nikki knew were no more than a couple of years older than herself seemed to be so much more mature and informed about everything.

And the girls. They were everywhere! Nikki knew girls nowadays were attending college, but it seemed they'd *all* chosen Lafayette. And they all knew Donald. They couldn't enter a coffee shop or diner, the campus library, bookstore, or the football stadium without some chick waving, "Hi, Don, Hey, Thompson," and once, this beehive blonde strolled over pressing her cone-shaped tits against his arm and breathing, "Hiya, big guy." She looked over at a stunned Nikki, "Is this little Rikki from back home?"

"Hi, Stella, this is *Nikki*. You going to be at Gimme Jimmie's after the game?"

The blonde batted her lashes affirmative.

"Great! We'll see you there. Bye."

"Bye, bye. Bye Rikki," the blonde drawled, swinging her hips as she sauntered off.

"What the hell was that?" Nikki asked Donald.

"Just Stella. Don't worry about her, she's the same with everybody. She likes to flirt."

"Really? I hadn't noticed. Do you have other friends like Stella at college? Rikki wants to know."

Donald sighed,

"She flirts. Does she do anything else? I thought maybe she used that fat ass for more than just sitting on."

"I don't know, it could be. Yeah, she does, but not with me, okay? I mean, come on, would I have told people I had a girlfriend at home if I wanted to play the field? Would I have invited you to visit?"

He put his arm around her, "Come on, let's go to the game." She nodded and they went. The rest of the weekend was a bit of a blur, but some of the awe she'd felt upon arrival had worn off. The game was a success, Lafayette beat Holy Cross by three, they attended the party afterward and had a good time. No sign of the dreaded Stella. Maybe she's 'flirting' with the first string, Nikki'd said. Donald just shook his head and went to get them drinks. Nikki had her first experience with pot and while she didn't dislike it, she thought she'd stick to cigarettes and a few beers. Safer, she thought.

Boarding the bus on Sunday though, she felt a bit queasy. Maybe it had been more than just a few beers. She had a fuzzy memory of confronting Donald about 'whoring around' on campus. God, had she really said that? He'd assuaged her fears, and was polite as always when they walked (her unsteadily) to the bus stop the next day. He hugged her and told her how much he loved her and he would be home to see her soon. But something was there, dividing them that hadn't been there before. And he hadn't invited her to come back for another visit. The ride home consisted of brief naps and fits of nausea. Nikki was able to control her stomach until she reached home where she flew into the bathroom, bruised her knees on the floor, and was violently sick into the toilet. As her cramping stomach heaved she thought, Fuck you, Stella.

There were phone calls the next couple of weeks, each with Nikki apologizing again for her behavior. Donald always dismissed her apologies, but the calls became more perfunctory and brief. Then one evening after returning from the drug store she received a call from Donald's stunned parents.

Donald and several of his friends had been involved in a car accident. It had been one of the first snows of the year, the car was going too fast, apparently they had been drinking. They missed a turn and went off the road into one of Pennsylania's many rock outcroppings. The driver was killed instantly. Donald was in the passenger seat and he probably died immediately, as well. Another boy who had been sitting in the back seat died on the way to the hospital. Only one of the four occupants in the car survived.

Nikki lived the following week in a fog; she had vague, half-memories of consoling Donald's parents, and being consoled by the Gormans. She could not escape the unbearable guilt she felt for having caused the rift in the relationship with Donald, unknown to anyone, save her. All blindly assumed that she was the grieving, nearly, but not quite, fiancée of the fine young man. Only Nikki knew this rosy prognosis, in all likelihood, would never have come to pass.

The funeral was well attended. Saint Margaret's was nearly full. Pendale knew how to turn out for a funeral, with the war and all, especially an untimely death like this. Distant family, childhood friends and new ones from college came to pay respects to the family. Nikki was asked by Donald's family to sit in the front pews with them. She rode with the family to the cemetery near the highway. Under the iron November sky, around the squared off hole in the ground, Father Dwayne murmured words that were lost in the wind and the whine of the distant turnpike traffic.

The reception was at Donald's parents's house. Nikki kept herself occupied making sure the ice buckets were full and the food table bountiful. Everyone had the necessities to mourn in comfort. She was pulling the foil off a platter of cold cuts when Donald's father touched her arm.

"Nikki, hon, there's someone who would like to offer you their condolences. Donald's classmate that was in the accident with him. Probably the last person to see him before…anyway, I guess you've met. Miss Mortenson?"

From behind Donald's father stepped Stella, beehive hair perfectly in place and her arm in a sling of black crepe. "I'm so sorry for your loss. The accident was devastating," she lifted her arm an inch or so, "to us all. At college we all know what you're going through. We all know exactly what you meant to our Donald. Exactly." The corners of her mouth twitched.

If Donald's death had been a catalyst for Nikki's downward spiral, then Stella's presence at the reception was the instant her true descent began. Nikki sprung at her, she scratched Stella's face, tore her arm from the crepe, and even managed to dislodge some of that seemingly immovable hair, yanking out a hank of it. Her screams of frustration and accusation were unintelligible to all but Stella and herself. Nikki tried to jam the sling's black cloth into Stella's painted mouth. Stella, eyes bulging, clawed at Nikki, both arms suddenly working very well. She tore Nikki's dress from the collar to her shoulder, ripping the material open and exposing her brassiere. It was this moment that Donald's stunned father and several other men broke their tableau and pulled Nikki away.

Stella played the part of the bewildered and wronged guest beautifully. Here she was, trying to offer solace to the close friend of a classmate after nearly dying *herself*, and she's attacked. But she was fine, she assured Donald's parents and the others. Yes, it was unfortunate and a shame, but Donald had said Nikki was rather high strung and a bit overemotional.

"I'll be fine, thank you," she smiled bravely to the knot of concerned guests, primarily male, surrounding her. "Yes, I would love to have a glass of wine if that's possible. Just to steady me. You're so kind, Donald always said so and now I see why. I can't blame poor Nikki. She's been through so much. The awful scenes at college when she visited, Donald's decision, and now the accident. Hmm? Donald hadn't said anything about that weekend? Oh, I guess I'm speaking out of turn, putting my foot in my mouth. I'll just be quiet now, oh, thank you so much for the wine."

As Stella was being administered to, Nikki sobbed incoherently on the hall stairs, her face in her hands, curls of displaced hair helping shield her face. Someone put a glass in her hand and she drank without thinking. The alcohol seared her throat and for an instant forced her mind from Stella. And Donald. But only for an instant. "More," she sobbed, pushing the empty glass back at whoever gave it to her.

Another glass was shoved in her hand and she tossed it down as quickly as the last one. "There now, Nikki dear," she felt a hand on her knee. She opened her eyes and looked up at Donald's sleazy Uncle George, his eyes on her torn dress. "Yes, You'll be fine." His patted her knee.

Nikki looked at him through red, glassy eyes. "Fuck you, Uncle George."

Uncle George pulled his hand away as though burnt. He attempted a smile. "No Nikki, you don't mean to say you think–"

Nikki rose from the stair she'd been sitting on. Uncle George's face changed from pasty pale, to beet red. He backed away from Nikki. She shoved him into the hall wall, knocking a photograph of Donald in his Boy Scout uniform to the floor.

"You're drunk," Uncle George hissed, "as well as crazy! We all saw you attack that woman. Get the hell away from here. What on earth did Donald ever see in you!"

Nikki threw her glass at his head. It shattered against the wall over his left shoulder bringing a gasp from the living room and then sounds of confusion.

Nikki stumbled past several people as she ran through the kitchen to the back door, trying to get some air.

"You wouldn't believe what she said, what she did," she heard Uncle George's voice behind her.

She pushed open the door and stood on the enclosed porch, gasping in the frigid air. She brushed by a tray of foil covered cold cuts, staying cool on a bench, and pushed her forehead against the freezing glass window. Oh, Christ, Donald, what the hell happened? I miss you so much. I'm sorry for what I said. I'm so, so sorry.

She heard footsteps in the kitchen coming toward her. I guess I better start trying to make apologies, she thought. Except to that asshole, Uncle George. She pushed back from the glass and turned around.

"You sure know how to liven up a party. Maybe that's what Donald saw in you. God knows," Stella said, looking down at Nikki's torn dress, "there's not much else to see. It's hard to believe he stuck with you…for a while anyway. I mean, what are you," she laughed, "just a bony little whore." Stella looked back to check if they were alone, then continued, "How pitiful, they're all talking about you in there, you know. That drunk, how could she act that way? They'll want no part of you anymore."

Nikki looked beyond her into the house in disbelief. "Yeah, Rikki, they're practically erasing you from history right now. You'll just be that crazy bitch Donald used to know before he outgrew you and went off to college. But you know Rikki, you know who'll never forget you, never stop talking about you? Ever? Old Uncle George. You gave him something to gossip about until *he's* planted." She touched her newly repaired coiffure. "It was worth a bit of a headache." She turned to reenter the reception with a swing of her hips and said over her shoulder, "Run away, Rikki. You're not welcome or wanted here."

Nikki stood mute on the cold porch, her breath visible in the air. She slowly turned, pushed open the porch door and walked down the dark driveway. By the time she reached the corner she was running. Her life as she had known it, over.

It wasn't long before reality caught up with people's perceptions. She was just some crazy girl Donald used to know, a fling he had before heading off to school. No one remembered she hadn't always been that way. As the weeks and months passed the Nikki of the couple, Donald and Nikki, seemed to fade to nothing, while the image of Nikki, the promiscuous barfly grew. A persona had been created for her, courtesy of Uncle George and Stella. She was a drunk. She was nuts. Her mind was a gutter. You wouldn't believe how she was acting toward the other guys that weekend at Lafayette, according to Stella. While visiting Donald! No wonder he wanted to end the relationship. Thank God Donald was never serious about her, because he wasn't, you know, just a case of weakness in the face of temptation. Look at her, dragging herself down to Broadway every night. Who knows how many men she's slept with? Anyone willing to buy her drinks and desperate enough go home with her.

And it was true, all of it. It was so much easier than dealing with reality. It was easier to make it through the day as Nikki the drunk whore than address the pain of having wrecked the relationship and then losing Donald forever. Not to mention the loss of her own life as she had known it. Waking and confronting the agony of a screaming hangover was a walk in the park compared to having to actually live through a day clear and sober. The alcohol was her shield against anything and everything that could cause her to stop, think, and feel. Men, well, they were a means to that shield.

Nikki had long since lost her job at Rexall. Showing up half in the bag, reeking of beer and vomit at ten o'clock on a Saturday morning quickly put an end to her employment. With no income, the only way to a drink was to rely on others. Who was going to support a raggedy-ass girl's alcohol habit? The answer was obvious. As long as Nikki had something to barter, she'd never be wanting for a drink. So she bartered.

"Hey, Mrs. G, you home?" Nikki poked her head around the kitchen's screen door. "Any chance of scaring up some toast for breakfast? I'm all out of bread."

Mrs. Gorman was at the sink, her back to Nikki. It's almost lunch time." She didn't turn. "You're always out of bread. The kind you eat and the kind you spend, isn't that right?"

"Come on, Mrs. G., not this morning, please. I really don't feel well." She slumped against the door jam.

"You never feel well in the morning. And I said, it's almost afternoon, not morning. If you went to bed earlier, if you didn't go drinking, if you went to bed alone, you wouldn't feel like you do."

Nikki sighed, "Mrs. G-"

"Don't you Mrs. G. me anymore!" the woman shouted, turning. There were tears in her eyes. "Don't you dare! Do you have any idea how much it hurts me to see what you do? To hear you every night? You with different...men all the time? You sick all the time. You crying in your sleep. Yes. That's right, most nights after whoever leaves you alone, you moan and cry almost until dawn. It is so wrong, Nikki. It hurts me so much to see you try to drink and shame yourself to death, because that's what you're doing. My God, what would Donald say-"

"Stop right there, Mrs. G. No more talk about Donald. I don't know what you think you're hearing at night, it's probably the Edmunds' cat going at it in the back alley, but it's sure as hell not-"

"It's you. Crying."

"Sure, you might hear me entertaining a friend on occasion," Nikki admitted. Mrs. Gorman cocked an eyebrow, "But there's no crying. Unless I leave them crying for more, right?" Nikki tried a weak smile. "Hey, I missed out on the Summer of Love last year, I'm playing catch up. You understand, right? One girl to another?"

"What you do is wrong," Mrs. Gorman said quietly. "I fear for your health, your life, your repu-" She stopped.

"I guess it's too late for my reputation at this point, huh?"

"Nikki, come here," Mrs. Gorman took her hand and sat her down at the kitchen table where they had sat with their men long ago. "Do you ever wonder why I still let you live here? With the terrible things you do with terrible men? With the mess you have made of the apartment? With the fact you haven't given me a dime for rent in who knows how long?" She looked into Nikki's eyes. The younger woman staring down at the table. Nikki tried to answer, but couldn't, she simply nodded her head.

"You are all I have. After Carl died I didn't know what I would do. I thought I would go crazy missing him so much. I even thought, God forgive me, of joining him. Don't look at me that way. I felt there was no reason to wake in the morning. Do you remember when he died? It was like being in hell."

Nikki nodded. She had actually stayed sober that day, in a pathetic gesture of respect toward the Gormans.

"But I couldn't join him. I couldn't because I had you living in my house. I had to make sure the utilities were paid on time so your power wasn't shut off, the garbage went out on Tuesdays and Saturdays, banking the rent on time. Not that *that* has been occurring recently."

Nikki grimaced and whispered, "I'm sorry, Mrs. G…"

"The point is, silly as it sounds, I had to keep myself together, keep myself alive, because you were in my life. I was responsible for you. I had to maintain your home for you. And now," she inhaled, "I feel I'm failing you. I can't seem to give you what you were able to give me. I can't make you want to go on living. I can't keep you from slowly killing yourself."

Nikki slumped in the chair.

"I don't know what to say, I know you care for me, I mean hell, like you said, I can't remember the last time I made the rent and you still let me stay here. I bet the neighbors are thrilled about that. And you're always trying to shovel food down my throat–"

"You eat less than a bird."

"I'm sorry I've made it so hard for you. I guess it's no picnic living in the house with a train wreck. And I know sometimes I sometimes I bring home a friend or two–"

"Oh, Nikki, I hate those men! I have never laid my eyes on any of them, but I hear them. I recognize some of their voices. This is a small town. Some are married, with families." Nikki winced. "They are not good men, Nikki, they only want to humiliate you so they can feel better about themselves. Big men, hurting a young girl. Oh, that one last night sounded so evil. What a horrible, horrible laugh he had."

"Let's not talk about that, okay, Mrs. G? Just please know I'm really sorry about hurting you. And please, please don't think you're failing me. The only one failing me is me."

"Oh, Nikki."

"Anyway, I promise to change things around here. First, about the rent, I'll talk to some friends–"

"No, Nikki, you will not. Your 'friends' will want something in return for the money they give you. That sort of thing must stop. Now."

"Okay. But Mrs. G., I really don't have two dollars to rub together. I'm flat busted," Nikki smiled ruefully. "Seems the only thing I have of value, I'm sitting on."

"Don't worry about rent. We will let that slide for now. Carl left me comfortable, so it isn't a worry." She smiled, "Besides, I've been spending a fortune in coins at church lighting candles and praying for you. I'll probably be better off paying your rent and saving on candles."

"Ha, ha."

"And now you can come with me to church. And confession."

"What?"

"Confession is good for the soul."

"Confession? Are you kidding? Mrs. G., if I walk in a church the steeple will be struck by lightning. I mean, there are sinners and there are sinners. And then there's me. I could be like that Rosemary chick, carrying the devil's baby. Where would you and all the nice people of Pendale go to pray if I caused the church to collapse onto itself? I don't think so, but thanks for the thought."

Mrs. Gorman reached across the scratched linoleum of the table and put her hand on Nikki's. "We will go to church. And we will take you to a doctor. I am worried about your health, and while I am certain you are not carrying the devil's child, I do worry because you have been with so many men. You should be examined for diseases. You may have caught and spread something bad."

"Jeez, you make me sound like Typhoid Mary."

"You know I'm right."

Nikki looked at the table top, sighed and said, "Yeah, I know. Christ, half the male population of this crummy town could have the clap by now."

"And their wives."

"Yeah, and their wives." Nikki looked up, wiped her eyes and smiled. "Thank you, Mrs. G," she whispered.

"It is my pleasure, my dear. After all, you saved me once."

Nikki sat silent for a minute. "Now," she cleared her throat "how about that toast?"

"Toast is for breakfast." Mrs. Gorman nodded toward the wall clock. "It's now afternoon. How about I make you a nice club sandwich?"

"I don't think I'd be able to keep it down. How about we start small on this new, healthy, holy life of mine. Toast?"

"Toast." Mrs. Gorman smiled.

⤕ 10 ⤔

MacDougall pulled up to a small, well-kept bungalow on Prospect Street and double checked the number. Yup, three seventy-two. The single story home had been repainted recently, reminding him the trim on his own little house needed to be scraped and painted sometime in the near future. As he climbed the front porch steps he noted the potted geraniums on either side of the front door. They were flourishing. He checked his reflection in the door knocker, pressed down his ever-present cowlick, took a deep breath and rapped with his knuckles.

He heard a muted rumble of running steps on bare floors, followed an instant later by the door being flung open by a small, grinning boy in a green number twelve football jersey. The grin disappeared the second he saw MacDougall.

"Hi! Are you," MacDougall glanced at his notebook, "Alfonso?"

After a second's silence, the small dark face nodded once. Even at this young age these people knew the presence of a police uniform was never a positive sign, MacDougall thought.

"I'm Police Officer MacDougall." He grinned. "You know, I have a niece that I bet is in your grade. Patty Stephenson, second grade. Do you know her?"

The look of suspicion changed to one of contempt. "I'm in fourth grade, not second." Unsaid were the words, 'you jerk'.

"Oh, sorry. You like the Jets, huh? Joe Namath? I like football too. I'm a big Giants fan."

It hardly seemed possible, but the look in the boy's eyes, darkened.

"Is your mother at home? I'd like to speak with her, please."

"Wait on the porch. I can't invite in…," the boy looked at the police uniform, "'strangers'."

"That's smart," MacDougall said to the already half-closed door. He turned and regarded the geraniums again, tucking his shirt in tight with his thumbs. He ran through various scenarios of the upcoming conversation, each one concluding with a middle-aged, matronly woman dissolving into quiet tears, which he patiently waited out before escorting her in a dignified manner to the police car.

His musings were cut short by a sharp, "What?" from behind him.

He turned and could not keep the surprise from his face or voice. "Mrs. Anita Donez?" he asked. The woman in the doorway looked to be no more than thirty years old, though he knew that if indeed this was Mrs. Donez she was certainly older than that. Her eyes were dark and cheekbones pronounced, there was no sign of gray in her thick, shining hair. She wore blue jeans and a bright red T-shirt which accented her bronze skin. She could have been the older sister of the girl in the photo.

"Yes, what?" she repeated.

"I'm Officer MacDougall of the Pendale Police Department. I need to speak to you about your daughter, Rosaria. May I come in, please?"

At the mention of Rosaria's name, she blinked and her look of hostility shifted for a split second to one of concern. "Yes, Rosaria is my daughter." She hesitated. "Come in." She stepped back before turning and leading MacDougall into the small living room. MacDougall's eyes couldn't help following her hips as she moved. He heard a grunt and looked up to see Alfonso staring at him from the entry to the kitchen. MacDougall felt his face coloring.

She sat on the edge of a small sofa and gestured him to a chair across the coffee table. The room was immaculate.

He cleared his throat. "Rosaria Donez...is your daughter?"

A muscle in Anita Donez's jaw twitched. "Yes, she is. Is she in trouble?"

"She isn't here for me to speak to?"

"No, she's...why do you know to ask that?"

"I have some bad news, Mrs. Donez–" he began.

"What happened? Is she in some kind of trouble?" she interrupted. "Did that boyfriend of hers get her into some kind of trouble? I told her to keep away from him! He's only looking for one thing, like all boys that age."

"Ma'am it's nothing to do with...that, you know, ah, sex, or anything." His voice dropped to a whisper on the "s" word. No way could he equate Rosaria's horrible mutilation to anything in any way having to do with sex. "In fact, we just found out that there was no–" He stopped. Fresh sweat broke out at this near slip up.

"What? What are you saying? Tell me," she said fiercely. "Tell me! Where is my hija?" Her mouth dropped open for an instant, then, "Oh no. Not that...the muerta on the beach...," she whispered. "Tell me."

"I'm so sorry, Mrs. Donez. We believe that Rosaria was a victim of an attack at the waterfront. We would like you to come down to the police station to identify her...belongings."

"No," she whispered. "That was not my Rosaria! No, my Rosaria is too smart. The waterfront? No, no! It's not her! She knows not to be out alone at night. She knows!"

"Maybe she was troubled with something. When did you last speak with her?"

The woman's eyes were glassy, looking toward the silent black and white television in the corner. "My God," she whispered. "We argued about that Marcus, her boyfriend, his taking advantage of her. I know he is, always with his arm on her, treating her like a possession. Boys like him…" She shook her head, grasping at her hatred of Marcus, attempting to avoid her worst fear.

There was a noise from the direction of the kitchen. "I told her if she didn't stop seeing him, she would have to move out. You see," she looked to MacDougall, still a trace of hope in her voice, "she doesn't make enough money to live on her own and I know that boy wouldn't want her there all the time, weighing him down. He would not let that happen." Her eyes filled with tears. "I know he wouldn't, I was right, wasn't I? Wasn't I right?" she pleaded.

"I'm sure I don't know, ma'am," MacDougall said quietly.

"What did he do to her? What did that bastard do to my hija?" she whispered.

"No!" A high scream came from the kitchen. "No, Mama, Marcus would never hurt Rosaria. He loved her, he told me. He was going to marry her and we were going to be brothers. That's what Rosaria told me." He ran in from the kitchen and threw himself into her arms.

Anita Donez turned to her son, as though surprised at his presence. She squeezed him tight.

"He loves her. He loves her," Alfonso whimpered into his mother's neck. Mother and son quietly cried in each other's arms. MacDougall looked out the front window to the street.

He learned the argument between mother and daughter had been a bitter one. Rosaria stormed out threatening to never return. Anita had called her some choice names and made it clear she believed her daughter's behavior was a negative influence on Alfonso. That parting shot was one she knew would strike home with her daughter. There was no one on earth Rosaria cared for more than her little brother.

"Alfonso," Anita whispered. "Was Rosaria staying with Marcus?"

"Yes."

She bowed her head. "I thought she was with Cousin Rose. She's gone there before when…oh, God…."

"She was really happy, Mama. She was sad about the fight with you, but she wanted to be there. She wanted you to be happy, too."

"She was smart, my Rosaria, she could see how hard it was. Raising a family with no man. Life changes so fast; you're young, the world is a long road in front of you, with so many possible directions to take, and then you're not young, and the road leads just one way. She knew… she should have known…" she trailed off.

Those were the last words she spoke before the three of them got into the police car and drove to the station. The boy whimpered as the hot vinyl seat burned him; Anita didn't seem to notice the car's temperature or its upholstery. The two sat in silence in the back seat. MacDougall radioed to the station that he was on his way with the victim's mother and brother.

"And brother?" squawked the radio.

"Yes," he said deliberately into the microphone. "Her, ah," he did some quick mental arithmetic, "nine-year-old brother."

"Got it. Over."

After pulling into the station parking lot, MacDougall got out of the car and opened its back door.

"Go inside, hijo. I need to speak with the policeman for a minute," Anita said.

"No, Mama, I'll wait with you."

"Inside. I'll be there in one minute." She pushed him gently toward the station.

Alfonso walked reluctantly toward the door.

When he reached it Anita quietly said to MacDougall, "Marcus Rodriguez. He lives on Highland Avenue. Get the bastardo. If he didn't kill my little girl he may as well have. He's the reason she left us. My Alfonso will never be like that." She turned and walked to the station, a devastated mother with just one child left to watch over. MacDougall couldn't help but watch her hips again as she walked away.

"Take all the time you need, Mrs. Donez." Officer MacDougall discreetly closed the interview/coffee room door and stepped into the hallway that bisected the Pendale Police Station. He didn't have much experience in dealing with the bereaved. He had no idea what to expect.

He entered the squad room to check on Alfonso. He sat in MacDougall's desk chair, feet dangling a foot off the floor, glumly fingering one of the menus stuck into the blotter.

"How about a soda, Alfonso?"

The boy shook his tear-stained face and returned to the menu.

Mrs. Donez identified the purse and its contents, scowling a bit at the transistor radio before pushing it away. She cried openly at the picture of her two children in the wallet. Captain Clarke had thought to remove the strip of photos from its hiding place. Inside a brown paper shopping bag were the victim's leather sandals, pants, and top. Anita nodded through tears at the sandals and pants. At the sight of the stained halter she seemed to choke and MacDougall was afraid she was having some sort of seizure. He bolted to the adjacent men's room and filled a coffee mug with lukewarm tap water. He put it on the table next to her. Through hands clenched at her mouth she silently nodded thanks. After a moment she sipped.

"We're almost done, Ma'am."

She shook as he looked into the paper bag. "There's just her, uh, these," he stammered and produced a pair of soiled white cotton panties. "Are these hers?" he asked.

Anita looked at the underwear with no expression. "Maybe. I don't know. She has....she had underwear like this, I don't know if it's hers, though. Same with the handkerchief."

"Alright, thank you Mrs. Donez, that's all. I'll take–"

"I want to see my daughter now."

"No!" MacDougall blurted before he could stop himself. He mentally cursed for not anticipating this. "It's not necessary right now, I'm sure you and your son want–"

"Take me to my daughter."

"Mrs. Donez," he said, grasping wildly for the right words in this oh, so wrong moment, "you don't want to do that. There was...trauma. She was hit. Repeatedly. And she was also...ah... cut. You probably wouldn't be able to recognize her. You won't want to remember her like that."

"Officer, if this is my daughter, I'll know. If it's not...God knows, I need to know that, as well. Don't drag this out and make it any harder than it has to be," she pleaded quietly.

He hesitated and nodded. "You don't want your son there. He can wait here." She nodded. "The coroner's office is two blocks down in back of Saint Mary's Hospital. It's not far." She nodded again.

The air conditioning in the mustard-colored hospital hallway sent a shiver through MacDougall. He couldn't help but take a quick look at the front of Mrs. Donez's T-shirt to see if the cold affected her, too. Before he could tell, they were greeted in front of a pebbled glass door by a green-smocked Dr. Avery. He offered condolences to Mrs. Donez and ushered them into a large tiled room. There was a portable privacy screen, the type you'd see in a doctor's office, blocking the view of most of the room.

"Usually I drape the entire body and show the deceased's face." He looked at MacDougall, and seeing panic there calmly continued, "There was quite a bit of damage to the face and head in this case. I think it would be better if we didn't do that. Mrs. Donez, are there any distinguishing marks on your daughter's body that would help in identifying her?"

Anita no longer looked as determined as she had at the police station. Perhaps the surroundings and the smell of formaldehyde had affected her. She was silent looking at the white screen before her.

"Her stomach. By her navel, can you show me that?"

"Certainly," Avery said, to the great relief of MacDougall. "Just one moment." He disappeared around the screen.

They could hear the sound of sheets rustling and sliding over the body. The sound caused MacDougall's stomach to roll.

Avery appeared and took Mrs. Donez by the arm. MacDougall reluctantly followed. A human form lay under several green folded sheets atop a stainless steel gurney. Dr. Avery had folded back a section of sheet and revealed the torso, from a few inches below the rib cage to the hips. The belly was flat, the body was very fit. The skin, though obviously once a shade of brown, was now closer in color to gray. Just to the right of the naval was a triangle comprised of three small birthmarks. Each one barely bigger than a grain of sand, this entire constellation was no more than an inch across.

Mrs. Donez moaned and for a second, MacDougall was afraid she'd fall onto the gurney, bringing it and its contents crashing to the cold tiled floor. Instead, she fell back into him.

He caught her as she began to buck and flail. Her screams bounced off the hard, indifferent walls. Kevin MacDougall had never heard, and would never forget, a sound filled with so much pain.

The identification was complete.

✦ 11 ✦

Captain Clarke riffled through Officer MacDougall's more than copious notes on the details of the killing. He squinted at the cramped scrawl and held it up to the window for better light.

"Looks like a drunk chicken dancing," he muttered under his breath. But he knew what it lacked in legibility it more than made up in detail. MacDougall might appear to be Pendale's answer to Mayberry's Barney Fife, but he was a cop who, when not feeling overwhelmed or reacting to a life-long distrust of those who were different, could be relied upon to do a thorough job, and then some.

The coroner's report had recently been added to the file. Rosaria Donez, age eighteen, died of massive head injuries. She appeared to have been struck on the back side of the head just behind the right ear, near the hairline in front of the same ear, and repeatedly in the face. The nose and jaw were broken as well, and one eye socket was shattered. Her palms and the undersides of the forearms were scratched and contained bits of sand, gravel, and specks of broken glass. Pretty much what you'd expect to find on the ground down at the waterfront. There were no wounds on her hands or broken bones other than those already identified. It did not appear she put up any struggle, something a young, healthy girl would normally do unless she was taken by surprise. Maybe that blow to the back of the head came first, knocked her out, she never saw what hit her. That would be the most merciful scenario, thought Clarke, but if she was out with the one blow, then why the rest of the damage to the face? Why not just one more roundhouse to the head to end it quickly? No, she may have been too stunned to fight back, but she knew what was happening to her. Clarke didn't doubt that.

But the breasts, why did the killer take the breasts? Were they some sick trophy to fondle in the dark night? For as long as they lasted, that is. Was this hatred of some kind? Hatred of this woman, of women in general? There certainly seemed to be rage of some kind. Clarke was out of his depth when it came to answering these questions and he knew it. The mutilation, though, was one fact they would certainly keep from the press. He didn't need his entire town turning sleuth and pointing the finger at every neighbor who owned a pair of hedge clippers. Also, he didn't want the killer getting any thrill from the fear he generated through the mutilation and thus feel encouraged to kill again. There would be more than enough fear anyway.

Thank Christ there was no evidence of sexual molestation.

He flipped a page. Apparently, the attack took place near the breakwater. There were blood spatters and evidence that Rosaria's hands had made imprints in the ground. A transistor radio and ear jack were found near a large rock at the water's edge. The radio was turned on and its batteries were dead, but it didn't appear to have been outdoors for any length of time. The plastic wasn't stained and there was no rust on the tiny metal screw heads. There was also evidence the body had been dragged from that location to the World War II bunker about twenty yards away. The trail between the two locations was pretty obvious, dried blood and bits of brain matter. How difficult would it be to drag weight of about…he flipped another page, one hundred and ten pounds, across twenty yards of beach? The ground was pretty solid there and relatively flat. There were a few large rocks, but the route to the bunker was direct. How strong would a man have to be? Could a woman do it? Clarke couldn't imagine a woman inflicting that kind of damage on the victim. But he'd seen enough evidence of what a killer, jacked up on adrenaline and God knows what, could do. No way he could discount the possibility.

That damn bunker. It was far past time to block that thing up, if for no other reason than to keep kids away. God only knows how many drunken, drugged out trysts...or rapes, those dirty graffiti-covered walls had been witness to over the years. It's a shock this was the first body to turn up there. Horrible as this was, imagine if the victim had been a little kid. Clarke didn't want to think about it.

Time of death was difficult, everything accelerated by the heat, moisture, salt air, etc. The crabs, rats, and snapping turtles hadn't made it any easier to figure. Jesus, what a way to die. What a thing to see. That boy, Edward McConnell, was going to have a lifetime of nightmares. Clarke didn't put in much for that psychology stuff, but the kid was sure to need some counseling.

And MacDougall's handling of the situation needed to be addressed. The poor kid shouldn't have been brought back to the scene. Kevin knew better than that. Sometimes he got so damn eager, he couldn't see the forest from the trees. Well, he'd take care of that later. Clarke had spoken with the boy's parents and told them that Officer MacDougall would be dealt with. It was a situation which was, needless to say, far from ordinary. Clarke had been away and Kevin did not handle it as well as he should have.

That said, the McConnell guy didn't need to be such an ass. All that talk about getting a lawyer and suing the department... please. He should be concerned with his son, not a lawsuit.

Sounded like both the guy and his wife were wrapped pretty tightly. Sure, they were upset, but Clarke was certain there was more going on there.

Christ, he thought, looking through the dust-streaked window of the police station at Broadway Avenue, what was there not to be upset about? The whole crazy country was going to hell, why should little Pendale be exempt? Damn war scaring the president right out of running for re-election, kids looking like vagrants burning draft cards and the flag. The Flag! They had no idea what their parents went through to keep that flag flying over this country. What the whole country went through so they could live free, express their opinions, go to college, be successful. And they were crapping all over it, like it was some sort of joke. Like this country wasn't worth the effort. Jesus, he wondered, when did all this start? It seemed like everything was just like always and then, pow! Nothing made sense anymore.

It was Kennedy's assassination, he thought. When he went down in Dallas it was like the whole country took a kidney punch. Maybe we never recovered. Clarke was no big fan of the former president. Hell, he thought, I may be the only man in this Irish-Polish burg who voted against him. It's not that he was in love with Nixon, it's just that Kennedy seemed so damn young. Clarke was afraid he would rely too much on the advice of his father, and Joe Kennedy was a man Clarke felt belonged in prison, not bending the ear of the most powerful man in the world. But it shouldn't have ended the way it did. Blown away by some disenfranchised Communist during a parade. And then the shooter getting blown away on live TV. While in police custody! What a screw up. If there was ever reason for a cop to surrender his shield in disgrace, it was that.

He shook his head, trying to clear away the thoughts. Later, that crazy Negro, Malcolm X. What the hell kind of name was that? X? Some of the things he said, well, Clarke would never say that a man deserved to be shot down in cold blood, absolutely not, but some of what that guy said was plain scary. And now, just a couple months ago, Martin Luther King assassinated. Life seemed to be getting cheaper. Like it's alright to permanently silence anyone you don't agree with. Don't like what you see or hear? Kill it. Maybe that was it. The whole country was so accustomed to seeing and hearing about that damn war and all the killing that went with it every night on the news. Maybe, since they couldn't kill the war, they were taking out their frustration on each other. The Negroes in the the cities, the Puerto Ricans right here, hell, everybody. He sighed.

Well, there's another Kennedy who might make it to the oval office this fall. Maybe he'll be able to figure things out. Bobby seemed pretty good that awful night King was shot, kept what calm he could. There could've been a bloodbath. And if Kennedy didn't make it to office there was always Dick Nixon ready for his long-delayed moment in the sun.

Clarke sighed again and wondered for the thousandth time why he hadn't taken early retirement five years ago when his wife begged him to. Judith made it clear she felt she'd waited long enough. Waited the long nights by the phone when he was on duty, waited for the kind of life she always imagined she was deserving of. She was tired of this tiny burg with its small-town ways. Appeasing her, he had said being a police officer meant respect, it was a stepping stone to city politics. Clarke had always imagined he would one day be chief of police and maybe, with some college and law school, district attorney. He'd been young, intelligent, ambitious, The sky was the limit. With the right woman supporting him, well, let's just say that Pendale was to be the first in a long line of stepping stones. She needed to believe in him and practice a little patience. But it hadn't worked out that way.

Sure, for the first five years of his career he'd been the golden boy on the force. Even had his picture taken receiving awards from old Mayor Finnigan. Twice. Judith loved the local limelight. The light, however, faded, and with it so did his wife's patience. Where was the money? Where were the Florida vacations? Christ, another crummy week in August at the shore? Was that it?

Eventually Judith's patience reached its end and the marriage was over. She moved out and headed, belatedly, to Florida. Shortly thereafter, Clarke received a letter from her attorney petitioning for divorce. Clarke was shocked his Catholic wife would want this, but apparently the Florida sun had worked some magic and she wanted the freedom to 'do her own thing'. Christ, he thought, she's starting to sound like the kids today. He did as she asked, and a portion of each paycheck went south to Tampa, keeping Judith in Coppertone comfort.

Enough.

Right now, Clarke had a murder to think about. He turned his attention once again to the report in front of him, wondering once more what in the world an eighteen-year-old girl could have done to deserve such a fate.

⇥ 12 ⇤

Will McConnell lay on his back and stared at the ceiling tiles in his dark bedroom. One hundred and sixty-eight. Twelve along each side wall of the room and fourteen along the walls that ran parallel to the front of the house. God knows he'd counted them enough. None of that multiplying length times width, he counted each and every one. One at a time, night after night. They were easier to count than sheep. Will tried to remember if he'd ever even seen a real, live sheep. Maybe when he was a kid on on one of those Sunday afternoon drives into farm country. "Exploring the Garden State" his father used to call the excursions.

Those were real family days, the three of them, driving around South Jersey, Will asking questions about nearly everything they saw, Dad always with the answer, and Mom having packed a lunch in a wicker picnic basket. They'd stop at some country lane in the middle of nowhere and chow down on chicken, deviled ham, or whatever was on the menu that day. Idyllic.

One hundred and sixty-eight. Will followed the progress of a pair of headlights crawling across the bedroom wall as tires whined on the pavement. Damn kids, he thought. Hot-rodding. He looked at the curves of Lynn's shoulder and hip under the thin cotton sheet.

He reached over and ran his hand over her hip. Lynn muttered in her sleep and rolled away as far as the double bed would allow. Christ. Enticing as a corpse. He threw his legs over the side of the bed, pulled on a pair of shorts, walked down the narrow hall and stairs. He used to hope the sound of his bare feet slapping against the worn risers would wake her. No more. A damn bomb detonating wouldn't rouse Lynn. It used to irritate the hell out of him. But not anymore.

Will grabbed a bottle of Yoo-Hoo from the fridge, popped the cap, and carried it to the front screen door. He stood gazing at the shadows cast by the street lights. Quiet. He unlatched the door, stepped out onto the porch, and sat on a porch rocker. The fabric stretched over the aluminum frame scratched his bare back. Will settled in and propped his feet on the rusty porch rail. He'd need to wire brush and paint it soon. Hell, it should have been done last year. The landlord would wait until the roof fell in before shelling out for any repairs himself. Cheap bastard.

Will thought he heard footsteps behind him from inside the house. He held his breath for a moment. After a few seconds he turned. The screen door hadn't closed and whatever air current there was must have caused it to bump gently against the frame. He reached back and pushed it. Nothing. Shit. He got up and leaned against the door, pushing it to the frame with his shoulder. The latch finally caught. Great, something else messed up that needs fixing. He sat again, picked up his drink and listened to the quiet of the night.

But no night was ever really quiet. He heard the squeal of tires again from a couple blocks over, a solitary dog barking in the distance, the sound of a radio, pretty near, maybe just across the street. Old man Edmunds might be up looking for that damn cat of his. Maybe it was that crazy drunk girl who lived behind the Gorman house. One of her many Romeos might want some music to fuck by. Could be the Wilson house.

He thought about Vern and Nora. How the hell she lived in the same house with that psycho was beyond him. Will knew Vern was up many nights, sitting on the porch killing beer after beer. Insomnia was something they had in common. In Will's opinion, that was all they had in common, well, almost all. Pretty soon Vern would pass out and Nora would turn off the radio and put her brother to bed. And it would be still. This was Will's favorite moment of the day. It was worth the late, lonely vigil. He'd wait. He had, after all, things to do in the night.

→ 13 ←

"I honestly don't know what I can tell you, Captain Clarke," Minna Cooper said, as they walked up the driveway toward her small garage.

"Here, let me help you, ma'am." He grabbed the handle of the heavy wooden garage door and pulled it open to the side. The bottom scraped along the gravel of the driveway.

"Why thank you Captain, that's very kind of you. I must say that I've always been very impressed with our police force here in Pendale. They have always been very proper and polite. Why, I remember Captain Delaney, a lovely man, but that was before you arrived. Now there's Kevvy MacDougall. I've known him since he was a baby. In fact, I remember his first communion at St. Agnes. I had a nephew in the same class. It was a lovely ceremony. I remember the little ones marching up Bordentown Avenue from religious education to the church. Their heads bowed, hands folded, walking in two straight lines. One for the boys, the other for the girls. Not a single child out of step. Of course the nuns wouldn't have tolerated a single misstep, they were no-nonsense then." Minna walked into the relative darkness and heat of the garage. "They were better times, Captain."

"I often think you're right, Mrs. Cooper."

"Do you know the march of the first communion students from the school to the church isn't a part of the ceremony anymore?" The voice came from the shadows in the garage.

"I do, ma'am."

"Do you know why that is?"

"Actually, I do–"

"It's because older children, teenagers and such, have disrupted the march. They ridicule the youngsters. Those with cars honk their horns and make an awful racket. These young children, trying to enter into a holy sacrament, being made fun of, can you believe it?"

Clarke could. It had been an issue for the last couple of years. Beyond setting up a couple saw horses to close off the street and citing the guilty parties for disturbing the peace, there wasn't much the department could do beyond appeal to a sense of community and decency. And lately there wasn't much of that around.

"It's hard to believe, ma'am. Society seems to be changing and there's very little we're able to do about it."

"That's it exactly! Society *is* changing. It wasn't like this when we were young, was it?" The voice in the darkness was adamant.

When *we* were young? Clarke knew Minna had at least dozen or so years on him. He made a mental note to take up an exercise routine, jogging maybe.

"It all just seems to be crumbling," the voice from the darkness continued. "Everything we fought for in the war. None of it matters to the young people. They're just selfish and crude. All they do is make noise about what they want and how they want it *now*. They have their drugs and sex and all they do is complain about the country. None of them want to try to make things better, they just want to tear it all down!"

"Can I give you hand in there, Mrs. Cooper?" Clarke peered into the dark garage, worried the old woman might get too worked up with the heat and all.

Minna stepped into the light, pruning shears in her gloved hand. There was a serene smile on her face and a thin bead of perspiration running down her left temple. "Not at all, Captain. This is my relaxation. I'm out here every day the weather permits. The exercise is good for me. Some women watch Jack LaLanne on television, I work in the yard." She waved her arm holding the shears before them. "Isn't it lovely?"

He noticed thick beds of flowers along the back of the house and side of the garage. The beds were about four feet deep and flowering shrubs supported by stakes rose five feet from the ground. Most of the beds were covered with a layer of wood chips.

In a back corner of the yard, sheltered from view of the street, was a small raised platform, with a roof and latticework surrounding the four corner supports. Flowers, mostly roses, Clarke noted, were threaded through trellises which ran from floor to roof around most of the perimeter of the structure. Inside, was an ornate garden chair and foot stool. It was the single most feminine structure Clarke had ever seen.

"I see you're admiring my gazebo, Captain," Minna's voice interrupted his thoughts.

"Gazebo?" Clarke wasn't sure he'd heard her. "That's what it's called?"

"Yes. It's my little oasis. I sit inside, surrounded by the beauty and aroma of my flowers and there's nothing in the world that can touch me. All the ugliness of which we've been speaking is a million miles away. I don't see or hear the world outside."

"Really?" Clarke looked doubtfully at the gazebo's latticed sides. "I guess those flowers really soak up the noise."

"I guess they do indeed. This is a lovely visit, how is it I can help you, Captain?"

Clarke looked around the yard for a place they could sit. All he saw was the single chair in the gazebo and no way in hell he was going to sit in there even if she produced a second chair.

"Would it be more comfortable for you ma'am, if we went indoors to talk?"

"There's no place I'm more comfortable than my yard, Captain. Please, go ahead."

"Okay." He reached into his breast pocket for his notebook and pen. "I'm sure you heard about the murder down at the waterworks."

Minna frowned. "Of course, it's all people seem to want to speak of."

"Well, according to the deceased's aunt, her niece, Rosaria, said she had been to see you. It was the day before she was killed. Is that right?"

"Yes, I suppose. She stopped to ask me what I charge to do hair, but why is this important? Surely, wanting her hair done has nothing to do with her death."

"No ma'am, but what we're trying to do is piece together the last days of her life to see if anything out of the ordinary occurred. Anything that in any way might have a bearing on her death. Can you tell me what time she was here?"

"I was working on the bed in front of the shop at the time and I didn't have my watch on. I never wear it when I'm gardening. I think it was early afternoon. She approached me about setting up an appointment for her. She said something about an outing with her boyfriend. I told her I didn't have time for her. She was quite rude, I'm afraid."

"Why do you say that, Mrs. Cooper?"

"When I told her I couldn't do her hair she asked if I was afraid of catching something."

"Catching something?"

"Yes, she said since it seemed I don't cut any of the Puerto Rican women's hair, was it because I was afraid of catching something."

"I see."

"I told her that if she felt like that she shouldn't have come to me in the first place. There are plenty of her own people who cut hair. Maybe not as well as me, but they do."

"What did she say then?"

"She called me a name I will not repeat and left, probably off to see her boyfriend. They're often together on the street. They can't seem to keep their hands off each other. It's disgusting."

"The young people today are very demonstrative with each other," Clarke said.

"Hmmph," Minna said, her lips a flat line.

"I know this is difficult, but I really do need to know exactly what she said to you. If you'd feel better about it, you can write it down instead of saying it."

"I would *not* feel better writing it down, it's not a word I'm comfortable speaking *or* writing."

"Mrs. Cooper–"

She sighed impatiently. "It rhymes with 'witch'."

"Pardon?"

Minna stared at Clarke in exasperation, "She called me a fat, old rhymes with witch."

"Ah, I see."

"And then she made an obscene gesture as she left. Surely I don't have to show you *that*?"

"No, not at all. Is there anything else you can add to your statement?"

"I wasn't under the impression I was making a statement. I thought I was simply assisting my local police department, but since you ask, no, there is nothing I care to add to my statement."

Clarke flipped close his notebook and pocketed it along with his pen. He wiped some perspiration from his brow with the shoulder of his short sleeve uniform shirt. "Thank you for your time, Mrs. Cooper, you've been a big help."

"I seriously doubt that, but you're very welcome Captain. If there is more I can do, please just call." She bent down and slashed through the bag of topsoil with the pruning shears. She tossed the shears to the ground, grabbed the bag, and dragged it toward a nearby bed.

Clarke headed down the driveway.

"Captain?"

He turned.

Minna stood before the flower bed, hands before her, gripping a mound of top soil between them. "I'm a Christian woman and I realize this is not a very Christian thing to say, but, she will not be missed. She was not someone who made the world a better place, quite the opposite. She was selfish and uncaring. Our town is better off without her." She dropped the top soil in the bed and rubbed her hands together, brushing the dirt from them.

Clarke stood still at the bottom of the driveway. "Her family might feel differently." As he drove away he looked in the rear view mirror at the old woman standing in the yard, still brushing her hands clean.

⇥ 14 ⇤

"I'm headed over to St. Margaret's church," Clarke said into his car microphone. "It's time I spoke with Father Ryan. If he's not there I'll head over to the rectory. I can be reached there if I'm needed. Over."

"Yes, Captain Clarke. Over. Have a good day now."

Clarke sighed. The department had a new dispatcher who was still getting her feet wet when it came to protocol. Mrs. Barton was a retired school teacher who nearly went batty after her first full year away from the job. She was ready to do anything that necessitated human contact, even if it was just by radio. The department scooped her up for next to nothing. It was a classic example of you get what you pay for. He'd have to speak to her when he returned to the station. Maybe, Clarke smiled, he'd order MacDougall to speak to her. Apparently little Kevvy had been one of her star pupils a decade or so ago. Maybe tie it to a punishment for how he'd handled the McConnell kid. Thoughts of Eddie McConnell brought Clarke back to the murder and he wondered why exactly he felt the need to speak with Father Ryan.

True, the man had ties in the Negro and Puerto Rican communities. He was often seen at neighborhood functions there, and he knew many of the town's young people, especially those in the Catholic groups he ran, but why did Clarke feel there was more? The man wasn't a suspect, not at this time, anyway. Why bother? Maybe, thought Clarke, when he got to the church God would provide that answer for him. Clarke pulled up to the granite steps in front of the church just as Father Ryan was exiting. The middle set of heavy wooden doors thudded closed behind him.

The tall blond priest stood at the top of the granite steps and reached into his breast pocket for a cigarette. Clarke watched the young man blissfully exhale a stream of smoke. Clarke reached behind and peeled the sticking shirt from the small of his back. He looked up at the Father, dressed head to toe in black, collar wrapped around his neck, looking like he'd just stepped out of the air-cooled Palace Theatre downtown. He reminded Clarke of that actor from the movie "Barefoot in the Park." The one with Jane Fonda, Henry's girl. Damn…what was the guy's name? Redford, yeah, Robert Redford. The priest grinned at Clarke and waved. Asshole, thought Clarke.

"Hi, Captain," the priest said, sliding his hands into his pants pockets, thumbs hooked over the edges.

"Mind if I speak with you in private, Father?"

"Not at all, Captain. I know you're not a regular churchgoer, but please step into my office, as they say," he said turning back toward the wooden doors.

"Huh?"

"These aren't our regular hours for confession, but I'm more than happy to bend the rules a bit for our boys in blue. A high-ranking boy, at that. I know your schedule must make it difficult for you to make regular hours." Smiling, Ryan held the door open and made an elaborate "after you" gesture.

Clarke shook his head, not certain if the younger man was putting him on. "No Father, I guess I didn't make myself clear enough. I don't want to talk to you about me, I want to talk to you about *you*. Specifically, about what you might be able to tell me about Rosaria Donez and her murder." He was gratified to see the smile slip for an instant from Ryan's face.

"Rosaria's murder? I don't see what I could possibly say that might be of any help."

"I was thinking that exact same thing when I was driving over here, Father. I was asking myself, why do I want to talk to that priest? What could he possibly tell me that I need to know? I figured by the time I got here maybe I'd have it figured out." Ryan raised his eyebrows in question. "Nope. Sweating like a pig in this old squad car-hey, sweating like a pig-get it? A pig in a squad car? I know lots of young people would agree with that. Anyway, sweating like a pig and feeling every pothole in the road on account of bad shocks. So, I pulled up here, parked by the damaged step, hopped out, and *still* wasn't sure what I'd ask about. But then, you told me." Clarke smiled broadly.

"I told you?"

"Yes, you did. You asked me in to hear my confession. Confession. It all came clear. It seems the Lord really does provide."

"Captain, you know that confession is a holy sacrament and I cannot reveal what I hear in the confessional. I would be violating church tenet."

"I realize that, Father, but there is confession and there are things which are confessed. Now, can we please get out of the sun and talk about this?"

The ceiling fan in the rectory's kitchen was a blessing from above. Clarke leaned back in the kitchen chair and let the breeze hit him in the face.

"May I get you some iced tea, Captain?" Father Ryan asked, reaching into the large refrigerator. "I'm going to have a glass."

"In that case, Father, I'd love to have one." Clarke's face still upward, eyes closed, soaking in the air.

He heard ice cubes clink into one glass and then another, followed by the sound of liquid flowing over the cubes. A glass was thunked down in front of him. "Father Dwayne around?" Clarke asked, eyes still closed.

"He's upstairs, napping."

Clarke nodded. "Not a bad way to spend the afternoon. Well, I guess he's earned it. He sure put in the time."

"He certainly has. How is your tea, Captain? Don't let the cubes melt and dilute it."

"Sure won't." Clarke picked up the sweating glass from a placemat embroidered with the Ten Commandments. Where the hell do you find Ten Commandment placemats, he wondered? He looked at the other ones on the table. One with the Our Father, one Hail Mary, and the Creed. Wow, that one must have taken a lot of time. He sipped from the glass. "Delicious, Father. I can't stand it when people load sugar into it."

"Nor can I, Captain. Sometimes it's better to take what comes straight, not sugar-coated."

"Um, I agree."

"You know I won't violate the sacrament of confession. I wouldn't be much of a priest if I did. I make no claims to being the most pious man to ever wear a collar, but I won't do that."

"And I'm not asking you to."

"Then why, Captain, as much as we're each enjoying the other's company, are we here?" Ryan smiled again, showing his perfect teeth.

Clarke looked at the priest. He unbuttoned a breast pocket and pulled out his notebook. He very deliberately turned one page after another until he found what he wanted. He read from his notes. "You were arrested in August, 1965 in Trenton. Is that correct?"

"Yes, it is." The smile was still intact.

"Then, in November of the same year and again the following March."

"You certainly know your facts, Captain."

"Hell-oops, sorry, it's my job."

"And I'm sure you're very good at it. I'm also sure you know each of those occasions you've mentioned were either anti-war demonstrations or rallies for the civil rights of Negroes."

"I do know that, Father."

"And I'm sure you also know that after each demonstration I was fined and released."

"Yes, I know that, too."

"Then why do you feel the need to bring it up? It has no bearing at all on what happened to Rosaria Donez. Am I right?"

"You probably are."

"So?" Ryan questioned.

"So, I brought this up because I want you to be certain that I'm one hundred percent serious about this. I don't need some smart-ass, placard-waving, jailbird priest getting cute with me when I need to ask a few questions. People look up to you because of who you are, they ask advice, maybe they say more than they think they say."

Ryan opened his mouth to speak.

"I'm not finished yet, Father. I don't want you to violate any sacraments. What I want is for you to realize that poor girl was murdered, *murdered*, and I want to do her justice. If there's anything you can remember that in any way might help me do her justice, I expect to hear it. Are we clear on that?"

A sheen had appeared on Father Ryan's upper lip. "Clear."

"Good!" Clarke drained his glass, licked his lips, and sighed. "Any chance of getting another glass of tea? I swear it's heaven on earth."

Clarke rose to leave forty-five minutes later with several pages worth of information scrawled in his notebook. Whether any of it was worthwhile was another question entirely. In the rectory's front hall he noticed another piece of embroidery, this one framed and hanging in the entryway. A quotation from the Bible. "An eye for an eye" and so on.

"Where do you get these things? Is there some sort of religious embroidery clearing house somewhere I've never heard of?" Clarke asked.

"No," laughed Ryan, "these are made by parishioners."

"The same person makes them all?"

"I'm not certain, these were all here when I arrived. I can ask Father Dwayne about it if you like. He should be up soon."

"No, just curious, this one doesn't seem all that heart-warming and love thy neighbor and all."

"No, it doesn't, but there are many parts of the Bible that are very bleak and unforgiving. There's pretty much something there for every belief, from forgiveness to penance."

"I suppose so. Thank you for your time, Father."

"Captain, I *was* trying to pull your leg a bit at the church. I meant no disrespect to you. I think I may be a bit jaded by my track record in dealing with the police, but don't be mistaken, I want to help in finding Rosaria's killer any way I can."

"I'm sure you do, Father."

"Sometimes we take everything and everyone we see at face value and we never look beyond the surface."

"Beyond the surface to what?"

"To what's beneath, to what really comprises us, our essence." The toothy smile returned.

Our essence, huh? "Well, thanks, Father. I'll be in touch with any other questions. Thanks again for the iced tea."

Father Ryan closed the rectory's front door and leaned back against it. He looked at the framed embroidery on the wall. The truth is, before Captain Clarke brought it to his attention, he'd barely noticed it. The heavy block letters looked very forbidding.

He walked into the kitchen to rinse the glasses they'd used. He looked at the clock and knew their part-time cook would be arriving shortly to prepare dinner, also, Father Dwayne would be rising in any minute. Picking up the glasses from the table he examined the placemats. The lettering was done in cursive, it seemed a much lighter hand than that which had embroidered the hall hanging. Different people, we're all God's creatures though, no forgetting that.

He reached for the phone, then hesitated. He walked to the foot of the stairs and listened. Silence. Ryan returned to the kitchen, grabbed the receiver from the wall and began to dial. After a moment he said, "It's me.

"Listen, the police were just here. Listen! They don't know anything. They're just flailing around like they always do." After a moment, "It was the captain, Captain Clarke. Just wait! He wasn't questioning me about my whereabouts or about yours, he has no idea about you, not yet. He only wanted to know if I'd heard anything from any parishioners. Hang on."

He pressed the receiver to his chest and stretched the coiled cord as far as it could go to the bottom of the staircase. He cocked his head and listened.

Walking back he whispered, "Look, the father is getting up from his nap, I don't have time. Keep your head together. If you're questioned just act the part of–okay, okay, I get it. It won't be an act." Father Ryan listened and nodded. "I know, babe. It's got to be hard, but choices were made, right? By both of us. I'll talk with you soon. I love you."

Father Josh Ryan gently hung up the phone and turning to Father Dwayne as he slowly descended the stairs, greeted him with a wide smile.

⇥ 15 ⇤

"**D**ammit, Will, don't you turn away from me when we're talking!"

"Nobody here is talking, it's just you yelling. Who needs to listen to that?"

Eddie got up from his bedroom floor and pushed the door closed. He sat down again, picked up his G.I. Joe, and got back to the task of ridding the world of the Third Reich. He increased the volume of gunfire and grenade explosions to drown out the background noise from his parents.

"Great, just great, he heard us arguing all the way upstairs and shut his door. Aren't you proud of yourself?" Lynn said.

"Hey, *I'm* not the one screaming here. You sound like a goddamn shrew, you know that?"

"I don't deserve that and you know it. And what's more I won't stand for it!"

"RAT-TAT-TAT! KA-BAAMMM!"

Lynn dropped her face into her hands. "Oh, God."

Will, hands in his pockets, stood at the foot of the stairs looking up toward the door of Eddie's room. He turned to Lynn and shrugged. "Nice job, hon."

"Will," Lynn got her voice under control, "please, we have to talk about what's been going on. It's been three days and

Eddie's afraid to go outside. He can't just spend the summer up in his room playing G.I. Joe."

"I'm not the one who got him that damn doll, Lynn. No boy sh–"

"Will, I'm not talking about the doll. I'm talking about our son. He's terrified. He hasn't spoken since the day he found that... since that day. We can't help him if we're at each other's throats. He'll just withdraw even more. We have to be united on this.

"Christ, that sounds just like that mumbo jumbo crap that's springing up everywhere. Let's *unite*, not *withdraw*. You're not some tie-dyed eighteen-year-old, Lynn. Act your age."

Deliberately she said, "This isn't about me, it's about Eddie. Can we please, *please* think about him?"

Will crossed to the coffee table, grabbed a pack of Marlboro's and felt his pockets. "Where are the damn matches?"

She sighed. "In the kitchen, on the counter by the toaster, I think."

In the kitchen Will lit his cigarette and looked out the screened door to the bathmat-sized back yard. To the right, was the side of the Murphy's house, last painted just after the Japanese surrendered. Behind, and on the left, protected by a six foot high lattice fence, that old Cooper broad's yard. The fence design pretty much obscured any view of the yard, but Will knew she had heavy duty gardens in there, her own private Versailles. Will sometimes heard her humming to herself well after dark, just the light of a lantern flashing through the fence, like an old bloated firefly.

Christ. It wasn't ever supposed to be like this. He was smart. He worked hard. Why were they living in this dump?

"Will?"

"Coming." Damn wife, buying that doll for Christmas, yeah, it was a soldier doll, but it was still a doll. Those idiot kids she lets him hang around with, and then acts all indignant when there's trouble. Now he finds out, from that damned Murphy, for Christ's sake, that Eddie's also been spending time with some fairy Puerto Rican kid. And the kid is the brother of the tramp at the waterfront! Will thought of his father. Thank God the old man isn't here to see this. After slapping Will in the head, he'd want to know where the hell his son's balls went. Dolls, PRs, shit. Time to pull it together, Will thought.

Lynn was sitting on the second-hand sofa, a hand me down from her parents, her hands clasped together between her knees, dark circles under her eyes. He sat beside her.

She said, "I know we don't agree on everything, but I also know we both love Eddie. We need to do what's best for him. Somehow, I'll get some extra time off from the nursing home to be here more. At least until he's able to get through this thing and regain some normalcy. It would be great if you saw more of him, as well. You always talk about the time you spent with your dad and how important it was to you. It would be great if you could be more of a presence in his life."

More of a 'presence?' "Are you insinuating that I'm a bad father? If you are, you can just–"

"No. Please, listen. I'm saying you're a huge positive in Eddie's life, and right now, he needs even more of that." Lynn took a breath. "I know you've been putting in long hours at work. I know it's necessary to get ahead, but we've really been missing you around here. Not just Eddie, me too."

"You know this extra work comes with the territory, we talked about it when we first married. No. Listen to *me* now. If we're ever going to get out of this house, off this street, and even out of this town that seems to be going right to hell with the rest of the country, then I'm going to have to climb the company ladder. And that's what I'm doing."

"But Will, there's no extra money coming in for all the effort."

Exasperated. "I'm not paid by the hour, you know that. I'm on salary. It's not like your little job at the home where you punch a clock. I'll be rewarded down the road for the time put in now."

"Don't put down my 'little job'. Without it we wouldn't be eating because even with all this *necessary* time at work for you there's not enough money for the three of us to live on. I swear, it seems the more time you put in, the less money you make. Is that part of the climbing the ladder plan?"

"I don't need this crap, Lynn." He jumped up and strode to the door. "The reason Eddie is so screwed up," he pointed to the stairs, "is because he has no mother at home nurturing him. He's out playing with spics and, and…wandering alone at the waterfront. Get off my back and just look at what you're doing for him. Excuse me, what you're *not* doing for him. Don't bother with dinner for me." He pushed open the screen door and it slammed back, bouncing against the doorframe.

"BAMMM! ACK ACK! POWWW!"

Lynn leaned forward and cried into her hands.

→ 16 ←

"Please tell me you didn't drag a traumatized child back to the scene of a violent crime," Captain Clarke said, rubbing his face with both hands, elbows resting on his desk.

"Well, it sort of looks like the actual attack didn't take place right there. The body appears to have been dragged–"

"Stop," Clarke said from behind his hands. "You know what I'm saying, don't split hairs. Why Kevin, why the hell did you do that?"

"We needed to be sure of the exact location of the victim. The boy didn't have to go inside the bunker and ID the body or anything."

"He told that old fisherman–"

"Retired fisherman."

"Kevin!"

MacDougall shut his mouth and looked straight ahead at the wall.

"You grew up in this town. As a kid you played down by the water, right?"

"Yessir."

"You *know* where that damn bunker is. You didn't need anyone to lead you there by the hand. What the hell were you thinking?"

Clarke watched as a range of possible responses passed over Kevin's face. This kid better not be a poker player.

"I just wanted it to be by the book," MacDougall finally said, defeated. "You were in the city and I just wanted to follow procedure. Be sure nothing was overlooked."

"But a nine-year-old boy?"

"Yeah, I know. I didn't think it all the way through. I'm sorry, Captain. Do you want my badge?"

"What? Hell, no, just don't do it again."

MacDougall stood at attention and almost clicked his heels. "I won't sir. Thank you sir."

Jesus. "Get the boyfriend in here. What's his name?"

"Gonzalez, sir, Marcus Gonzalez."

"Right, get him in—hell." Clarke's eyes were on the report in his hand. "Rodriguez. His name's Rodriguez! Jesus, Kevin! Get it right!"

"Sorry, sir. Those names all sound the same to…"

Clarke glared. "Get him in here and park him in the interview room. Let him sit for awhile. In domestic slayings nine times out of ten it's the spouse."

"They were just seeing each other, they weren't married, sir."

Clarke glared again. "Check around too and see if anyone's seen her with other men. Maybe Marcus heard about it, blew his top, and went after her. Wouldn't be the first time. See if *he's* got anyone on the side, as well. That's sometimes the case, too."

"Yes, Captain."

"And officer," Clarke said quietly, "suspect or not, Marcus Rodriguez deserves the courtesy of you at least making an attempt to get his name right. Got it? No more 'those names sound the same' bullshit. Understood?"

MacDougall gulped and nodded. "Yessir."

An hour later Marcus Rodriguez sat in the coffee room of the Pendale Police Station which also doubled as the interview room. There was a white spray of non-dairy creamer on the well-graffitied table that Kevin MacDougall could swear had once done duty in Hoffman High's library. He'd even scrutinized the scratches once to see if his own name was there. Nope. A stack of saucers, mugs, a jar of instant coffee, and a few battered spoons sat on a shelf. Water came from the men's room down the hall. MacDougall had thought about suggesting renting a water cooler, but didn't want to make trouble. Especially now.

After having Marcus sit in the windowless room for forty minutes, MacDougall entered and sat across the table from him.

He opened the file he carried, examined some notes there, pulled a pen from his breast pocket, looked up and smiled. "Hi, Marcus."

"Why'd you call me that?" The young man from the strip of photos glared at him.

"It's your name. Says right here." He pointed to the file. "Marcus Rodriguez, 717B Highland Avenue. That's you, right?" Still smiling..

"Yeah, it's me. What I'm saying is, if my last name was O'Malley, or McNulty, or even Smith, would you walk in here smiling and say, 'Hi, Marcus'? I got a feeling it would be, 'So sorry for your loss, Mr. O'Malley,' or, 'I know this is a hard time for you, Mr. Smith', instead of a dumb-looking grin and, 'Hi, Marcus'."

MacDougall looked at the young man across from him. Three or four years younger than him but seemed so much more sure of himself. The fact that the kid was so good-looking didn't help matters. Marcus had a good build beneath the blue golf shirt he wore with chinos and brown loafers. Better dressed than Kevin usually was when not on duty. He preferred beat-up blue jeans and T-shirts along with his beloved Yankees cap. This guy looked like a young Ricky Ricardo.

"Marcus Rodriguez," MacDougall said, and cleared his throat. "You're the boyfriend of the victim, Rosaria Donez?"

"I was."

MacDougall looked up. "Was? When did the relationship end?"

Marcus looked away. "When she died."

"Oh. Yes. But you were together until that time?"

"We weren't together when she died. If I'd been there she'd still be alive. No way anybody would have laid a finger on her. I'd have killed them first." His eyes shone under the fluorescent lights, daring MacDougall to contradict him.

"You mention killing. Would you say you've got a temper, Mr. Rodriguez?"

Marcus leaned over the table toward MacDougall. "Of course. We all do. You know that. Just a bunch of hot-blooded Latins not able to control ourselves. Just as soon kill someone as look at them, right? Fucking animals. You can only hope we all kill each other off. World would be a better place, huh? Ringing any bells with you?"

MacDougall felt his face getting hot. He had heard this, almost word for word, his whole life.

"Let me ask you this, then. Were you, in any way, responsible for the death of Rosaria Donez?"

Tears shone in Marcus's eyes. "I'm responsible because I wasn't there, but if you're asking did I kill her, then you've got to be even dumber than you look. I loved Rosaria." Again, that 'dare to say I don't' look. "She was my life, my whole universe. She made me a better person. Without her...Jesus..." He appeared overcome.

MacDougall sat quietly taking in Marcus's show of grief. Was this genuine, he wondered, still questioning how well he could read these people. He thought back to Mrs. Donez, and having to drag her bucking and screaming out of the coroner's office. *That* was genuine grief. He almost shuddered thinking about it. But this…he wasn't certain.

"Why are you just sitting there?" The young man had found his voice. "Find who did this to her. I know to you she's just a PR, one of those girls you sneak looks at, grin to your buddy and say nasty things about," again this rang familiar in MacDougall's ears. "But she was a person, a beautiful, beautiful person. Don't just let this go because she's different from you. Find the bastard, please."

"Was she seeing, romantically, anyone other than you?"

Marcus barked a bitter laugh and fell back into his chair. "My God, do you hear *nothing* I say? Do I have to be white for you to listen? Rosaria was a good person. She'd no more see another man than I would another woman." Again his eyes dared MacDougall.

"That brings us to our next point. Are there any other women in your life who might be angry you just wouldn't cut those ties with Rosaria? Someone not willing to share?"

Marcus stared at the table, shaking his head.

MacDougall looked at his suspect for a minute then leaned forward, elbows on the table.

"Hey, you're a good-looking guy, Marcus. Why be tied to one girl, no matter how attractive she is? I bet you've got a little going on the side. Yeah, you could have the pick of the litter, right? Come on, Marcus, man to man, you can tell me."

He looked up, eyes dry. "We're back to 'Marcus', huh? There's no 'litter' I'm picking from. Tough as it is for you to understand, we're not animals. As for 'man to man', don't make me laugh. There's only one man in this room and he isn't wearing a uniform."

MacDougall's face flushed again as he looked down at his notes.

"Do you have any more questions for me or can I go and be with Rosaria's mother and brother? You see, we have families that grieve and hurt, just like other people."

You may not be as welcome with her family as you think, MacDougall thought. "Yes, I do. Where were you the night of May 30th?"

"Okay, now we're to it." He stared at MacDougall. "From three in the afternoon till after one a.m. I was working and then cleaning up at my uncle's restaurant on Lodi Street. You can check that out if you want to."

"I do. We will. What time after one?"

Marcus looked at his hands on the table in front of him. "I locked up about ten, ten-twenty. Then I had to clean; the place was a mess. Dishes were stacked up from the whole day. Water pressure was crap, everybody watering their lawns or something. Only time we're able to do the dishes is late. That took a while, the grill was a damn mess too, I remember. After sweeping, mopping, man, I probably didn't get out till about almost two o'clock."

"Do you own a car?" MacDougall knew it was about thirty minutes on foot to the waterfront from Lodi Street.

"Poor spic like me? You know better than that."

"Do you have access to a car?"

"Sometimes my uncle loans me his, but not that night." He was quiet for a moment.

MacDougall was pretty sure no buses ran that late, but made a note to double check. That and the town's only cab company. He closed the file and pushed back from the table. "We're finished. Just be available if we need to speak with you again."

Marcus got up and went to the door. He stopped and turned to Officer MacDougall. His mouth moved, but no words came out. Then, "We drove to Roseland that day, you know?

"If you had half a brain," he went on, "you'd be out looking for someone who doesn't like people like Rosaria, and me. In this town, you got your pick." He glared at MacDougall. "From the cops on down." Marcus was quiet for a second.

"I tell you, that crazy bastard over on Augusta Street, the one who came back all messed up from the war? Rosaria said a couple days ago he was on his porch screaming at her, calling her Charlie, gook and shit like that when she and Alfonso walked by. Said he threw a beer can at her. Didn't hit her because it was empty and fell short. That guy empties a lot of beer cans. I wanted to kill him, Rosaria said why bother, he's pretty much dead inside anyway, poor guy. See? She was like that. He screams at her, throws something at her, and she feels bad for the guy.

"She shouldn't be dead. Find who did it, or I will. And I'm not as forgiving as Rosaria. She was all I...she was a good person."

He left MacDougall sitting at the table, wondering again at the extent of Marcus's grief.

17

Vern squinted as the sun flashed off the chrome of the police cruiser sliding up to the curb. His feet rested against the weatherworn porch rail. He gently pushed against it, rocking back in the old chair. His hands worked the can of Schaeffer resting against his crotch. The can turned as the chair rocked. Around and around, back and forth. The car door opened and that little pissant Kevin MacDougall got out. Vern remembered him from school. Despite the fact he was a year or so older than Vern and his crowd, they had loved tormenting him. Vern smiled at the memory of him and the guys giving ole Kevvy a swirly. Washing that pizza face of his in the boys' locker room toilet. Holding him upside down, arms pinned to his sides, face pressed against the bottom of the bowl, giving it a flush or two. It was a howl. He chuckled at the recollection.

"Hey, Vern," MacDougall said. "What's so funny?" He stood one foot up on the curb, thumbs hooked into his belt. A real gun slinger.

Vern laughed again. "Just thinking about old times, Kevvy, that's all."

"Uh, huh. It's Officer MacDougall now, Vern."

"Oooh, yeah, right. Officer MacDougall. Sorry about that, Kevvy. How's those zits been treating you, Officer MacDougall? Ever get them cleared up?"

Vern leaned forward in the chair and myopically inspected the officer. "Nope, doesn't look like it. Gotta be sure you keep washing, Officer MacDougall. That's the key. You know what they say, 'cleanliness is next to Godliness' or something like that. Let me know if you need a hand there. I sure do remember helping to wash that ole mug of yours."

MacDougall remained at the curb for a moment and then slowly walked up the porch steps. "I'm not here to talk about the past, Vern. I need to speak to you about the murder down at the waterfront."

"Yeah?" Vern's eyebrows rose. "Some slut spic got herself bashed up I heard."

"A Puerto Rican girl was killed, yeah."

"Jesus, those people," he shook his head. "Bunch of fucking animals, aren't they? Either killing each other off or fucking like bunnies, making more. Keeps the population level, I guess."

"The girl's name was Rosaria Donez, Vern."

"Yep, just killing or fucking." He took a long swig from the warm can and belched. "Actually, that don't sound too bad. Some bad craziness and then some of the ole in and out." He gave his hips a thrust as best he could while still seated in the chair. "Maybe those spics are onto something."

"Listen to me, Vern. The girl's name was Rosaria Donez."

"So? So she got a name, who cares?"

"Apparently, you had an altercation with this girl recently."

"Huh? What the hell are you talking about, Kevvy? An altercation?"

"We've been told two days before she was killed, while she and her younger brother were walking by your house, you verbally accosted her and threw a beer can at them."

"I verbally what? Shit, Kevvy, talk English, will you?"

"You yelled at them, Vern. You yelled something about them being the enemy, or Charlie or something like that, and then you threw a can at them," said MacDougall, slowly and clearly.

Vern's eyes widened a bit. "Yeah?"

"Yeah. But you didn't hit them. The can was empty and your aim was pretty bad."

Vern smiled and opened his arms wide, sloshing some beer onto his wrist. "Then what's the problem? No harm, no foul, huh? Besides, these are a couple PR's, right? Maybe I was just making sure they don't get no ideas about knocking over my place. Can't be too sure with them. It was like a public service."

"No, Vern, it wasn't. This was an eighteen-year-old girl and her nine-year-old brother. You insulted them and tried to injure them. And now one of them is dead."

Vern's smile vanished. "Hang on, Kevvy–"

"You hang on, Vern. I told you, it's Officer MacDougall. This isn't high school, this is real life. It's not the 50s, and you're not one of the bad-ass boys roaming the halls of Hoffman High. It's 1968. I have a badge and you're a first class fuckup who was known to have accosted a young girl less than forty-eight hours before she was brutally murdered. You're going to listen to my questions and you're going to answer them to the best of your impaired ability or I'll have you cuffed and in that car before your beer can hits the ground. Got it?"

Vern shrugged and shook his head once. "Life sure is strange, huh? Seems like only yesterday I was flushing your ugly pizza face down the toilet, now you're like fucking John Wayne." He shook his head again and smiled big. "Okay, *Officer MacDougall*, ask away."

MacDougall took a deep breath, pulled his notebook from his breast pocket, and flipped through several pages. "Why did you verbally accost Miss Donez?"

Vern drained the last of the beer and flipped the can over the porch rail into the tiny front yard. MacDougall opened his mouth and then closed it. "Who said I 'verbally accosted' her?"

"She told her boyfriend about it and he told us."

"Shit, Kev-Officer, you going to believe what one of them says? They don't even know what the hell the truth is, been brought up liars, you know? What the hell's going on in the world? A goddamn foreigner telling–"

"*And* we verified it with several of your neighbors. They were more than happy to point the finger at you. Seems you're not the most popular guy on the block. It happened, Vern. Now tell me why."

"Shit, you grow up on a street and you think you know your neighbors–"

"And they know you, Vern, too well."

Vern shook his head, glaring up and down the empty street. "Fuckers," he mumbled.

"Vern!"

"Huh?" he started. "I don't know, maybe I did it, I don't remember."

"You don't remember."

"No. Hell, I have a few beers, the day gets away from me, nothing to do but sit around waiting for that bitch sister of mine to get home and make supper. Nothing on the tube but fucking soap operas. Mom called them her 'stories'. Half the crap on the radio is that jungle music shit I heard enough of in 'Nam. So, I get a buzz going, just trying to keep it level, sometimes it works, sometimes it don't." He looked down the street at nothing. "Anyway, maybe I did throw something at the bitch and her brother, I don't know, and I don't really care. Since when is a dead spic such a big thing anyway? Wouldn't have been before, back when we were in school. Things were a lot better then, simpler. It's all wrong now, you know? It's just wrong."

He looked up at MacDougall, honestly puzzled. "What happened?"

MacDougall wrote a few words in his notebook and slowly closed the cover. "Nothing happened, Vern. Life just kept on going, that's all." He slid the notes back into his pocket. "Did you kill Rosaria Donez, Vern?"

Vern slowly stood and stretched before brushing past MacDougall and heading for the screen door. "I got no problem with one less PR on the streets, but no, I didn't do it."

MacDougall turned and walked down the porch steps into the heat of the day. He heard the screen door slam behind him.

"So what are your thoughts, Kevin? Was he telling the truth or is he someone we should invest more time in?"

"I don't really know, Captain. He sure isn't the most stable of people. I could see him losing it one night, thinking he was back in the jungle, bashing in the head of a Viet Cong. Maybe even cutting up the body to send some message to the enemy. I got the feeling from the neighbors they wouldn't be heartbroken if Vern was locked up for a good long time."

"It'll be a real good long time if he's the one. He'd never see the light of day again."

"I think that's the wish, Captain. Vern's been a jerk all his life. As a kid he probably broke into or vandalized more than a few of the houses on Augusta Street. His dad was a city worker. You know how it goes, a few words here and there and little Vern gets off with a warning or suspended sentence, maybe a fine. That was always the extent of it. When he finally went off to war I'd bet half the congregation of Saint Margaret's said a prayer of thanks and the other half prayed he'd get his head blown off. When he came back and moved into his old house the neighbors must have about died. His current mental condition doesn't help matters. Spends most of the time drunk or trying to to get there. He's out on the porch a lot, doing his drinking there. From what I understand he harasses quite a few passersby, it's not just the Donez girl and her brother."

"You've known him since you were young, haven't you?"

"Um, yeah, pretty much most of my life. Why?"

"It's important that we use all the tools available to us. You say you've known him awhile. Let's use your knowledge to help us. Do you think the person you've known most of your life is capable of a crime like this?"

Clarke was aware of MacDougall's discomfort. He wasn't sure what it was he thought MacDougall could give him, maybe nothing. He was looking for something else right now. Perhaps some sign of maturity or growth that Clarke knew MacDougall better provide if he had any prayer of being successful in this job.

MacDougall sat quietly for a minute. He seemed to make up his mind. "Okay, Captain, I'll give you my opinion of Vernon Wilson. Before I do though, I need to tell you something." He hesitated and then went on. "I don't like Vern. I think he's a piece of garbage and this town would be infinitely better off if he was locked up somewhere. Hell, the *world* would be better off with him locked up. He's cruel, dishonest, and a bully. I've heard stories about how he treats his sister and I wish to God she'd call in just one complaint so I could nail his ass. I know he killed one of his own platoon mates in the war. I don't know any of the specifics, but when I first heard about it, I can't say I was surprised. He's had a screw pretty loose for as long as I can remember, maybe the damn thing fell right off over there."

Clarke remained silent, not moving.

"You asked if I thought he could do this murder. He's cruel. He and his low-life buddies, some we've had the pleasure of arresting, did their best to make school miserable for a lot of kids in this town. Beating them up… humiliating them any way they could think of."

He looked directly at Clarke. "I was one of those kids he and his gang enjoyed picking on. You should know that, know where I'm coming from."

Clarke nodded. His boyish junior officer looked about ten years older at this moment.

"They w ere c ruel, y eah," M acDougall c ontinued, " but I think they were also cowards. They fed off each other's cruelty, trying to outdo one another, but on their own, they were lost. Individually, none of them had the brain power of a hamster. It was like they could almost sense they were going absolutely nowhere in their lives and this was their only shot at having any control. And I think Vern was probably the most scared of the group. He was the cruelest, the most likely to strike out, hurt someone, but it was like he knew he'd better do it now because sooner or later it'd be too late for him."

Clarke listened to this astute observation by his very young officer.

"So, I guess my answer to your question is I don't think Vern Wilson did this. He's a bastard; he practically said he was glad another Puerto Rican was dead, but I don't think he has it in him to do this. He's just too...weak, I guess. Not physically, but just about every other way."

Clarke nodded, his first movement in several minutes. "He still in touch with any of those old friends of his?"

"From what I heard, he pretty much drove them all off with the way he acts. Nobody wants to be near him. The only one with any real contact to him is his sister, Nora."

"What's she like?"

MacDougall thought for a moment. "I don't think I've seen her in years. From what I remember she was a quiet little thing, usually doing the bidding of her father or brother. She never struck me as being a happy sort, never really unhappy either. I guess she was just sort of there. Someone you were vaguely aware of, but didn't really notice. She works in the kitchen over at Children's Hospital."

"Talk to her. Away from her house, either at work or here. We don't need Vern around, intimidating her. I don't expect her to put a noose around his neck, but maybe she can tell us something we don't know."

"Right, Captain."

"Kevin, nice job on that analysis of Vern Wilson. I haven't known him as long as you, but from what I heard I'd have to agree with your assessment."

Kevin MacDougall grinned, the acne marked face of a kid again. "Thanks, Captain. See you tomorrow!"

"Ugh," Clarke grunted.

⇥ 18 ⇤

Lynn McConnell dropped several Chips Ahoy cookies onto a plate and placed it on a tray. She poured some milk into a jelly glass bearing the stone-age image of Barney Rubble. Barney had always been Eddie's favorite character on the cartoon show. Lynn put the milk on the tray with the cookies.

It had been four days since Eddie's discovery and it didn't seem her only child was making any progress at putting it behind him. She doubted she would have been able to get over it that quickly herself; she tended to dwell on the maudlin as Will often reminded her. But you always heard about how much more resilient kids were supposed to be and despite his small size, Lynn had always believed her Eddie was less a child than most.

She carried the tray up the twelve worn stairs, then to Eddie's bedroom. She'd asked several times if he wouldn't rather play outside in the yard, but he was adamant in his refusal. He did not even want to go downstairs and play in the living room. He left his room to use the bathroom and nothing else. Will was beginning to lose tolerance with Eddie's refusals. No son of his was going to hide his entire life. Lynn begged for patience and, at last, Will had relented. For now.

She tapped on the door and turned the knob. As she entered she was aware of both the dimness and the stagnant air.

"Hey, Eddie, you in here somewhere?" she asked, a false smile in her voice. She saw him lying on his small twin bed in the room's corner, farthest from the window. The shade was pulled down blocking out any intrusion from outside. Her heart tightened seeing her son hiding like this. He was holding a book in front of his face as though reading. How he could see the page in front of his nose was beyond Lynn. "How about we throw a little light on the subject?" she said, and clicked on the overhead light illuminating the bright orange cover of Dr. Seuss's "Green Eggs and Ham" in Eddie's hands. His tiny hands. God, he was so small.

"Glad to see you're nourishing your mind, my good man, but now it's time to nourish the body. Milk and cookie time!"

Eddie dropped the book to his chest. He was pale and there were dark circles under his eyes.

"Cookies? Nourishing?" he asked with a small smile. A smile. Thank God.

"Why not can the questions and just take advantage of your old mom's generosity? Deal?"

"Deal." The smile spread.

"Mind if I let in some sun, hon? It's kind of weird turning the lights on at ten in the morning."

His hand hesitated over the plate of cookies. "Okay."

Lynn pulled up the shade and pushed open the window. The sounds of the street wafted in . She returned to the bed and sat next to her son. "Better drink that milk before it gets so hot it curdles. Mr. Rubble wouldn't like that." She brushed Eddie's forehead, feeling for a fever while doing it.

"Aw, Mom, stop it. I'm okay." He pushed away from her hand.

"You're on to me, huh? I keep forgetting what a smart kid I've got. What did Mrs. Westcott say this year?" She feigned trying to remember. "Oh, yes, 'one of the most intelligent young men

I've ever had the pleasure of teaching. And I've been teaching here at Hoffman Elementary since–'"

"Since Barney Rubble's time," Eddie interrupted.

"Edward Sean McConnell," Lynn admonished, silently thrilled at his attempt at humor, "that is not nice at all. Mrs. Westcott has been teaching quite a while, it's true, but show respect. She hasn't been at Hoffman anywhere near that long. In fact, I know that during her first year as a teacher she had little George Washington in class."

Eddie looked at her and sadly shook his head, "Oh, Mom, George Washington is from Virginia, not New Jersey. Everybody knows that."

"You see!" she exclaimed. "My son is soooo intelligent! You must have genius parents or something!"

Eddie rolled his eyes, pried a chip off a cookie, and popped it into his mouth. After picking the cookie chip-clean he got rid of the remainder in three quick bites. "Hey, don't choke. Here, wash it down with some milk." Lynn handed the jelly glass to her son.

He drank and handed the glass back, a Groucho-sized milk mustache on his upper lips. Lynn smiled and felt tears coming. She fought them back and wondered if she could ever love anyone or anything more than she loved her son at that moment. She lifted the tray off the bed and placed it onto the floor, then slid over to him, putting her arm around his narrow shoulders. The two of them leaned against the wall, felt the heat of each other and looked across the room to the square of light coming through the bedroom window.

"It's been a rough few days, huh?" she asked.

She felt her son shrug.

"It's not fair you have to go through this, Eddie. What you saw, no one should ever have to see, especially a nine-year-old boy. I'm sorry. I want to help you any way I can. Is there anything you want to tell me? About anything that scares you, maybe?"

She felt Eddie's shoulders relax, just a bit.

"Your dad and I love you more than anything else in the world. If we could make this all go away, we would."

Eddie pulled away and reached to the floor for another cookie.

"They're pretty good, aren't they? Mind if I steal one from you?" she asked. She took the last one from the plate and nibbled. "If you're afraid of something bad happening to you, hon, let me tell you, your dad and I would never, ever let anyone hurt you. You're our number one son, our little prince. We'd nev–"

"I'm not afraid."

"You're not?" Eddie shook his head. Lynn proceeded slowly. "Okay, that's good. Is there something else on your mind?"

Eddie shrugged and ate the last of his cookie. He drained his Barney Rubble glass and put it back on the tray.

"Got yourself a stash there, big guy," Lynn said. "Better wipe your mouth."

"There's no napkin."

"Here," she pulled the bottom of her shirt out of her pants and used it to wipe his face, "Don't tell anybody."

She held him at arm's length and inspected his thin, pale face. "An Adonis, just like his dad," she declared. He rolled his eyes again and leaned back against the wall. They sat in companionable silence for several minutes. Lynn wondered when the last time was they had been so physically close for so long. Depressed, she couldn't remember. God, how had she allowed life and its everyday obstacles come between her and her son? She slid to the floor so she could have a direct view up into her Eddie's eyes, even if he hung his head, as he so often did.

"Hey, Ed?"

He raised one eyebrow and met her gaze.

"Oh, very Mr. Spock-like. Well done, my man, those hours of practicing in front of the mirror have really paid off."

A genuine smile spread across his face. She could have cheered.

The arrival of the long-awaited smile almost caused her to hesitate before asking her next question. Almost. "Eddie, you said you're not afraid, and I believe you."

The smile vanished.

"But if you're not afraid, and you know Dad and I would never let anything happen to you...." He squirmed and reached down to the plate, found nothing and began playing with his Barney Rubble glass. Lynn handed him the remaining half of her cookie.

"Why is it you don't want to go outside or even downstairs? This is a great room and all...," she looked around at the G.I. Joe doll crammed into the bookcase with his read-to-tatters Dr. Seuss books, his baseball mitt, the yellow Rockem' Sockem' Robots boxing ring in the corner with its two combatants poised to knock each other's block off, lightweight fighter plane pajamas hanging from the bedpost, and, of course, the pile of dirty laundry inside the closet's gaping door. Such a little boy's room, *her* little boy's room. "But hon, I've got to tell you, with the door always closed and the window and shade down, it's starting to get a bit smelly. And nine-year-old boy isn't the greatest smell in the world, you know?"

Eddie continued rolling the glass between the palms of his two small hands.

She gently took the glass from his hands and put it on the tray. "Won't you please tell me why?" She looked up into his downturned face. "I love you more than anything else in the world, Eddie. Anything."

He continued staring down, but whispered, "Anything?"

"Anything."

He looked into her eyes. "Anyone?"

They were a tableau, mother gazing up into her son's intense stare.

"Anyone," she whispered.

"Something is going on with Dad."

Lynn blinked, taken aback. This certainly wasn't what she'd expected to hear. "Of course something is going on, Ed, he's worried sick about you, just like I am. We want you to be your old happy self again."

"No, this is from before."

"Before? Before your…what you found?"

"Yeah."

"Eddie, he's been working very hard. Your dad has had to spend a lot more time at work than before. He wants to move up in the company so he can give us all we'd ever want. You know, a nice house of our own, vacations to Disneyland, stuff like that."

"I know about that. You both told me about it. That's why he can't coach Little League this summer."

"That's right."

"It's not that. I miss not having him home all weekend, but it's not that."

"Then what is it you mean, Eddie?"

He sighed. "I mean his secrets."

Lynn slowly shook her head. "What do you mean, Eddie? Your dad doesn't have secrets from you. You're his number one guy, his little prince, there are no secrets kept from the prince."

"Not from *me*, from *you*, from *us*."

She didn't know what to say. She sat in silence looking into her son's nakedly earnest blue eyes. They were starting to fill with tears. Eddie's eyes didn't spill over, it was like he had done all his crying and though he was pained to have this conversation, he would not cry over it.

"From *us*?"

Eddie nodded in silence, a bead of sweat slid down the left side of his face, sweat, not tears.

"Why don't you tell me what you mean, hon. I'm really lost here."

"Sometimes he goes out at night. After you're asleep."

"Oh, Eddie," Lynn felt herself relax, "your dad is an insomniac. Do you know what that means?"

"Yeah, we learned that in school. It means you can't sleep."

"That's right. Your dad's been like that for as long as I've known him. He gets up and reads or listens to the radio, or sometimes, and I think this is what you're talking about, he'll go out for a short walk. Even though it's the middle of the night, he'll take a stroll. Before you were born sometimes we'd take a walk together, around the block or to the old school and back. He would sleep better after that." Lynn thought of what else she and Will would do to help relax him during those long nights. It had been a while though.

"Okay," said Eddie, "but why would he be gone for so long?"

"Well, maybe it was just a long walk."

"A couple times he wouldn't get home until it was almost light out. Once he got home and I heard the milkman on the porch just a couple minutes later."

"How do you know this, Eddie? I bet maybe this is some kind of dream."

"I don't think it's a dream. I guess that I'm a insom…, insun…"

"Insomniac."

"Yeah, I guess I'm one, too, like Dad. I don't get up and go out though. I think about what happened during the day. Then I change a few of those things and I try to figure how the day would have been different with those changes. Like, if I had just gone home when I first thought about it instead of going on and checking out the bad smell in the bunker at the waterfront. *That* would have been a good change."

"It sure would have, but Eddie–"

"But what I'm saying is Dad makes it a secret. When you ask him at breakfast how he slept he always says–"

"Like a lumberjack," she finished with him.

"Yeah, and one time you asked that was the morning he got home right before the milkman. Remember how you said he sure looked like a tired lumberjack and Dad got all mad about it?"

Lynn did in fact remember the occasion. It had been about a month ago. After she'd made her small joke Will had become extremely angry. He'd said something about not needing to be told he looked like hell before going off to work to provide for his family. Lynn had been surprised at his reaction, but Will could always be moody. She chalked it up to the long work hours he'd been putting in.

Thinking about it now she also remembered how tired Eddie looked that morning. She'd asked him if he'd been up late reading comics or maybe the Hardy Boys and he'd said no. Lynn remembered not quite believing him and giving him a quick scolding, reiterating the importance of sleep to a growing boy, and then moving ahead in her day. If what Eddie said was true, he had gotten almost no sleep at all that night. How many similar nights might there have been?

"Eddie," she said, "are you sure you didn't just *think* you heard your dad coming in? I don't remember anything like that, and we're in the same room, same bed."

"Mom," he rolled his eyes, "a bazooka couldn't wake you up."

It was true enough, Lynn knew. She'd been like that all her life, and if it was a night when she took a pill, well then, forget it. Janis Joplin could be wailing in the same room and she wouldn't budge. But still, on a regular, no-pill night she would at least notice if Will left the bed, wouldn't she? Sure she would. Eddie must be exaggerating, or at the very least, dreaming. Still….

"When do you remember this first happening, Eddie?"

He thought for a moment. "I think around Thanksgiving time. Yeah, I remember, it was the weekend after Thanksgiving, Friday or Saturday night."

Will had been incredibly moody. Something was obviously on his mind. About the third time Lynn asked about it, he erupted. She'd never seen him that way. She really feared he would do himself damage. He raged about her parents and how he would be damned if he'd ever put up with their condescension again. He raged about her job 'wiping the asses of fossils' who'd be better off dead than remaining a drain on society. He raged about his job where he sweat blood and brought home next to nothing. He raged about the town, the country, where everything was going to hell and no one knew why. The long haired agitators were stirring everything up, spics and niggers were taking over the towns, the music was awful, and there was just no respect for anything anymore. He stormed around the small living room and screamed loud enough, she was sure, for Eddie, and probably half the block, to hear him. Eventually he calmed down, and after two hours, fell asleep on the sofa in Lynn's arms.

It was this episode that moved Lynn the following day to speak to her doctor, feign a difficulty with sleep, and get a prescription for sleeping pills. If an outburst similar to this ever occurred again she would slip a pill into some food or a drink of Will's. It would need to be on the sly, Will had some crazy aversion to anything stronger than aspirin. Didn't want to become part of the 'drug culture'. Thankfully, it hadn't been necessary, and the only person using the pills had been Lynn on one or two occurrences of a killer migraine. The bottle sat, almost full, in the medicine cabinet hidden on the bottom shelf behind a box of tampons. An absolute no-man's land for Will.

Yes, it had been awful. In fact, it may have been that Friday or Saturday when she'd taken that first pill, trying to escape the stress. It was damn selfish of her, she thought now, thinking of herself and not her son.

"I think he sat on the porch for a long time." Eddie's voice brought her back to the present. "The old porch rocker squeaks a lot. I listened to it squeaking back and forth for a long time and then it stopped. I heard him come back in, and I think put on some shoes. Then he walked away. His steps got quieter and quieter until they were gone." Eddie looked at his hands in his lap. "I was scared he wasn't coming back. I laid listening until I heard steps again and the screen door open. When I knew he was back home I could go to sleep."

"Oh, Eddie," Lynn whispered, "Your dad would never leave us. You don't have to worry and stay up listening for steps all night. Your dad loves you too much to ever leave you. He loves us both too much."

"Then where does he go, and why does he lie about it?

Lynn looked at her son. She had no answer.

✦ 19 ✦

They sat in a small alcove off the large institutional kitchen which, judging by the number of cigarette butts in the ashtrays and empty soda bottles littering the table, also served as a sort of break room for the kitchen staff of the Children's Hospital. Nora fished a pack of Virginia Slims out of the pocket of her white smock and extended it toward Officer MacDougall.

"No thanks, not while I'm on duty. Actually," he grinned, "I don't smoke anyway. Guess I should've just said that in the first place."

Nora shrugged, shook a cigarette from the pack and lit it. With a Zippo, he noticed. Nora inhaled and looked to her left, out the scratched window, which overlooked a small, litter-strewn courtyard behind the hospital. She exhaled through her nose, enveloping her profile behind a veil of gray. She seemed to almost vanish behind the cloud she'd created. MacDougall studied her through the smoke.

He saw the girl he vaguely remembered years ago from school. Brown hair that could be described as no way other than mousy. She'd always worn it pulled back with a rubber band he recalled, or thought he recalled. It was tucked into a hairnet now so he couldn't tell if she'd changed the style over the years. It looked a little shorter. He had no recollection at all of her figure. She'd been a kid when he was in high school. The woman sitting in front of him was thin with rather prominent, pointed breasts. MacDougall didn't have enough experience with women to know if this dramatic a transformation occurred naturally, or was a fabrication owed to the mysterious world of women's undergarments. He made an effort to maintain eye contact.

When she knocked an ash into a small, foil pie tin he noticed several burn marks on her wrist and forearm. She saw this and said, "Industrial dishwasher. The plates and pots and things come out really hot. If you're not careful you can get burnt." Her lips moved into what MacDougall guessed was a smile. "I'm not careful."

The temperature in the kitchen, even in this corner away from the ovens and other machinery, was stifling. It was like being in hell, if hell consisted of stainless steel, tile, and the odor of steamed broccoli.

The cigarette smoke dissipated and he got a good long look at her face. It was familiar, but not. She could have been any number of girls a year or so behind him in the long procession from kindergarten to high school graduation. At first glance, she struck him as being rather plain, but certainly not the gruesome troll he remembered Vern denouncing in high school. Her nose was broad. Two unexceptional brown eyes looked at Kevin. Her thin lips gripped the cigarette for another pull. Small ears hid beneath the hairnet tucked behind wide cheekbones.

"What can I do for you, Officer? As much as I'd like to stretch this break out as long as possible, I'm low man, or woman, here. I'd better get back to the dishwasher soon or Lavinia will be all over me. And I really don't want to have to put in extra time."

"Can't say I blame you. Lavinia. Say, is that Mrs. Ottman?"

"Yeah, that's her, although I doubt it's missus; no way anyone would ever marry that one."

"When I was a kid she used to scare the heck out of me and my friends. If we ever strayed off the sidewalk and onto her lawn she'd really tear into us."

"She hasn't mellowed."

"Do they still refer to her as–"

"The Nazi? Yup." Nora smiled, this time broadly. The transformation was amazing. It was almost as though her face had been completely altered. The unexceptional face became, almost, beautiful. There was a flicker behind the eyes, the cheekbones seemed to lift the corners of the mouth to reveal an expansive and, despite the cigarettes, dazzling white smile. MacDougall wondered if she'd always had a smile like that. But then if she had, what would she have had to smile about back in school?

It knocked him off stride for a second. "Yeah, um, the Nazi. Frau Lavinia."

"Fräulein."

"Huh?"

"No husband. Fräulein."

"Right." He reached into his pocket for his notebook.

"So," she asked, all business, the smile a memory, "what is it you want?"

He fiddled separating stuck pages, grateful for a brief reprieve as he collected himself. "You're aware of the murder of the young woman at the waterfront?"

"Of course." She crossed her arms over her middle, and gripped her elbows as though protecting herself or trying to ward off a sudden chill.

"I need to ask some questions that might be tough for you. Would you rather we went down to the station instead of doing it here?"

The small, tight smile from earlier was back. "There are very few places in the world I'd less rather be at than here, but I'd guess the Pendale Police Station is one of them. Besides, like I said, I really don't have a lot of time. So, shoot."

"Can you tell me where you were the night of May 30th? It was a Thursday."

"I know it was a Thursday," she said, "it was only a few days ago. Am I a suspect? Do I need to get a lawyer or something?"

"You're not under arrest, you're not being charged. I'm just asking if you can tell me where you were that night."

Nora looked at him for a long minute. "I was where I am virtually every night of my life. Home. In bed. What's it to you?"

MacDougall made a note on his pad. "Can you tell me the whereabouts of your brother during the same time period?"

"Ah," Nora crushed her cigarette into the mound of similar ones in the tin. "That's what this is about. Your real target here is Vern and you want me to narc on him, do your work for you." She shook her head. "Nuh-uh, ain't going to happen, Kevin."

"Miss Wilson—"

"Don't 'Miss Wilson' me, Kevin! Cut the shit! We know each other. You and me have been in this crummy town our whole lives. Sure, you went off to some damn cop school for a couple years, but you're still a townie, just like me. We were born in the same hospital, went to the same church for a while, attended the same school, got teased, put down, and bullied. By the teachers as well as the kids. We got to learn everything there is to know about everybody in this stinking town, whether we wanted to or not. Who they are, what they are, what they think, who and what they hate and what they're afraid of. Some lucky ones, like you, got away for a couple years, but you were too damn weak to stay away. You let the town suck you back, like a…a sludgy whirlpool. Letting you flail around its edge for a while, long enough to get some hope of escape, before slowly pulling you back in for good. You may have a badge, Kevin, but you're weak as hell.

"Some of us were destined to live in this hole forever because of who we were, who our parents were, or maybe because of *what* we were. I know this for sure though, 'Officer MacDougall', if I had the chance you did to get out, I would have had the balls to grab it and run. So don't expect me to do or say anything that's going to make your job any easier."

Nora was breathing hard now. Their shared smile concerning Lavinia Ottman long over. This cop, this guy, this fellow sufferer at the hands of her brother, someone she tried to reach out to once years ago, and made no impression at all…this bastard who didn't even appear to remember the gesture of one victim asking another for help, well, fuck him.

"I didn't know you were so devoted to your brother, Nora."

She snapped her head away from him and gazed out the dirty window, collecting herself, her words.

"There's a lot you don't seem to know, Kevin," Nora said, still looking at the gray, scratched window. "And don't think just because my brother is a sadistic creep who gave you swirlies in school, that you know him. Hell, I've lived in the same house as him all my life and I don't know him. No one knows what happened to him in that damn jungle over there. He's not the same creep you knew, he's not the bully I lived with. He's something different. There's a lot more than you can see, and sometimes, I think, a lot less than there was."

Her gaze met his, "So, I'm telling you this, that night you're asking about, my brother was down the hall from me, asleep."

"What time did the two of you turn in?"

"We watched Johnny Carson's monologue and went to bed."

"Were you together?"

"What the fuck are you insinuating?" she snapped.

"I mean," he said quickly, "were you watching TV together?"

She stared hard at him. "Yes, we were. A happy little family. Until I went to bed. On my own."

MacDougall dropped his eyes to his notes. "Could he have left the house at any time during the night without your knowledge?"

"I'm a very light sleeper, I would've heard him."

"That's all for now, Miss Wilson. I think there's more you could be telling me, but that's it for today. Thank you for your cooperation and I'm sure we'll be in touch again."

Nora slowly shook her head and gave a weary smile. "All your cop show politeness, *Officer MacDougall*, is just so much crap. 'Miss Wilson' isn't going to live the rest of her life knowing that she destroyed the life of her only living family member just to help the likes of you."

MacDougall rose from the table and looked to the window Nora had been staring at. It was so scratched, smudged and gray, it was impossible to discern a thing through it. "Rosaria Donez had *her* life destroyed in a major way. I bet her mother and little brother's lives are pretty much destroyed, too."

Nora reached for another cigarette. MacDougall plucked the lighter from the tabletop and lit it for her. "We'll talk again, Nora," he said, over the flame. He snapped the lighter shut, dropped it into her hand and walked out of the stifling kitchen.

Nora watched his thin, sweat-soaked back disappear around the tiled corner and turned again to the window. There was some comfort to be found in the innocuous gray there. She inhaled deeply on the cigarette, feeling her throat and lungs absorb even more heat. At this rate, she thought, she'd soon be no more than an old cinder. Why had she just lied? Sure, part of it was resentment, resentment he had thought so little of her that he did not seem to even remember her approaching him in school and asking for a minute to talk, to maybe help each other and find comfort together. Unforgivable. Despite what she'd said about him being weak and being sucked back into the town, the truth was he *had* gotten away and been able to make a huge change in himself. Now here he was with the power to alter her and her brother's lives in such a dramatic way. No, she couldn't easily forgive that either.

Was it the fact that, despite what Nora had said to him, Kevin MacDougall *did* know about her, her life on Augusta Street in Pendale? How much did he know? Did he know about her father's heavy hand when it came to disciplining his 'ugly, retard daughter' as she'd heard so many times growing up? About the shame of being the younger sibling of a brother who publicly referred to her as a troll? Or worst of all, the shame of having a father who trudged down the short hall to her room late at night? Seeing his whale-like bulk backlit in the dim night light of the bathroom, knowing in the next seconds she'd feel his weight and hear the scream of the bedsprings beneath her?

Once, after finishing, he'd fallen asleep on top of her. Nora could barely breathe. She thought she was going to die. She thought of what it would look like in the morning, her dead body, splayed wide and crushed under the mass of her father. What would he say? How would he explain it to her mother? Later, Nora realized it wouldn't matter. Her mother would simply refuse to acknowledge it, just like for years she refused to see, hear, admit to her husband's ponderous footsteps in the hall. Just like she never heard Nora's initial cries of fear, pain, and pleas for help until Nora learned it was better to keep quiet than have a meaty palm clamped over her mouth for the duration of the act.

In the beginning, Nora prayed to the Virgin Mary to make her father stop, to make him go away and never come back. Daddies weren't supposed to do that. After a year or so of her father's visits Nora figured no sainted virgin was going to come to her rescue. Mary probably wanting nothing to do with her now, damaged goods and such. That's when she stopped going to church. Mom hadn't said a word.

She exhaled and hid for a moment in the comforting cloud. The two happiest days of her life were those of her parents' deaths. Her happiness only slightly marred by the fact that she couldn't outwardly revel in it. Now, if only Vern....

Maybe she'd lied because of all of this. Or none of it. The truth was, Nora could not honestly say that her brother was home late Thursday night. This was because she was not there either.

Driving from the hospital MacDougall reran the interview with Nora Wilson in his mind. He did not know what to make of it. Going into the meeting he felt he might be able to establish some sort of rapport. The two of them being victims of Vern's malice. *That* certainly hadn't happened. Instead, he generated a lot of antagonism. She seemed to resent him and MacDougall wasn't sure why. She certainly jumped on him for his slip of the tongue regarding watching TV together and going to bed. Made him wonder. Had Vern ever made advances toward his sister? The very thought made him shudder. Could be it was exactly what she'd said. Kevin had the opportunity to leave town and she hadn't. Actually, he'd done worse; he'd left and then returned. Perhaps that was the unpardonable sin. Maybe Nora's life had been even more miserable than he'd thought.

MacDougall tried to picture the Wilson family of his high school years. The father, Rex, was a tub, probably over three hundred pounds. He drove a snowplow or something for the town. Probably did something else, too, in the warm weather. Kevin pictured a red face resting on three or four chins atop a body as wide around as it was tall. He had absolutely no memory at all of Mrs. Wilson. Then there was Vern, of course. God knows how many times Kevin had seen him in his nightmares. And Nora. Shy, quiet, unattractive...as a kid, anyway, almost non-existent, sort of like she was hiding, trying to vanish from sight. A non-entity. For the life of him, Kevin really couldn't come up with much more.

Whatever was going on with her, he was sure she wasn't being truthful. Hell, he thought, let's be honest, she was lying. About *something*.

20

C larke and MacDougall compared notes while lunching on subs and lemonade from the deli down the street. The department had an account there and Clarke blamed his expanding middle, in part, on their drop-dead delicious potato salad. He'd done without it today and, instead, asked for some extra provolone and oil on his sandwich. He watched Kevin shovel forkful after forkful of the potato salad into his mouth. He seemed to barely breathe before biting off another hunk of sandwich, chomping once or twice, swallowing, then chasing it down with a gulp of lemonade.

"JoJo sure makes good lunches, huh, Captain? Only way this could be better is with a big bottle of Mountain Dew instead of the lemonade."

Mountain Dew looked like nuclear waste to Clarke. Its bright yellow color non-existent in nature, in nothing that should be ingested anyway. "Doesn't seem to be slowing you down any, Kevin." He glanced at MacDougall's waistline in envy.

"Oh, I've always been a good eater. Mom always said I was the farthest thing from a finicky eater."

"She did, huh? Have I ever met your mother? I can't seem to recall."

"No. She died the year before I entered the academy. Hit and run." He took another bite and a dollop of mayo and shredded lettuce fell onto the table.

Clarke was genuinely surprised. How could he not have known this about one of his officers? Or had he known and just forgotten? "I'm sorry, Kevin."

"That's okay." He shrugged and gulped down some more lemonade. "She was coming back from Foodtown with stuff for dinner."

Clarke remembered the case now. Unsolved. He hadn't known the victim was Kevin's mother.

"They never got the guy," said MacDougall. "He's still out there somewhere. That's just not right. Stuff like that shouldn't be allowed to happen. Makes me realize I made the right career choice. Trying to put away people like that." He looked up quickly. "Not that I ever had any doubts."

"It's alright, Kevin, we all have doubts."

"I don't. Really, not ever. We're here to protect good people from bad people. It's that simple. It's really important. Good people deserve our help."

Like your mother, thought Clarke.

"I'm proud doing what we do, and I know even if we don't always get the respect we deserve, people are glad we're here."

Clarke wished he felt the same conviction.

"Say, the victim, your mom, had a different last name, didn't she? I seem to remember the victim in that accident was Polish."

"Well, her name was, but she wasn't. My real dad died in Korea and she remarried a couple years later. Paval Solciek. Pretty much right off the boat. Back in Poland he was a blacksmith. Neat, huh? They still had them there. Went to work at one of the factories near the bay. Breyerton Refinery. He wasn't my real dad, but he was a great guy. May as well have been my father.

Taught me to swear in Polish." Kevin grinned. "Want to hear some?"

Clarke smiled. "Maybe later." After a moment, "He's gone, too?"

Kevin nodded. "Just me and the law now. I dream sometimes of catching the guy who killed Mom. Crazy, huh?"

"Not so crazy."

They ate together in comfortable silence for several minutes. When finished they crumpled up the greasy paper wrappers and MacDougall shot each paper wad toward the waste basket, and despite the close confines of the room, missed every shot.

"Guess I better practice more."

"I'd say so," said Clarke shaking his head. "Okay, time to get to work, let's see what we've got."

They each pulled out their pocket notebooks and pencils, and Clarke produced a fresh legal pad from his office on which to consolidate the information.

MacDougall began, "Sometime during the night of Thursday, May 30th, eighteen-year-old Rosaria Donez was–"

"Friday, May 31st. Dr. Avery said that the murder likely occurred sometime after midnight," Clarke corrected.

"Right. Early in the morning of May 31st, eighteen-year-old Rosaria Donez was bludgeoned to death at the Pendale waterworks. It seems she was sitting on a large rock near the water's edge listening to her transistor radio when she was struck from behind."

"Those things aren't very loud, are they?" Clarke asked. "Even with the ear plug in?"

"You mean would the music have drowned out the sound of someone, the killer, approaching?"

"That's what I mean."

"No, they're not loud at all. I've got one at home and they sound pretty tinny. Even with the volume way up she'd probably be able to hear. Anyway, the plug only goes in one ear. It could be she was daydreaming or just lost in the music. You know how that happens."

It had been a long time since Clarke had felt 'lost' in any music. "Okay, go ahead."

"She was struck from behind and knocked to the ground. While there she either turned to face her attacker or he moved to the front of Rosaria, because the majority of the blows hit her in the front of the head and face. My guess would be when she hit the ground she rolled back around a little."

"Maybe, but let's keep the speculation to a minimum."

MacDougall nodded and continued. "There were no defense wounds. This indicates that she was stunned and unable to defend herself. After several more blows to the face, Dr. Avery believes there were seven of them, a couple just glancing, but the majority direct hits, the killer may have knelt beside the body."

"Why don't we know this for sure? There certainly ought to be indentations from the knees."

"The problem is, Captain, Rosaria's body–"

"Keep it professional, officer. She was the victim."

"Right. Sorry." MacDougall blushed to match the color of his acne scars. "The problem is, the victim's body was dragged over the spot where the killer may or may not have knelt, obliterating any potential marks in the dirt. We just can't be sure."

"Alright. What else?"

"The victim was then dragged to the cement bunker, thirty-six feet from where we believe the attack took place. It was there Dr. Avery believes the breasts were cut away. There was evidence of some tissue on the ground there. She was placed in a rear corner where she'd least likely to be seen from the outside. When the sun's out, the shadows are pretty dark in there."

"Any sign of the weapon?"

"You mean what he hit her with?"

Clarke nodded.

"None. It appears the killer took it with him. Same with the breasts and what was used to cut them off. The weapon could have been anything blunt. A baseball bat, shovel handle, even a rolling pin. Avery isn't sure what was used on the breasts. It was sharp, but not like anything surgical. Maybe a machete. Something like that."

"How difficult would it be to drag a dead body for that distance?"

MacDougall was ready for the question. "Not too difficult. The ground in that part of the waterworks is pretty hard. I don't have to tell you it's been real dry and it's almost baked solid in the heat. Sully and I grabbed a couple equipment bags from the lockers downstairs. You know, the P. B. A. baseball team's stuff? Weighed them both, tossed them in the trunk and headed down to the waterworks. One was–"

"Where'd you weigh them?"

"Oh. We stopped at my place and used the bathroom scale. I held each bag in my arms. I know how much I weigh so we just subtracted my weight to get the bag's."

"How high does your scale go?"

"Two-twenty."

"And it didn't go over with you and the bag?"

"Not even close."

Jesus. "What do you weigh, Kevin?"

"Well, in uniform and sidearm, I'm around one forty-five."

"*Pounds*?"

"Yup."

"Wait, you weigh yourself with your gun?"

"Um, sometimes."

"Never mind. What did the bags weigh?"

"One was forty-nine pounds and the other was a little over sixty-three. I think that was the one with home plate and the bases in it."

"So you've got a hundred and twelve pounds."

"Wow, that was quick. Anyway, we used our belts and sort of tied the two bags together and it wasn't tough at all to drag it for that distance. Sully's a lot bigger than me so obviously, he had no trouble with it. I didn't strain much either."

"Well, that tells us that the murderer could have been just about any size, but it doesn't–"

"I know where you're headed, Captain."

"Do you?"

"Yup. You're wondering if a woman could've done it. Done the dragging, that is."

"And?"

"And we grabbed ole Mrs. Barton–"

"Mrs. Barton from dispatch? *That* Mrs. Barton?"

"Well, yeah."

"Jesus, she's got to be almost eighty years old! Were you trying to kill the old bird?"

"Oh, no, Captain. I know for a fact she's only in her early sixties. It's years of teaching those darn kids that makes her look so old. She's one tough woman, though. I remember once when I was in school she jumped in the middle of a fight between two kids. I swear, she almost broke the arm of one of them. She could be downright scary. Trust me on that," MacDougall said with such conviction Clarke couldn't help but believe him.

"Anyway," MacDougall continued, "she was tickled to be able to help us out. We drove down to the waterworks and had her drag the bags back and forth between the bunker and the murder site."

"Back and forth?"

"Yup. She was sort of showing off, I think. She'd probably still be doing it if we hadn't told her we had to get her back to dispatch. I think she was disappointed."

Clarke tried to picture the tiny bird-like creature he'd seen this morning with headphones pressing down her permed gray curls dragging over one hundred pounds. Impossible. But then he couldn't picture her leaping into the middle of a school brawl, either.

"Alright. So we know the killer could have been of either sex. That just makes our job twice as difficult. Continue."

"The body was found in the bunker at approximately 4:30 p.m. by Edward McConnell, age nine. He said he was hunting for snapping turtles."

Clarke nodded. He remembered similar hunts from his childhood. "He was alone?"

"Yes. It seems that it's a cause of friction between his parents. They didn't come right out and start arguing in front of me, but I get the impression the father didn't think the boy should've been left alone and he blames the mother. She works herself and feels the father has been neglecting the boy. I got the feeling the kid was sort of caught in the middle. They were both pretty upset."

"That's not really our business. And maybe that's not *all* they're upset about." Clarke glared at his officer.

MacDougall cleared his throat. "Although dead for less than a day, because of the salt and moisture down by the water, the body quickly became pretty ran–, uh, decaying. Insects and vermin, too. Smelled awful."

"What do we know about the victim's recent past? Was she targeted or was she a random victim?"

"Well, we know that earlier in the day she had a fight with her mother concerning her boyfriend, Marcus Rodriguez. The mother, Anita Donez, felt that Marcus was taking liberties with her daughter."

Taking liberties. Clarke wondered what police show MacDougall had recently been watching.

"She felt they spent too much time together and he, Marcus, was a bad influence on Rosaria's little brother, Alfonso. Apparently things got pretty nasty. The mother called her a tramp or something like it, and that's the last they saw of each other. Alive anyway."

"She was staying at the boyfriend's before the attack?"

"Yup. Mom didn't know it, though. She thought she was at her aunt's. Marcus has a place of his own. Claims he was putting in a lot of hours working at an uncle's restaurant. Says he was there cleaning up the night of the killing."

"Be sure to check on it. I know there are often a lot of aunts and uncles in these families. Get the facts."

"Right. Also, sometime earlier in the week of the killing, or maybe the week before, I'm still trying to nail it down exactly, Miss Donez and her brother were accosted by Vern Wilson."

"But your feeling is he's not capable of the crime?"

"That's my feeling, Captain, but I'd hate to rule out our most obvious suspect just on my gut feeling."

"I agree. I've got something to add to the victim's recent history." Clarke flipped through is notes. "Apparently on the twenty-eighth or earlier in the day on the twenty-ninth, she stopped at Minna Cooper's Hair Salon."

"Really? I didn't know Minna cut their hair."

Clarke looked up. "Why did you say that?"

Uncomfortable, MacDougall reddened and said, "I guess I just don't think of her as doing that. I don't recall her ever cutting the hair of anybody...different, you know, not white."

"Turns out the only reason Rosaria Donez stopped to ask was because she promised her aunt she would. Mrs. Cooper refused for one reason or another and they had words. It ended with the victim calling Mrs. Cooper a bitch and giving her the middle finger."

MacDougall's eyes widened. "Holy moly, I bet Minna nearly had a conniption. She's not one to take any crap from any...uh, young folks. No sir, she's real old-fashioned. She'd still be living in 1950 if she could. Maybe 1940."

"Why didn't you say what you started to say?"

"What do you mean, Captain?"

"You were going to say Mrs. Cooper would never take crap from any Puerto Rican, right?" MacDougall was quiet.

"Kevin! This is a murder investigation! What gives?"

MacDougall fidgeted before answering. "I'm sorry, Captain. It's just I've known Mrs. Cooper my whole life. She cut my hair more times than I can count. She's always real nice to me." Clarke waited. MacDougall took a breath and went on.

"Sometime around the early 50s Mr. Cooper, Arnie his name was, managed Greene's downtown, a real nice man, was a volunteer fireman–" Clarke made an impatient noise.

"Anyway, around that time, Mr. Cooper must have been in his early forties, he sort of...well, they say when a man gets that age he sometimes gets an urge to look around for something new, something exciting, something he'd never done before."

Clarke grunted.

"So," MacDougall continued, "there was this new clerk hired down at the store. Brand new to town, a woman, and Puerto Rican. How about that? Who'd of thought Pendale could be so progressive? Hard to believe now, jeez, back then she must have been the only one around." He noted his captain's look. He stammered, "Only Puerto Rican around, I mean. You know, there were lots of women around then and–"

Clarke cut him off. "How do you know this, Kevin? What were you, two years old?"

"Oh no, Captain. I was born in forty-three, so I must have been, gee, about eight, maybe. I heard most of it from my mom, though. She and Mrs. Cooper had been pretty good friends and mom said it was a shame that some foreign...some outsider could come into town and cause such trouble."

"This woman caused trouble?"

"Oh, yeah. Well, not just her, Mr. Cooper was part of it, too. He was looking for something different, I guess, and this pretty young woman shows up at just the right time." MacDougall shook his head. "They carried on for a few weeks, under the radar, so to speak. But in a town like this, nothing like that stays quiet long. I understand Mrs. Cooper was truly fit to be tied. I remember Mom saying that there's no way Minna would ever divorce Arnie, being Catholic and all, but she sure might kill him."

"So what happened?"

"Oh, I guess it worked itself out. The woman probably figured there were more inviting places in the world than Pendale and she left town one night. Without even saying a word to Arnie, I heard. He came back to Minna, tail between his legs, she forgave him I suppose, and they moved on with their marriage. Since then though, I don't think Minna has any love in her heart for the Puerto Ricans. It must really gall her to see so many living in town now. It's hard to imagine a time when there was just the one of them." MacDougall hesitated. "And she sure was beautiful."

"Your mom tell you that, too, Kevin?"

"Oh, no. Didn't I say? Once Mom took me down to the store when the woman was working. Mom was a great lady, but she could be as nosy as the next person. She pretended to be shopping for gloves for my Uncle Joe and Mr. Cooper's woman waited on us."

"She was pretty, huh?"

Kevin was quiet for a moment. "She was stunning," he said quietly. "That's really the word for her. I was stunned by her beauty. Her hair was black as the coal in our basement bin and she wore it in a braid hanging over one shoulder. I remember thinking that her skin was the color of my mother's coffee after she put in the cream. And it was flawless. Her eyes looked like the night sky way out in the country where the lights don't ruin it." He blinked and looked at Clarke, embarrassed. "You have to remember, Captain, this was 1951 or 2. We didn't have a TV yet. I was too young to look at newspapers; all I saw was what was in front of me. My whole world was my family, my street, my school. And there was nothing like this woman anywhere in my life. Looking back, I don't know if I even knew people that weren't white existed. She was the first I ever saw. I'll never forget her."

MacDougall sat quietly looking at the surface of the old table. Clarke made a note in the legal pad. "Why didn't you tell me this before?"

"That I'd never seen anyone not white before?"

"You know what I'm talking about, Kevin."

"About Mr. Cooper having a fling with a Puerto Rican girl fifteen years ago?"

"Yes, that."

"I guess I didn't see the relevance. I had no idea about Mrs. Cooper's recent encounter with the victim. I can see now how it may be important. Sorry."

Clarke sighed and threw his pencil to the table. "Shit. I should have briefed you on my interview with Mrs. Cooper earlier. It's my fault. From now on, let's be sure we confer on every point as quickly as possible. Lunch and just before leaving for the day. Okay?"

"You think this is going to take some time to figure out, Captain? Days? Weeks?"

"Let's hope not. It's not exactly news there's a lot of unrest going on. I know it's been building everywhere for a while, in Washington, other big cities, but it's present here, too. People are frustrated and angry and they don't really know why. Sure, the war is like a giant black cloud hanging over us all, slowly choking off the light, but it's even more." MacDougall had never heard his captain talk like this before. "People in town, people I've known for years, people you've probably known your whole life, they hear a Puerto Rican girl has been killed and their first response is almost glee. Unless they're an asshole like Vern Wilson they won't come right out and say it, but it's what they feel, you can tell. I was walking by Frank's Barber Shop earlier today. The door was propped wide open and I heard some old boys talking. 'Tramp probably deserved it,' they said, 'Good, thin out their ranks some'. One joker even added he hoped whoever did it had some fun with her first, seeing that's what those girls are best at.

"Kevin," Clarke said, almost imploring, "this was a girl, a young girl, someone's daughter and sister. And these men were trashing her like she's no better than dirt. How does this happen?"

MacDougall stood mute.

"Yesterday afternoon I got a call from Reverend Altiz, the guy who runs the youth center that so many of the Puerto Rican kids hang out at." MacDougall snorted, disgusted. "He demanded to know what progress we were making on the case. Wanted to know why we were dragging our feet. He didn't come out and say it, but he intimated that if the victim had been a white girl we'd have the whole thing tied up in a bow by now."

"Wow," MacDougall whispered. "What did you say?"

"I told him the investigation is progressing and he would hear the results when everyone else did. He finished the conversation by letting me know that there were people in his community who believed Pendale put a higher value on the lives of white people than brown."

MacDougall just shook his head, not surprised.

Clarke pushed back his chair and rose. He paced the miniscule room before turning to MacDougall. "And the worst part? The worst part is that bastard Altiz, with his mail order degree, is right. As long as they're safe themselves, most folks couldn't care less about a Puerto Rican girl dying horribly. They view her as less than human.

"I'm sure that's how Vern Wilson feels, and Minna Cooper, and you can be certain that's how the idiots at the barber shop feel. Hell, if I was a minority in this town I'd be upset; I'd wonder if anyone gave a damn about keeping me and my family safe. That asshole, Altiz, has a point."

"But Captain, we don't feel the way those others do. We're trying our best to catch the killer. I mean, okay, they're different and sometimes I don't get them, but that doesn't stop us from doing our jobs."

"Protecting good people from bad people. That's what you're saying."

"Yeah."

"No matter race, skin color, or what."

"Well," MacDougall hesitated, remembered the pain of Mrs. Donez, "yeah, that's what I mean."

"Good," Clarke sighed, "I'm very glad to hear that, but it may not be what's perceived out there." He pointed toward the street. "And sometimes, Kevin, perceptions become realities." He slumped down into his chair again. "Coming to the station this morning I turned on the radio. God knows why, but I tuned in to a popular music station. There was a guy singing about revolution. Something about wanting a revolution. It was mostly noise and I could barely hear the words, but I'm sure that's what he said. Christ, what's going on? Why would anyone sing about having a revolution?"

"Yeah, I know the song. The Beatles."

"That was The Beatles? I just saw them on the Sullivan show last year. They seemed like nice kids. Sure, they looked ridiculous with those haircuts, but they were smiling, having fun. Jesus. What happened to them?"

"Actually Captain, I think they were first on Ed Sullivan almost five years ago."

"Really?" Captain Clarke looked bewildered. "Five years? What happened to the time? What happened to them?" He shook his head. "What the hell's happening to us?"

MacDougall had no answer.

❖ 21 ❖

Minna Cooper was in her yard, as usual, working at one of her flower beds. It was early in the year, but she was already having difficulty with fungus on the leaves of her rose bushes. An old Eight O' Clock coffee can contained a solution of warm soapy water which she gently rubbed into the leaves with her bare fingers. When she finished with the bushes at this end of the bed she would bathe them in a gentle spray of the hose. Minna knew to keep them looking and feeling their best required constant vigilance on her part. They didn't just grow into healthy adulthood on their own, you know. They needed regular care and nurturing. Leaning back on her heels for a moment, she surveyed her domain. Lovely. And she would do what was necessary to keep it so.

She heard the sound of wheels on gravel followed by the slam of a car door and Minna rose slowly to her feet. She gradually straightened and felt her spine crackle. Ah, that's better, she thought. She turned and saw young Kevvy MacDougall walking up the drive, all dressed in his uniform. How quickly they grow up, she thought, feeling the familiar pang of regret that she'd never had children of her own.

She smiled. "Hello, Kevvy, I'm sorry, *Officer* MacDougall. It's been a while since you've stopped by. Looking for a quick trim?"

"Uh, thanks Mrs. Cooper, I've been going to Frank's Barber Shop for a while now." Maybe not anymore, though, he thought. "I'd sort of feel funny going to a lady's salon for a haircut at my age."

"At your age! Why it's only been a few years since you came here with your mother, Kevvy. But don't worry, I completely understand, you now being a law officer and all. It probably wouldn't seem right. Remember though, I always have time for you if you need me. In fact, I'm not busy at all these days."

"Sure, thanks anyway, Mrs. Cooper." He remembered Captain Clarke saying Minna had told him she'd been too busy to take Rosaria's business.

"Would you like something to drink?"

"What? Oh, I'm not allowed to drink on duty, it's against–"

"No, no, Kevin," she laughed, "I mean something cold. Certainly you're allowed a cool drink?"

"I'm sorry, Mrs. Cooper. Sure, I'll have something if you are."

"I'll be right back then. Why don't you have a seat in the gazebo while you wait. It's so lovely and cool in there. There aren't any blossoms yet, but it still smells nice and fresh."

"Sure. That's the, uh, over there?"

"That's right, be right back."

He walked to the rear corner of the yard and surveyed Minna's gazebo. "Wow," he muttered.

He stepped onto the white decking and turned to sit in the ornate chair. He felt foolish and oddly vulnerable. He could only hope to quickly wrap up this conversation, he couldn't think of it as an interview, and then be on his way. He had to say, though, it was a pretty comfortable chair despite its looks. Felt nice in the shade, too.

He heard the back screen door slam and saw Mrs. Cooper walking stolidly toward him, tray in hands. He rose to help the older woman. On the tray were two large plastic cups, decorated in a tan plaid design. Kevin had to smile. He remembered his mother having cups exactly like them. The two women had probably shopped at the same store. Maybe even made the purchases together. They'd been pretty good friends, Kevin recalled.

"What have you got for me, Mrs. Cooper?" he called out when she got near. He could hear the sound of ice cubes thunking against the plastic. The sound bringing pleasant memories from the past.

"I'm sure you'll like it, a young fellow like you. I certainly can't seem to get enough of it with my sweet tooth."

"I never knew you enjoyed sweets, Mrs. Cooper," he said reaching for the tray.

"Oh, yes, ever since I was a young girl. My figure wishes I didn't enjoy them so much."

Kevin laughed politely and shook his head.

"The house is usually full of chocolate, cookies, candy, and whatnot. So I always make this extra sweet, just the way I like it. I hope you like it, too."

She lifted one of the cups from the tray and extended it to him.

"It's my absolute favorite," she beamed, "cherry Kool-Aid."

MacDougall stood frozen, plaid cup now in his hand, looking down at the deep red liquid in which floated pink-hued ice cubes. One of the nagging details of the homicide kept undisclosed to the public, along with the breasts, of course, was the red stain on the halter of the victim. He wasn't rash enough to believe that because Minna Cooper enjoyed Kool-Aid she was in any way tied to the murder. Heck, there was probably a pitcher of Kool-Aid in over half the refrigerators of Pendale. And cherry was certainly a popular flavor. But coupled with the fact that Minna'd been in contact with the victim shortly before the attack, and that the encounter had been disagreeable, along with what MacDougall knew about her marital difficulty, brief and in the past though it was, well, no way he could ignore it. He wondered how to best go about drawing information from this woman he'd known all his life and had always looked at as a friend.

He took a sip from the cup and almost gagged. God! Was it sweet! "Mmm, it's great Mrs. Cooper, nice and cool."

She took a delicate sip of her own. "I'm glad you like it, Kev–, I'm so sorry. I keep doing that, don't I? It's so hard not seeing you as the shy little boy I had to hoist up on a booster seat to cut his hair. I promise to make more of an effort from now on to remember that you're Officer MacDougall, not little Kevvy."

MacDougall realized he'd probably receive more information as Kevvy than Officer MacDougall. He smiled and leaned toward Minna. "I tell you what, Mrs. Cooper," he said in a low voice, "when it's only you and me, Kevvy is just fine."

Minna laughed, "Oh, Kevvy, it's so nice to hear that. It reminds me so much of years past. Good years." She looked at him for a moment, making up her mind. "And seeing as you *are* an adult now, if you wish to call me Minna instead of Mrs. Cooper, you may."

"Absolutely not, Mrs. Cooper, it wouldn't be proper. You'll always be Mrs. Cooper."

She beamed and MacDougall knew he'd handled the situation well. Anything to keep her thinking he was still the naïve seven-year-old he was in 1950. He wondered how to move forward when he was forced to decide.

"It's lovely to see you, Kevvy, but to what do I owe the pleasure? Surely you're not just stopping to visit an old lady?"

"An old *friend*, Mrs. Cooper," he said, thinking furiously about what to say next. As he scanned his surroundings in a near panic the answer presented itself. "Last year I bought a little place over on Douglas Street, did you know that?"

"You know, I may have heard something about it, I'm not certain, Kevin. Oh, yes, I remember. I believe Lucille Spencer mentioned something about it while she was in for a perm. It's nice for you to have a place of your own. It's a bit too far from shopping for me and too close to Browntown, but who knows, once you find yourself a nice girl, maybe you'll be ready to move up to a better address."

Browntown. He'd forgotten that's what the Puerto Rican section of town used to be referred as. He'd heard it enough times from his mother, MacDougall thought uncomfortably. Was it still called that?

"Yes, who knows? I want to make the most of what I have though, and I thought I'd do some landscaping to spruce up the place, you know, increase its value for when I eventually want to sell." He saw Minna's eyes light up. "And I thought, who would be the right person to get advice from? Who has the most beautiful yard in town? Who else, but Mrs. Cooper?" She clasped her cup with both hands against her chest, looking almost as though she was in prayer. Tears filled her eyes. "That makes me *so* happy Kevin, to know when you needed help you thought of me." MacDougall felt a stab of guilt which was quickly erased by the image of Rosaria's ravaged face and savagely torn chest. "We old friends need to stay together in these awful times, don't we, Kevin?"

He looked into her earnest, trusting eyes. "Absolutely."

"You're out here most days, aren't you?" MacDougall asked, the two of them walking arm in arm, surveying the yard.

"Whenever I can. It's good for me, keeps me busy now that the hair business has slowed down some." He thought again of Rosaria Donez. "Plus, it really takes quite a bit of effort to keep up. Most people think you plant some seeds or bulbs and just let them 'do their own thing', she said with a slight sneer. "That's not the case, I assure you.

"Of course, it's up to the gardener how much effort she, or he," she added quickly, not wishing to discourage Kevvy's plans, "wants to put in. Perhaps you could have several perennial gardens, or some annuals that don't require so much maintenance. It's your choice, and of course I would be more than happy to help in any way I could. I know your job keeping the peace you must be very busy."

He sensed an opening. "That's true Mrs. Cooper, we're especially busy now. The murder down by the waterfront is taking most of our time."

"What a shame, and I'm sure there are so many other duties you may be forced to neglect because of it. Is it necessary to devote so much time to that? Surely it's something which involves their community, don't you think?"

"Their community?"

"A feud or gang altercation. Like that show on Broadway." She sniffed, "A musical about gang fights. Hmph. Imagine!

"You hear about them and their violence on the news all the time. she was probably at the center of something between several men. Oh, those people, they have absolutely no self control. They're so volatile. Sometimes I wonder, living so near them, if we're really safe ourselves. There are people in town who wish they would just go ahead and finish themselves off, that way we could all rest easier. I don't know that I would agree with them, but I see their point." She shuddered. "Awful people."

"The townspeople?"

"No, silly!" she laughed, "The Puerto Ricans and the rest of them."

The rest of them? How had he ever looked at this woman as a friend, he wondered? And more to the point, how had his mother, an adult, who would have been aware of her friend's beliefs? Had his mother shared these views? He pushed the thought from his mind. They stopped in front of a wide bed, the earth freshly turned.

"Why is it this bed hasn't been planted yet? It seems to be lagging behind the others."

"That's because I've been mixing some manure into the soil. Oh, don't look like that, Kevin," she laughed, "I washed my hands before getting our Kool-Aid. I always keep very clean hands. And, of course, I wear gloves, as well. This bed is one I can see directly from the window in my sitting room." She nodded toward the small addition at the rear of the house with jalousie windows. "On inclement days I sit inside and read while still enjoying the sight of my garden. It is also right along the sightline with my gazebo, see? I want what's growing in this bed to be extra beautiful and satisfying to me. It needs to be every bit as attractive as the roses around the gazebo. I take great pride and satisfaction in them."

"I bet you do. I'm sure when they bloom they're stunning."

"If I may be so bold as to agree with you, they are."

"Did Mr. Cooper build the gazebo for you when he put in the hair salon?"

"No." They walked toward the garage. "It wasn't until years later. In fact, when you first began having you hair cut here, the yard was empty. First, the flower beds were planted and later, Arnie built the gazebo for me."

"Well, it sure is beautiful. What a nice thing to do."

"My husband loved me very much."

MacDougall took another sip and hid his grimace. "Do you ever get lonely here, by yourself?"

"Very rarely. I see a few customers from time to time, I'm in my garden daily, and being on a corner I see lots of people going by. There's no time to be lonely."

"Do you ever get tired of the people walking or driving by? These are two pretty busy streets. Is it ever annoying?"

"Well, now that you mention it, sometimes late at night, teenagers in their cars speed by and make an awful racket. I've often thought of making a complaint." She smiled. "I suppose that's what I'm doing now, isn't it, *officer*?"

He returned the smile. "I guess so, I'll be sure to mention it down at the station. Do people on the sidewalk ever bother you? Being on the corner you've got them on two sides of the house."

"On occasion, maybe, but it's rare."

"Say, didn't the victim of the killing, Rosaria Donez, stop by and give you some grief? I think Captain Clarke said something about that."

Minna stopped and looked up at Kevin. "Did he? As you said, her death seems to be monopolizing your time. To the exclusion of all else," she added.

MacDougall stood silently and waited.

"Yes, as a matter of fact, she was very nasty to me. I know it's not considered polite to speak ill of the dead, but she was rude and obscene."

"That's awful."

"It was. It's bad enough I'm forced to watch her walk by day after day, week after week, wearing those trashy clothes. Do you know that her blue jeans were so low you can see…well, never mind. And lately there was some kind of radio plugged into her head, like she was in a world of her own, no thought at all about others." Minna shook her head, agitated. "It's one thing putting up with her trampy looks, but I will not be rudely spoken to. Especially not by one of them."

"Young people today." He shook his head.

She made a noise of disgust.

They stood together in silence before Kevin said, "Maybe it's better you won't have to see her anymore."

They gazed over the serene lawn and botanical splendor of the flower beds. The beauty washed over them like a warm wave.

Minna sighed before saying, "Yes, I just wish someone would do something about all the others."

⥤ 22 ⥢

Yesterday had been one of the healthiest days she'd experienced in months. Today though, first thing out of bed, Nikki was dry as a chip and craving a cold beer. She opened her refrigerator door with no real expectation of finding said beer, she'd long since drunk her apartment dry. She was surprised to see a six pack of Coca Cola. No way she'd ever have squandered precious booze money buying it, must be a gift from Mrs. Gorman. Nikki smiled. How the heck did her landlady know she'd be so parched? Must be psychic.

Not quite the wished for beer, but she cracked a soda anyway. Once the sugar hit her tongue she chugged down the entire bottle and reached for a second before erupting with a colossal belch. Holy shit. Bet they heard that one over in Perth Amboy, she thought. Better slow down.

Half an hour later Nikki sat at her kitchen table, foot tapping against the linoleum floor and listening to the radio while gulping down her fifth Coke. It had been a day since her heart to heart with Mrs. Gorman and while yesterday hadn't been too difficult, today was another story.

Yesterday, after some toast and juice (bleah) with Mrs. Gorman, she'd taken a shower, at her landlady's insistence, and gotten dressed for church, also at her insistence. Nikki'd been shaky and not at all sure she could make it through the afternoon. But apparently God, as Mrs. Gorman told her, helped those who helped themselves. After searching for, and finally discovering, a long forgotten dress hanging jammed against the wall of her bedroom closet, she slid on a pair of shoes and presented herself before Mrs. Gorman.

One look at Nikki and Mrs. Gorman shook her head. "Slip."

"Huh?"

"You need a slip. The light goes right through that dress."

"Right. Um…Mrs. G., I don't think I have–"

"Never mind, I have one you can use. You must be presentable in God's house, Nikki." She again examined her tenant. "We need to fix your hair. It looks like it was cut by a blind barber."

Pretty close, Nikki thought. She'd been blind drunk when she cut it herself using nail scissors.

"Well, we won't worry about that right now, no one will see your hair," Mrs. Gorman said walking into her spare room.

Am I going to wear a bag on my head? Nikki wondered. When Mrs. Gorman returned she had her answer. "Oh, no, Mrs. G. No way."

In one hand was the promised slip. In the other was a round, light green hat, festooned with small silk daisies. The very thing for the stylish female churchgoer of the early 50s. "I know I've been a really bad person, but are you trying to kill me with embarrassment? What are people going to say?"

"Nikki, put this on." She passed her the slip and Nikki stepped into it sliding it up under the dress. "Let me see, alright, it looks fine." Mrs. Gorman sighed and took Nikki's hand. "Wearing this hat will embarrass you? You ask what people are going to say?" She looked into the younger woman's eyes. "What do you think they say now? What do they say when they see you stumbling up the street in broad daylight? What do they say when you are at the grocery store, asking for credit, unwashed and smelling of vomit? When they see you night after night leaving some bar with different men, what–"

"Okay, Mrs. Gorman, I see your point." There were tears in her eyes. "I guess my reputation's withstood worse than a silly hat."

"How well it's withstood is another question, but," she said, placing and pinning the hat on Nikki's head, "it certainly can't do any more harm. There. We'll deal with the hair another day. Now, about a brassiere?"

"What about one?"

"Put one on."

"But–"

"Nikki, you're going to *church*."

"What, is God going to sneak a peek?"

Mrs. Gorman glared at her and Nikki retreated, mumbling, to her apartment.

By the time the short drive to the church was over Nikki was openly perspiring. She knew, despite the open windows, the interior of the car was permeated with the odor of last night's alcohol leaking from her pores. It would take more than a single shower to remove the smell. If Mrs. Gorman noticed, she didn't say a word and Nikki was grateful. It had already been an emotionally trying day and she expected the worst was to come when they arrived at Saint Margaret's. But it didn't.

Inside, the stained glass windows muted the harsh light and the temperature was cool and soothing. The two women were alone in the pews save for an ancient couple in the second pew, each with a rosary draped over their fingers, their lips moving in silence. On the altar was a woman replacing flower arrangements on each side of the tabernacle with fresh ones. Despite being absent from any church for years, the feeling of the pew beneath her as she slid over making room for Mrs. Gorman was familiar to Nikki. The air itself seemed to have a different consistency; it felt more substantial. It wasn't heavy like the humidity outside, but comforting and consequential.

Probably because all the big time sinners never come in and pollute it, Nikki thought. She gazed up at the gray, blank-eyed stares of the statues, feeling helpless and vulnerable. "Mrs. G.?" she whispered.

Mrs. Gorman's eyes were shut. Her hands were clasped in front of her and her lips were moving. They continued for a moment before stopping. She opened her eyes. "Yes, Nikki?"

"What do we do now?"

"We pray."

"Okay." Nikki looked forward briefly before turning back. "What for?"

Mrs. Gorman narrowed her eyes at Nikki.

"Oh, yeah."

After about fifteen minutes of what might constitute prayer, Nikki turned and again whispered to Mrs. Gorman. "Mrs. G.?"

She silently nodded.

"Mrs. G., please don't make me go to confession. I really don't feel good. I know you probably think I'm saying it to get out of going, and I probably would say it to get out of it, but it's the truth. I'd hate to be in the little closet and be sick. I bet God hates it when people barf while confessing. In fact, we better get out of here soon or I'll be puking in the baptismal font."

The two women crossed themselves and quickly departed, Nikki trying to keep the hat from sliding off her head. Back in the car she thanked her landlady for not forcing the issue of confession.

"I was never planning to make you go to confession today, Nikki," she said putting the car in gear and carefully nosing out into the street.

Lifting the dreaded hat from her head and rubbing her fingers over her sweaty scalp, Nikki asked, "Then why did you say so back at the house? I was terrified."

Mrs. Gorman smiled in satisfaction. "I suppose I was, what do they say today, messing with your head?"

Nikki stared at her and slowly shook her head. "You're evil, Mrs. G., I guess I've been too messed up to notice, but you're the devil."

"Mmmm," she smiled. "Maybe so, I guess I'll have to confess it tomorrow when we come back."

"Man," Nikki sank into her sticky seat, "You sure don't mess around, do you?"

"No, I don't."

After arriving home in barely enough time to sprint to the bathroom, Nikki spent the rest of the day napping on the sofa in front of a fan lent to her by Mrs. Gorman. The two women had a light dinner together sharing an omelet and Nikki was in bed and asleep before dark. Alone.

Today however, in the absence of a hangover, and now that she'd substituted a sugar rush for alcohol, she didn't know what to do with herself. She sniffed her armpits and decided a quick shower was in order. There was nothing like a coating of alcohol sweat and BO to really gross you out. She quickly brushed her teeth before jumping in the shower, hoping the toothpaste taste would leave her mouth by the time she was finished so she could enjoy another Coke. Booze and now sugar, she thought. Man, I'm just a walking addiction.

Wrapped in a clean towel, with another on her head, she examined her small apartment. She remembered the quaint set of rooms she and Donald had first visited. The carpeting had been new, the appliances spic and span, fresh flowers were on the table. No more. The carpeting and table tops were stained and cigarette burned, the appliances were dented and God knows the last time they were cleaned. There were two holes punched in the paneling above the headboard in the bedroom. What the hell...let's not even go there. Worst though, the entire apartment reeked of stale sweat, smoke, booze and sex. It was as if she was seeing it for the first time. "Christ. I'm a pig."

Nikki ran from window to window, opening them wide. She dragged in Mrs. Gorman's fan and turned it on high. Then, grabbed debris from every surface and tossed it into the silver galvanized trash can from the back porch. She swept the kitchen and bathroom floors and dumped the waste. Nikki was shocked at the quantity of dust, dirt, sand and plain old garbage she shoveled away.

And in the bathroom, jeez. The amount of hair on the floor made her wonder how she had any at all left on her body. She threw every piece of dirty clothing she could find on the bed and made a large bundle of it with her sheets before carrying it to the back porch. Maybe later Mrs. Gorman would let her use her washer, or loan her some quarters for the laundromat. Nikki could not remember the last time she'd been there.

Still in her towel and turban, she sat fiddling with the radio dial, searching for the last cigarette in the pack with her free hand. Ooh, "Gimme Some Lovin'". Nice tune! She bent over the stove and lit her cigarette off a burner. Sitting back down she turned to face the fan which was now in the kitchen. That thing's following me everywhere. It's like an appendage.

At Penny Lane the barber was shaving another customer. God, that Paul McCartney was groovy. He could take her away to rainy Liverpool any day. She ran a hand up her calf. Jeez. Talk about needing a shave. The natural look was convenient, and truth was, Nikki hadn't given grooming much thought in a while, but man, it was time for a date with the razor. It was looking like she had two cactus trees protruding from beneath her towel.

After hearing the opening "dee, dee, dee, dee, dee, dee's" of "Mrs. Robinson" she gave the radio dial another half turn. No need to get depressed about the fact a horny middle-aged suburbanite got to bed down with quirky, but cute Dustin Hoffman, and she didn't. After a second thought she searched for the mid-day news. Time to get socially aware. Hell, new life, might as well expand our horizons. She zeroed in on a news station. Damn. Vietnam, Vietnam, Vietnam, Vietnam. The never ending background music of the day. At least that cracker Lyndon Johnson would be gone soon. She hadn't liked him as vice president and she certainly didn't like him now. Although, in truth, for the past couple years Nikki and the news had been strangers, she may as well have been living under a rock.

The California Democratic Primary was kicking off any minute now. Maybe there'd be another Kennedy in the White House come next year. The radio said with a win in California Bobby'd be on his way to overtaking Humphrey for the nomination. Try as she might, Nikki couldn't from any mental picture of Humphrey. It was easy picturing Bobby Kennedy. He looked like a twelve-year-old altar boy. That probably didn't bode well for him with voters, she knew, but Nikki remembered her father once saying that Bobby was tough as nails and he'd hate to have to face him in a street fight. Hmm. Cute, but tough. Not a bad combination.

Nikki looked over at the door separating Mrs. Gorman's kitchen from her own. She slid down a fraction in the chair and opened her legs slightly, letting the fan blow under the towel. Nirvana.

"Hey Mrs. G., can I give you a hand with that?"

Nikki had dressed and she heard the tread of her neighbor on the back porch. Mrs. Gorman had obviously walked to the grocery store. She was lifting several brown paper bags from the wheeled cart she used to transport her purchases. She set them on the porch deck, collapsed the cart, and leaned it against the railing.

"Why'd you walk? How come you didn't take the car?"

"It's only a few blocks, and I always used to walk when Carl had the car. It was a little nostalgic."

"Yeah, nostalgia's great, but it's pretty muggy out there.

Mrs. Gorman waved her quiet. "Thank you, Nikki," she said, handing her a paper bag. "I bought us some cold cuts at Baronowski's and I'll make us some nice sandwiches for lunch," she said, handing another one of the bags to Nikki.

"This can't all be cold cuts."

"No, I also went to Foodtown for household groceries and I bought you some cigarettes."

Touched, Nikki said, "You didn't have to do that, Mrs. G. I was just thinking earlier about giving them up. You know, why not make a complete lifestyle change while I'm cleaning up my act? The new, improved Nikki."

"Hmm. I like the sound of that, but I know how difficult it can be trying to quit smoking. My Carl tried again and again, but the hold on him was too strong. Carl smoked since he was fourteen though, you're young yet and I'm sure you can stop. But let's take one thing at a time for now. Here." She handed Nikki a carton of Lucky Strikes.

"Luckies! You don't mess around, Mrs. G."

"I couldn't remember what you smoked. This was Carl's brand. I hope it's alright with you," she said, turning away, carrying a bag into the kitchen.

"They'll be fine, thank you Mrs. G." Nikki lifted the other bag and followed her landlady. She deposited the bag on the counter and couldn't help but notice how despite the cleaning job in her own kitchen, Mrs. Gorman's kitchen somehow seemed to almost shine. Ah, well, she thought, maybe cleaning is an acquired talent. "Is it hard without Mr. Gorman?"

Mrs. Gorman's back was to her as she emptied a grocery bag's contents into a cupboard. Nikki heard a sigh before Mrs. Gorman replied. "I miss him very much, but I speak with him every day. So even though he's not here making a mess on my kitchen table with his crumbs and cigarette ashes, he's with me."

It was quiet as the women unpacked the remaining groceries. Nikki noticed that much of what was purchased seemed to be destined for her own apartment. "You're lucky to have had Mr. Gorman for so long. I mean, I'm sorry he's gone and all," she quickly added, "but still, you know."

"Yes, Nikki, I do. We were together almost forty years and they were, for the most part, happy ones."

"For the most part?"

"Yes. Sit down Nikki, that's what I want to talk to you about."

"Uh-oh, this sounds kind of heavy. Maybe I will have a smoke after all, you mind?"

"Just let me get an ashtray." She dragged a chair from the table and placed it in front of the refrigerator. Stepping up, she opened the cabinet above and pulled down a large, beige glass ashtray. Nikki noticed the cabinet held several others of various shapes and styles.

"How convenient," Nikki said.

"After Carl died I put them all away."

"Sorry," Nikki mumbled. She busied herself opening the carton and tearing at a pack while Mrs. Gorman sat back down. The older woman handed her a box of kitchen matches. Nikki's hands shook as she struck the match against the side of the box. Swilling six Cokes was great, but...well...they weren't exactly what she craved most. Nikki tossed the spent match into the ashtray and saw the image of Niagara Falls on its bottom. She looked up at Mrs. Gorman.

"Our honeymoon," she said, simply. "I want to tell you something. It's something I haven't spoken to anyone about in, oh, twenty-five years or so."

"Wow, that's a long time to keep a secret."

"It's not a secret, just not something that was necessary to speak of."

"I'm all ears, Mrs. G."

The older woman sat, folded her hands before her, and leaned forward against the table. "Several years after Carl and I married, he developed a drinking problem. It didn't happen overnight, it was, looking back, a very gradual thing. He always drank, but never more than others. Or so it seemed, anyway. But eight or ten years into the marriage it began to change. Instead of a beer after work, it turned into three or four. When going out with friends he was the one that had to be dragged out of the bar and almost carried up the porch steps to be put to bed. Sometimes he missed work. On a couple occasions his supervisor stopped by the house to speak with him. I say speak, but he did more yelling than speaking. The only reason Carl wasn't let go, was because the two of them were brothers at the same lodge. A lodge," she added grimly, "where quite a bit of the drinking took place."

Nikki had difficulty picturing the kindly old guy she'd first seen sitting at this very table, wreathed in smoke, screwing up to the extent where he almost lost his livelihood.

"His personality changed, as well. Instead of going out with friends, he spent more time alone, puttering in the basement in his workshop, drinking beer after beer, and later, bottle after bottle of schnapps. Ugh!" she shuddered. "To this day, the taste of peppermint reminds me of that terrible time. He cut himself off from most of the outside world. The only time he went out, aside from work when he was able, was when he needed to get more to drink. Does this sound familiar to you, Nikki?" Nikki took a deep drag and looked at her hands in silence. "All this was bad, very bad, but the worst was he isolated himself from me, as well. Oh, he was physically here, but emotionally, he may as well have been in China. His feelings seemed to dry up and blow away. The drink seemed to be a shield he'd raised to stop feeling. It protected him from what he felt could hurt him." Nikki squirmed in her chair. "It wasn't until I said I would leave him that he got help."

"This is hard to wrap my head around, Mrs. G. I can't picture the man I met doing that to you, to himself."

"I know. He must have felt tremendous pain."

"What was it? Did he ever tell you?"

"As he was able to recover from this sickness, he did. It's not important to us now. It was something shameful that happened to him when he was a boy. Something he carried guilt for, unnecessarily, for many years. My point is, Nikki, when he hit rock bottom, he was finally able to get help."

"I guess having his wife say she's leaving is pretty rocky, alright." Nikki stubbed out her cigarette on Maid O' the Mist. "Would you have really left him?"

Mrs. Gorman looked into space for a minute before facing Nikki. "Absolutely."

"Wow, you're pretty brave. Did women actually do that back in what, the 30s?"

"Bravery had nothing to do with it. It was more cowardice than anything else. I simply didn't have the strength to watch someone I loved so completely destroy himself. I was helping myself as much as helping Carl."

"You've got to tell me, Mrs. G.," Nikki leaned toward her over the table, a hint of desperation in her voice, "what was the secret? How did Mr. Gorman do it?"

"You're willing to do what he did, Nikki?"

"God, yes, Mrs. G. Believe me, this life of mine isn't as glamorous as it looks."

Mrs. Gorman smiled grimly. "Sometimes I think *your* shield is your joking. It's easier to hide behind that and the alcohol than deal with the pain you refuse to face."

Nikki lit another cigarette, buying time, hands no steadier than before. "How did I ever get such a smart landlady? You should be on Jeopardy. Really, what's the secret to this, so I can stop before I'm actually legal age to start drinking?"

"Alcoholics Anonymous."

Nikki slumped back. "Aw, Mrs. G.," she said, "that's not what I wanted to hear."

"I suppose not," she smiled. "A few seconds ago I asked if you were willing to take the steps Carl did to help himself and your response was, 'God, yes', right?"

"Yeah, but you can't hold me–"

"You promised me, Nikki, and I take you at your word."

"Mrs. G., you're way too trusting a woman. It's going to be your downfall one day, really. You can't be–"

"Enough, Nikki." She said this quietly, but with such intensity Nikki immediately shut her mouth.

"Well," Nikki asked after an uncomfortable pause, "how many of those meetings did he have to go to? My social calendar is pretty full, you know."

"I'm sure. He went to them his entire life. The first several months he was there every day, sometimes more than one meeting a day. After that, it was less, but he never completely stopped."

"What! His entire life?" She jumped out of the chair. "Are you fucking kidding me?"

"Nikki!"

"I'm sorry Mrs. G., but you're telling me these meetings are some kind of life sentence. No way I'm signing on to that."

"Sit back down, dear. Carl continued attending because he *chose* to, not because he had to." Mrs. Gorman looked Nikki in the eye. "You promised me, and I'm holding you to that promise."

"Look, I have nothing to wear; there might be a dress code."

"I think not. I'd guess what you have on now would be fine, although…," Mrs. Gorman eyed Nikki's cut offs and tie-dyed T-shirt with disdain.

"Come on, Mrs. G. This is the requisite wardrobe of a 1968's single woman on the move."

"With no bra?"

"What's with you and bras?" Nikki pulled out the collar of her shirt and peered down. "Not much in need of support here. Why not save it for a more formal occasion?"

Mrs. Gorman rose. "Get some plates from the cupboard, please. It's lunch time. We'll talk about this more afterwards, deal?"

"Deal." Nikki smiled and reached for the plates. "I really prefer the nice, 'let me feed you' Mrs. Gorman to the evil toughie."

"Evil, that reminds me, confession is two to four o'clock. Dress nice, *with* a bra."

Nikki sighed and pulled down the plates.

23

Marcus Rodriguez stepped out of Rexall Drug Store, bag in hand, and was headed down Lexington when a black and white police car pulled up to the curb. "Mr. Rodriguez, can I have a word with you?"

Marcus bent, shielded his eyes from the glare off the chrome, and peered into the car. It was that skinny, red-faced cop from before. "What now? You here to arrest me on the charge of being the PR boyfriend?"

"I'm asking for a word with you," MacDougall repeated.

Marcus straightened up and thought about the walk ahead of him. "Sure, what the hell. Front or back?"

MacDougall hesitated. "Better make it back."

Marcus grunted a laugh. "Of course, can't have one of us sitting anywhere but there." He opened the rear passenger door and got in. "Bit short on leg room."

"They're not exactly made for comfort."

"Where to, James? Polo? Perhaps a stop at the club before we're off to the Hamptons?"

MacDougall pulled away from the curb and slid into traffic. "I just want to tell you one thing. We talked to Vern Wilson about his altercation with Miss Donez. Whether you believe me or not, we're not ruling out anyone as a possible suspect, especially someone who accosted her just days before her death." They turned up David Street and MacDougall saw an older woman get out of her car and start up the stone steps of St. Margaret's. With her was…jeez, was that the crazy redhead who seemed to live in the bars downtown? It couldn't be, but yeah, it was, he was certain. He'd scraped her off the sidewalk in front of the Bottle Cap enough times to know. What the hell was she wearing on her head? The car was past the church before he could get another look. He'd been so distracted he almost missed what Marcus said.

"Why are you telling me this?"

"Hmm? Oh, I just thought you should know." MacDougall blushed and knew he looked like a damn tomato. "Look," he quickly continued, "what you said at the station the other day about how I dealt with you versus how I might deal with someone who's…someone else. Maybe you were right. I just felt I owed you something. This car ride is it. We're even now. Okay?" He looked into the rearview at Marcus who, blank faced, looked back.

"You dumbass, you just don't see, do you? We're not even now, we were never even and we'll never be even. That's the whole fucking problem. Me, or somebody else like me will always look right at home in the back of a cop car. Somebody like you will always have the uniform, the gun, the power. Don't think you're doing me any favors here. Stop the damn car. Your sociology experiment is over. I don't want to be seen in my neighborhood in the back seat of a cop car. Come on. Now!"

"What about people around here seeing you in the car?"

"Don't you listen? Look out the window."

The few people out on the street went about their daily business. An octogenarian sat on her porch gazing listlessly across the pavement at a circle of teenagers hanging out and smoking on the corner. A raggedly-dressed six or seven-year-old boy whizzed down the sidewalk on a gold Stingray with a white banana seat and worked on his wheelies. A dazed-looking young mother struggled down the street, one arm holding a baby on her shoulder, the other wrapped around a brown paper grocery bag she helped support with her protruding stomach, well into a third trimester. White. Each and every one.

Why doesn't she have a stroller wondered MacDougall?

"They don't see *me*," Marcus said, interrupting his thoughts. "They see a brown face, that's all. Hell, probably makes them feel a little safer seeing another PR right where he belongs."

They had circled several blocks and were back in front of Rexall. Marcus reached for the door handle, found none, and swore. "How about letting me out of here, Officer Fife?"

MacDougall got out, opened the rear door halfway and blocked the exit. "I mean what I said. No one has been ruled out. The spouse, or closest thing to it, is usually the most likely suspect, no matter what color they are." He stepped back and opened the door the rest of the way. "Here you go. Keep in touch."

Marcus strode away, not looking back.

MacDougall watched him reach the corner and turn out of sight. Jesus, he thought. Why even bother trying with these people?

When he got home Marcus threw the small Rexall bag on the counter and dropped onto the sofa. He clenched his head between his forearms and tried to breathe. After several minutes he got up and fumbled open the paper bag, unscrewed the top from the Anacin bottle, fished out the cotton, and dropped it on the floor. He filled a glass half-full of tepid water and, grimacing, swallowed several tablets. He filled the entire glass and drank it down, choking toward the end. God, his head was killing him. How long could he keep this up? He was being torn in half, each half needing, though despising, the other. The glass dropped from his hand into the sink and shattered. Hell.

There were things to do, things to ensure his safety. They had to wait, though. He stumbled to the bedroom and opened the bottom dresser drawer. He pulled out one of Rosaria's blouses and held it to his face breathing in her scent.

Oh Rosaria, I really did love you, I really did. I'm so sorry I...

Marcus crawled onto the bed and curled into a ball, blouse still pressed to his face and began to sob. He cried for Rosaria, himself, and what might come.

A few minutes later the phone rang. Like an automaton, he answered, listened for a moment, and quietly said, "But I – " He listened. "I know what I need to do. Don't worry. I know it's not worth it. No way I'm going to prison. No." He listened again, a ghost of a smile on his face. "I'll take it. Love you." Marcus gently hung up the phone and slumped against the wall.

He knew exactly who he needed to speak to first. Before the cops got there, if it wasn't already too late. He needed to create an alibi. Fast.

24

"We've got to talk, Will," Lynn said, after clearing away the dinner dishes and piling them in the sink.

Terrific, he thought, just what I need after a crap day of work. He looked pointedly at the dishes in the sink. Letting her know his feelings. God knows, his mother never would've just left the dirty dishes to harden. She would have them washed, dried and put away before dad was halfway through the Star-Ledger's sports section. He shook his head and walked into the living room.

"Okay, what have we 'got to talk' about?" He dropped onto the sofa, lit a cigarette and let his head fall back against the cushion. He looked up at the ceiling. He'd been home from work for about an hour. He'd told Lynn he'd be back early to check on Eddie. Make sure the little guy knew his dad was thinking about him. He'd kept his word, but Eddie was still not coming out of his room. If anything, instead of getting over his experience he seemed to be withdrawing even more. He barely made eye contact with Will during dinner. Great way for a kid to show respect for his father. Now this, Lynn's 'listen to what I have to say, it's important' voice. Well, okay, he'd listen, get through whatever the hell it was. He could do that. Because he had later. Thank God for later. The thought was a ripe piece of fruit hanging from a branch before him, keeping him moving forward.

"...with Eddie."

He tipped his head forward. "What, hon? I'm sorry. I missed that."

"Jesus, how the hell can we communicate when you refuse to even *try* to listen?"

"Lynn, stop. My head was at work, I apologize. *Please* repeat what you just said."

"I *said* this afternoon I had a long talk with Eddie. I got Celia to cover my shift at work so I could be here."

Great. Another dig at him. *She* got away from work. "Good. I'm glad he's talking to one of us anyway. He could barely spare me a glance. Nice way to treat old Dad."

"He's been through a lot, Will." She hesitated, "And he may feel he has reason to act as he does. That's what I want to talk about."

Will allowed his head to drop back again. "Look Lynn," he addressed the ceiling, "I've told you, there's not a lot I can do about my work hours. Christ, you know I try, I mean I'm here now, right? What is it, seven o' clock, seven-thirty? That's not bad."

"This has nothing to do with your work."

"Well, that's a nice change."

Lynn stood in the center of the living room, looking at the underside of Will's upturned chin. This man she met eleven years ago while on a girl's night out at the Boardwalk and fell madly in love with. Her girlfriends were astonished. He's so square, they said. He's like Ozzie Nelson. Me Tarzan, you Jane, get in the kitchen, make me a baby. Lynn saw this, but she also saw Will's firm belief in what he felt to be right and true. But really, she wondered lately, just how well do I truly know him?

The last few months their lives had dropped into an established pattern, or let's be honest, rut. Will worked more and more hours, sometimes weekends. Lynn put in her time at the oldsters' home, as Will referred to it, and seemed to get more and more worn out by each week's labor. If Will was home, there'd be dinner for the three of them, maybe a story or two read to Eddie, perhaps a drink, and then they'd drop into bed. This routine was only interrupted by the frequent quarrels about Will's work schedule.

"I was in the medicine cabinet today."

Will exhaled, sending a plume to collect at the ceiling.

"My head was killing me and I thought I'd grab some Excedrin."

"Good idea, it really works. I've got a bottle at work. Only stuff I'd ever use."

"Yeah. When I was rooting through the medicine cabinet I noticed something."

"Oh?"

"My bottle of sleeping pills."

"You have sleeping pills?"

Lynn was silent for a second, watching the underside of Will's chin and throat.

"I got them after Thanksgiving. Couldn't sleep, you know."

"It certainly was a stressful time."

She ignored that. "The bottle had been moved."

"Really. So?"

"I'd put it on the bottom shelf behind some of my feminine stuff. Out of your way."

Will hadn't moved. "Very thoughtful of you."

"It was on the top shelf today."

"Mmm."

"Why would it be up there, Will?"

"You must have moved it without thinking about it. Didn't want to risk Eddie getting into it. You're a careful mother."

"I don't think so. Eddie knows not to open anything from the medicine cabinet. He's a smart boy. Anyway, the top shelf is too high. I can barely reach it on my tiptoes. I'd never put anything of mine there. That's why it holds most of your shaving stuff."

"It does, doesn't it?"

"Yeah, it does," Lynn said quietly. "But I did get on my tiptoes and take them down. Something else was strange."

Silence.

"The bottle was half empty, Will. Over half. How can that be? I took one pill the weekend after Thanksgiving and maybe one or two since then, but that's it, no more. I know you don't approve of prescription drugs, so you certainly didn't take them." There was a long pause. "Where did they go?"

Will slowly brought his head forward and smiled at his wife. "That's easy, you must have taken some and then forgot you took them. That's the danger of those things, Lynn. You come to rely on them without realizing it. If I knew you had them I would have flushed them. They're bad news."

Lynn stared at her smiling husband.

"No, you wouldn't. You knew and you didn't flush them."

"What are you talking about?"

"The day Eddie found the body. We brought him home and he was so upset. You were worried, Will. You were scared for your little prince."

"Of course I was, you were, too. No one should go through that, especially not our Eddie."

"I know. You felt that because you're a good father. We wanted him to calm down, to sleep, but he wouldn't, couldn't. Remember? Remember what we did next? What you said we should do?"

A light seemed to dawn in Will's eyes.

Lynn sat on the rocker next to the sofa. She sat on the seat's edge, her palms flat on her thighs. She spoke quietly. "You said we should mash up a sleeping pill and give it to Eddie dissolved in a glass of warm milk. I was so upset I didn't even think twice. I sat, here in this chair, rocking him against my chest while you heated some milk, walked to the bathroom, got a pill, mashed it up, and stirred it into the milk. Our little boy drank it down and we put him to bed." Lynn sat, still. "You knew, Will, you knew the pills were there. You were so upset about what happened to Eddie, when you replaced the bottle you put it on the wrong shelf. Your shelf, the one you automatically reach for without thinking."

Will leaned forward and slowly stubbed out his cigarette. "Was the pill my idea? Are you sure?" Lynn nodded. "Maybe I did know, maybe I knew and didn't realize I knew. You know, one of those subliminal things. They say that stuff is all over advertising. A picture of a glass of Chivas on the rocks has some naked girl hiding in the cubes. Makes you crave a scotch. Theater owners flashing pictures of popcorn so fast you don't even realize it. Makes you want to buy the stuff. Happens all the time. That's probably it, I've been sort of seeing it, but not noticing until I needed it, then I forgot it again."

"I don't think so, Will, and it doesn't explain where all those pills went."

"Jeez, Lynn, didn't we just cover that? *You* took them and now you don't even realize it. Watch it, babe," he wagged a finger and smiled at her, "You'll end up with a monkey the size of King Kong on your back."

"I think you're right, partly right, anyway."

"See?" His smile broadened. "Willy knows."

"Yeah, I think he does. You're right, I took them, but I didn't know I took them."

Will tilted his head, looking curious, his smile tight on his face.

"I took them alright, but you were the one giving them to me. During the past few months, every now and then we've been having a drink before bed, a beer, maybe a seven n' seven, always, I think, at your suggestion. You know I'm no drinker, never have been. It all tastes pretty much the same to me. I wouldn't know if the flavor of my Pabst is a little off. I'd never know if something was dissolved in it."

Will slowly shook his head in disbelief. "Hon, why would–"

"Wait. You've got to let me finish this. I've thought about it for hours and hours today. You listen."

Will shrugged and leaned back into the sofa.

"Some mornings the past few months I wake up and I'm exhausted. Yeah, I know I'm a deep sleeper and all that, you know it, too. Usually I can sleep through almost anything and I'm hell to wake in the morning. But I've been feeling like, well, like I've been drugged or something. It made no sense. I wouldn't snap out of it until I was hours into my day. Being that heavy a sleeper, why in the world would you give me pills, is that what you're going to say? I'll tell you why, because you needed to be absolutely, one hundred percent certain that I wouldn't wake during the night. Isn't that right, Will?"

He blinked, "Oh, I'm allowed to talk now? Why, thank you, Lynn. Your 'hours and hours' of thought have really produced a whopper, but I have a question. A pretty simple one, but an important one."

"Why?"

"Yes, Lynn, why?"

Lynn slid slowly back into the rocker until the small of her back pressed against the rear. "Remember what I said earlier about Eddie? Our talk today?"

"Yeah?"

"Eddie is a lot like his dad in some ways. Your insomnia, tossing all night, having to get up and read, listen to the radio, sometimes take a walk? Eddie's like that, too. Oh, he doesn't get up and walk or anything, he lies in bed and imagines what his day would have been like if certain circumstances had been different. Isn't that cute? He has some imagination. I bet maybe he'll become a great writer some day."

"Maybe."

"He hears you, Will. He hears you get up and he hears you leave the house at night." She looked calmly at her husband. "I don't. I don't because I sleep like a hibernating bear and because I've been fed a sleeping pill in my beer. What about it, Will? Is our little prince hearing things in the night?"

"You already answered your question, Lynn. Of course he hears me, because, as you said, I'm an insomniac. You've known that since we've been married. Actually, since before that," he said with a slight leer. "Remember the summer we got engaged? Those were some steamy nights while your folks were at the Cape."

"I remember."

"Yes, I can't sleep. I get up, I read, I listen to the radio, if the TV broadcast all night I'd probably watch that. And yes, I take little walks. I imagine that's what Eddie hears, me taking a stroll to work off tension. Is this why he's been so cold toward me? He doesn't like the fact I abandon the nest for a few minutes once or twice a month? Jeez, he's more neurotic than I thought. Maybe he does need one of those shrinks you like to talk about."

"He's not neurotic, Will. And the fact that you leave for walks wouldn't upset him, he's too bright for that. Like we're always saying, he's a smart boy. No, he's upset because he hears you go out...and he's still awake when you come back. Any encounters with Ronny Bronicki lately, Will?"

"Ronny Bronicki? Who the hell is that?"

"Yeah, that's right, that's one of those little household chores that fall under the category of wife's work. You wouldn't ever have had to deal with him. Eddie says you two almost met at the front porch one morning."

Will stared at her.

"He's the milkman, you bastard. The fucking milkman. The guy who delivers the milk you splash onto your corn flakes at breakfast when you tell me you slept like a goddamn lumberjack the night before. And I'm so dazed by the drugs you've fed me I don't even think twice about it. You bastard, you fucking bastard!"

He looked at her for a long moment and said, "I know you don't like it when I say this, Lynn, but is all this hormonal or something? You've got this crazy scenario set up and obviously you believe it, and it's also obvious you've convinced our son of it. I think Eddie's discovery at the waterfront has knocked you both off your rockers. Think about it, Lynn, if all this crap you just spilt is true, that I secretly drug you and sneak off into the night, only to return just before dawn, just in time for breakfast, how the hell do I function at work, huh? I may be an insomniac, but I can't function on zero sleep. Have you thought about that?"

"I have, and I don't have an answer. Maybe you're sleeping elsewhere, then making up the missed time at work. I think all these extra hours you've been pulling have something to do with it, I don't know."

"So I'm doing all this clandestine stuff *and* working overtime? Jesus, I must be Superman."

"No. Maybe you're working those extra hours to compensate for others that are lost. I don't know! But you've been lying to us, Will. To me and Eddie."

"Christ. Then tell me, please, just where the hell am I during all these lost hours at night? I'm dying to know."

"So am I. I don't have an answer, but I have a suspicion. And I have a fear."

"Well, let 'er rip, love of my life."

"Shut up. I think…I know that for the past six months or so sex has been almost non-existent."

"No kidding."

"It's been so rare that now it makes me wonder if there's a reason other than your crazy work hours and my exhausting job. With me wiped out and drugged half the time, are you maybe going elsewhere?"

"Jesus, does that sound right to–"

"No! It doesn't sound right! It sounds wrong. Wrong! Wrong! But if what I'm thinking is true, suspecting is true, it's what's happening."

"Oh, Lynn, this is crazy. Is this what you've been afraid of?"

"No. You slipping out at night to meet some woman isn't my fear, it's my suspicion. My fear is worse."

"What could possibly be worse?"

"What's worse is Eddie said you were gone nearly all night last Thursday. The night before he found the body at the waterworks. The night that girl was murdered."

There was silence as the two stared at each other.

"You're crazy. Right out of your ever-loving mind." Will leaned forward and gripped the coffee table. "How can you sit there and accuse your husband, the father of your child, of such a thing?"

"I'm not accusing you of anything. I said I was scared. After Thanksgiving, the way you just blew up, mad at everyone and everything. I never heard you say things like that. It was, oh hell, I don't know, scary."

"How can you even think that's a possibility? Jesus, Lynn, what have I ever done to make you think–"

"I don't know! I only know that you've been lying. I never would have thought you'd do that, but here we are. I'm confused and scared. It's like I'm living with someone I don't know."

"You don't know," he said incredulously. "Come on, Lynn! You're not a kid, you're an adult. Act like one. What you're thinking is impossible."

"No! No, it's not impossible. It's incredible, almost unbelievable, but not impossible. That's the damn problem! It *is* possible, and the way things look, maybe it's even probable."

Will shook his head, "Christ, what did I do? What the hell did I do to warrant this? What can I do to…what can I say… Jesus, I can't even talk I'm so mad! You're nuts, and so help me God, Lynn, if you have Eddie thinking this, too, that his father might be a–"

"A what?"

"I can't even say it! But if you've got my son thinking this, I swear I'll–"

"What Will, you'll kill me? Is that what you swear you'll do?"

"Don't put words in my mouth. Anyway, it's just a figure of speech and you've got me so upset I can't be held responsible for what I say."

"You have to be responsible for it, for what you say and what you do, no matter how angry you get. That's why I'm so scared. You may have just lost it, like after Thanksgiving and–"

Will stood and walked into the kitchen, cutting her off. Lynn heard the water run and Will drinking. He returned and glared at her. "Are you afraid of me, Lynn? Are you really afraid that I would harm you or Eddie?"

She sighed. "No. No, I don't think so."

"What are you going to do? Should I expect a police cruiser pulling up in front of the house any time soon?"

"No. I don't know what I'm going to do. I haven't thought it through, yet. It's so hard to imagine you…that poor girl…." She sighed again. "It still doesn't change the fact that you've been lying. Something's going on at night. I don't know what, but I'm sure of it."

He remained standing in the doorway.

"I don't want us in the same bed, Will. Please pull out the rollaway bed in the spare room next to Eddie's."

"Christ, Lynn, I'll never get any sleep on that thing. My feet hang off and that metal bar–"

"It's not for you. I'll sleep there. Just outside Eddie's room. I want to be near him."

Realizing what she was implying, he said, "You don't think I would–"

"I'll tell him I'm concerned about his insomnia. You don't have to worry about me saying anything about you. No matter what he may wonder, he loves his father. I won't do anything to take that away from him. But you need to know two things, Will."

"And what's that, hon?"

"If anything else comes up, any piece of evidence, whatever, you better watch for that police car."

"And?"

"No more drinks at night for me. And you can bet that I won't be doing much sleeping on that rollaway, either."

⤙ 25 ⤚

"Okay, Kevin, how did the interview go with Mrs. Cooper?" Clarke and MacDougall were in Clarke's small office. Clarke was behind the desk, leaning forward, arms on either side of the Donez file open in front of him. MacDougall stood on the other side of the desk, fumbling with his small notebook, and to Clarke's irritation, blocking the breeze from the fan.

"Sit down, Kevin," he said, nodding to the chair in the corner. "This isn't the military, take a load off."

"Thanks, Captain."

"Ah," Clarke groaned as he leaned back and laced his fingers behind his head, stretching his back. The top pages of the file caught the breeze from the fan and threatened to blow off the desk before Clarke quickly leaned forward and weighted them down with his pencil can. "What did dear Mrs. Cooper have to say this afternoon?"

MacDougall played with the pages of his notepad for a minute. Clarke noted that those particular pages were blank.

"She's not quite like I remember her."

"How so, Officer?"

MacDougall looked up quickly. "Well, I guess the main thing is I don't remember her being such a hateful bigot. It's got me sort of wondering about things."

"You don't say?"

"She didn't have much nice to say about anyone who wasn't white as you or me."

"Were you able to bring up the topic of Rosaria Donez?"

"Yeah." He flipped some more pages and stopped at one covered in his minute scrawl. "I mentioned what you told me about Rosaria, er, the victim, stopping by to make an appointment. Mrs. Cooper feels that we've been wasting the department's time on this case. Feels that it's just a matter of PR on PR violence. A love triangle between promiscuous kids, a West Side Story kind of thing. You see it every day in the news."

"So we do. What else?"

"Miss Donez isn't a stranger to the corner of Augusta and Bordentown Avenue. Mrs. Cooper stated that she was sick and tired of having to watch her strut by day after day, swinging her hips, listening to her radio."

"Surely the radio wouldn't have bothered her?"

"It was more the hips, I think."

"I think so, too."

"I said something along the lines that it was probably nice not having to see her anymore. You know, trying to draw her out more. Mrs. Cooper agreed with me, but said something that sort of caught me up short. She said, yeah, it's nice not to see her now, but somebody should do something about all the others."

Clarke raised his eyebrows questioningly.

"I don't know what others. Maybe other Puerto Ricans, or Negroes, Mexicans, I just know non-whites."

The two men sat in silence, MacDougall shaking his head, looking at the floor.

"Interesting, Kevin. I have more to add to the file on Mrs. Cooper. After our conversation earlier I did some research in the basement file room."

"Ugh, what a mess."

"It wasn't so bad. I dug out some useful information. Interesting information, anyway."

Clarke slid on his reading glasses, opened the file on his desk, and looked at his junior officer.

MacDougall waited.

"The year is 1952. Our little Kevvy MacDougall is nine years old. The same age as Eddie McConnell, incidentally. There is a report of a missing person filed on October 10th. A woman has vanished and no one is sure of the exact day. She lived alone in an apartment over on Oak Street. In those days not a lot of people had phones, she didn't at any rate. Her family wasn't in daily contact with her. There had been a falling out. There's a window of about five days when she may have disappeared. It was that long before she was reported as missing."

"Must have been rough tracking her down. Five days is a long time in a disappearance."

"It sure is."

"Did she work? Is there a record of her employer missing her?"

"A good question, Officer. It turns out that she did indeed work, but her employer did not make any attempt to track her down when she failed, day after day, to show up for work."

"That's odd, isn't it?"

"It certainly is, unfortunately, my predecessor, Captain Delaney–now don't roll your eyes, as I was saying, Captain Delaney didn't pursue this oddity as thoroughly as I would have wished."

"From what I heard growing up, the only thing he really pursued came out of a bottle."

"At any rate, he seemed to accept the word of the woman's employer who said she was irresponsible and when she failed to show up it came as no real surprise. It was probably...," Clarke moved the pencil can an inch or two on the file, "…'just a matter of time before she blew town' was his response."

MacDougall frowned at the file, wondering what was going on.

"Arnold Cooper went on to say that since his employee, Angela Castille, had just received her weekly pay," MacDougall sat up straight, "he was not at all surprised she left when she did. Whatever day that was, of course. Apparently she was a very flighty woman, seemingly unable to handle a pocketful of money. Mrs. Minna Cooper adds," Clarke read from the file, "'Arnie said he thought she might have stolen some items while working there.' When asked about this, Mr. Cooper agreed and stated that yes, she may have, and no, he had not confronted her about it because he simply could not be certain. Didn't want to appear like a suspicious racist, no doubt. One interesting sidebar to this file, Kevin. Your Captain Delaney–"

"He's not mine, sir."

"Okay. Captain Delaney may have been a drinker, but he was also a pretty keen observer." MacDougall doubted this, but kept quiet. "He notes in the margins of his report that Mr. Cooper seemed quite distraught during the questioning, not nervous, as you may think anyone would feel when speaking with the police, but actually distraught. Delaney states that he seemed to be almost mourning. He found this odd since Mr. Cooper didn't feel concern enough to report the woman missing when she failed to show up for several days at work. Unfortunately," he closed the file and weighted it down again, "his curiosity ends there. There was very little else done. Miss Castille was never found and the case was never solved, just filed in our basement."

"Hmm," MacDougall chewed his thumbnail.

"Yes, one other point I thought you might be interested in. It turns out that in 1952 Miss Castille was not the only Puerto Rican in Pendale, despite what you believed as a child.

Her mother and brother lived here, too. Not too far from her apartment on Oak Street. The three of them had lived together until Miss Castille felt it was time to spread her wings a bit. Apparently, her mother wasn't happy with this. The daughter had been a financial contributor to the family. Mother didn't like the fact that some money would be siphoned away for rent elsewhere. The daughter still contributed, just not as much. It was when rent day came and went that Mama Castille finally reported her daughter as missing. Kind of tragic, isn't it? It wasn't the daughter that was missed, it was the rent money. Anyway, she doesn't sound all that irresponsible and flighty to me, what about you?"

"I'd have to agree with you, Captain."

"I find the fact of Arnold Cooper's statement not matching his demeanor to be significant. Mourning. Maybe he knew something Captain Delaney didn't. At any rate, we have another incident where a young Puerto Rican woman may have come to harm and one of the parties involved, indirectly or not, is Minna Cooper."

MacDougall nodded and stood. "Something I probably ought to add. When I talked to her today we were out back in the yard, she was working on one of her flowerbeds."

"No surprise there, she seems to spend the majority of her time doing that."

"Well, it's really humid back there, you know? She went in to get us something cold to drink while I sat and waited in her gazebo."

That must have been a sight, Clarke thought. The image of Kevin MacDougall sitting on that fancy, and oh, so feminine deck chair under that ornate roof caused him to cover his mouth to hide a smile.

"She came out with the drinks and it really gave me a start. I think I hid it okay, though."

"What was the problem?"

"She served cherry Kool-Aid. Real sweet. It was cherry Kool-Aid we found on Ros–, on the victim's halter. It's hard to imagine, but maybe she was a guest at Minna's before she died. Maybe they had a couple cups of Kool-Aid together and she spilled some. Who knows? But it's something else that sort of ties Minna to this. Right?"

Clarke scribbled on a sheet of yellow legal paper which he then added to the file. "You're right, Kevin, it is hard to imagine Rosaria Donez calling socially on Minna Cooper. It just doesn't seem kosher, but you're also right when you say that it's another fact which can tie Minna Cooper to this whole mess. Good job. Anything else?"

"Yeah, again it might be nothing, but…,"

Clarke raised his eyebrows.

"Right before I left we were near her garage. I don't think she really uses it as a garage, more like a big shed for all her gardening stuff. Along with all the tools she uses I could see a wheelbarrow full of dirt, power mower, one of those seed spreader things that you push around. I couldn't be sure though, because it's pretty dark in there and it was shadowy–"

"Where are you going with this, Kevin?"

"Sorry. There was a stack of four or five bags of wood chips against the right hand wall, near the front. I saw that each of them was a fifty pound sack."

Clarke stayed silent and let his officer finish.

"I said bye and walked to the car. I kind of waited a second before getting in, thinking about the conversation, when I heard a little grunt. I looked back toward the garage and there was Minna, dragging two of the sacks, each one had a sort of looped handle on its corner, dragging them around to the flower bed on the far side of the house. Didn't appear to be straining much, either. I know two bags of wood chips isn't the same as a dead woman, but there it is."

Clarke just nodded.

"Something else, too, Captain. I think she waited until I was down the driveway before grabbing them. No way I'd let her do that on her own if I was still with her. I would've offered to carry them, right? It's the way I was raised, heck, she knew that. Well, I can't swear to it, but I think she was showing off. Like, look here, Kevin, see what I can do. Who knows, maybe she wasn't even thinking that, I don't know. But it sure made *me* think."

"About the possibility of her dragging a hundred ten pound body across a stretch of hard ground?"

"Yeah…about that."

26

"Minna Cooper certainly appears to be at the head of the suspect list, for the moment at any rate," said Clarke. "We need to be careful, though. We can't concentrate on her to the exclusion of others. Speaking of the others, anything new on Marcus Rodriguez?"

"There is, that was next on the list. When he was brought in for questioning he said on the night of the murder he was cleaning at his uncle's restaurant. I stopped out to see the uncle after lunch. He owns a little place over at the corner of Lodi and Oak, probably not too far from where that Castille woman lived. A lot of the business is take-out food. Bills itself as, 'authentic island food', whatever the heck that is. What is Puerto Rican food anyway?" He got no response from Clarke. "Anyway, it's a real dump. Doesn't look like a mop's hit the floor in over a year. If Marcus did any cleaning I doubt it took as long as he said.

"The owner, Uncle Bernardo Nuñez, didn't strike me as the sharpest knife in the drawer. He confirmed his nephew did indeed work there, but as far as supporting Marcus's alibi, he stopped it dead in its tracks. Yeah, Marcus worked that night. Alone. After dinner hours there's usually just one employee. The place was open until ten or thereabouts. Apparently some of the locals like to hang out at the counter, reminiscing about the island days, nursing coffee, or whatever they drink, until closing time. I guess it gets to be a chore some nights pushing them out the door. Anyway, the door is usually locked by ten-fifteen and cleanup begins. Like I said though, it sure doesn't look like much more than a surface cleaning. The counter and tables are cleared and wiped, dishes are done, grill scraped, though from what I saw, not too enthusiastically. Floors are swept, and trash put out back. According to Uncle Bernardo, cleanup never lasts beyond midnight. It's rare when it even hits eleven thirty. And if you saw the place, you'd believe it."

"Why wouldn't he confirm his nephew's alibi? Did you get a sense that there was some bad blood there?"

"The only sense I got was Uncle Bernardo was dumb as a rock. I don't think he realized he was messing up Marcus's story. How this guy runs a business is beyond me, I'm surprised he knows how to work a flush toilet. Maybe he doesn't." Captain Clarke said nothing. "Where does somebody like him get the money to start a restaurant, even a hole like that? It's crazy."

"Minority loans. Johnson's Great Society."

"You think?" MacDougall shook his head in wonder. "It's like everything is just handed to them. I was born the wrong race, in the wrong time."

"I seriously doubt you mean that, Kevin."

MacDougall sighed. "Yeah, you're right. Sorry. Marcus was probably out of the place by eleven-thirty or twelve, not the two o'clock he said."

"So, we're looking at a window of possibly an hour and a half, two hours, when he wasn't accounted for which also happens to coincide with the estimated time of death."

"Right."

"As much as I'm coming to dislike Minna Cooper as a human being, I think we have to return to our original suspicion. The boyfriend is looking more probable. People don't intentionally lie unless they have something to hide." He paused to make more notes in a different folder. "Did you get a feeling he was covering up something when you spoke with him?"

"I'm not sure. Like I think I said before, the first time I talked to him he really seemed to be laying on the grief awful heavy. The more I think about it it's almost like he was behaving the way he thought he *ought* to. Sort of acting." MacDougall thought of the grief Anita Donez exhibited when she identified her daughter. No question of authenticity there.

Clarke's head came up. "First time? When did you speak with him again?"

"Ah," MacDougall's face reddened, "I, ah, saw him on the street and spoke with him for a couple minutes."

"On the street."

"Yeah."

"Not in the controlled confines of the station." Clarke's face was now getting red as well.

"Well, it was pretty controlled. He was in the back of the squad car."

"You picked him up in the squad car?" Clarke threw his pen down. "Jesus, Kevin, what the hell is going on? Why didn't I know about this? Why the hell did you *do* this?"

MacDougall's mouth opened, paused, and shut. How could he state this young suspect had made him feel uncomfortable and even guilty about his own behavior?

He cleared his throat. "When I interrogated him in the station he seemed to feel we were concentrating solely on, ah, non-white people as suspects. It sort of put him on the defensive. I couldn't get much from him at all. When I saw him coming out of the drugstore I figured why not take a minute, assure him we were following various avenues, maybe get him to relax a bit. I thought maybe he'd be more forthcoming if he was a little more relaxed." Yeah, that sounded pretty plausible, he thought.

"You wanted him to relax, feel comfortable."

"Uh, yeah."

Clarke shut his eyes and rubbed his forehead. "Kevin, you realize the reason we interview suspects at the station, the reason why we leave them sitting to stew in their own juices for a while, is to make them feel decidedly *un*comfortable?"

Hell, MacDougall thought. "Well, yeah, but the back of the cruiser is pretty uncomfortable, too. I mean, there's almost no legroom at all. Have you ever been back there?"

Clarke continued rubbing, eyes still closed. "I've been a cop for over twenty years, Kevin. Yes, I'm aware of what the back seat of a squad car is like." Jesus, he thought, what is this kid thinking? "So what you're saying to me is that you interviewed a suspect you-"

"Really just talked to, not interviewed."

Clarke opened his eyes and glared, hand still at his forehead. "So what you're saying to me is you picked up a suspect to talk to and stuck him into the back of a squad car. And your reason for doing this is because you wanted to reassure him and make him feel relaxed?"

"Um, yeah."

"You see how this makes absolutely no sense, at all?"

MacDougall nodded miserably. "Our job is not to make suspects relaxed. It's to make them the exact opposite of relaxed." Clarke's voice was rising. "We want them on edge, we want them uncomfortable, we want them to feel vulnerable." He leaned back in his chair, deflated. "Kevin, come on, this is first year police academy stuff."

MacDougall was silent, he just looked at Clarke. After a moment of silence he sensed maybe the Captain wanted some sort of response. "Sorry."

Clarke picked up his pen and rolled it between his fingers. "Okay." He took a deep breath. "Tell me what you learned."

MacDougall spoke quickly. "Like I said, he was really showing a lot of grief when he was here in the station. Almost too much, you know."

"How much is almost too much, Kevin?" Clarke asked wearily.

"Um, well, I don't know, but it seemed over the top, forced." He was quiet for a few seconds. "Although, it sure seems like they're a pretty emotional group of people. I mean, you kind of see it a lot...like they're always yelling and stuff...." He tailed off. "Maybe I misread him," he finished quietly.

"Maybe. It's a strong possibility you did, but you said your initial reaction was one of disbelief."

"Maybe not disbelief, something just seemed off."

"Okay. Something seemed off. You felt it in your gut, right?" MacDougall nodded.

"Sometimes you need to trust your gut. That's not to say it can never be wrong; it can. But often first impressions are right on the money. You think something just wasn't quite right with him."

"Yeah, Captain, something just wasn't quite right. I don't know what, but it was something. It's like he was mad having to be questioned, but then he remembered he was supposed to be grieving, so he figured he'd better make sure I saw that, as well."

"But it didn't seem genuine to you?"

"I wouldn't say that, he seemed really upset she was dead, but it was almost like that was only part of what he was feeling. And whatever else he was feeling, he was hiding." He shrugged. "Sorry, I know it doesn't make a lot of sense."

"Maybe not, but don't discount it. Now, what about this second *talk* in the squad car?"

MacDougall blushed again. "Not really anything, Captain. More anger than before, but that's it. You're right, it really was a waste of time."

"Maybe, maybe not. There's no such thing as too much information." He paused, "Next time though, let's all be on the same page, okay?"

MacDougall nodded.

"Let's keep Marcus at the top of our list. Who else?"

"Vern Wilson."

"Ah yes, Mr. Congeniality. You have new information on him?"

"Yup. Nothing real definite, but after speaking with his sister, Nora, at work, I got the feeling she wasn't being totally honest with me either. So, I grabbed Sully and the two of us canvassed the street again. We didn't catch everyone at home, but we did pick up some interesting information about Vern. Apparently, sometimes whole nights go by when the guy doesn't sleep."

"How do the neighbors know this?"

"Knew you'd ask that," Kevin grinned.

So tell me, Clarke thought.

"As you face the house, the left side is awful close to the house next door. Sully walked between the two and he couldn't raise his arms without hitting the sides of the houses. The close proximity makes it easy to see in. Sometimes, Vern sits in front of the TV all night, just staring."

"Who says this?"

"Mrs. Madigan, next door neighbor. Believe me, there's no love lost between her and the Wilson family. She says living next door to them have been the worst twenty-seven years of her life." MacDougall grinned again. "You should see, the side of her front room facing the Wilson's, she's got big plants in front of all the windows, to block out the view. Says no matter how hard she tries, at night, when its dark, you can still see him there, propped up in front of the tube. She says the shades are never pulled. I guess Vern doesn't care much about privacy."

"What the hell is on TV all night?"

"Beats me. Maybe he stares at the test pattern. Probably blind drunk anyway. Lately, in the warmer weather he's been sitting on the porch all night. According to her he just sits there, drinking, staring into the dark. Sort of like he's looking for something."

"Like what?"

"Don't know. That's what Mrs. Madigan said, 'Like he's looking for something,'" he read from his pad.

"Mrs. Madigan sounds like one of those busybody neighbors who has the dirt on everyone around them. For the police, they're a gift from the Gods. Anything specific for that night?"

MacDougall sighed. "Unfortunately, no. Believe me, I'm sure she'd love to produce something to help put Vern away for a long time, but she said she had a bad headache Thursday night so she took a pill and went to bed early. She says Vern was in regular form the following night, screaming at Nora about supper being late or something, but nothing on Thursday."

"Damn."

"Sully's back trying to catch the neighbors we missed earlier. He might get a nibble."

"Let's hope so. The fact that Wilson 'sometimes stays up at night' doesn't do much to build any kind of case against him."

They heard the rear door slam and the quick thumping of heavy footsteps down the corridor leading from the small back parking lot.

"Speak of the devil," Clarke said. They then heard the bathroom door slam shut, followed by a relieved groan. They waited, after a flush the door opened. What they did not hear, Clarke noted, was the sound of any hand washing or drying.

Sully lumbered into view and leaned against the doorjamb of the small office. He was a big man, maybe six three or four, usually slow in thought as well as movement. His uniform shirt was heavily stained under each arm, the chest, and probably the back. He grinned and leaned his face directly in front of the small fan's current.

"Oh, man, that's good. Chugged a couple cold Mountain Dews on my way over." Clarke made a face. "They hit my bladder and all hell broke loose. Barely made it in time."

"Just be sure you don't leave the empties in the squad car. There'll be ants in no time at all."

"Sure thing, Captain," Sully said, his eyes closed, ruffling his hair with a huge hand, trying to dry it in the breeze. "Oh, man, oh, man…,"

MacDougall saw that Captain Clarke was getting impatient. He jumped in, "So Sully, any luck with the neighbors after I left?"

"Yeah, Kevvy, I think we got something interesting from an old guy named Edmunds. He's a couple doors up the street on the same side as the Wilsons. Just on the other side of the Gorman place." He stopped and again leaned in the fan's breeze.

"What exactly did he say, Sully?" MacDougall asked quickly before the captain could speak.

"He saw Vern Wilson sometime Thursday night. He's not sure of the time, but it was late."

"Saw him? Where?"

"On the street, the sidewalk, he was walking down the street. Sneaking, was what Mr. Edmunds said."

"You better grab a chair and drag it in here, Sully," Clarke ordered. "Give us all you've got and don't leave anything out. And get the hell away from my fan," he snapped.

The extra chair, along with Sully's bulk, drastically dwarfed the small office. The big man read from his notes.

"Paul Edmunds was out sometime late that night looking for his cat, Westy."

"Westy?" asked MacDougall.

"Short for Westmoreland."

"You're shitting me," said Clarke.

"Seems little Westy is in heat and all the neighborhood cats are screaming their furry little lungs out trying to get at her."

"Westy is a her?"

"Yeah. A pound kitty. Turns out Edmunds didn't check her out all that carefully when he adopted and named her. Anyway, sometimes when she's in heat, she gets out and there's this noisy cat orgy in the alley. Seems old man Edmunds is sick of Westy staggering home in a family way and dropping another litter of kitties every three or four months. So he went out after her Thursday night, trying to find her before, you know."

"Get to the part that concerns Vern Wilson."

"Almost there, Captain. Mr. Edmunds was out for about an hour or so, but was having no luck finding little Westy. Seems back in the alley behind his place all the yowling bounces off the sides of the houses echoing and you can't tell exactly where the sound is coming from. He gave up, said he'd just have to deal with getting rid of another litter. Thought he'd sit on the porch and have a smoke before heading back in. That's when he saw Vern.

"He said Vern was walking down the street real slow and a little hunched over. He was walking sort of tip toe. Putting his toes on the ground before the rest of his foot followed. Like he was trying not to make noise. Seemed weird to Mr. Edmunds, walking down the sidewalk like that, but, well…this was Vern, after all. His shoulders were sort of hunched and his head was turned a little to the side. The way someone would do when they were listening real hard for something. His hands were clenched in front of him like he was holding something, but Mr. Edmunds says there wasn't anything in his hands. It was all pretty strange. The old guy didn't know what to do. He didn't want to scare Vern, but at the same time, Vern was a neighbor, a crappy one, but still a neighbor. So, real quietly he said, 'Hi, Vern.'"

"What'd Vern say?" said MacDougall.

Well, Mr. Edmunds said Vern jerked so hard in surprise. Took him a minute or so to focus before he recognized the old man. During that time Edmunds says he didn't know if Vern was ready to attack him or run off screaming down the street.

"'What'cha up to, Vern?' he asked, 'Pretty late for a stroll, isn't it?' He said he asked it real friendly because he was awful scared himself. Said he was trying to," Sully peered closely at his notes, "'diffuse the situation', whatever that means." "Now here's where it starts to get weird."

"It's just starting now?" asked MacDougall.

Sully grinned, glad to have such a captive audience. "Vern then told Mr. Edmunds why he was out and about. Said he was on a re-con mission."

"A re-con mission?" said Clarke.

"Yeah, old man Edmunds knew what Vern meant. Edmunds fought in the war in Europe. Hell, he named his cat, Westmoreland. He asked Vern if he was talking about a reconnaissance mission. Vern nodded and said it was up to him to get something on those gooks before daybreak. Without news on the enemy, he seemed to think all would be lost."

"Jesus."

"Got that right, Kevvy. Anyway, Mr. Edmunds didn't know what to do. All he knew was he wanted to get away from that loony, and fast. He said something like 'carry on soldier', and scurried back inside. To hell with having a smoke on the porch and to hell with Westy, she was on her own. Last thing he saw was Vern continuing down the street, slow and careful, until he was out of sight." Sully flipped his notes closed and sat silently, eager for a response.

Clarke asked, "You say that Mr. Edmunds watched him walk down the street?"

"Yes."

"He's sure of the direction?"

"No doubt about it. He walked down toward Broadway."

"Toward Broadway. And the waterworks is a couple blocks past that."

The big man nodded and sat still for a moment before turning and looking longingly up at the fan.

"What exactly did the sister say about Vern being in the house that night?" Clarke asked MacDougall.

MacDougall flipped furiously before finding the right page. "Uh..., Nora Wilson said that she and her brother watched the monologue of the Johnny Carson Show and then they both went to bed."

"The show starts at what, eleven-thirty? So the monologue runs ten, fifteen minutes, brush their teeth, change for bed... so it's no later than midnight. That sound right to you two?"

"Sure, more or less," said MacDougall. Though he seriously doubted Vern brushed his teeth. Sully nodded.

"This Mr. Edmunds says it was late. What does that mean? Late could be ten-thirty or an hour before sunrise. Get on the phone and get a better estimate of the time, Sully." The big man nodded and headed toward the squad room, flipping pages.

"Kevin, could Vern have gone to bed, but then gotten up later in the night and left the house without the sister's knowledge?"

"Asked her that myself and her response was that she's a light sleeper and she doubts it's possible. But, like I said before, I didn't feel she was being absolutely truthful."

"You think there's any chance she's being threatened by Vern in some way? Being forced to cover for him?"

"I didn't get that feeling. The impression I got was she just wasn't going to do us any favors by fingering her brother. It seemed her problem was with me, not him, I have no idea why.

I don't think I ever said two words to her in school. It was definitely strange."

Sully plodded back into the room and plopped into his chair. "Edmunds was a little miffed that I kept pushing him for a more exact time, but he finally said he was sure it was later than midnight because he had to hit the john around then and he remembers the time."

"Okay, so we know it was *after* Nora Wilson said they went to bed. I think we need to speak with her again, as well as her brother. We'll do it here, not somewhere at her convenience. Kevin, call her. She may still be at work, tell her we need to speak with her now. She can stop here on her way home. If she gives you any trouble, say we'd be more than happy to pick her up at the hospital and bring her here."

Captain Clarke leaned back in his chair and looked at his two officers. He wondered, not for the first time, if they had what it took to solve this thing. He had no idea.

"Okay," he said quietly. "It appears that Vern Wilson is back on the radar screen. There doesn't appear to be a clear motive, but he certainly seems unstable, and we have the fact that he threw a beer can at the deceased. We also have a witness who puts him on the street at the approximate time of the killing. Marcus Rodriguez seems to have lied about his whereabouts at the time of the murder. We need to find out why. We also need to find out if there's any reason he may have wanted Rosaria Donez out of his life. Sully, you get over to his place and drag him back here. If he's not there try the Donez house, and if necessary, his uncle's restaurant." He rubbed his forehead again. "And there's Minna Cooper. She seems to have a strong dislike of Puerto Ricans, women in particular." That's an understatement, thought MacDougall. "We need to find out if this dislike is strong enought to drive her to kill. We know she's strong, physically capable of it, now we need to know the rest." He sighed. "My head is killing me. Sully, before you take off after Marcus, clean up the car. Get rid of those soda bottles." Clarke rubbed his eyes. "Would you give me a few minutes?"

Sully and MacDougall scattered. He did not mention it to his men, but Clarke was reopening the sixteen-year-old case of the disappearance of Angela Castille. He wasn't sure there was a connection with the current case, but there was certainly one with Minna Cooper.

✦ 27 ✦

Clarke sat, eyes closed, rubbing his temples, fervently wishing the pressure behind his eyes would relent and give him a few minutes respite. He didn't know how long he sat there, but after a while he sensed he wasn't alone. He looked up and saw a young woman standing in the entrance of his office. She looked to be about thirty. She was slim and wore her dark hair cut short. He would have said she was very attractive except for the fact her nose was red and it appeared she'd been crying very recently. As if to confirm his suspicions, she pulled a wrinkled hanky from the pocket of her pants and brought it up to wipe her nose.

"Captain Clarke?"

"Yes, did anyone from the squad room help you, miss?"

"Officer MacDougall is on the phone. His back was to me when I came in. The truth is, I'm not a fan of his. I'd rather not speak with him." She stopped and wiped her nose again. It was on its way to becoming raw.

Clarke couldn't imagine anyone being upset with MacDougall, anyone except.... He rose from behind his desk. "Are you Mrs. McConnell?" The woman nodded. "The boy who found the body was your son, Eddie." She nodded again, tears in her eyes. "I'm so sorry for what your son had to go through. It must have been an awful experience for him. I don't want to make excuses for my department, and I know it's water under the bridge anyway, but I am very sorry we may have made the ordeal more difficult for him, and for you, as well. I've spoken with Officer MacDougall about how he handled the incident. I realize it may be of little solace to you, but Officer MacDougall is a fine police officer and a good man. This wasn't his best moment, but I can promise you, he will never make the same mistake again."

Lynn McConnell nodded silently, wiped her nose again and stuffed the hanky back into her pocket. "Thank you, Captain. I'm sure I'll get over my feelings toward him eventually. A matter of time."

"I'm no expert, but I'm sure as time goes by Eddie will emerge from this healthy and well."

Lynn nodded her head and looked at the floor. She stood there and Clarke saw tears dropping from her face. He came around his desk and led her by the arm to the chair recently occupied by MacDougall. "Mrs. McConnell, please sit down. I'm sorry, I don't know where my manners are. Can I get you some water?"

She shook her head and wiped her eyes with the heel of her hand. "It's not Eddie. He's still jittery, but I think he'll be okay. We've talked and he says he's not afraid. I know he's small," she said, smiling through tears, "but he's really a tough little kid."

Clarke nodded, waiting.

"No, Captain Clarke, I need to talk to you about something else. I need to talk to you about my husband."

Clarke sat waiting as she dissolved into a fit of sniffles and muffled tears. After a moment he said, "I'll just go get that water for you." He left his office and quietly closed the door behind him. He didn't know what to make of Mrs. McConnell. His only experience with the family thus far had been some brief sparring over the phone with Mr. McConnell about their handling of his son the day of Eddie's grisly discovery. She wouldn't be crying about her husband's threatened lawsuit against them, would she?

He entered the squad room just as MacDougall dropped the phone into it's cradle. "Well, that was a waste of ten minutes of my life."

"What happened?"

"That was the Children's Hospital. I called for Nora Wilson, like you asked. They went to get her and I sat there forever, listening to the sound of plates and utensils rattling. You'd think someone would invent some recorded music or something that could run while you're waiting. Something to pass the time. Would that be so hard? I bet people would love it."

"What did she say?"

"Nora? Nothing."

"What do you mean, nothing? Did you tell her to get down here or we'd send a car for her at work?"

"I couldn't, she wasn't there. Turns out after all that time looking for her someone remembered that she hadn't been feeling well today and she went home early. I called her house and got no answer. Who knows where she and Vern might be."

"Yeah, who knows, but we'd better find them, and fast. On another topic, I've got Mrs. McConnell in my office crying a small river."

"What? Now, you mean?" MacDougall asked, his eyes widening and face beginning to redden.

"Of course, now," snapped Clarke. "Is there anything else I need to be told about the events of Friday afternoon?"

"No! I swear, you know it all."

"Have you had any contact with the family since then?"

"Not a word! If anything, I'm trying to avoid them."

"Alright," Clarke said, "Get over to the Wilson house and get either Nora or Vern down here. Not," he stressed, "together."

"Yessir." MacDougall scurried out.

Clarke walked into the interview room and found a relatively clean mug. He allowed the cold water to run a while before filling it. He wiped the bottom on a paper towel and carried it to his office where he knocked gently and walked in. Mrs. McConnell seemed to have collected herself. She sat very erect, her back straight in the chair, hands clasped between her thighs. Next to the IN/OUT basket, on the corner of his desk nearest the woman, sat a neatly folded hanky. Where had he seen one similar to it?

"I'm sorry about that, Captain Clarke. I'm not normally such an emotional woman. Not in a tearful way, at least."

"Don't think twice about it, ma'am." He eyed the hanky and set the mug next to it.

"You're very kind." She sipped from the mug. "Tastes a little of Mountain Dew."

"Oh, one of the officers must have been using it. I'm terribly sorry."

"Don't be, I like it."

He'd never understand young people.

"You mentioned your husband," he prodded.

She nodded. "Sitting here, I'm half-thinking I'm crazy. There's no reason to be talking to the police at all, maybe just... maybe just a priest or marriage counselor or something."

Clarke leaned back in his chair. Surely this woman was intelligent enough to know the police couldn't do anything about marital troubles. Not unless there were signs of abuse, and that didn't appear to be the case. Even then, their hands were pretty much tied. He looked at Lynn McConnell. Her eyes dropped to his desk, looking at the folded hanky with tiny pink roses at the corner.

"That's not mine."

Jeez, is that what this was about, a straying husband? Was McConnell fool enough to bring his fluff's hanky home with him? Clarke leaned forward and began, "Mrs. McConnell, while I'm very sorry for you, there's not–"

"Please, let me finish."

He leaned back again and waited.

"We've been going through a difficult time lately. Not just with what happened to Eddie, though that certainly added to it. I work as an aide at Golden Twilight Home several days a week. I know it doesn't sound like much, but it can be exhausting."

"I would imagine so, old folks are extremely demanding. They can be like children, but of course, they're not. It must be draining to care for them while still trying to allow them what dignity you can."

"Yes," she said, eyes widening, "That's it exactly. It's hard emotionally as well as physically. Will could never understand that. He habitually refers to those of us who work there as the bedpan brigade." She shook her head. "Well, he works hard, too. He's on the train to the city every morning and not back until six thirty or seven. And that's on regular days. Lately there's been an awful lot of extra work." She paused. "Sometimes he spends the night in the city."

Here we go, he thought. She's afraid McConnell's got a chippy in town.

Almost reading his thoughts, she said, "I know you're thinking I'm afraid he's getting something on the side in New York. He might be, I wouldn't be surprised, but I don't think it's as simple as that. If it was, I wouldn't be here talking to you." She took another sip and glanced at the hanky before continuing. "Things have been very tense for months. I know this isn't really a concern of yours, but please bear with me. Thanksgiving was awful. Something seemed to snap inside him. He raged about everything that was wrong in the world today. When I say raged, Captain, I mean it. I was afraid for him."

"You thought he might harm you or your son?"

"No, I wasn't afraid *of* him, I was afraid *for* him. It was like a Dr. Jekyll, Mr. Hyde thing. The bad one, Hyde, I think, was loose. It took what seemed like ages to calm him down. I was so frightened the next day I went to my doctor and got some sleeping pills. I lied to him, I'm afraid. I said I wanted them for myself when in reality I planned to slip one to Will if he ever got that crazy again."

Jesus, who wasn't taking some sort of pills today? Clarke wondered. Maybe he was missing out on something.

"It appears that Will turned the tables on me. I think…I'm certain he's been sneaking the pills to me at night."

"Why do you believe your husband is doing such a thing?"

"The pills are almost all gone, about two thirds of them anyway. I've taken a couple myself, but since November when I got them, it's only been two, maybe three, tops."

"Perhaps Mr. McConnell has taken them, after all. Maybe your plan worked out without you having to dose your husband."

"No," she shook her head, "Will has strong feelings about prescription drugs. I don't know why, he has no problem with aspirin, but anything else, forget it. Maybe he looks at it as the first step on the road to addiction." She sighed.

"I know this is difficult to consider, but could it be–"

"I know what you're thinking, but no, it's not Eddie. He would never do such a thing." How many times had he heard those words from parents? Clarke thought. "Just to be certain, I asked him. There is absolutely no possibility of Eddie having taken them."

"Perhaps then, Mr. McConnell changed his views, and he felt the need to use the pills."

"No," Lynn McConnell said sadly. "That's where I caught him lying again. He claimed he was entirely unaware the pills were in the house. I put them in the medicine cabinet behind some of my things. I hadn't even looked at the bottle for who knows how long. After Eddie's...after he found the young woman, Will thought we should grind up a pill to help make him sleep. He went to do it while I stayed with Eddie."

"Obviously your husband found the pills, Mrs. McConnell. He probably did this without thinking to tell you. How else would he know of their existence?"

"You're absolutely right, Captain, he had found them. But he told me *after* he gave the pill to Eddie that he was unaware of them being in the house. You see, he was so upset about what had happened, he wasn't thinking. He even replaced the bottle on a shelf I can barely reach." She shrugged. "He lied."

Captain Clarke picked up a pencil and tapped its eraser gently against the desk blotter. "Assuming he did this, Mrs. McConnell, what could be the reason?"

She lowered her head for another sip and when she straightened Clarke saw her eyes glistening. "Eddie, like his father, is an insomniac. Apparently, my son has been awake on occasions when Will leaves the house after I'm...sleeping. Eddie's still awake when he gets home in the early hours. At breakfast Will claims he slept like a log."

"Could your husband just be out talking a walk?"

"When I confronted him, that's what he said. Despite the missing sleeping pills, despite the fact that I've felt like a damn zombie so many mornings, my husband is shocked I'd have such suspicions," she said bitterly. "Eddie said he's sure Will was gone most of the night. Right now, I believe my son, not my husband."

"I see why you have doubts about your husband, Mrs. McConnell. On top of what happened to your son, this must be awful for you, but I don't see what it is you feel I can do for you.

I think you were right, perhaps a marriage counselor might be in order."

Lynn continued as though not having heard him, "I was doing laundry earlier today. Trying to take my mind off this, just wanting to get lost in some mindless household routine. I was sitting on the bed, making sure there was nothing in the pockets of anything going into the washer. My husband is forever leaving change, matchbooks, whatever in his pockets. It's a nuisance. Does your wife complain about that, too?"

Clarke remembered when Judith had lectured him on the very topic. "Guilty."

"While emptying the pockets of the slacks he wore last week, I found that." She nodded again to the hanky. "It's not mine. Mine aren't so…dainty." She produced hers, wrinkled from her pocket, resembling a rag more than anything else. "I don't know where he got it, but he was wearing those pants Thursday. That was a night Eddie said he was out until almost dawn."

Clarke stopped tapping his pencil.

Rosaria Donez's purse. That's where he had seen a hanky like this. Maybe not identical, but similar.

"If you could have heard him on Thanksgiving, it was so hateful. Anything, anyone different…God, it was awful, he just went on and on. It wasn't the man I married. I don't know who it was." She shook her head slowly. "I told him my fears yesterday. He seemed incredulous. I so much wanted to believe him, but the pills, what Eddie said he heard. I can't, I just can't." She sobbed again.

"I promised him I wouldn't go to the police with my fears. I gave him my word, but that was yesterday, before I found the hanky. I know it's probably nothing. Part of me honestly hopes it belongs to some little free love groupie he found in the city. That would be simpler. But I have to know it's not from that poor girl at the waterworks. I want to believe my husband, but it's so hard. I promised, but…but…," she shook, sobbing. "Am I a bad person for thinking this? Am I a bad wife? I should stand by him, I know. I'm just so scared. So scared for Eddie and me. I'm so scared for Will, too."

Captain Clarke asked her to repeat all the salient information while he took notes. Mrs. McConnell sat quietly, almost listlessly, and cleared up any questions he had. She sipped from her mug and twisted her wrinkled hanky in her lap. After an hour they were through. A thought suddenly dawned on Clarke. "My gosh, Eddie! He's not home with–"

Lynn shook her head. "No. Will's at work. He phoned earlier and said not to expect him tonight. Lots to do at the office, you know," she said quietly. "No, I don't expect he'll be home until tomorrow. I really don't know…we're kind of in new marital territory at the moment. Every minute's a new adventure…," she trailed off. "A neighbor is at the house with Eddie. She looked at the wall clock and said, "I've got to get going. I told her I'd be back by about six, I'm late." She pushed herself out of the chair. It was the movement of an old woman.

"What are your plans now, Mrs. McConnell? I mean, for tomorrow, when your husband comes home."

"When my husband comes home tomorrow, Captain Clarke, he'll find a letter telling him if he wishes to speak to me or his son he'll have to call or visit my parents downstate. They don't know what exactly the trouble is, but they're waiting with open arms. Amazing, isn't it, no matter how old, how 'grown up' you are, when trouble arises, the instinct is to head for the safety of home. I wonder, will Eddie ever think of home and feel that way?"

Clarke made certain he had the addresses and phone numbers of Will's workplace and her parents. He walked her to the front door of the station. The sinking sun peered over the facades of the buildings across the street, causing the two to squint as they said farewell. As Lynn's car crept into the sparse dinnertime traffic Clarke wondered what this visit had cost her. Probably her marriage, and Clarke believed she was very aware of that.

He returned to his office to make an attempt at reaching Mr. McConnell at work. If no one answered the switchboard at this hour, he'd try again first thing in the morning. Reaching for the phone, he noticed for the first time since reentering the room the dainty handkerchief with the tiny pink roses, neatly folded, still sitting on the corner of his desk. Could it actually belong to Rosaria Donez? Could she and Will McConnell have been in a relationship? Had it gone bad and he killed her because of it? Had he killed her for some other reason? A lot of questions. Time to dig for the answers.

28

MacDougall tried to put the McConnells out of his mind as he drove to the Wilson house. He wasn't looking forward to accusing Nora of lying, and it was never pleasant dealing with Vern. He grabbed his cap, shoved open the car door, and headed toward the porch. As he reached the bottom step he saw the front door gaping open. The screen door, which he vaguely remembered seeing hanging in the doorframe two days ago, was lying on its side, leaning against the porch railing. Its hinges looked like they'd been ripped from the casing. Climbing the steps, MacDougall examined the rotting wooden doorframe. Probably hadn't taken Charles Atlas to do the job.

"Hallo!" He called into the entryway leading into the living room. "Hallo! Nora, Vern, it's Officer MacDougall! Kevin MacDougall!" he added. "Anyone home?"

There was no sound, save for the barking of a neighbor's dog, a few backyards over. Kevin's thoughts went briefly to Westy, Mr. Edmunds' wayward cat. He wondered how her night on the town had gone.

He knew he should call for backup. It was absolutely against all training to enter alone, but...he'd joined the force to help set things right. This was his opportunity. MacDougall took a breath and stepped into the house. Unsnapping his holster he rested his hand on the gun butt. He walked as quietly as possible, probably, he thought, looking a lot like Vern had looked several nights ago on the street.

The house seemed to be empty. Though he'd assumed Vern wasn't much of a housekeeper, he was stunned by the condition of the place. Wallpaper hung in strips where leaks from above had long since dissolved the glue holding it to the wall. It seemed every surface was covered with dirty dishes, empty bottles and cans, or overflowing ashtrays. MacDougall could not see a single piece of furniture that hadn't been scarred by cigarette burns. Crushed butts littered the floors, along with stained newspapers and an occasional magazine. Stepping carefully through the front room he saw the dining room table was a mass of plates, cups, silverware and empty cartons, all of which were caked with dried food. The fingerprint-stained swinging kitchen door stood open and the smell of spoiled meat permeated the rear of the house. Crossing the threshold he froze. A patch of the wall near the phone was stained red. He inched forward, eyes sweeping the room, the palm of his gun hand suddenly slick with sweat. He crept closer and closer to the stain. The stain's texture looked rough, not uniform. MacDougall's eyes dropped to the floor and saw…a chunk of meatball. Jesus, spaghetti sauce. His shoulders relaxed a degree. He wiped his hand on his pants leg. Turning, he noticed the sink full of dishes beneath a swarm of circling insects. He opened the refrigerator. It revealed next to nothing, some lunch meat gone bad, a half-full bottle of cola, and very little else. He retraced his steps until he reached the staircase leading to the next floor. He looked up into the shadows.

"Vern? Nora?" Shit.

Last chance to call for backup. He thought of his mom, her killer never found, still out there. No, MacDougall thought, I'll handle this.

He drew his revolver from its holster, grasped the rough and rather shaky banister with his left hand, and climbed.

The layout of the house was nearly identical to the one he'd grown up in. He knew straight ahead at the top of the stairs was a small bedroom. Usually reserved for the youngest child, or when they'd grown and fled the nest, used for storage. To its right was the second largest of the rooms. In his house there had been an entrance to the attic off this room. The master bedroom, such as it was, was in the front of the house facing the street. Next to that, accessible through the short hallway, was the home's single bathroom.

Kevin took a deep breath and turned toward the master bedroom. He had no doubt which of the siblings would have laid claim to this largest room. He pushed the door open with his foot and his suspicions were confirmed. This was Vern's habitat, alright. The bed clothes were in a tangle and the bottom sheet was stained with God knows what. An ashtray the size of a hubcap balanced on the nightstand overflowing its contents onto the scratched wood veneer. The floor of the room was a sea of empty bottles and cans. It smelled like closing time at the Bottle Cap. Well-handled copies of Playboy and skin magazines MacDougall didn't recognize splayed open on the bed and room's only chair. Stepping back and crouching low, being careful not to touch any filth, he saw there was also a collection of them under the bed. He straightened, and noticed what appeared to be the focal point of the room.

On the wall opposite the foot of the bed hung a centerfold, several feet above mattress level, in direct sightline of anyone lying on the bed. An almost obscenely endowed young Oriental woman gripped both long, dark nipples between her thumb and forefingers. Her dazzling red fingernails a contrast to their darkness as she lifted her breasts up and out, their weight a heavy drag on the pinched and stretched nipples. She smiled coyly at the camera.

MacDougall felt himself blushing while at the same time becoming aroused. He quickly left Vern's room and stepped next door. He again pushed open the door with his foot and was surprised. This room, the one he knew to be next in size, and had assumed would be Nora's, seemed to be used expressly for storage. Boxes and brown paper bags were stacked everywhere, some having spilled to the floor and burst open. The room, despite the disorder, was the least repulsive to MacDougall so far. He quickly scanned for any sign of life. Finding none, he turned to the final bedroom. He knew the dimensions of the room couldn't be much more than six by eight feet, probably closer to six by seven. His own mother had used this space in their house as a sewing room and always complained how cramped she was. He pushed against the door. It opened halfway, bumped against something, and stopped.

Oh, God, thought Kevin, please, please don't be a body, just be a piece of furniture. God, I'm sorry I looked at that picture in the other room, I'm sorry I looked at Mrs. Donez's butt and boobs. Please God, I'll be a better man, just please, no dead person.

God, it turned out, was listening. MacDougall inched his gun first and then his head slowly around the edge of the door. It bumped against the footboard of a narrow twin bed. Both headboard and footboard were white and painted with a faded design of what Kevin believed were brown-eyed Susans. The bed was neatly made, a light yellow cotton spread pulled up and anchored under a flat, white pillow. It was impossible to get into the room without squeezing between the partially open door and the left wall. No way the captain would've made it, he thought. Why was the bed against the short wall, making entry so difficult? Immediately, the answer came to him. Would anyone living with Vern want to make it easy for him to enter their room? Maybe his sister had another motive. Maybe something in the past gave Nora a reason to partially barricade herself in. MacDougall wondered again about the possibility of Vern sexually abusing his sister. Jesus.

There was no doubt this was her refuge. He stood in the center of the tiny room, holstered his gun, and slowly turned in a circle. Against the short wall was the bed, next to that was a low nightstand which barely reached above his knees. A small lamp and a Nancy Drew book sat on top. Kevin recognized the blue cover and silhouette of the young sleuth with her magnifying glass. "The Secret of the Old Clock", the first of the series. Next to the nightstand was a narrow dresser with a pair of small drawers up top, and three wider ones below. The wooden knobs on these drawers were each painted with images of different wildflowers. On the dresser's top sat a white doily on which perched a stuffed Pooh-Bear. Windows were cut into the third and fourth walls. A small cedar chest sat beneath the one which faced the littered backyard. There was little else in Nora's sanctuary: pegs, on which hung two white smocks she must have worn at work, a small trash can containing some crumpled tissues, and a shelf of books. Mostly kids' stuff he noted, a few more Nancy Drews, Bobbsey Twins, and a couple others.

Pushing aside feelings of guilt for invading her retreat, MacDougall read the spines of the stray volumes. Nothing of importance. In this room that looked like it belonged to a fourteen-year-old junior high school student, he'd hoped to find some clue as to what transpired in the house, a journal or diary of some sort. He knew his search was on shaky legal ground at best, but hell, he figured he'd already entered the house uninvited. Why stop now? Besides, he told himself, thinking of Rosaria Donez's horrible death, as well as his mother's unsolved homicide, the ends more than justified the means. He dropped to his hands and knees and peered under the low bed, nothing, not even dust balls. He marveled at the disparity in housekeeping between the siblings. He dropped to his elbows in an effort to peer under the nightstand when he noticed a shallow recessed shelf had been added just a few inches below the nightstand's upper surface. If he, or anyone, had been standing upright, the shelf would have been invisible. MacDougall saw small nail heads under each corner of this shelf protruding from the nightstand itself, acting as support for the secret hideaway. On the shelf was a small book about the size of a stenographer's pad and almost an inch thick. Bingo! He smiled and reached for Nora's diary.

Marcus couldn't believe it! What the hell was the matter with that asshole? He slammed the restaurant door behind him and strode up Oak Street. How damn hard could it be to just back up his story? Marcus looked over his shoulder, almost sensing a black and white cop car on his tail. Christ. "Tell them I was working late. No, you're not sure what time I left the place." That's all he had to say, the dumb bastard. Instead, his uncle gives the cops a list of the chores and an estimate of when his nephew probably finished up. Jesus, if he had a time clock he probably would've handed it over to them.

"Marcus, I love you like you were not my sister's son, but my own." Bite your tongue, thought Marcus. "But I'm not going to lie to the police for you. "After all," he gestured with his arms at their surroundings, "I have much to lose." Marcus followed the gesture and scanned the fly-speckled interior of the restaurant. Jesus, this moron thinks he owns Schrafft's or something. "Sorry nephew, you are on your own. I don't know where you were and I don't want to know." Uncle Bernardo crossed behind the counter and punched a button on the register. The drawer shot open and he pulled out several bills.

"Better not come back for a while. Here," he pressed the folded bills into Marcus's shirt pocket, "take this, you might need it." On top of everything else, Marcus thought in wonder, I'm being fired from my shitty job. He turned and left.

Marcus crossed the street and ducked into Regent Terrace, a short one-way passageway connecting Oak to Pine. The trash barrels of apartments adjacent to the grandly named alley lined either side of the dingy, sun-starved strip of pavement. He stopped and sat on the top step of stairs leading to a basement apartment. He reached to his breast pocket and pulled out the money from his uncle. Thirty bucks. Great. He fished a pack of Marlboros out of the same pocket, shook the pack, squeezed it with his fingers, crumpled it and threw it away in disgust. Empty. Shit. He sat, staring dully at a cat sunning itself atop an overfilled trashcan. There was no choice, only one place to go. He rose and jogged down the alley toward Pine. Time to seek sanctuary.

Marcus was short on both patience and calm by the time he rounded the corner near Saint Margaret's. He stopped dead in his tracks. A police car was just pulling away from the curb in front of the church. Marcus jumped back around the corner, counted to ten, then peered down the street. The car was gone. Thank you, Jesus.

He needed to get off the street *now*. He looked at the church down the block then at the rectory, just a house away. Keeping his head low he quickly climbed the front steps and rapped on the door. An elderly woman answered and he asked to see the father. He was invited into the sitting room while the housekeeper went to fetch the priest. After taking a couple deep breaths to calm himself, he scanned the room. He'd never been here before. Pretty plush. Even had what looked to be a drinks cabinet in the corner. Not a bad gig, if it wasn't for that celibacy thing. He shook his head and almost laughed. Celibacy my ass.

Marcus heard steps coming down the stairs. He turned and waited what seemed forever before the priest walked into the room. A wrinkled face smiled at him and motioned to the sofa. "Please sit down, my son," said Father Dwayne. "I'm so glad you came. I rarely get visitors nowadays and it's a pleasure I sorely miss."

Shit. Where the hell was Father Ryan?

The old man shuffled to an easy chair and gingerly lowered himself, placid smile on his face. "Now," he nodded again to the sofa, "tell me how I may be of help to you."

Marcus stood for a second, uncertain. Should he get the hell out of here and leave the old guy to drool over himself until he nodded off? The way things in his life were going though, the last thing he needed, was to piss off a priest. Especially one so close to entering the pearly gates. Besides, he doubted the Pendale police would think to look for him here. Marcus smiled at the ancient priest, and sat down.

After an hour of inane conversation during which the priest reminisced about his missionary days in Kenya, and continually referred to him as Javier, Marcus figured screw it and escaped, assuring the father that he would return shortly.

He ran down the block to the church, took the front steps two at a time, pulled open a heavy wooden door and stepped into the narthex. The door thudded closed behind him and it took several seconds for his eyes to adjust to the dim light. He walked into the nave. The stained glass windows allowed for muted sunlight to help guide him. Along the walls between the windows were the Stations of the Cross. For as long as Marcus could remember, these had made him extremely uncomfortable. Why anyone would want to immortalize the last moments of suffering in anyone's life was beyond him. He pulled his eyes from the plaster representations and scanned the church. The pews were empty save for a few old timers, rosaries clasped as though their lives depended on it. The temperature inside the church sent a quick shiver through Marcus. Man, if folks knew how cool it was in here the place would be packed to the rafters. He jogged down the aisle, earning a frown from the old folks, and yanked open the door to the sacristy.

The last time he'd been in there was when he'd been an altar boy years ago. The room had always given him a feeling of lightheadedness, having a peek behind the scenes at the church's machinations. Like seeing the wizard behind his curtain in Oz. He felt none of that today. The empty room was just a room. Marcus opened the door to the narrow hall which ran directly behind the altar. Hanging on pegs were the cassocks and surplices worn by the altar boys, ranging in size from that which might fit a munchkin, to one, unused for many years, that could have been comfortably worn by Officer Sully. This hall, too, was empty. Where the hell was he?

Retracing his steps and reentering the nave, Marcus slowly gazed from left to right. He stopped and raised his eyes. The choir loft. Hurrying by the praying pensioners he heard a, "Tsk, youngsters." He thought he saw movement between the ornate lattice-like scrolling of the loft railing. Opening a side door in the narthex, Marcus ran up the winding steps to the choir loft. There, on the organ bench, staring dully at the polished golden organ pipes, sat Father Ryan.

"I think I'm in trouble. We've got to talk."

The priest looked toward Marcus, smiled, and extended a hand.

⤜ 29 ⤛

Nikki stood at the curb while Mrs. Gorman walked up the driveway to Mrs. Cooper's yard. She could just make out Minna's chubby legs resting on a footstool in that weird looking hut in the corner of her yard. Nikki hadn't been keen on the idea of visiting Mrs. Cooper, but Mrs. G. had been adamant. "Your hair looks like it's been nibbled down by mice. We're going to get it taken care of. Minna has cut my hair for ages, and while she sometimes may seem strident in her beliefs, she certainly knows her craft."

"But I don't have the bread to pay her," Nikki tried to protest.

"It's my treat. And since I'm paying, let's not look at this as just a suggestion, hmm? I'm tired of spending all day talking to a wire brush."

In truth, it was easier to let someone else make the little decisions which comprised the day. Dealing with the craving was hard enough, actually thinking, feeling, and making decisions on her own, was a terror Nikki just wasn't ready to face.

Uh-oh. Looked like trouble. Minna was now standing, and judging by her body language it didn't look like Nikki was going to be shorn at Minna's Salon any time soon. Nikki watched the woman shake her head and gesture toward downtown. Nikki turned and slid a Lucky between her lips. She cupped her hands around the light by habit, though there was no breeze at all. She sucked in a lungful of smoke. Jesus. No wonder poor Mr. Gorman's hanging out with the angels. These Luckys'll kill you.

She heard Mrs. Gorman walking toward her. "Sorry Mrs. G., it was really kind of you to offer, and I'm starting to think I could use a little trim, but I guess it's just not going to happen."

Mrs. Gorman smiled. "Of course it is, Nikki. Minna is getting ready for you. Just give her a minute to wash up and open the salon."

"What? It sure didn't look like she was in the mood a minute ago."

"Nikki," said Mrs. Gorman, taking her arm and leading her toward the house, "haven't you realized how very persuasive I can be?"

When they reached the side door to the enclosed porch, Mrs. Gorman said, "Just come on back to the house when you're through. I'll make up some lemonade to celebrate your new look."

"Whoa, wait, Mrs. G., aren't you coming in with me?"

"You're a big girl, Nikki. I think you can handle getting your hair cut on your own. I'm just up the street, you know."

"Yeah, but what about paying the lady? I'm flat busted, I don't want any close friend of yours getting mad because I stiffed her on a haircut."

"Don't worry, dear. Here is some money." She pressed it into Nikki's hand. "And Minna and I are more neighbors than close friends." She stepped back and looked at Nikki. "You're not afraid of her, are you?"

"Come on Mrs. G., you know I chew up and spit out old ladies all day long."

At that moment the porch door slammed open. It seemed to be the signal that Minna was open for business. Great, thought Nikki, she heard me and is insulted. Just what I need, an angry woman working with sharp instruments around my head and face.

Mrs. Gorman leaned toward Nikki and whispered, "Her bark is worse than her bite. See you later," she said and waved over her shoulder.

Nikki climbed the porch steps and entered the salon. It was like walking into 1945. The walls were hung with black and white photographs of Judy Garland, Rosemary Clooney, and entertainers and actors Nikki vaguely recognized, but couldn't name. A giant beehive hairdryer and chair sat against one wall. Music was coming from somewhere. Nikki thought she recognized the singers, no, yes! Was it the Andrew Sisters? Holy shit, this really messed with her head.

"No smoking in the salon."

She started. "What?"

"I said, you need to get rid of that cigarette," ordered Minna.

"Oh, sorry," she reached for the door, "I'll just–"

"No, you won't throw it out onto my driveway. I'll just have to clean it up later. Get rid of it some other way."

Nikki looked around for a moment, then stepped outside, pinched the end of the cigarette, and knocked the ash to the ground. She toed some dirt over it and smiling up at Minna in the doorway, slipped the butt into her hip pocket. "Okay, Mrs. Cooper, it's snipping time."

Minna grunted. "Sit."

"This is quite a setup you have here," Nikki said, sliding back into the barber chair. "Must be great being able to go to work and never leave your own house. I don't know how I missed coming here before."

There was another grunt from behind Nikki's head. A large bib ballooned out over her. Minna cinched it tight around back. "I think you were otherwise occupied."

Nikki blinked. "What's that, Mrs. Cooper?"

"I said," she intoned, as though speaking to a slow child, "I don't believe you were paying much attention. Don't move." The sound of scissors furiously snipping was heard. "Your mind... and everything else, was on other things."

Nikki took a deep breath, "You're probably right."

"You're not the type of person whose hair I would have cut anyway." She thrust Nikki's head forward. Snip, snip.

Staring into her lap, her chin against her chest, Nikki asked, "So why are you doing it now?"

"My God, what did you do to this hair?" Minna yanked at a tuft. Nikki winced. "There are parts that look like they've been burnt." She shoved Nikki's head to the right until she had a clear shot at the area behind her left ear. Snip, snip, snip.

"I said–"

"I heard you, be quiet and keep still unless you want to lose an ear." She worked in silence, furious snips accompanying the 1940's soundtrack.

"I know who you are," said the quiet voice behind Nikki's head. "This is a small town and there are very few secrets. Especially when one behaves as you do."

"Okay, that's–"

Nikki tried to rise from the chair and Minna roughly pushed Nikki's shoulder down. "We're not through yet. Sit." She tightened the bib around Nikki's neck until it pinched the flesh. "I didn't want you here, but Rose Gorman forced me into taking you. Stupid of me, allowing myself to be taken advantage of. A Christian act she said it was, ha! My guess is she wanted you off her hands for a few minutes."

Nikki tried to shake her head.

"I said still! You're just the latest reclamation project in her life, you know. The first was that drunk husband of hers. She said he'd stopped the drinking, but I don't believe it. Once a drunk, always a drunk. You'd know all about that, wouldn't you?

And you can never trust what a man will tell you anyway. He was in the same lodge as my husband. Oh, what my Arnie told me about that Carl Gorman! Drank like a whole school of fish, he said."

"Look, I don't want to hear this," Nikki began.

"I don't care what you want to hear, you will hear what I say. You're just another drunk like him. Rose probably feels she can dry you out, but we know better, don't we? Aren't you thinking about drinking this very minute? Something cold, something to put out the anger you feel toward me, something to blunt the hopelessness you feel each minute of every day?"

Nikki looked forward, breathing heavily, not moving. She swallowed, afraid to say anything.

"I said I know who you are, and I do. I've known the Thompson family for many years." A small sound escaped Nikki's throat. "I remember Donald Thompson as a boy playing on the swing set and seesaw at the Peter Street playground. He sat on the floor in this very room with his Lincoln Logs while I permed his mother's hair." Minna's fingers found a twist of hair at the nape of Nikki's neck and pulled. Nikki gasped. "I know the family well enough," Minna whispered into Nikki's ear, "to have attended the funeral, and later, the reception for dear Donald. I was there when you caused that awful spectacle, upsetting the family even more. The best thing you ever did for them was run away when you did." Minna snipped, a fraction of an inch from Nikki's left eye.

"Why Donald gave you more than a glance is beyond me. Of course, he was a man, and when tempted with cheap trash he did what all men do. My God! They are so weak! They can't see beyond the next minute, the next few seconds. And you, and all those like you, preying on them, destroying what is good and decent. Thank God he didn't have to spend his life with you. I would have to say he was blessed to have died when he did.

Death would be preferable to a life sentence with a woman like you." Minna yanked some hair to one side and snipped madly. Nikki sat immobile, gasping, tears spilling down her cheeks.

Nikki cried quietly as Sinatra crooned "The Very Thought of You" while Minna hummed along, scissors a blur. Minna grabbed an electric razor hanging from the wall and ran it against the nape of Nikki's neck. The pressure on the razor raised pinpricks of blood. Nikki shuddered in silence.

"There!" Minna stepped back. "Not one of my more inspired efforts, but there was little of quality to start with. Minna untied the bib and yanked it off Nikki, the nylon fabric burning the side of her neck as it was jerked away. "You're not much to look at, and you never will be, but your hair looks one hundred percent better than it did twenty minutes ago. Now get out of my shop and never come back again. Whores aren't welcome here. They may be welcome in your bars downtown, but not here. You should go where you belong."

Nikki slowly slid forward and stepped to the floor. She wiped her eyes with the back of her hand, but still had difficulty seeing. She reached to her pocket, "I have…I have some…," she stammered through tears.

"I don't want your money. I thought I was clear, I want you out of my salon. Your kind are not welcome. Ever."

Nikki stumbled down the steps to the walkway. The door slammed behind her and a series of sobs shook her to the bone. Crossing her arms over her thin middle, she leaned against the house for support until the quaking passed. She pulled a Lucky from the pack and after several shaky attempts, lit it. Nikki inhaled deeply, crossed her arms again over her chest, cast her eyes to the pavement, and walked toward downtown.

⤜ 30 ⤛

Will McConnell gazed at the menu before him, seeing nothing. He sat in a booth in the side dining room at the Peterson Diner. It was forty minutes out of town, far enough to avoid seeing any familiar faces. He picked up his fork in his fist and with his thumb pushed back each tine until they were perpendicular to the handle. He then flipped the fork over and pushed them back. The waitress sidled over and asked if he was ready to order yet. He declined, saying he was waiting for someone and asked for another coffee. She looked at the fork in his hand and left. He pushed his shirt cuff up and glanced at his watch. Christ.

After Lynn's ultimatum of the night before, Will cancelled his plans to slip out of the house. He didn't want to do anything that might push her to involve anyone else in what was going on. The very last thing he needed was the police tailing after him trying to place his whereabouts at an inconvenient moment. How she'd arrived so close to the actual truth was a mystery. He shook his head. The fact that Eddie had so much to do with her discovery was maddening. He loved that kid more than life itself, and what does he do? Screws up everything for his old man. Why hadn't Will thought maybe Eddie would know he skipped out in the dark? He was like Will in so many ways, why didn't Will realize maybe his son would have difficulty sleeping,

241

too? Instead, he's slipping pills to Lynn who'd probably sleep through a nuclear war. Dumb. Now he was paying for that mistake. And other mistakes as well. Why the hell couldn't he have put the bottle of pills back on the right shelf? And why, even after he'd given one to Eddie dissolved in milk, did he deny he knew about them? Shit! He was smarter than that! A lot smarter!

The waitress looked over from her station where she was waiting for another pot of coffee to finish brewing. He must have made some noise. Calm, Will, calm down. He busied himself with the menu again as she brought the coffee pot. Wordlessly, she poured him a fresh cup, picked up his crooked fork, and replaced it with a new one before walking away.

Sleep had been elusive last night, and his insomnia had nothing to do with it. The double bed, always slightly crowded with the two of them, felt foreign and odd with just him in it. He couldn't get Lynn's discovery and its possible ramifications out of his mind. He doubted he would have gotten less sleep on that damn rollaway bed. The only consolation he had was the certainty that Lynn's night had been sleepless as well. He'd heard the creaks of that old cot from down the hall as she tossed, trying to find some comfort on its uneven mattress. Haven't been able to get her to take a day off work for months, but here she is, standing guard, like there's some monster loose in the house. What's the word? Ironic. Yeah, pretty freaking Ironic, Miss 'Let Me Work' and 'Do My Thing.' now won't leave her kid's side.

Will peered out the window again, wondering about the delay. Two young, caramel-skinned girls were walking by the parking lot, each with a book or two cradled to their budding chests. School kids on their way home for a quick lunch. His eyes stayed on their teenaged asses swinging beneath skin-tight denim. Each girl had a long dark mane which swung left and right, in time with each provocative stride. Jesus. Home for a quick lunch my ass, he thought, more like a quick fuck. Those people, no wonder they're reproducing like a colony of rats. The girls practically advertise for it on the street. He watched until they turned the corner just past Vonny's Used Cars. Ten more minutes, he decided, that's it. He couldn't be expected to wait any longer.

This morning, he'd left the house after a solitary glass of juice. Lynn hadn't deigned to speak to him. He thought of saying a quick goodbye to Eddie, giving him a kiss, let him know his dad loves him no matter what, but decided to hell with it. He'd probably have to go through Lynn to get to him and he was in no mood. He walked the two blocks to the train station, but instead of boarding he turned to a bank of pay phones where he found an unoccupied booth with a phone that actually worked. He folded the glass doors closed hoping they muffled the noise of the station and dialed an inside line at work. The switchboard operator picked up and connected him to his department. Just an ant in a colony, Will thought as the line rang. It was picked up by his immediate superior's secretary.

"Mr. Minnifield's office. How may I help you?"

"Adele, this is Will McConnell," he rasped into the receiver.

"Oh, hello Mr. McConnell."

"Hi, Adele. Is Mr. Minnifield in? I need to speak with him."

"No, not for another forty minutes or so. I thought you knew that."

"Oh, Jeez, yeah, I'm sorry. I'm so out of it I wasn't thinking. I really wanted to talk to him, too." Just outside the phone booth a man in a gray suit shouted a hearty good morning to a fellow commuter. Will winced and pressed the mouthpiece against his chest. He coughed several times and lifted the phone again to his mouth. "Sorry, Adele, my chest. I caught something somewhere and I can hardly breathe. Didn't sleep a wink last night. Uh, would you let Mr. Minnifield know there's just no way I can make it in today? I'm a mess and I sure wouldn't want to infect anybody."

"If you call back in about an hour you'd be sure to catch him yourself, Mr. McConnell."

"I just took something to make me sleep, I'll probably be dead to the world by then."

"Would you like me to have Mr. Minnifield call you at home when he arrives?"

Shit. "Um, no, that's nice of you, Adele, but like I said, I just took something. I was going to take the phone off the hook so I could get some rest. Got to get better, you know, don't want to miss any more time."

"Yes, Mr. Minnifield has mentioned he's concerned about the time you've been missing."

Dammit. "I always make up any missed time, don't I, Adele?"

"I'm sure you do, Mr. McConnell. I think it's the break in continuity that Mr. Minnifield is concerned with. It's difficult for a group to make headway on a particular project when one of the members is often absent. I believe that's what he said."

Hell. "When did he say this, Adele?"

"I believe it was last week during assessment meetings. A copy of the assessment report is waiting on your desk right now. Reviewing the reports with employees is part of today's agenda. But you won't be here for that today. Will you?"

You pinched-faced hag, thought Will. "Unfortunately, no. I'll try to make it in tomorrow."

"Thank you, Mr. McConnell, I know Mr. Minnifield is worried about your... 'delicate constitution' I believe is how he put it. He was expressing this concern to Mr. Carpenter just yesterday."

Will felt himself going red. Aiden Carpenter was the glad-handing bastard that started at the firm a year after Will did.

He was Will's junior and here it sounded like he and Minnifield were yucking it up together at Will's expense.

"Thanks for the concern, Adele. See you tomorrow."

"Goodbye, Mr. McConnell."

He hung up and sat with his hand on the receiver. A sharp rapping on the glass door broke his trance. He stood and pulled the doors open.

"Come on, pal, it's not a public toilet," a paunchy, middle-aged man slid by him into the booth. "This is one of the few of them that work, don't set up shop here."

"Sorry," Will mumbled.

"Dumbass," he heard as he moved away.

Will bought a paper and sat on one of the benches deciding what to do next. He opened it up, shielding himself from passersby. Unable to avoid it, bold black print caught his eye. Still more casualties in Vietnam with no end in sight. Riots in Poland, students in France, as well as those in the U.S., seizing campus buildings, the aftermath of race riots in Boston, Detroit, and Newark, Humphrey and Kennedy holding their breaths for the California primary, no new news on the Pendale Waterworks Killer. Jesus, what a messed up world. Will flipped through pages. Photos of men with hair to their shoulders, women, emulating that skinny British model, their hair shorter than any woman should ever wear it. Maybe they were trying to *be* men. Wouldn't surprise him. Everything was topsy-turvy.

How could this happen to the world he grew up in? Men not willing to fight for their country, fleeing to Canada where those commies welcome them with open arms. Women abandoning their families, kids having to raise themselves while mom's working or 'finding herself,' rich kids refusing to go to classes at college and seizing administration buildings, doing drugs and looking like Skid Row residents, police now called pigs and lampooned in the press, skinny, greasy weaklings held up as the idols of the day. Long haired singers, poets, actors, my God, where were the heroes he remembered? Patton, MacArthur, Wayne, Ike, Glenn. These were men who made you proud to be an American male. Now who was there, Bob Dylan? Dustin Hoffman? Life was going to hell.

A train pulled out of the station and left behind it momentary quiet. Will ducked back into the booth he'd occupied earlier, which now reeked of cigar, and dialed. He spoke quickly.

"It's me. Yes, I know it's early. I know, that's a risk I thought I'd take. We need to talk, face to face, it's important. No, everything's fine," he lied. He waited a moment and interrupted. "You'll have to find a way. Something's come up and we've got to get our stories straight. Now's not the time, you can tell me later. Look, I'm at a pay phone and I'll be cut off in a minute. No, I called in sick. Yeah, I *know* I might get in trouble if I keep it up. Will you just listen? Meet me at the Peterson on Rte 9 at eleven, okay? Yeah, in the back. Right, bye."

Will walked along the water to kill time and think, then caught a bus to the shopping center located behind the diner. He browsed aimlessly for awhile before throwing in the towel, heading to the diner, and waiting.

He looked again at his watch. Eleven-fifteen. He grabbed his fresh fork and began bending once again. Two of the four tines were pushed back when a familiar car pulled into the side lot.

"Thank Christ," he said under his breath. He motioned for the waitress to bring another menu. "And how about a decent fork, huh?"

⇥ 31 ⇤

Captain Clarke could not contain his frustration. "You're kidding." Once again his hand went to his head. "What did he say *exactly*?"

Sully's voice came through the receiver. "His uncle said I missed him by about ten minutes. Marcus stomped off, mad at the guy, and that's the last anybody here saw of him."

"No idea of where he might have gone?"

"I asked. The uncle said he might be with his 'girlfriend.' He said it like he was trying to be funny, but then he stopped when he remembered she's dead and that's the reason why we want Marcus. He really doesn't seem to be too bright, Captain." This, coming from Sully, Clarke thought. "Oh, Captain."

"What?"

"He also said we might want to look over on David Street. He could be there."

"What's on David Street? Why would he say that?"

"I asked, but he just sort of smiled and shrugged and all of a sudden his English got really bad."

Christ. "Did you go there?"

"That's where I'm calling from. I'm parked in front of the church. No sign of him anywhere."

Clarke sighed. "Okay, cruise the area for a while, we may get lucky."

"Got it."

Ten minutes. Dammit.

"Dammit! You did what?" Clarke asked Kevin MacDougall.

"I, um, went over to the Wilson place–"

"I got that part, Kevin. That's what I asked you to do, right?"

MacDougall nodded.

"What I specifically didn't ask you to do was to enter and search the premises. Do you have any idea the position you put this department in? Anything you found, anything that might help us catch Rosaria Donez's killer, may not be admissible. It's all going to depend on the mood of whatever judge eventually hears the case. Christ, there's a motion in the courts now to have anything obtained from what's deemed an illegal search thrown out of court and moved to be inadmissible."

"No way! Even if it helps solve a crime?"

"Yes, Kevin! Even then! Do you understand what you've done?"

MacDougall was quiet, examining his thumbnail.

"Kevin?"

"Yeah, I understand, it doesn't seem right though. I mean, we're supposed to solve crimes, right? Not just…just…" He shook his head.

Clarke rubbed his forehead with the palms of his hands.

"Kevin, sit down." His head still in his hands. "First, close the door."

The office was silent.

"Do you have any idea how dangerous your actions were?"

"I proceeded with caution, I had my gun at the ready. Before I entered any room I–"

"You don't know that house as well as the people who live there."

Kevin thought of his childhood house and doubted this, but said nothing.

"There may be a closet you don't notice, a turn in a hallway, hell, even a piece of furniture they could hide behind. You went in there *alone*. That is an unforgivable mistake. This isn't mishandling a kid who finds a dead body, this is a direct violation of rule number one. What could you have been thinking?" Clarke spoke quietly.

MacDougall was about to open his mouth.

"Let me finish first. I put my trust in you, as does this entire department. The citizens of this town look up to you. Sure, I know some of them still see little Kevvy MacDougall, but with each passing day, that changes. Your actions, how you represent the department, the respect you show the citizens, all that goes into the transformation from skinny kid to valued officer. I know it's not an overnight process and I've been willing to invest my time and energy in you because I believed you're the kind of man who will make a good cop." He paused. "For the first time since you've been under my command, my belief is wavering. This isn't just you deciding what's legal or acceptable, this is you putting your *life* in danger for no good reason other than to satisfy a curiosity, or maybe, and I hope like hell I'm wrong, to show off a little. Kevin, I know your actions might be somehow connected to your mother, her unsolved death, but we can't afford to lose you. This simply cannot happen again."

MacDougall nodded, swallowed several times and whispered, "Yessir."

"Okay, open that door and let's get some air in here. Since we have it, let's take a look at this diary, huh? We'll worry about what we can actually use from it later." He opened a desk drawer and pulled out the small book. It was a bit larger than his flat hand on the desk. The cover was light green with a design of flowers, daisies. The book had no lock as some diaries did, but there was a strap with a snap button that held the cover tightly closed.

"Have you looked through this yet?" Clarke asked.

"I skimmed through quick. There's some real surprises."

"Okay," Clarke reached into his middle drawer for his reading glasses, "Let's see what we have here." He unsnapped the strap, opened the small book, and began to read the rounded schoolgirl script.

About twenty minutes later he closed the back cover, tossed his glasses down and rubbed his eyes. His back was sticky with sweat and aching from leaning over the desk. "Jesus."

"Yeah," agreed MacDougall.

"I feel like a damn voyeur. This isn't information she would have ever shared with us, or anyone else for that matter. Except one other person. Some of it."

"Yeah."

"It answers some questions, at any rate. I think with confirmation of this," he gestured at the book, "we may be able to rule out one of our suspects." Clarke looked at his young officer. "Kevin, you ought to be thankful this didn't spell out the whole damn solution to the Donez killing for us. How would you feel if it did and we couldn't use any of the information?"

MacDougall just shook his head.

"You know, I've never met this woman, Nora Wilson. I'd never recognize her on the street. Yet, I feel awful for her, imagine the life she leads. Shackled to that crazy brother her entire life, both his slave and provider. Walking in the footsteps of a mother that may as well have never existed. And the father…," Clarke trailed off and rubbed his eyes again. "Now, the poor girl thinks she's the luckiest girl on the planet. Christ, talk about deluding herself." He looked down at the diary and shook his head. "And she thinks…."

"Yeah," MacDougall said again.

"Find her." Clarke said. "Jesus, you have no memory of her from school? Some of the childhood…hell she writes about?

"God, no! I had no idea!"

"Find her," he repeated, slumping back in his chair.

Rose Gorman eyed her wall clock again and brushed the flour from her hands onto the pie crust below them. She had a hankering for some pumpkin pie and thought she'd throw one together. Well, sort of, she thought, glancing at the can of pie filling on the counter. It won't be quite like she used to make for Carl, but it'll be close. She often thought about the "good old days" and how much better things seem to have been, but thank God for modern conveniences. She certainly wasn't up to cutting up an entire pumpkin, and wherever would she get one this time of year, anyway? No, some things were better now, no doubt about it. Running her hands under the faucet, she wondered again where on earth Nikki could be. It had been almost an hour since she left her at Minna's. She hoped it had gone alright. Mrs. Gorman had no illusions that Minna and Nikki might be lost in deep philosophical discussion. She'd barely been able to persuade her neighbor to do the job. Calling up the past had helped, as she knew it would.

She dried her hands and decided to let the crust sit for a few minutes while she walked down the street. It wouldn't take long. Just as she reached the crosswalk, she saw Nora Wilson of all people, opening Minna's porch door and stepping into the salon. Who would have thought? Perhaps she and Nikki know each other, considered Mrs. Gorman hopefully. Maybe Nora saw her through the window and wanted to say hello. There was another poor girl in need of a friend. That crazy brother of hers…. It would be nice if she and Nikki had each other. Mrs. Gorman smiled and turned back toward her house. Everything was fine. If Nikki wasn't back in another hour, she'd worry then.

"This is certainly a surprise. You may as well sit down, Nora. How long has it been since you last stopped in? I can't remember."

"It's been a while, Mrs. Cooper. I guess I get caught up with work, being busy, you know, just life in general." She sat in the barber chair and laced her fingers over her stomach. "I've been neglecting things."

"Oh, I understand how that happens, the pace of today is just insane. No one is able to enjoy themselves, to take part in what's important, the good things."

"You may be right."

"I must say, Nora, you're looking very healthy and happy."

"Thanks, Mrs. Cooper, I feel pretty healthy," she smiled shyly, "most of the time, anyway. And I am definitely happier than I can ever remember being."

"Oh? That's just lovely, dear," Minna said, thinking that the entire time she'd known Nora she could not recall a single instance before today when the girl had looked happy at all.

Minna billowed the bib over her and tied it off at the neck as it settled onto Nora's lap. "When I was young, there was only one thing to make a girl as happy as you seem to be. Tell me, is there a young man in your life?"

"Mrs. Cooper!" Nora smiled. "Why would you ask that?"

"When you've seen as many women as I have over the years, it's not difficult to see when there's a change in their life. There's a kind of satisfied glow."

"I'm blushing." Nora slid her hands from under the bib and touched her cheeks. "In fact, I *do* feel a little bit glowing."

Minna reached for a comb and pair of scissors. "I certainly don't want to embarrass you, that's not my intention at all." She combed and clipped the back of Nora's head.

"I know, Mrs. Cooper. All this is so new to me. I was never one of those girls in school who had boyfriends buzzing around all the time. The fact is… there's someone who likes me, who loves me." She shook her head as if unable to believe it herself.

"Keep still, dear."

"Sorry."

"Hmm. He loves you? You're a very lucky young lady. It seems there is painfully little love around anymore. I didn't know young people actually fell in love today. I thought it was all just…well…."

"Oh, it's love, he tells me all the time." Nora's smile glowed.

"Who is the fortunate young man? Is it anyone I might know?"

Nora's smile vanished. "I don't know, Mrs. Cooper. Probably not. She was quiet for a moment. "We're not ready to go public yet."

"Oh? Is that your idea or his?"

"It's his," she said, but added quickly, "I agree with him, though. The timing isn't right."

Minna snipped and combed in silence for a while. "Does this have to do with your brother?" she asked.

"With Vern?" Nora asked, puzzled. "No. It has nothing to do with *my* family, it's…," she stopped and briefly smiled. "They say there are no secrets between a woman and her hairdresser, right?"

Minna stopped clipping and looked down on Nora's head. "That's right, dear."

"This is so hard. I want to talk to somebody about it, but I really don't have anyone. Vern scares away most people and I guess I'm not exactly Miss Personality. Sometimes it feels if I don't get to share stuff, I'll just explode. Thank God for my diary," she laughed. "It's probably kept me out of the loony bin."

"You go right ahead. "I'll just keep right on working and not interrupt you."

"Thanks, Mrs. Cooper. My mom liked you. I remember that. I think I remember you cutting her hair. We weren't as close as some mothers and daughters, but…I'm pretty sure you did her hair."

Minna smiled and nodded. A completely forgettable woman, a nobody, not even worth the air she breathed. She gently tilted Nora's head left and began clipping.

Nora took a breath. "The reason nobody knows about us yet is because he's in a…well, I guess you'd say he's in a relationship right now." The clipping paused briefly and resumed. "It hasn't been going well for a while. He wants to end it, but there are complications. He's been unhappy for such a long time."

"You've known each other long?"

"Not so long, but long enough." She smiled. "We bumped into each other at Jo Jo's. Pretty romantic, huh?" She rolled her eyes.

"So he's a local man?"

"Huh? Oh, yeah, he is. I wasn't going to say, but I guess the Jo Jo's kind of gave it away. You should be a cop, Mrs. Cooper. You're good at ferreting out information. We'd seen each other before, but that was the first time we met and really talked. He's such a sweet man. We left and took a drive. We must have talked for an hour. When I dropped him back at Jo Jo's it felt like I'd known him for years."

"Why did you drop him there, instead of his home?"

"I couldn't drop him at his house because he's…um, like I said before, he's sort of spoken for."

Minna tilted Nora's head to the other side and snipped. She said nothing.

"It's not the greatest situation, I know, but well, it just happened. We'll be talking about what to do next a little later today. That's why I wanted the haircut. I want to look extra special when I see him."

"What is your man planning on doing? Divorce?"

"It's complicated. We're still at the talking stage. We'll move on from there."

"Marriage is not something you can just shove under the bed when you don't want to see it. It doesn't just go away," Minna said.

"I know, I'm sorry I told you about it. I don't want you to be upset, Mrs. Cooper. Please, you won't tell anyone about this conversation, will you?"

"Of course not, dear" She snipped once more and said, "There!" Minna untied the bib from the back of Nora's neck and gently pulled it off her body. "Don't move." Minna lightly brushed the back of Nora's neck, her forearms, chest and stomach with a soft camelhair brush. "Some stray hairs sneaked under there," she said, gently brushing Nora's stomach.

"Oh, thanks, Mrs. Cooper." She looked critically in the handheld mirror, turning her head from side to side. Minna stood quietly looking in affirmation.

"Looks great, Mrs. Cooper. What do I owe you?"

"Let's say it's a gift. For a special occasion," she said quietly.

"That's so sweet! It *is* a special occasion, isn't it?" Minna

nodded. "Thank you so much, Mrs. Cooper."

Nora pushed open the door, her free hand resting gently across her stomach, and bounced happily down the steps.

Minna stood staring at her as she walked by the front of the enclosed porch and up the street.

✦ 32 ✦

I t was just after four o'clock when Mrs. Gorman rapped on
the door of Minna's front porch. She squinted and peered
between the louvered window slats. No one. She hurried
around the house to the driveway and then to the yard. There
was no one to be seen. Mrs. Gorman walked to the yard's back
corner to check if Minna was behind that crazy gazebo of hers,
she wasn't. The yard was deserted. No sign of Minna, and more
ominously, no sign of Nikki. She looked toward downtown,
thinking the worst, and cursing her own stupidity. Giving a
weak and shaky alcoholic a pocketful of money and leaving her
alone. What an idiot she was. But Nikki hadn't been alone, she'd
been with Minna. And Nikki wasn't weak. My God, thought
Mrs. Gorman, most people wouldn't survive what that girl has
put herself through. The hardships, both physical and mental…
no, she may be shaky, but certainly not weak. There was a core
of iron in that girl.

Halfway to Broadway, Mrs. Gorman wished she'd thought
to use her car. If she did find Nikki, and if she was drinking
again, how did she intend to get her home? She might have
a prayer of doing it if she could coax her into the car, but
otherwise…she didn't want to think about it. She stopped for
breath and looked in each direction. It had been so long since
she had to worry about anyone's drinking, she couldn't recall

exactly where the taverns were. She turned north and started walking.

The Bottle Cap was her third stop. She stepped through the door into the darkness, stark contrast with the harsh light outside. My God, she thought, people actually come here to socialize? The brown tiled floor was unswept and a trail of dried mud disappeared into the gloom. Six barstools with red vinyl seats, all of which looked to be repaired with masking tape, lined the bar. One, at the end, was occupied by a large man in stained jeans and a gray T-shirt, the others appeared empty. Two of three tables in the back of the room were also empty. On the third table was a large tool box which appeared to belong to a fox-faced man who was working on the back of the cigarette machine. Every few seconds there was a clank of metal against metal and a long string of profanity.

"Can I get you something, ma'am?" The bartender sounded young, although it was difficult to actually see his face under his full beard, ponytail and Mets cap with the visor pulled low.

"No, no thank you, I'm just looking for someone."

"Hey!"

Nikki leaned out from behind the large man sitting at the bar. Apparently there was another stool back there Mrs. Gorman had missed. Nikki leaned against the man's shoulder and waved an empty shot glass with her free hand.

"Welcome to my home away from home, Mrs. G.! We got it all here, TV," she nodded at the ball game over the bar, "food," she rapped her knuckles against a large jar of pickled eggs, "drink of course, speaking of which, Jonesy, please pour Mrs. Gorman one of your finest and I'm about ready for a refill myself. The facilities are in the rear, but," she leaned toward to Mrs. Gorman and whispered, "I'd only use them if I really, really had to, if I were you." She wrinkled her nose and shook her head.

Dear Lord, thought Mrs. Gorman, help me to help her.

"So, what do you think of the place?" Nikki swung her arm around wide and would have fallen to the ground if she hadn't been caught by the large man at the bar. She broke into a giggling fit, "Why thank you, my good man. Mrs. G., this is my benefactor today, his name is Rocky."

"Stony," said the man.

"He's doing roadwork on Route Nine, right?"

"Route One, right. Here you are, Nik." He handed a full shot glass to Nikki, which she tossed back in a gulp. She followed it with half a mug of beer.

"Ahhh. A man after a girl's heart, huh Rock?" she grinned blearily at him.

"That's right, Nik, your heart." He laughed and drank down his own beer.

He was a mound of flesh that gave off a strong reek of sweat and alcohol. His gray T-shirt may once have been white, it was impossible to know. The blue jeans he wore were grimy and Mrs. Gorman saw his work boots were the source of the mud on the floor. A large gut hung over his belt, while in back his pants rode low enough to expose more than anyone would ever want to see.

He slid a hand around Nikki's hip and pulled her close. "Almost time we took a walk, right, Nikki? Let's check out my new truck out back," he whispered in her ear loud enough for Mrs. Gorman to hear.

Nikki closed her eyes, smiled, and pushed away gently. "Soon, Rocky, soon. Let me visit with my friend, huh?"

"I haven't been shelling out for your drinks half the afternoon for nothing, doll," he complained, good humor on the wane. "You can talk to the old lady later, you got a business transaction to think about now."

"Hey, a promise is a promise, Rocky," Nikki slurred, and made a cross-my-heart motion.

"It's Stony, babe, and it better fucking well be."

"Jonesy, tell him Nikki never breaks a promise, huh? Her word is as good as–"

A baseball bat slammed down on the bar, splashing spilt beer over all of them.

Mrs. Gorman gasped. Her hands flew to her breast. Stony's head snapped around. "W-What the fuck?" he stammered.

The only person to express no reaction at all was Nikki.

"Get the hell out of here, pal," Jonesy said quietly.

"What? No fucking way!"

Jonesy lifted the bat and jammed the fat end into the big man's chest. Hard. "You don't want to make me say it again, believe me."

"I ain't been pouring money into this bitch for nothing. She owes me!"

"How much money have you spent?" interrupted Mrs. Gorman. "I'll pay it."

"No, you won't," said Jonesy.

"I don't want *you* to pay me, grandma, I want this little slut to do like she promised."

"That's it." Jonesy was on this side of the bar so quickly Mrs. Gorman wasn't sure if he'd gone around or over. He grabbed Stony by his wiry brown hair with one hand and prodded him in the kidneys with the bat in his other. Despite his threats and protestations, Stony was out the door in seconds. The bar was quiet except for the occasional noise from the cigarette vendor.

"Thank you so much, Mr. er, Jonesy," said Mrs. Gorman. She gingerly eased herself onto a stool and passed a shaky hand across her face. "What a terrible man. Are there many like him?"

Jonesy set the bat on the bar and nodded his head toward Nikki who appeared almost oblivious to the proceedings. She perched on a stool and drained the last of her beer. "Unfortunately, she attracts them. Take her home, please."

Mrs. Gorman carefully stepped down from the stool and took Nikki by the hand. The girl followed like an obedient child. "Thank you, again," she said as they reached the door.

Back behind the bar, Jonesy said, "Please take care of her. I should have stepped in long before today. I was a friend of Donald's and I met Nikki before...the accident. She hasn't always been like this."

"I know."

He nodded, lowered his head, and went back to work wiping down the bar.

The two women walked home in silence. They passed Minna's where Mrs. Gorman again looked for signs of life in the yard but again saw none. "What happened here today, Nikki?" she asked. There was no reply. "I see she cut your hair, it looks nice." In reality, it looked, and smelled, like Nikki's beer-drenched fingers had repeatedly raked through it. Still silence. As they reached home and left the sidewalk to walk toward the back porch, Mrs. Gorman tried again. "Did she say something to you, Nikki?"

Nikki sighed quietly. There were tears in her eyes. "Nothing I haven't said to myself a million times, Mrs. G." She walked up the steps to her own apartment and turned. "Thanks for coming to my rescue, you didn't have to, you know. This was just another day for me."

"No, Nikki. Not anymore."

"Yeah, well...," Nikki smiled sadly. She slid her thumb and forefinger into a tight hip pocket. "Here, this is yours. Mrs. Cooper didn't want it." She held out the money Mrs. Gorman had given her earlier.

"She didn't take it? Why not? What did she say to you, Nikki?"

"She didn't want it," Nikki repeated, and she pressed the bills into her landlady's hand.

"Why didn't you use this money for drinks, Nikki?"

Nikki faintly smiled again, "Mrs. Gorman, I don't need money to drink, and besides," the smile faded, "that was money from you. I couldn't use it for that."

She opened her kitchen door and stepped in. "I think I'm going to lie down for awhile."

Mrs. Gorman listened for the sound of the bedsprings through the open window of Nikki's apartment. It came followed by the sound of sobs that tore at the old woman. She waited until they finally faded and the sound of long, deep breaths reached her ears. Once she was sure Nikki was sleeping, she turned and marched down the street to Minna's.

This time she saw Minna in the yard, on her knees next to a wheelbarrow full of topsoil, scooping out handfuls and leaning to spread it over one of the flowerbeds.

"Minna. I need to speak with you," Mrs. Gorman said to her neighbor's wide bottom.

"Can it wait, Rose? I'm working on this last bed right now," she said, not turning around.

"No, it can't wait. I need to speak to you immediately." Hearing Minna use her first name angered her, she couldn't say why, but it certainly did. "What happened here earlier today? What happened with you and Nikki?"

Minna leaned back on her heels, still facing away, "I cut her hair. Isn't that what you wanted? Isn't that what you basically forced me into doing by questioning my Christian charity? I did it, a good job, too, considering what I had to work with." She slowly rose and turned to face Mrs. Gorman. "Why in the name of God you care about a piece of filth like that amazes me. She's trash, Rose, a cheap whore, not worth the effort or thoughts of either of us. Why?" she asked again, truly puzzled.

"Did you say that to her? Did you call her those names and make her feel worthless? Did you?"

Minna shrugged and turned to walk behind the wheelbarrow.

"Dammit, look at me!"

"Rose, really," Minna scolded.

"How could you? How could you do this to a girl who has been through so much?"

"Been through so much, oh please! She's a tramp, Rose. You should know that better than anyone. How many nights have you heard her dragging home her latest bedmate? My God, the number of times I've heard, and seen, yes seen, her with a different man staggering by my house, loud, profane, inebriated. It's a disgrace! Women like her shouldn't be allowed in town. They prey on men and use them to get whatever they want. That one, why, she'd entertain the entire male population in town for a drink. How many husbands have fallen prey to her? How many marriages may be in tatters because of her? She's evil! She ruins people! Ruins marriages!" Minna was out of breath.

"That's what this is about, isn't it, Minna? It isn't about Nikki, not really. It's about men who stray from the marriage bed. Because face it, Minna, there are no women like Nikki without the men who want them. It's about men choosing to find what they want elsewhere." She paused. "This is about Arnie, isn't it?"

Minna gripped the wheelbarrow's handles, her knuckles turning white. She breathed heavily. "You don't know what you're saying."

Rose Gorman looked at Minna, the woman she thought she'd known for over thirty-five years. "This is about him. What he did, am I right?"

Minna stiffly walked the wheelbarrow toward the garage doors. "Get out of here, Rose. I don't want to see you again. Leave."

"I feel so sorry for you, Minna. How long have you thought this? After all these years, you're still not able to truly face what happened, are you? You just refuse to see it."

"Go! You're not welcome here. And keep that little whore of yours out of my sight!"

33

"McConnell isn't at work, he called in sick."

"Damn. Alright, then get over to the Wilson house. And don't go alone, Kevin. Contact Sully and have him meet you there. He's in the cruiser. He just missed Marcus at the uncle's restaurant and it looks like the kid's on the run. That bumps him toward the top of the suspect list. Get moving. And we need to speak with that nutcase Vern and his sister. Then, once we get a line on Marcus, we're all over him." As MacDougall left Clarke's office the black phone started to ring.

At that moment Sully walked into the interview room carrying a fresh box of StarLite Bakery donuts. "Come on, Sully," MacDougall called to him. "You're with me. We're hitting the Wilson place. Aren't you supposed to be looking for Marcus Rodriguez?"

Sully looked down at the box of donuts and sighed. He took a bite of one, grabbed another, and wrapped it in a paper napkin. He quickly chewed, swallowed, then opened his mouth to speak. "I tried, but–"

"Wait!" called Captain Clarke, dropping the receiver in its cradle. "We know where Vern Wilson is. The ticket master at the train station just called. Seems Vern's down there screaming about ghosts in the trees or something. Grab him and we'll throw him in a holding cell until we know who to call at the VA.

If his sister ever turns up, maybe she can help us out. Be careful. This guy is nuts and possibly dangerous. Got it?"

"Yeah, Captain," said MacDougall. Sully nodded, powdered sugar on his lips.

"Use the damn napkin," MacDougall muttered to his partner as they moved to the car.

When they reached the train station the ticket master told them they'd missed him by about five minutes. "Was yelling his brains out for a good while. Couldn't get him to shut up. He got his free speech and all, but he got no right to bother the commuters. Was saying we had to drop the bomb. Wipe them off the face of the earth, stuff like that. Who the hell's he talking about? All he said was, 'ghost, ghosts in the jungle.' Jesus, what a loony."

"Which direction did he head?" asked MacDougall.

The man nodded east. "Toward the water, said he had to finish them off. Had his hands in front of him all clenched, like he was holding something long and kind of thin, like a club, or stick. But wasn't nothing there."

"Thanks. Let's go," he said to Sully.

They sped the block or so to the entrance near the waterworks, the car kicking up a cloud of dust as it skidded to a stop. The two men unsnapped their holster covers and proceeded down the same path Rosaria Donez had walked. They separated, Sully taking the area near the breakwater and MacDougall moving south toward the old bunker.

As he approached the bunker Kevin could swear he smelled the stink of decaying flesh still clinging to the concrete structure. He breathed through his mouth, not wanting to risk losing his breakfast. When he reached the bunker's nearest wall he hesitated. The structure was the perfect hiding place. He could picture Vern inside, crouching in the dark shadows, oblivious to the smell around him, waiting for MacDougall to walk by and then spring out, clubbing him from behind.

MacDougall drew his gun and held it ready. He stepped away from the entrance, distancing himself from Vern's possible attack. He strained to see inside. It was too dark to glimpse a thing. "Vern?" he called softly. "Vern, it's Officer MacDougall. Come out with your hands on your head. All I want is to talk to you. Don't do anything to make things bad for yourself." There was a skittering sound and MacDougall dropped to a crouch, ready for confrontation. A water rat the size of a small cat raced out the entrance and around the back of the bunker. MacDougall eased his finger from the trigger, stood straight, and allowed himself to breathe. He felt a fresh trail of sweat moving down his back. Jesus. He hated rats.

He inched toward the entrance, allowing his eyes time to gradually adjust to the gloom. Finally, he poked his head in and turned each way. It was empty. A bit of trash clinging to a wall at his left, and the stains left by Rosaria Donez in the furthest corner. He sighed and leaned against one wall, oblivious to any residual odor in the place. After a moment, he pushed himself to move again and stepped back into the glare of the sun. He hadn't thought to let his eyes readjust to the intense sunlight and was momentarily blinded. With an arm over his eyes, he staggered to the far exterior wall of the bunker. It faced the side of the waterworks that was more secluded with bluffs sheltering it from the town and the bunker itself obscuring the view north. MacDougall looked directly at the ground after uncovering his eyes. After a minute or two he was able to raise his head and look up the stretch of beach. "No," he whispered, "not again."

About fifty yards from him lay the body of a woman face down on the ground. Her head was turned away and her long, dark hair was in a tangle. She appeared naked above the waist, her cut off blue jeans barely covered her bottom. The left arm stuck straight out, perpendicular to her body, pointing toward MacDougall, as though beckoning for help. Oh, God, he thought. That damn psycho did it again.

Clarke sat at his desk, fingers pressed against his temples, gazing at the open file on his desk. Who had the strongest motive to kill Rosaria Donez? Marcus Rodriguez professed to love her, but he lied about his whereabouts at the time of the murder and he's since disappeared. Vern Wilson? Probably a certifiable nut who recently accosted her and was seen moving toward the scene at about the time of the killing. He too, can't be located. Minna Cooper was a bitter old woman with hate for anyone who reminded her of her dead husband's infidelities. At least they knew where *she* was. He sighed and pushed the folder away, squeezing the bridge of his nose to ease the pressure there.

The phone rang and he answered with an irritable, "Yes?" He listened. "How long ago was this, Mrs. Barton? Mr. Edmunds? A neighbor? Contact officers MacDougall and Sullivan. They're in their cruiser. Alright, I'm on my way. If any emergency calls come in before we check back be sure to route them to Sayreville. Yes, I'm sorry, I know you know. Right, good bye."

Clarke grabbed his gun belt from his lower right hand drawer and strapped it on as he pushed open the back door and jogged to the squad car. He thought about hitting the siren and lights, but decided against it. Instead, he drove as quickly as traffic allowed and came to an abrupt stop in front of the Wilson house. Mrs. Barton radioed and told him she was unable to make contact with the other officers. Hell.

He exited the car, unsnapped his holster and proceeded to the porch steps, aware he was about to do exactly what he'd admonished Kevin for doing just yesterday. As his foot hit the first riser, a wail emanated from the house, so full of pain that, despite the heat of the day, sent a chill through him. He pulled his gun free and warily inched up the steps. He stopped at the gaping front door, noting the detached screen door and splintered threshold frame. Another wail reached him, this one louder than the last, ending in a choked gasp. Clarke couldn't decipher what, if anything, was being cried. His heart beat at a crazy rhythm as the noise continued. He stood, anchored, against the doorframe. The noise, seemingly non-stop now, siren-like, with almost no pause for breath. It sounded like the word "no" being drawn out forever. Clarke couldn't discern if the source of the sound was male or female. He *was* sure it was human.

"This is the police!" he shouted through the entry. He waited. The only response was another drawn out wail of anguish. "This is the police! Put your hands on your head and come out!" Another wail, followed by a snuffling sound. The noise seemed to be coming from the first floor and rear of the house. Clarke had been in enough houses in town to know that meant it was the kitchen. Christ. He'd have to go in. His only comfort was it didn't sound like the source of the noise was in any state to offer resistance.

He took a breath and willed his feet to move. He entered the living room. Knowing what he did of Vern, the home's squalor barely registered. The sound of another wail swept over him.

"Nooooo!"

It seemed to be even louder, but that may have been because he was closer to its source. He paused at what looked to be the dining room. A large table, its surface completely hidden under who knows how many days or weeks worth of trash, stood in the center of the room. There was no doubt now. The wails were coming from the other side of a grimy, swinging door leading to the kitchen.

Clarke reached with his left hand, pushed the door open, and stepped into the kitchen. What he saw would remain with him for the rest of his life. Like a photograph, every sharp detail visible for as long as it's gazed at. Except that sometimes, after awhile, photos faded. This never would.

As he pushed the door open, Clarke first saw the grimy cabinets on the far side of the room and the stained, brown ceiling. A wall clock hung askew over a sink full of dirty dishes. Its face was so smeared and spattered Clarke could not decipher the time. As in the rest of the house, he noticed each surface was covered in filth. Near the wall phone, a large red stain caught his eye, drawing his focus. Later, he was thankful for this split second reprieve of the horrors to come. He thought at the time, my God, a blood spatter on the wall. If only that had been the full extent of the carnage.

There, in the center of the filthy kitchen floor, slumped back on his heels, fists and forearms pressed to the sides of his head, knelt Vern. As his identity registered with Clarke, Vern cut loose with another scream.

"NOOOOOOOOO!"

As the sound spewed from his mouth, it was as though his insides were being shredded and cast out of his body. He choked and made a frenzied retching sound. From the knees down his pants were wet and stained dark. Vern's shirt was an abstract in various shades of filth. From where Clarke stood, he could see Vern's eyes were screwed shut in his pain. His arms fell from the sides of his head. Clarke thought for a second the man had grown a set of long, red sideburns. It was not until he saw what was behind Vern that he knew the truth.

Lying on the dirty linoleum, shoved against the refrigerator door, was Nora. What was left of Nora. Her face was unrecognizable. The bone beneath the flesh had been shattered in so many places the entire head seemed misshapen. Bits of bone tangled in her hair, flies crawled on the red-gray jelly of the brain. As Clarke stood, transfixed, he now saw specks of the substance stuck to the cabinets, refrigerator and floor. Pieces of what was once Nora Wilson's head.

Her smock was torn from her shoulders, yet still buttoned at the waist. It spread under her, around her hips, like a dancer's twirling skirt. Her brassiere, its original color unknown, hung like a twisted, crimson sash from her right shoulder. Her chest, oh God, her chest. Beneath her a pool of red covered nearly a third of the room's floor. The source of Vern's stained pant legs now apparent.

Vern's next keen almost split Clarke's own skull. Tears rising, he lowered his gun, stepped forward and, using his foot, shoved Vern face down on the floor. His cheek made a wet splat as it landed in his sister's blood. Through the tears, Clarke kneed Vern flat to the ground and cuffed his hands behind his back. As Vern screamed yet again, the pressure of the floor against his diaphragm muffled the volume, yet caused the wail to sound more recognizable. He wasn't screaming "nooo," he was screaming "Nooooora." Clarke stepped away and looked again at the disfigured body of Nora Wilson, her barely recognizable skull, and her raw, mutilated torso. Jagged, vaguely circular wounds where her breast had once been, now attracting the attention of the flies. Through the horror, one question surfaced in Clarke's mind. The breasts. Where were they?

⤜ 34 ⤛

larke shoved Vern in the backseat of the cruiser and, between screams, radioed for an ambulance, cognizant of the fact it was for transport, not medical assistance. He stood on the porch, his own pants now soaked red with Nora's blood from the knee down, collecting himself as best he could before re-entering the house. Trying to detach from his horror, Clarke knew he needed to record every detail of the crime scene before it was disturbed. He crossed through the front of the house and hesitated at the kitchen door. Okay, let's do this, he thought.

He began at the side of the room furthest from Nora's body. None of the accumulation of dishes, trash, and junk seemed to have been disturbed in a while. The food appeared dried on. Steeling himself, he approached the phone wondering how such a large concentration of blood could have made it this distance from the body. As he neared the stain he became aware of another smell, which earlier had been unable to penetrate that of the gore. It was, no, it couldn't be, could it? Garlic? Clarke leaned toward the telephone, and for the first time since entering the kitchen, risked a deep sniff. He jerked his head back and sniffed again. Spaghetti sauce. He laughed. It was fucking spaghetti sauce. In addition to the garlic, he identified basil and parmesan cheese. Jesus, spaghetti sauce!

He shook his head and laughed. He laughed until he doubled over. Tears ran down his face and Clarke thought his sides would burst. Look! Behind the coiled cord, a dollop of meatball! His wild braying echoed off the hard kitchen surfaces and continued long enough for Clarke to fear he would lose his breath and black out. He knew his reaction was a symptom of shock, but could do nothing to suppress it. Finally, as he felt himself getting lightheaded, the absurd laughter passed. He was weak and grabbed the back of a greasy kitchen chair for support. He wiped his face on his shoulder sleeve, took a deep breath which he immediately regretted, and went back to work.

Despite the overall cluttered condition of the house, in the kitchen there was very little, save the table and chairs, and a large, overflowing metal trash can. Clarke crouched and examined the floor under the table. Nothing but filth. The back door was ajar and he could see there was nothing behind it. The sink was jammed tight with dishes. Most of the cabinets hung open. Those that weren't he peered into, finding nothing but dirt, a couple dead ants, and a few stray pieces of crockery. He opened the oven. Just years of baked-on grime. That left the trash can and the refrigerator. If Nora's severed breasts were still in this room, those were the only hiding places left.

Clarke looked at the trash can and knew he'd better wait for help before searching through that mess. He now forced himself to look down at Nora. He'd never met the girl, didn't even know what she'd looked like. Without the smock and the location of the body, he would have been unable to discern the victim's identity. Truthfully, he had no positive ID now, but he knew, there was no doubt. Vern had snapped and done it again. Would the results have been different if only they'd come to the house earlier instead of being summoned by the phone call from the train station? Of course they would have. Clarke knew that and knew he would have to live with that thought forever.

The poor woman, what they had learned from her diary added to the knowledge he had of her pitiable existence. Sexually abused by a hateful, overbearing father, her pleas for help ignored by a timid, frightened mother. Finally free of both only to find she was now the sole support of her malicious sibling who lived in a hell of his own, punctuated only by outbursts directed at her. A true life sentence, no relief at all until quite recently. Until a chance meeting gives her a glimmer of hope. The deluded girl snatched at it like a drowning person would a life preserver. The man of her dreams. Tells her she's beautiful. Clarke looked at the pulpy mass that was her face. Tells her she understands him, she's the woman he should have met years ago, one day they'll be together and truly be a family. A family like one Nora never knew or dared imagine she could have. It gives her a reason to look forward, something to live for, a meaning to her otherwise worthless existence. He even gives her what would have been their child. Clarke recalled the excitement she recorded in her diary when she realized she was pregnant. She would have his child! Clarke's eyes teared. Not now. Not ever.

He stood over her, his feet set and unable to move, blood adhering his lower pant legs to his skin, itching. The now swarming flies moving from her body to his legs and back again. He closed his eyes and waited for the sounds of the ambulance.

When Clarke heard the sirens he crossed through the house to meet them at the door. He gestured to the kitchen with his head and stepped out onto the porch. Behind him, he heard, "Jesus Christ, what a mess," as the crew walked through the first floor and then a muted, "My God," as they reached the kitchen.

He rested a hand on a porch pillar more for support than anything, and looked up and down the street. Neighbors stood in their yards whispering to each other about the latest goings on at the Wilson house. Arms crossed over their chests almost as if trying to shield themselves from whatever terror had just occurred there. How many of these same faces had, over the years, turned away and closed windows when they'd heard cries of rage or perhaps screams for help coming from this house? We've become a nation of scared sheep, frightened of the changes speeding by us, clinging to the past with both hands, all the while decrying those responsible for those changes. Clarke knew he was as guilty as any of those people standing on their postage stamp lawns, shaking their heads, wondering about this crazy world they were living in.

Was life truly better in the past? Nora Wilson was being molested by her father, her pleas for help falling on deaf ears. If anyone with any power *had* heard them, would they have been able to make a difference? Clarke seriously doubted it. She would've been put through bureaucratic hell before eventually being returned right back to where she'd started from. Angela Castille disappears from town and no one, not even her own family, cares enough to feel outraged that almost nothing is done to find her. The woman's reputation is tarnished in a police report by those with nothing to risk and no reason to really give a damn. Simply because of the color of her skin. The former police captain files it as an unsolved missing person and washes his hands of it. Besides, she was one of *them*. God only knew what happened and who really cared? Certainly not the good citizens of Pendale. The ones in the barber shop, those same neighbors he'd heard buying rounds of drinks for each other when they'd heard the news of Martin Luther King's assassination. Hell, it wasn't better in the past, it wasn't better now, it was exactly the same. The town was static. It never changed. The same people say and do and think just as they did ten, fifteen, twenty, a hundred years ago. Clarke felt forgotten as the rest of the world moved on while he and his town remained, rooted, forever unchanged.

Several doors up the street he saw an old man holding a large, tawny cat in his arms. He held it to his chest and scratched behind its ears. The cat's eyes were closed in ecstasy and its head was tilted back to receive more pressure from its master's fingers.

Clarke descended the porch steps and looked in the car at Vern. He was slumped against a back door and a low moaning had replaced the wails of earlier. Clarke gave the wire mesh screen between the front and rear seats a solid shake before double-checking that the two front windows were wide open. Couldn't have Vern die of suffocation before…whatever happened to him. Clarke straightened with a small groan, felt his sticky pants peel from his shins, while even more sweat rolled down his back, and walked toward the man with the cat.

"Mr. Edmunds?" he asked.

"Yes, Captain," the man answered, knowledgeable of Clarke's rank.

"Thank you for calling, sir. I just wish you'd done it a little sooner," Clarke said, aware he sounded like he was shifting the blame he felt for himself to the old man.

Mr. Edmunds looked questioningly.

"The sister, Nora Wilson, is dead." Why the hell try to keep it quiet, he thought. The news would be out in minutes anyway. "There's not anything I can add at the moment." He paused. "It was…it was an awful thing."

"Ah, dear God," Edmunds hugged his cat closer. "I was afraid it was something like that. I heard him screaming and I knew something terrible happened. Such a pained, lonely cry. The poor, poor boy."

Clarke could not believe he'd heard right. "Sir? Did you say, 'the poor, poor boy?'"

Mr. Edmunds nodded. "I know he's always had his problems, no, I'm referring to his war experience. Something happened and it affected him deep. I had buddies in Europe, same thing happened, it's awful. They were never the same and their lives were completely ruined."

"What about Nora Wilson? Her life was completely ruined, too." Clarke couldn't believe this guy.

"Yes, you told me, but why–"

"This piece of garbage bashes in his sister's face and you say, 'poor, poor boy.' Are you fucking kidding me?" Clarke was seconds away from screaming at the man, and felt himself growing even more flushed.

The cat squirmed. Mr. Edmunds fumbled for a better grip.

"No! What are you saying? You believe Vern is responsible for this?"

"Of course he is. His booze-addled brain finally snapped and he killed her, just like he killed Rosaria Donez."

"No, Captain," Edmunds shook his head. "It's impossible. I don't know about the killing at the waterfront, but he couldn't have killed his sister, that much I know."

The man is soft, thought Clarke. "Why couldn't he have killed her?"

"He didn't have time."

Clarke just looked at him.

"Captain, I've been on my porch for hours. I was grooming Westy, she's prone to tics. I saw Vern sort of stagger across the street. He must have come up on the other side. If he'd been on this side I never would have seen him. Anyway, he crossed the street, almost got clipped by a bread truck, too. He went inside, and within maybe ten seconds the wailing started. For about a split second I thought about heading over to see if he was alright, but I figured, hell, let the experts handle it, and I called you folks. I'd say less than thirty seconds passed from the time he entered the house until I had the department on the phone."

"You're sure of the times?"

"Absolutely. I'm no expert, but I can't imagine someone killing a person like you said she was killed in just a couple of seconds. I think he walked into the house, saw her, and started yelling. Seems pretty simple to me. Sorry if it doesn't jibe with what you think."

Clarke shook his head. "We'll be holding Vern Wilson for the death of his sister. He was kneeling before the body, there was blood on his clothes. He was certainly capable of the crime."

"I'm sure you're right, Captain, but all of that doesn't make it so, and I think you know that, too."

He nodded to Clarke and walked back to his house, murmuring quietly to Westy.

Clarke watched him, then leaned and tried to peel his gore-soaked pants from his shins. He assured himself there was little uncertainty as to the guilty party, but...now he felt a worm of doubt. If indeed it was Vern, if somehow he'd been capable of committing this atrocity in only a few seconds, and if Mr. Edmunds could be believed about the time, then where were the breasts? Vern wouldn't have had the time to dispose of them. They had to be on the premises. Clarke said a fast prayer that they were in the garbage can or fridge. And immediately felt shame to be praying such a thing.

→ 35 ←

Vern put up no struggle at all. He was still during
fingerprinting and processing. Once in the small holding
cell in the station's basement, he sat on the cot, back against
the wall and hands folded in his lap. He let out a low moan or
two before slumping low and staring at the opposite wall, an
attentive expression on his face, as though listening for
something.

Clarke sat in his office and made the necessary calls to put
the system in motion which would, eventually, determine
Vern's innocence or guilt. He slammed the phone in its cradle
and sat back in his chair. A prime suspect was in custody, this
should have been a moment of intense satisfaction for him.
Instead, he couldn't put old man Edmunds out of his mind
and what he said about 'not making it so.' Dammit.

The back door slammed and he heard laughing as
MacDougall and Sully entered the squad room.

"I bet you almost shit, Kevvy!"

"Almost, but not quite. Good thing it wasn't you who found
her, you'd have been spewing StarLite donuts all over the
beach." There was more laughter.

"Get in here!" Clarke yelled irritably.

"Way to go, Captain, word on the radio is you got him!
Man, for a minute there I thought he'd done it again. I almost

tripped over victim number two." MacDougall grinned and shook his head.

"What the hell are you talking about, MacDougall?"

He hesitated. "You got him, didn't you, Captain?"

"Yes. What is this victim number two stuff?"

"Well," he began carefully, "down at the waterfront I thought I might've found another victim."

Sully, ever unaware, said, "This is great, Captain, you'll bust a gut."

Clarke glared at him before turning again to MacDougall.

"I'll ask again, what the hell are you talking about? What the hell were you doing down there anyway? Why weren't you at the train station?"

"Oh, Vern was gone by the time we got there. The ticket guy said he headed toward the water, so we followed. Thought he might be returning to the scene of the crime, you know," MacDougall finished with a grin.

"And?" Clarke prompted, an edge to his voice.

"He wasn't. But I thought he did. Scared the hell out of me." He shook his head and continued grinning.

"If you don't wipe that grin off your face and give me a succinct account of what happened I'll request a replacement from Sayreville and you'll be keeping our crosswalks safe for the local brats. Got it?"

"Yessir." MacDougall straightened. "I'm sorry, Captain."

"For the third time, what happened?"

MacDougall cleared his throat and began. "We proceeded to the waterworks at which point we split up to search for the suspect. Officer Sullivan went north, toward the breakwater, while I headed south in the direction of the old bunker. After searching the interior of the bunker, I stopped for a minute to allow my vision to readjust to the brightness."

Why the hell so many officers, when asked to speak clearly, felt the need to lapse into cop-speak, was a mystery to Clarke.

"After a moment, I proceeded south in the direction of the bluffs. There I discovered a woman lying prone on the sand. She was facing away from me, her bare back was exposed. My initial thought was that the killer had struck again. I assumed she'd been attacked and mutilated like Rosar–, like the first victim."

"Tell him what happened next, Kevvy," Sully eagerly chimed in.

"After a brief hesitation, I ran toward the woman. I guess I made some noise, kicked some loose stones or something, anyway," here he hesitated, "she jumped up, screamed, and ran."

"And…," prompted a grinning Sully.

"Miss Eleanor Nichols," read MacDougall from his notebook, "had been sunning herself near the shoreline. Because of the privacy the bluffs offered, she'd undone her top to get a smooth tan. When she screamed and jumped up, she uh, exposed herself. She took off down the beach pretty much topless."

"Pretty much?" asked Clarke.

"Well, completely. Once I got over the shock myself, I picked up her top and ran after her with it, trying to reassure her and get her to put it on. It took a while before she calmed down and stopped. She got about a hundred yards or so down the beach where some young boys trying to get their kite in the air got a real eyeful. She was, um, well-endowed."

"Why the hell did I pick the breakwater?" Sully muttered.

"Anyway, she wasn't dead, well, I guess that's obvious, isn't it? Once I was able to calm her and the boys down, I came back up the beach and met with Officer Sullivan. He hadn't found any sign of Vern either." '

Clarke sat with elbows on the desk, rubbing his eyes with his palms. Any other day the image of Kevin MacDougall chasing a 'well-endowed' woman up the beach waving her bathing suit top at her would have elicited at least a grin. Today though, it simply reinforced the feeling of chaos. From the self-imposed darkness behind his palms, Clarke heard MacDougall speak again. "I thought it best not to issue a citation."

Clarke dropped his hands from his eyes and saw a swarm of colors before they dissipated. "What? To who?"

"Miss Nichols. Indecent exposure."

Jesus. "Good call." He motioned the chair. "Sit. Sully–"

"Way ahead of you, Captain," said Sully, already dragging a chair in from the squad room.

"As you know, Vernon Wilson is in custody. What you may not know, or don't seem to show any knowledge of, is the fact that he killed his sister, Nora, shortly before he was apprehended." Here Clarke paused to run a hand over his mouth. "He was found kneeling before the victim, in a pool of what we assume to be her blood, wailing her name over and over."

"Jesus," whispered Sully. "We had no idea, Captain, we just heard he was in custody."

"Yeah," said Clarke. "There was severe trauma to the victim's head, just as in the case of Rosaria Donez, and also, as in her case, the breasts were cut off."

It was silent in the room.

After a minute, MacDougall asked, "What did he do with them?"

"We don't know, they're still missing. They were not in the kitchen where the body was found. The insides of cabinets, and appliances have been checked. There was a large galvanized garbage can in the kitchen. The call I just got informed me that its contents have been emptied and sifted through. Nothing."

"Do we know how long it was from the time of the murder until the body was discovered?"

Clarke looked at MacDougall with grudging admiration. "Kevin, you've hit upon the trouble spot. A neighbor, Mr. Edmunds, the same guy Sully spoke to, swears he saw Vern enter the house and begin screaming almost immediately. Edmunds then phoned us at once. When I arrived at the scene–"

"*You* found the body, Captain?" said MacDougall.

Clarke nodded, "When I arrived at the scene," he continued, "Vern was on his knees, back to his sister, from the knees down covered in blood. I doubt it was five minutes from the time the call came into the station." There was a pause. "You see the problem?"

Sully looked doubtful, but MacDougall spoke up. "First, was there time for the killing and mutilation? Second,–"

"Our Mr. Edmunds swears there wasn't," said Clarke sourly.

"Second, if Vern *did* do this, where are the breasts? He couldn't have had time to hide them someplace away from the body. They'd have to be right there. And from what you said, they're not."

"No, they're not. That begs the question: if they're not there, then where are they?"

"Another question, too, Captain."

"Yeah, Kevin, I know. If they're not there, and if Vern only began screaming when he saw his dead sister, then who was it that killed her and took the breasts with them?"

36

"Captain, I see how there's no way we *can't* hold Vern, but, well, what do you think we should do next?" asked MacDougall.

"I think we have a viable suspect in custody. I think we make the media aware of that. I also believe, however, that the investigation should remain ongoing. To that end, Kevin, get Will McConnell in here. I don't care if you have to drag him in from work in Manhattan."

"He's not there, Captain. He called in sick."

"Hell, that's right. Get back on the phone to his employers and find out if he left any information with them about maybe seeing a doctor or something. Say, who was the doctor that came here to look at his kid?"

"Silverman," MacDougall said sourly.

"Call his office and see if he knows who Will McConnell's doctor might be. Maybe there's some sort of fraternity of local docs or something. If you can't get an answer from either of those places, also put a call through to the number Mrs. McConnell left for her folks' house. She may know where her husband might be, probably not, but it's worth a shot. At the very least, she'll know his doctor's name. Okay? And Sully, get your ass back in a car and find me Marcus Rodriguez, got it?"

The two men looked at him, waiting for more.

"Move!" They rushed away.

With each passing minute, Clarke was becoming less and less convinced Vern Wilson was their killer. True, he was nuts enough to fit for both of the murders, but if he was guilty, where the hell were his sisters's breasts? And more to the point, *why* would he take the breasts of his victims? Was it some deep psychological thing from back when he was a kid? Maybe he wasn't breastfed or something. Sigmund Freud, help me out here. Christ, Clarke felt like a drowning kid flailing in the deep end of the pool trying to find a motive for such a thing. Could it be something to do with the war? He'd heard of soldiers taking 'trophies' from enemies they'd killed. Was this a twist on that? Mementos? It wasn't a trophy for sexual conquest because there had been none in Rosaria Donez's case, and by the looks of it, there'd been none with Nora Wilson, either. Apparently even Vern wasn't sick enough to rape his own sister's corpse. He needed to get in touch with someone at the VA who might be able to give him some insight into a case like Vern Wilson. Jesus, finding a rationale for something like this was like running through water, nearly impossible. He grabbed the phone and had Mrs. Barton put a call through to the Veteran's Hospital.

Fifteen minutes of being on hold didn't improve his temper when he heard a soft knock on the office doorframe. "What?"

"I called Dr. Silverman's office," said MacDoougall. "They were able to tell me that the McConnell's family physician was Dr. Epplestein. I called there and they hadn't heard from either of the adult McConnells since Mrs. McConnell ordered those sleeping pills last year. McConnell's employer didn't have a clue as to where he might be. I got the impression that his not turning up at work was becoming something of a habit. I don't think he's long for that job, and I'm sure the call from us didn't help him any."

"Too bad for him," growled Clarke, the phone's handset cradled between his ear and shoulder. "What else?"

"Mrs. McConnell and her son recently arrived at her parents', downstate. She states she believed her husband would be at work today, but I don't think she was too surprised to hear he wasn't. I think she's figuring out there's a lot more to her husband's life than she thought. I felt pretty bad for her. Her father or somebody was in the background yelling about what a bum McConnell is, a worthless loser. Her parents may be welcoming her, but I doubt she's in for an easy time."

Clarke thought of the fragile woman sitting before his desk yesterday, placing the handkerchief of her husband's supposed lover on his desk. Kevin was right, she was in for hell.

"Did she add any information to what we already know she suspects?"

"No. The conversation was pretty short. Like I said, her father was screaming at her. He sounded half in the bag. She just said she didn't know he was ill and she thought he went to work. Oh, she did tell me they slept in separate rooms last night."

"I don't doubt–Jesus Christ! They cut me off!" He stared at the receiver in his hand in disbelief. "I've been sitting here with this damn thing glued to my ear for the last twenty minutes waiting to talk to a headshrinker at the VA and they cut me off. Dammit!" He slammed the phone down.

"She doesn't know anything else?" Clarke glared at MacDougall.

"Nope."

Clarke picked up the receiver again and dialed once. "Mrs. Barton, get me the VA again and whoever their top psychiatrist is. When you have him on the phone put him through to me. If anyone gives you trouble, tell them it's police business and if we can't speak to him on the phone we'll be over there in an hour to haul him away from whatever he's doing. Understand?" He listened, then smiled. "Thank you."

He hung up and said, "I can definitely see her as a tough old school marm. She sounds ready to head over to the VA and drag that guy down here herself."

MacDougall nodded. "Oh, she had her moments."

Clarke took a deep breath and sat back in his chair. His sweaty shirt itched against his back, as did his sodden pants against his shins. He thought about a quick drive home for fresh clothes, pants certainly, then put it on hold. "Okay." He collected himself. "Okay," he repeated. "So Mrs. McConnell has her suspicions about her husband sleeping around, and she fears he may be involved in the Donez killing. Right?"

"Right."

"And, at first, she suspected perhaps an affair, but knew nothing specific, right?"

"Right."

"Well, we know she's correct on at least one count." Clarke reached into his desk drawer and pulled out Nora Wilson's diary. "For the last six months or so, Will McConnell has been sleeping with Nora Wilson. This could be one hell of a damning piece of evidence in a divorce trial." He turned several pages, scanning the writing. "It seems they were less than discreet about where they met. Motels when he was supposed to be at work, her place when Vern was at the VA or passed out, Christ, at night once in the kitchen where she worked! Talk about unsanitary." He paused, "And at the bluffs at the waterworks. I guess that's not a big surprise, it's pretty secluded."

He shook his head. "No wonder he's in trouble at work. When the hell did he have time to go there?" Clarke riffled toward the back of the diary. He reached into the same drawer that had held the book and produced his reading glasses. He slid them on his nose and turned a page. He read silently and turned another page. "Seems it was just yesterday that Nora decided she was going to tell Will the good news." He sighed. "Christ, this reads like a high school kid and her first crush."

MacDougall nodded. "I think maybe it sort of was." Clarke looked at him, over his glasses.

"I don't think she ever had any boyfriends or anything, Captain. In school she was always real quiet, almost unnoticeable. I don't think many people knew or cared she even existed."

"Why would anyone have an affair with someone that was basically a non-person?"

"I said that's what she was like in school. She's changed. When I interviewed her at the hospital she wasn't the same person I remembered from before. It was like she sort of blossomed. She still had the same features she always did, but it was as though the last couple years she'd, well…grown into them. She was pretty when she smiled. I think if I'd seen her every day from school to now I wouldn't have noticed, but the span of time made her seem a different person." He nodded at the diary. "Maybe that's what McConnell saw. He didn't know the wallflower from the past, or if he did, maybe he didn't care."

The two men sat quietly, each lost in their thoughts. After a minute, MacDougall continued. "Maybe there was something Nora had that he wanted and couldn't get from his wife." He saw the look on Clarke's face and continued quickly. "I'm not talking sexual or anything. I'm thinking maybe, I don't know, maybe he wanted someone to think he was the greatest thing ever. Someone to adore him. Nora never had any boyfriends to compare him to. To her, he probably was the greatest thing ever. Since I got off the phone with Mrs. McConnell I've been thinking about this. It doesn't sound like her family is too crazy about him. When I met her the day her son found the body I got the impression she could be a pretty tough lady. There's nothing wrong with that, but maybe McConnell wanted something else.

Maybe he wanted someone who would always agree with what he said, put him on a pedestal, even worship him. I think the days of his wife worshipping him, if they ever existed at all, were long gone." He nodded again to the diary, "It sure sounds like Nora did, though. She makes him sound like Jesus and Paul McCartney and Superman rolled into one."

"Yeah," said Clarke. "The question is, how did Superman react when he heard his adoring, number one fan was pregnant with his child? I kind of doubt he'd be as happy about it as she was. Maybe he'd be pretty damn *un*happy about it. I don't see him divorcing his wife, abandoning his son, and rushing off to live with Nora and Vern in that firetrap of theirs. Can you imagine? Vern Wilson…your brother-in-law? Maybe this news was like a slap across the face to him, waking him up." Clarke leaned forward and planted his elbows on either side of Nora's diary, his eyes now far away. "He's got to know what thin ice he's on at work. Right? He knows about his wife's suspicions…hell, she thinks he may have killed Rosaria Donez. Maybe he feels trapped. I know I would be in his shoes. The only means of escape is to get rid of what trapped him, right? Whether she adores him or not. Number one fan or not. He decides to make it look like the earlier killing. So, instead of going to work, he calls Nora Wilson, they meet and he kills her, getting rid of his problem."

"But Captain, what about the breasts?"

"What about them?"

"He killed Nora and then he took her breasts. Is that what you're saying?" Clarke nodded, a small smile on his face. "So how did he know to take the breasts? We've withheld that information from the press. There's no way he could know about it."

Clarke sat still smiling, silently looking at MacDougall.

Realization swept across MacDougall's face. "Oh my God. He'd know about the breasts if he was the one that killed Rosaria.

But why would he have killed her? Unless…oh man, he was getting it from her, too!"

Clarke nodded. The hanky Mrs. McConnell found. He now remembered a similar hanky in Rosaria's purse. They could both belong to her. Hell, the one Mrs. McConnell found could belong to Nora Wilson. They'd have to check both residences for similar ones. "And we never would have had anything to connect him to Nora Wilson without that diary. Forget I bawled you out about it, nice job, Kevin."

MacDougall blushed. "We would have found it when we searched the house after the second murder. Probably."

"He intentionally mimics the first murder. He wants us to believe they're both committed by the same killer. Maybe have us believe there's a maniac loose preying on random young women in town, some nut case like Vern Wilson. There's no random about it, though." Clarke placed his palms flat on his desk and said softly, "He doesn't know that his number one fan has kept a diary. And he doesn't know we have that diary. If we can place him at the Wilson murder, then we have him for the Donez killing, as well. It's because of the missing breasts. The sick bastard."

"But why kill Rosaria Donez? What does he have against her, especially if he's well, you know, having it with her, too? It doesn't make sense."

"You're right, Kevin, it makes no sense at all, but we're not talking about a sensible person here. We're talking about a guy who had a major meltdown about the state of the world, country, town, whatever, and the people he thought were the cause of it. A guy who drugs his wife so he can slink off into the night to have sex with another woman, or maybe *women*. And don't forget, Mrs. McConnell found the handkerchief in his pants pocket. One just like we found in Rosaria's belongings. I don't know about you, but I can see this sick bastard taking a certain

enjoyment having sex with someone he may want to kill later…
kill and mutilate. Mrs. McConnell was so concerned about his
meltdown she thought he might actually do harm to himself.
Maybe she was right about the harm, but wrong about to whom."

MacDougall nodded.

"We've got to find him, Kevin. Fast."

"Should we put it out on the wire?" MacDougall stood to
leave.

"Yeah. Let's get this guy behind bars before we discover
there's another woman he's been banging. We don't need that
kind of discovery."

Clarke's phone rang. He smiled. "Never doubt the tenacity
of a retired teacher, Kevin." He picked it up. "Yes, Mrs. Barton,
have you got him?" He stopped, a puzzled look on his face.
"Certainly. Put her through." He motioned MacDougall to sit
back down. "Hello, Mrs. McConnell, what can I do for you?"
Clarke sat silently, a look of surprise crossed his face and he
reached quickly for a pencil out of the can. "That's Millville,
right? And we have the address here? Alright. Please Mrs.
McConnell, don't say a word about this call. I'll explain in
detail as soon as I can. What we don't want is anybody to get
hurt, so the element of surprise will be important. As soon as
we hang up I'm going to get in touch with the Millville Police
Department. Once I hear they have him in custody I'll call you
immediately." He listened. "All I can say at the moment is that
your fears may have been correct. Now Mrs. McConnell…listen,
please. It might be a good idea to have your parents take Eddie
out for an ice cream cone or something, anything to get him
away from the house. It won't do him any good to have to see
this. Okay?" He smiled. "That's it, Mrs. McConnell. I have no
doubt you did the right thing. Yes. Goodbye." He hung up, hand
still on the receiver.

MacDougall looked questioningly.

Clarke lifted the receiver and dialed once. "Mrs. Barton, get me the Millville Police Department, fast, please. What? Well, the headshrinker will have to hold for a while. Let him feel what it's like." He hung up again. To MacDougall he said, "Forget the APB. The bastard just called his wife from the Millville bus station. He's taking a cab over to her folks' house. Says he wants to get everything off his chest, apologize, clean the slate and all that nonsense. Says he can't live without his wife and son. Sounds to me like he's taken care of his dirty work here and he's trying to set everything right again. The dumb jerk doesn't know he's basically walking into a jail cell. Thank God for that diary."

The phone rang and Clarke snatched it up in the middle of the first ring.

"Hello, yes Sergeant. This is Captain Timothy Clarke of Pendale. We need your assistance."

MacDougall left the office and headed to the station room. An older woman was tentatively entering from the street.

"Hello, I'm Officer MacDougall. May I help you?"

The visitor looked familiar. It was obviously someone from town he'd seen before. Kevin tried to place the face...he'd seen it recently.

"Yes. Thank you. I...I think I need to speak to a police officer. It's in connection with the killing of Nora Wilson. I don't know when exactly the killing took place, but I know who she was with for part of the day."

MacDougall grabbed a pad off a desk and offered a chair. "Come in and sit down. Would you begin please by telling me your name?"

The visitor sat. "Oh, I'm so sorry, I wasn't thinking. I live up the street from the Wilson house. My name is Rose Gorman."

⤜ 37 ⤛

I t didn't take long for the Millville Police to pick up Will McConnell. He and his wife were standing on the front lawn of Lynn's parents' house when they pulled up. His back was to the street and he was speaking animatedly.

"Hon, it's the pressure from work, I tell you. You know I'd never do anything to hurt you or Eddie. My God, you two are the whole world to me. This was…I don't know, some type of early mid-life crisis or something." He tried a weak grin.

Lynn's arms were crossed, her head down, Will couldn't see her face, couldn't see if he was getting through at all. "Babe," he reached toward her, but she quickly stepped away from the intended embrace. "I'm sorry." She lifted her head, looking over his shoulder. Will saw her eyes were dry and she had that defiant 'screw you' set to her face. Fuck, he thought, this was really going to be tough. Okay, let's try a different tact. "I want to speak to Eddie, Lynn. He's my son and I have every right–" It was then he became aware of the officers approaching him from behind. "What the hell–"

He was pushed to his knees and then his stomach in a single swift motion.

For a moment he was so shocked he couldn't speak. "What…what are…what the hell are you…" A knee pressed into his back, driving all the air from his lungs. His arms were

297

pulled behind his back and his hands were cuffed. From his position at ground level he saw Lynn's feet turn and quickly walk away. Then he realized what was happening. She'd told the police she believed he killed that girl at the waterfront. Jesus, how could she…?

"Lynn," he gasped, almost unable to make any sound. The pressure on his back then ceased as he was yanked roughly to his feet. "Lynn!" he shouted to her retreating figure. "What are you thinking? Are you out of your fucking mind?" From the corner of his eye he saw a neighbor woman staring, garden hose in hand, watching the spectacle. "You called the cops on me? You bitch! You fucking bitch!" he screamed at his wife's back as she climbed the porch steps. "This is why! This is why I did what I did! You fucking cold, cold bitch!" Lynn never turned. She slammed the door closed behind her as Will was dragged to the police car, then pushed into the back seat.

After Clarke hung up from speaking again with Lynn McConnell, he pushed his chair away from his desk, leaned back and closed his eyes. Thank God. Thank God it looked like it was over. He wasn't cut out for this crap. Maybe his ex was right. Maybe the truth was he was just a small-town cop unable to stomach whatever was necessary to make it in the big time. He'd risen as far as he ever would. Clarke sighed and opened his eyes. There was a brown stain on the ceiling tiles above him. Terrific. He took a deep breath and winced. He was sweating like a hog. And the office smelled like a monkey cage.

Let's run through the rest of the suspects, he thought. Do some eliminating while waiting on the Millville Police. Time to get Marcus Rodriguez in here and let *him* sweat for a while before letting him off the hook. Goddamn liar. First things first, though. He rose and walked around his desk to open the door and air the place out. He felt a hundred years old. The sound of the station's rear door shutting registered in his head as he trudged to the interview room. Maybe some caffeine was in order. He reached for the coffee pot and heard someone call his name. Turning, he saw Father Ryan and...well, how about that?

"We'd like to have a word, Captain." The priest nodded toward his companion, "Marcus and myself."

Clark was bewildered. This was too easy. "Sure, yes, have a seat. Both of you." He gestured toward the table, coffee pot in hand, slopping some onto the floor. "Hell." He shot a quick look at the priest who had a small grin on his face. "Sorry."

"No need to apologize, Captain. I do it too. We're all God's creatures, all of us, each very much the same as another."

That sounds contrived, Clarke thought. Where is he going with whatever it is he wants to say?

The two visitors sat while Clarke grabbed a pad and pen from his desk. He looked into the squad room and saw Kevin in an earnest conversation with an older woman.

"Now please, why are you here, Father?"

"I know you've been looking for me," Marcus interjected.

"We have, but that's not what I asked. I asked the Father, why *he* was here. To the best of my knowledge he doesn't have a law degree, so he's not acting as your attorney."

"Now Captain," the priest began, smiling, "why would Marcus–"

"He'd need a lawyer because he lied to police in the course of a murder investigation. He's lucky I haven't cuffed him already." He watched the smile evaporate from Ryan's face and saw Marcus gulp. And *that*, Officer MacDougall, he thought, is how to make a suspect uncomfortable. Another teaching moment lost.

The two visitors looked at each other for a long minute and something passed between them. "Captain," said Father Ryan, "I can tell you where Marcus was during the time in question."

"Please do." Clarke pulled the pad near him.

"He was with me."

"Father Ryan, I don't want to impugn the word of a man of the cloth, but I'll need more–"

"Captain," he said deliberately, "please listen. I'm saying he was *with* me." The priest's hand slid down the table and took Marcus's hand. "We were together."

Clarke looked at the grasped hands and then at the two faces. Ryan looked determined, Marcus, frightened, but no less willing to push on ahead.

"You realize, Captain, what consequences this admission can have for the two of us. It is not something we admit lightly. I, we, sincerely hope this information can be kept as private as possible." The priest looked at Clarke in earnest.

"Father, I realize the importance of your words. But *you* need to realize something. It's one thing for a priest to come in here and vouch for the innocence of a suspect. It's quite another for someone in a relationship with a suspect to try and alibi them. That person might do or say anything to get the suspect off, be it true or false. Am I right?"

Clarke took a small bit of satisfaction as this realization crossed Ryan's face. His admission, with all the ramifications it carried, did absolutely nothing to help Marcus's cause. It did, though, provide Clarke with a hell of a stick to use on them if he felt it necessary.

"I told you, I told you!" Marcus said. "I told you there's no way he would listen to people like us. People like him hate anyone different. And now we…now we…ah, Jesus," he moaned, dropping his face in his hands, "what did we do?"

Ryan was silent, looking at nothing.

Clarke wrote in his pad for a while then looked up and asked, "Can you prove it?"

Marcus looked up. "Prove what?"

"What are you asking, Captain, a demonstration of our feelings for each other? Would that be some kind of turn on for you? Would you get off on watching two men–"

"Father," he interrupted, "what I am asking is can you prove Marcus was with you, and not with Rosaria Donez, at the time in question." Left unsaid was the question of whether or not the priest was jealous enough of Rosaria's relationship with Marcus to want to do her harm. Another potential suspect. It's getting confusing. Thank God we have Will McConnell dead to rights, Clarke thought.

At the mention of the girl's name, Marcus's eyes teared up and he again dropped his head to his hands. Maybe he *did* still have some feelings for her, Clarke thought.

"I believe we can, Captain. There is an establishment, a tavern, that caters to, well, that caters to us. It's about halfway to the shore, off Route 9." Clarke had a vague recollection of hearing about the place. "Marcus and I were there until about one-thirty or one forty-five. I believe the bartender will remember us. It was a slow night."

Clarke nodded. "What's the name of the place?" he asked, head bent over the pad.

"Buzzy G.'s. It's a relatively well-known gay bar. Known to us, that is."

"A what bar?"

"Gay. A gay bar. A bar that caters to gays, to homosexuals. Gay means homosexual." The priest smiled at Clarke's confusion. "It's a commonly used term."

Not with me it's not, Clarke thought, scribbling down the name. Last he'd heard, gay meant happy, like that old movie, *The Gay Divorcee*. Not, well, queer.

"You're certain about the time?" he asked.

"Absolutely. We wanted to give it enough time for Marcus to…," Ryan stopped.

"We wanted me to get back late enough so I could tell Rosaria I had been working at the restaurant and got stuck cleaning up after hours. We'd done it before," Marcus finished listlessly, then burst into tears.

A beautiful girl like Rosaria Donez, Clarke thought, and he's lying to her so he could sneak around with…ah, some things he just couldn't understand. Probably never would. Also, the timeline didn't clear Marcus as much as Clarke was sure the two men would have liked.

They spoke for about ten more minutes before concluding with Clarke telling both men to remain in the vicinity until told otherwise. The two left, again by the back door. Clarke wondered. He'd heard of young men getting photographed being, well, gay, he guessed, with other men as a means to avoid the draft. Hard to believe, but they did. Murder was a lot more serious than being drafted, for most people anyway. Was that what was going on here? Was this convenient admission by the two men contrived to throw the law off the young man's trail?

Clarke found a relatively clean mug and poured some coffee. He heard his office phone buzz and hurried to his desk. Mrs. Barton put through Dr. Friedman at the VA Hospital. The doctor hesitated to speak about one of his current patients but when Clarke apprised him of Vern's situation, he became more forthcoming.

"Vernon Wilson is a near classic case, if there is such a thing, of battle fatigue. In the old days it used to be referred to as shellshock. I'm not going to get into details, but Mr. Wilson experienced an emotionally wrenching episode while in Vietnam."

"Don't most soldiers?" asked Clarke dryly.

"Not like this, that's all I'm willing to say on the subject. The result is that he is paranoid and sometimes believes he is back in the jungle."

"Sounds like he should be locked up."

"With medication he isn't a danger to anyone, not even himself. However, Mr. Wilson often forgets or refuses to take his medication. His alcoholism doesn't help matters. From his file, I see he was never a model citizen. He may have had emotional issues before the war. What happened over there exacerbated his problems and multiplied them tenfold."

"Doctor, there has been another killing in addition to the young woman found at the waterfront. Vern Wilson's sister is dead, as well."

"I'm aware of that, Captain, you told me as much at the start of this conversation."

"What I didn't tell you, what hasn't been released to the public, is the fact that in each of the killings the breasts of the victims had been hacked off and hidden. Thus far, they haven't been found. What I need to know, doctor, is does this sound, in any way, given his, uh, problems, like something that Vern Wilson is capable of?"

Clarke heard Friedman inhale and slowly release his breath. "I'm grateful you told me this, Captain. Since the start of our conversation I had been feeling very uneasy. The idea that Mr. Wilson may have killed two women while under my care, under my care to a degree anyway, is very disturbing. However, now that I am aware of this new information I can say I am extremely doubtful Vernon Wilson is your killer."

"Why do you say that, doctor?"

"Because, to put it simply, Vernon Wilson is afraid of women, specifically, he fears anything to do with sex."

"He didn't have sex with the victims."

"I'm aware of that, but the man would be incapable of *looking* at a live woman's bare breasts, much less touching them. He fears the feminine."

"But Dr. Friedman, the mutilation wasn't done when they were alive, also, he abused his sister for years, verbally anyway, and he threw a beer can at Rosaria Donez just a week ago. That sounds like hatred, not fear. Also, there was quite a bit of pornography found in his home. He certainly had no problems looking at *that*."

"I didn't express myself well, Captain. Viewing pornography is a very different thing than interacting with a human. Vern Wilson would be capable of the former, but the other…no. My guess would be the pornography acts as compensation for his inability to interact sexually with women. I would guess he never actually touched either woman. He's probably never touched *any* woman. Not as an adult, anyway. I haven't yet uncovered the reason, but believe me, Vernon Wilson is afraid of the female sex. Now that I know there was actual contact with a part of the victims' bodies that is viewed as sexual, I don't believe he can be guilty."

Clarke digested what Dr. Friedman said for a moment. "Alright, doctor, thank you very much for your time. We'll be in touch with you again, I'm sure. I don't have to tell you not to repeat the information about the mutilation to anyone."

"Of course not, Captain. As a doctor I understand confidentiality." He sounded offended.

"Thank you, doctor."

Clarke hung up and stared at his closed office door. Okay. That pretty much eliminates Vern. If Marcus was to be believed, and Father Ryan, they're clear, too. Thank God they had Will McConnell.

"Hell!" Captain Clarke slammed the receiver down. He'd just gotten off the phone with Millville. The police had arrested McConnell and would later have him transported back to Pendale. But there was a problem. A big, huge, hulking problem.

McConnell had his bus ticket in his possession. A ticket which had the departure time of twelve noon printed on it. It also had the estimated arrival time in Millville of four-thirty. It wasn't a direct trip, it made stops in a handful of towns along the shore. So, assuming the ticket was legitimate, and assuming Will McConnell was on that bus the entire trip, and they were now checking with the driver, there was no way he could have been in Pendale bashing in the brains of his mistress, much less slicing off her breasts and discarding them.

According to Millville, he'd seemed genuinely shocked when they pulled up and arrested him. When he was told he was under suspicion for the murder of Nora Wilson, he burst into tears. Apparently, while in the back of the squad car he swung from pleading for his wife and her forgiveness, to crying about Nora. The Millville Police weren't too impressed with him.

Jesus, Vern, in all likelihood was ruled out, if the headshrinker was right. Although, Clarke was struggling to believe it. Eliminated as well, was Marcus Rodriguez, according to the good Father anyway, though that would definitely need to be verified. And now, Will McConnell was nowhere near the scene at the time of the second murder. It *had* to be him. They'd been *so* sure with the diary and all. Shit. He dropped his face into his hands. Suspects were dropping like flies.

38

Kevin MacDougall looked at the notes in his hands in disbelief. It's not possible, he thought. He looked at the door of the captain's office, still shut. He knew he needed to tell Captain Clarke about this immediately. But still...they had been so sure. It simply *had* to be Will McConnell. He mentally ran through the interview with Mrs. Gorman again.

"Oh, I'm so sorry. I live up the street from the Wilson house. My name is Rose Gorman."

"Okay, just let me jot down your name, Mrs. Gorman. Now, how can we help you?"

"Well, I thought that maybe I might be able to help you. You see, earlier today, I know that Nora Wilson had been out visiting someone."

"Visiting?"

"Not exactly visiting, I suppose. I saw her go to get her hair done."

MacDougall felt a twinge of unease in his gut. "Her hair done?" he asked casually. "You saw her downtown?"

"No, I didn't. It wasn't downtown."

He asked, already knowing the answer, "Where was it you saw her earlier today?"

"She was walking into Minna Cooper's hair salon. It was about one-thirty," she added.

MacDougall wrote down the information. "Why did you feel you should speak to the police about this? We're not certain of the time of death yet, but it appears later than one-thirty."

Mrs. Gorman smiled apologetically. "I know I probably sound like a paranoid old woman to you–"

"Not at all, Mrs. Gorman."

"It's just, well, something happened today that made me wonder."

"Why don't you tell me, Mrs. Gorman. I'll take notes and then we'll run through it again to fill in any gaps I missed."

"Alright, Officer." She hesitated as if wondering whether to include what came next. "I suppose I'd better just begin at the beginning. I don't think I'll be offending anyone.

"I have an in-law apartment in my home. I rent it to a young woman, Nikki. She…she has a problem with alcohol. Her fiancé died several years ago and since then I'm afraid she's spent most of her time inflicting pain on herself. I don't doubt that you may have had some contact with her. She's a thin, red-haired girl. When she's not drinking she's one of the dearest people I've ever met. But when she drinks, well, she makes very poor decisions. In many areas, including the company she keeps."

MacDougall then remembered seeing Mrs. Gorman and the young woman over by St. Margaret's. The girl sure didn't strike him as the churchgoing type.

"Nikki has been trying to straighten herself out as of late. We've been spending quite a bit of time together. I guess I've been trying to act as a kind of support for her," she said, embarrassed.

"It sounds like a very selfless thing to do."

"Not at all," she waved aside the compliment. "At any rate, around noon today I took her down to Minna's to see if Minna would do something about her hair. It's been rather neglected." Mrs. Gorman paused here. "Minna wasn't very happy about being asked to do this. She had some strong feelings concerning

Nikki's behavior while drinking. I...I...oh, dear, I was able to convince her to take on Nikki. I wish to God I never had," she rushed. "I could have saved the poor girl so much pain."

MacDougall didn't know what to say. How bad could the haircut have been?

"I left Nikki there and went home to finish some work. After a while when she didn't return, I started down the street. It was then I saw Nora Wilson entering Minna's shop."

"Are you saying that your friend is now missing as well?"

"Oh, no. I found her. She was...she was, I'm afraid, downtown at one of the bars drinking again. I was able to get her home on my own."

"Mrs. Gorman, I'm very glad you were able to find your friend, but I don't understand why you came to the police. If she'd gone missing or was injured, I'd understand, but not now."

"Yes. Well, I guess that brings me to the main reason I'm here. After I returned home with Nikki and put her to bed, I went down to Minna's to find out what happened. She'd said some extremely hurtful things to Nikki. I don't doubt she called her some choice names and heaped quite a bit of guilt on her. I always knew Minna had strong feelings about what she believed to be right and wrong, but I never knew she would actively try to hurt someone the way she did Nikki.

"You see, years ago, when her husband was alive, there was some trouble with her marriage. He had an affair and while it eventually ended, I don't think Minna was able to completely get over it. She became a one-woman suffragette for marital fidelity. Poor Arnie. That's her late husband. I don't think she ever allowed him to forget what he did, even after the woman left town."

Mrs. Gorman shook her head. "I didn't realize her feelings had become so strident. She as much as admitted to me she caused, or at least encouraged, Nikki's relapse. My fear is perhaps she was in an extremely foul state of mind when Nora Wilson knocked on her door. I don't know the Wilsons well, but they seem to be a family Minna would strongly disapprove of. Was her disapproval strong enough to make her actually kill someone? Well, I don't know. I hope not. But I was frightened today when I spoke with her, Officer. She seemed capable of almost anything."

MacDougall dutifully recorded all the pertinent information. It was possible, he thought, but in no way was it stronger than what they had on Will McConnell. Sure, he now knew Minna Cooper was a racist and thoroughly unpleasant woman but all signs pointed straight to McConnell. Straight from Nora's diary, in black and white.

"I can almost, but not quite, bring myself to feel sorry for the woman."

"What's that, Mrs. Gorman?" asked MacDougall, his thoughts interrupted.

"I said I almost feel sorry for Minna. All this goes back to her trouble."

"Her trouble?"

Mrs. Gorman blushed. "It's rather personal, I know, but it's been quite some time since her operation."

"Oh?"

"Her mastectomy. Her double mastectomy, actually."

Clarke lifted his face from his hands and heard MacDougall saying, "Thank you very much, Mrs. Gorman. We'll be in touch with you soon. Best of luck with Nikki."

"Kevin," he called, "come in here. We've got a problem. Where the hell is Sully?" he asked. "Oh, yeah, he's out in the cruiser."

"Actually he just got back. He's in the john, stomach problems."

"StarLite Bakery problems more like it. Well, you get in here. I've got news."

"Me, too."

"Yours can wait a second."

He went on, "Millville tells us that McConnell has a bus ticket which, if accurate, means he couldn't have killed Nora Wilson. We still have the diary, but without him being here at the time of the killing, it's nothing. So he's effectively out of the picture. Plus, you're not going to believe this, but Marcus Rodriguez and Father Josh Ryan just paid us a visit."

"No way. I didn't see them."

"Through the back. Didn't want to be seen I suppose. The good Father has alibied Marcus." He waited for a reaction from MacDougall, but the young man seemed distracted and excited, looking at his chicken scratching on the pad on front of him.

"They were together at the time of the Donez murder, around the time, anyway."

"Really?" MacDougall said, still looking at his pad. "Wait." His head rose. "At one or two o'clock in the morning?" Clarke nodded. "What could they be doing at that hour?"

"Kevin, they were together." MacDougall still looked puzzled. "*Together.*"

"Whoa!" MacDougall's eyebrows shot up. "You mean they were, uh…doing…,"

"Not exactly. They were at some bar together where they think the bartender can vouch for them. The place is off Route 9 to the south."

"Oh yeah, I heard about that place, a queer bar."

"Gay, Kevin. It's a gay bar."

"Sure, I guess they have a bunch of fun in their own way."

"No. Gay is a commonly used term that means homosexual."

"It is?"

"Absolutely. You've got to get out more."

"I suppose," the younger man said, doubtfully.

"But the problem is," Clarke said, back to business, "if they're telling the truth and their story checks out, we're down another suspect. We started with too many and now we're about fresh out."

"Oh, no we're not," MacDougall began, excited again. "Listen and tell me what you think." He quickly looked down at his notes before speaking. "Mrs. Rose Gorman just left, she lives on Augusta Street, too."

"Who the hell doesn't it seems?"

"Yeah. She said that a friend of hers, a young girl, went to get her hair cut at Minna's earlier today. I guess this girl has a drinking problem and kind of sleeps around–"

"Maybe another buddy of Will McConnell's."

"What? I doubt it. Anyway, Mrs. Gorman said that Minna really tore into this girl. Loaded up on the guilt, caused the girl to relapse, practically poured the drink down her throat. A little later, Mrs. Gorman saw Nora Wilson go into Minna's shop. After pulling her friend out of the Bottle Cap, Mrs. Gorman went to confront Minna about what happened. She was stunned by how bitter and angry Minna was."

"So? I'm not following where this is going."

"Just wait, Captain. When we looked at Minna for the Donez killing, we thought she might be a viable suspect because of the fact her husband had an affair with a Puerto Rican woman fifteen or twenty years ago, right? So we thought Minna had it in for PRs, right?" He continued without waiting, "But what about this? What if sometime while she was getting her hair cut Nora says something about sleeping with Will McConnell or what if she says that she's pregnant by him?"

"Why the hell would a twenty-something-year-old girl say something like that to a woman like Minna Cooper? It makes no sense."

"I know it doesn't make sense," said MacDougall, impatient. "But you've got to remember, aside from Will McConnell, Nora has nobody. Don't you think she'd be aching to share her secret with someone? You read her diary, she was thrilled with the whole thing. If you were in her shoes, wouldn't you want to share your good news?"

Clarke was quiet for a minute. "Go on."

"So she says something to Minna. Whatever it is, Minna doesn't like what she hears and she follows Nora home to kill her. Because," MacDougall held up his palm as Clarke was about to interrupt, "because, it isn't women who are Puerto Rican that Minna has problems with, it's women who are promiscuous. Ones who cause trouble for married men. Home wreckers."

Clarke was shaking his head. "You're making a hell of a leap, Kevin. Her husband had an affair so she kills women she thinks sleep around?"

MacDougall sat back in his chair, a Mona Lisa smile on his face. "I have one more piece of information."

"Why do I feel like the audience at a magic show? Spill it."

Reading from his notes, MacDougall said, "Sometime in 1950 or 1951, Minna Cooper was diagnosed with breast cancer. It was fairly advanced and there was nothing they could do. She had a double mastectomy."

The office was silent save for the whirring of the fan.

"Back then, she and Mrs. Gorman were relatively close. Minna confided in her about how difficult the entire procedure was for her. I can only imagine, it was 1950, not 1968. I guess she refused to let her husband anywhere near her. Shame, embarrassment, who knows? Anyway, it was around the time Mr. Cooper had the affair with the woman at his store, the Puerto Rican woman. She later disappears–any new information on her?"

Clarke slowly shook his head.

"Maybe, like we thought, Minna did something to get rid of her. Maybe she's been harboring feelings of hatred toward those women she feels are evil, and the feelings have finally bubbled to the surface. Like you're always saying, things sure seem to have gotten weird in the world. Maybe Minna got pushed over the edge by something. Seeing Rosaria Donez walk by every day dressed provocatively. Nora admits to an affair and being pregnant by another woman's husband. Minna's a pretty loose cannon. And–"

"And the breasts."

"Right," continued MacDougall. "Maybe she somehow, uh, equates taking their breasts to replacing her own. Maybe she wants to mutilate them the way she was mutilated, I don't know. But I think there's something there, Captain, I really do. What do you think?"

Clarke stared at his officer in near disbelief. A smile spread across his face. "How did you get so damn smart, Kevin? You must be learning from the very best."

MacDougall blushed from the neck of his collar to his hair. "Come on, Captain. It's obvious."

"Maybe, Kevin, maybe. You know what else is obvious?"

MacDougall shook his head.

Clarke was serious again. "Even with this information, which is very damning to Minna Cooper, we need more. What is it we obviously need?"

"The breasts."

"Yes. Without them we have nothing, just a collection of circumstantial evidence." He paused, "If you were Minna Cooper, what would you have done with the breasts of your victims? Discarded them?"

MacDougall thought. "No," he finally said. "I'd want to keep them. I'd want to have them where I could enjoy them, knowing they were mine now and nobody else's. I'd keep them someplace that was special to me, someplace…her garden! In the flower beds! There was a particular bed in the yard that she was working on when I stopped to talk with her. She said it was important, one she could see when she sat inside on bad days. I bet that's it! She's got them buried in the flower bed. We've got to dig it up. We'll have her then!"

Clarke was already reaching for the phone. "Mrs. Barton? Please get me Judge Culhain. Yes, I know it's after five, but I need to speak to him immediately. It's concerning the murders. We need a court order to do some digging." He grinned over the mouthpiece at MacDougall.

They heard the sound of a toilet flushing. Sully strolled into the room. "Hi guys, I miss anything?"

❖ 39 ❖

By six-thirty the backhoe stood in Minna Cooper's driveway and Captain Clarke was at her front door with the court order.

"You're not serious, Captain Clarke," she sputtered. "You want to dig up my flower beds?"

"I'm very serious Mrs. Cooper. We're searching for evidence regarding the murders of Rosaria Donez and Nora Wilson. This court order gives us the authority. I'm simply letting you know the proceedings as a courtesy."

"Courtesy! Your tearing up my yard is a courtesy?"

"No, ma'am. My explaining to you *why* is the courtesy. I think it would be best if you stayed in the house while the operation was in progress. We don't want you in the way, and of course, we don't want to upset you any more than necessary."

"You will not place me under house arrest, Captain," Minna said coldly. "I will stand in my own yard if I choose."

"Alright, Mrs. Cooper, but I warn you, don't do anything to hinder our progress." He turned, walked toward the garage, and waved the backhoe to the yard.

MacDougall and Sully were joined by three officers from nearby Sayreville Police Department. Each man was equipped with a shovel, rake and work gloves. When Mrs. Cooper's eyes met Kevin's he could have sworn he saw her snarl. She walked by the men and machinery and stood by the garage, her arms folded over her chest, glaring at Clarke. He turned away and watched the machine.

The backhoe's treads lacerated the well-tended green of Minna's lawn, leaving behind ugly, brown scars. The long flower beds in the middle of the yard, the ones which had until very recently been unfinished, were the first to be excavated. The claw at the end of the extended arm ripped into the smooth, dark mound of earth and, swinging to the left, deposited the dislodged soil and plants almost at Minna's feet. MacDougall and Sully stepped forward and using rake and shovel, sifted through the soil looking for anything which might resemble a human breast. They had been told to keep their eyes peeled for any kind of packaging, container, even the bare breasts themselves. While they went at it, the backhoe operator tore up another section of the bed and swung to the right, dropping it for the men from Sayreville to examine.

After about fifteen minutes and finding nothing but several stones and clumps of earth that they broke up and examined, two more sections were dug up. All the while Minna stood silently in front of her garage, her lips pressed together and her arms folded. By seven-thirty, the middle flowerbeds had been dug down to the clay about three feet beneath the surface. Nothing.

The operator looked at Clarke questioningly.

"Take the beds next to the garage, and if necessary, those against the house. We know they're here."

The man nodded and trundled toward the garage leaving twin wounds in his wake.

Minna stepped through the dirt and muck and stood before Clarke. "Hasn't this gone far enough, Captain? Isn't it sufficient that you've caused so much damage? Why won't you admit you were wrong and let me alone? Why are you destroying what is so dear to me?" She was shaking in rage.

"Mrs. Cooper, we have the authority to dig up the flowerbeds in search of evidence. That is what I intend to do, not one flowerbed, not two, but all of them if it's necessary. Now, get out of the way or I'll have one of the officers remove you physically." He walked past her toward his men.

Jesus, please make us right on this one, he thought. We're certainly due. He approached MacDougall. "Anything yet?" he asked quietly.

"Nothing, not even a dog bone. I bet most dogs'd be terrified to come into the old bat's yard."

"Keep going. If necessary I'm going to call for some portable lights and generators. The highway department ought to be able to help us out with them. There's not much daylight left."

"There's not much yard left, either."

Clarke tramped to his squad car and radioed for the additional equipment. It arrived just before twilight and soon the hum of generators accompanied the sound of the backhoe.

A crowd of neighbors ringed the Cooper property line. Several times they had to be moved back, but they kept creeping forward, wondering what new bit of mystery was at hand on Augusta Street. First, a murder, now, an excavation. There were rumors of buried bodies. Every unexplained death in the last fifty years was revisited. There was a bomb shelter, buried deep under the roses. The entry was through a tunnel which opened into the garage. That's where crazy old Minna hid the bodies, amid the canned goods and bottled water. The house itself was cursed. Anyone who entered was marked for death. Forget the fact that half the women in town had had their hair done there at one time or another.

It wasn't until just before ten o'clock that the crowd began to dissipate. The yard was a total wreck. Every bed had been ripped up. Earth, topsoil, woodchips, manure, and of course, plants were strewn in every direction. The tracks of the backhoe crisscrossed themselves like a pile of pick-up sticks. Men's footprints headed in all directions. The officers, dirty and tired, leaned on their rakes and shovels looking at Captain Clarke. Minna remained, unmoved for the last two hours, in the garage's entry, dark shadows covering the upper half of her body. Only her sturdy legs were visible in the harsh artificial light.

Clarke walked to the center of the yard. His shoes feeling like blocks with the dirt stuck there. Hands on his hips, he slowly surveyed the damage. He turned to the men. "Okay," he said quietly. "Let's call it a night."

He remained in that spot as the lights shut down, the generators grew quiet, and the backhoe rumbled away. The last man remaining was MacDougall. He took a step toward Clarke, but the Captain shook his head and MacDougall walked away. Clarke stood for several minutes, wondering. How could they have gotten it wrong? It must be Minna, the breasts must be here. They've *got* to be here.

He turned as he heard a squelching on the dirt behind him. Minna stood there, glaring. "You stupid man. You're as stupid and weak as the rest of them. Look." She held out her arm to the carnage. "Look what you've done, and what have you proved? Nothing." Tears slid down the old woman's cheeks. "Get the hell out of my yard, Captain Clarke."

Clarke left her yard in silence. Driving back to the station was a complete blank. He thought of nothing until he was behind his desk staring sightlessly at the case file in front of him. He knew he should go home, shower and get some sleep. He'd need it for tomorrow. No doubt there'd be a lot of explaining to do to the town fathers. God knew who else.

The wall clock ticked in the silence. Maybe his ex had been right, maybe he'd risen as far as he ever would. Hell, after today, some would say he rose farther than he ever should have. He was really just a cop suited to walking a beat, no more. Clarke almost laughed. Maybe he and Sully would end up partners, best buddies.

The air in the office felt dead, even more so than earlier. What was the problem? He looked up and saw the fan had been unplugged. He leaned to the side and looked into his waste basket. Empty. The once a week cleaning people came, they must have unplugged the fan for some reason. Who knew why, it's not like they vacuumed or anything.

Slowly rising and navigating around the desk, he mused the cleaners must be the only people in town who hadn't been at the Cooper house watching the police make utter fools of themselves. He found the dangling cord and grunted as he bent to plug it into the outlet. Straightening up, he heard the fan whirr into life and almost immediately several papers piled high in his IN basket caught the breeze and fluttered to the floor.

Shit. Grunting again, he gathered them and placed them back where they belonged while scanning his desktop for something to weigh them down. The pencil can was already doing duty anchoring a pile. He grabbed a fistful of pencils from the can and dumped them on top of the papers. That did the trick.

He reached to the radio sitting on top of a bookcase and turned it on. Anything to serve as a momentary distraction. Static. He spun the knob, pausing as the signal cleared. "Nowhere Man". Talk about an accurate description of how he felt. He spun again, settled on the news, and sat.

The California Convention was in full swing. If Kennedy won he'd be on his way to the nomination. Another Nixon-Kennedy showdown. It was apt to be pretty bloody. Why should it be different from anything else today? Clarke thought. Listening to the words of the newscaster, hearing the oscillation of the fan, feeling its passing breeze, Clarke folded his arms on his desk. His sweaty forearms adhered to the Donez case file. He peeled them off, noticed the greasy marks they left, and tossed the heavy file to his IN box. Clarke then folded his arms again, put his head down, and closed his eyes.

❖ 40 ❖

ikki lay on her bed staring up at the cracks in her ceiling. At some point Mr. Gorman or somebody had attempted to repair and paint them over, but they still showed through. Their presence was a part of the room, part of the whole house. Once the damage was done, it seemed there was no getting rid of it. Ever. Too bad, she thought, somebody sure put in some effort here, it's a shame it was all for nothing.

She must have slept a couple hours. Nikki wasn't certain exactly when Mrs. Gorman came to drag her home. Before she had to pay off that fat-ass construction worker, anyway. Thank God for that. She'd heard Mrs. Gorman leave the house a little before dinner time. About an hour later she was back prattling around in the kitchen. Please, don't suggest dinner together, Nikki thought. She wasn't ready to face Mrs. Gorman. Not yet. Plus, she felt like puking.

She must have dozed off again. She woke to a sound of a low rumbling. The room was dark. Sitting up, Nikki felt a dull throb in her head. Hell, that's not so bad, she'd sure experienced worse. She noticed too that in addition to being extremely thirsty, she now felt hungry. Maybe if it wasn't too late, Mrs. G. could fix her a little something, after all. She walked to the bathroom, drank three glasses of cold water, ran a cool shower, and attempted to wash away the residue of her day.

The longer Nikki stood under the stinging spray, the clearer her head became. Minna Cooper's words ran through her mind, building tension in her neck, shoulders, and across her back. She turned and the water massaged those areas. She poured a dollop of Prell into her hand and rubbed it savagely into her scalp. She needed to rid herself of every last little snippet of hair left over from her excursion to Minna's. After shampooing twice and rubbing her skin to a raw red, Nikki emerged from the shower. She stepped into a pair of cutoffs and pulled on her Mets T-shirt. If anyone gave her any grief about her wardrobe, the hell with them. This was her, what she was, and the world could go screw themselves for all she cared.

She listened at the door to Mrs. Gorman's kitchen. Silence. So much for a snack. It's just as well, probably better to be feeling lean and mean, she thought. She left the apartment, noticing Mrs. Gorman's section of the house was completely dark. Maybe out taking a walk, she thought.

Down the block, near Minna's place, several knots of neighbors stood talking among themselves. Nikki wasn't sure, but she thought she saw Mrs. Gorman in the group. It was hard to tell. There seemed to be a lot of light coming from the back of Minna's place. As she puzzled over this, the odd illumination flickered for a second, and then when out. Weird, she thought.

Nikki turned and headed up the block. She had no intention of bumping into Mrs. Gorman. There were things to do and chatting with Mrs. Gorman would have to wait. He sandals slapped the concrete as she left the glow of a streetlight and entered the darkness.

Rose Gorman turned from Hazel Brodski and looked back toward her house. The women had been quietly discussing what impact the desecration of her beloved yard was going to have on Minna Cooper. Hazel believed the destruction to be a shame, an unwarranted act by the police. The department hadn't been the same since Captain Delaney retired. This new man, Clarke, seemed more concerned with keeping the immigrants happy than anything else. Rose was silent. She knew her visit to the station earlier surely had something to do with the current goings on. She certainly disagreed about Captain Delaney. He was a lazy drunk, no more, no less. He could have chosen to try and help himself like Carl did, but he didn't. No, Captain Clarke was a huge step forward.

She squinted into the darkness. Was that Nikki hurrying up the street? No. Why would she go in that direction? There were no bars there. Rose was instantly ashamed for thinking that, but, well, it was the truth. You couldn't hide from reality. Another thought struck her. Had Nikki seen her and wanted to avoid her? Was she circling the block so as not to have to speak with Rose? Her heart sank as she pictured Nikki taking a circuitous route simply to steer clear of her so she could get to the watering holes downtown. She turned again toward Hazel Brodski, but Rose was lost in her thoughts.

The phone rang and jerked Clarke out of his doze. "Christ!" Something pinched in the back of his neck. Why the hell was the phone ringing at this hour? Wasn't the damn switchboard picking up? He let it ring again before deciding to answer.

"Pendale Police, yes?"

"Hi, Captain. You okay?" It was MacDougall.

Jesus. "Kevin, what the hell are you doing calling now? Isn't the switchboard on? What time is it anyway?"

"It's almost midnight. Don't worry, the switchboard's picking up, I called and told them to patch me through. I tried you at home and got no answer. Thought you might be there. I was worried."

He was worried. Twenty-five-year-old, one hundred-forty-five pound Kevvy MacDougall was worried about him. Checking up. It's come to that. Clarke felt his throat catch just the same, and knew he was near tears.

"Captain, you there?"

"Yeah, Kevin, I'm here. Thanks. It was nice of you to call, but I'm fine, really. Just tidying up things. Tomorrow is going to be a hell of a day and I'm trying to get a jump."

"I bet you're right, about tomorrow, I mean. I feel really bad about this, Captain. I know it's all my fault. I'm the one who spoke with Mrs. Gorman and told you about Minna's breast cancer and everything."

"Don't be ridiculous, you did what you had to do. Anyway, the senior officer gets the praise when things go right and the blame when they go wrong. This'll be another learning experience for you. If you want to avoid my mistakes, watch and learn. Listen, while I have you, chances are I'll be busy with my superiors tomorrow, it'll be up to you to take care of some housekeeping. Let me jot a few things down to help you get organized."

Clarke looked for a pencil and found none. He opened his top desk drawer: paperclips, erasers, rubber bands, menus, and his reading glasses. "Shit."

"What's that, Captain?"

Clarke looked around and saw the empty pencil can. "Nothing, Kevin. Can't find a pencil."

"Try the pencil can."

"It's empty," answered Clarke, irritated. He slowly scanned his desktop from left to right. He stopped at his IN and OUT baskets in the far right corner.

He made a disgusted noise and lifted the Donez file from the top basket revealing a bunch of pencils. "Dumbass," he muttered under his breath.

"Sorry, Captain, I just thought I could help you find–"

"No, not you, Kevin, me. I used them to weigh down some papers and then buried them under the case file. I was stupid not to remember to look there. Okay, I'm going to leave a list for you to work through. Prioritize each–" He stopped.

"Captain?"

Silence.

"Captain, are you okay? Can you hear me?" Fear had crept into MacDougall's voice. Had tonight's disaster pushed the captain too far? Jeez, was he having a heart attack or something? "Captain!"

"I'm here, Kevin," Clarke said quietly.

"Oh, thank God," MacDougall said.

Clarke sat staring at his IN basket containing an array of paperwork and the fistful of pencils. He dropped the Donez file back on top and the pencils disappeared. In the basket, paper below, paper above, pencils hidden, out of sight.

"Kevin," Clarke said slowly, "when we were at the Cooper house tonight you searched through the garage, right?"

"Of course I did, first thing."

"What was in there?"

"Mainly gardening stuff, you know."

"Specifics, Kevin. What did you see?"

"Right, okay." Clarke could picture MacDougall screwing his eyes closed to better envision the garage interior. "On the back wall were a couple old bamboo poles. The kind ladies use to prop up their clothes lines. Along the wall on the floor were a bunch of ceramic flower pots. A couple stacks of them, the reddish-brown kind that sort of fit into each other. I was sure to look in the top ones. Empty. The left wall had a window and a work bench attached to the wall. The bench was cluttered with all kinds of garden hand tools, those little, ah, shovels-trowels, yeah, trowels. Also, those little claw things that you rip up hard ground with. I don't know what they're called, but I know I'd hate to get hit with one. There were jars of plant food and bug killer. A couple gloves and a floppy hat were there, too. On the opposite wall, next to a wheelbarrow were a couple bags of topsoil. They were still sealed, though. I banged into the wheelbarrow trying to get at them to check. There were some long, pointed sticks that I guess she used to stake up some of her plants. A spool of twine was hanging off a nail, too. The lawnmower was sitting dead center in the garage, a gas can next to it. I think that's it. Oh, yeah, one of those signs you see hanging in stores sometimes: Sorry I'm Closed, Be Back At and there's a clock. That was hanging off a nail, too. I guess she used to use it in the salon."

"You almost tripped over the wheelbarrow?"

"Yeah, nearly broke my neck. How would that be for embarrassing, huh? Like we didn't have enough as it was." He then realized what he'd said and Kevin quickly added, "I don't mean that we got embarrassed, Captain. I just mean, you know, we didn't find what we were looking for and everything."

"Tell me more about the wheelbarrow."

"Um, okay. It was standing next to the bags of topsoil. They were right up against the wall, so I kind of had to–"

"You tripped and almost fell."

"Right, it was–"

"But the wheelbarrow didn't tip."

"No, it–"

"Why not?"

"I was going to say. It was sort of weighed down. It was about half-full of topsoil."

"That's exactly what I remember, too."

"Um, okay," MacDougall said again.

"I walked into the garage just as the backhoe went to work. I saw pretty much what you did, though not in as much detail. The flower pots, workbench, lawnmower, bags of topsoil, and the wheelbarrow. Then Minna came up, trying to kill me with a glare and I looked away."

"Yeah, I remember that, too. She sure was smoking. Stood there in front of the garage the whole time we were there, arms folded over her chest. She was like a statue, wouldn't move."

"She *was* like a statue, wasn't she? I know I didn't want to go near her again."

"Heck, who would?"

"None of us, that's for certain. I avoided the entire area around where she stood. Including the garage." Clarke lifted the Donez file from his IN basket and looked again at the pencils. He let the file fall and they were gone.

"Kevin," he continued softly, "you're sure you gave the garage a thorough search before the digging began?"

"Oh, yeah, Captain. Top to bottom. I didn't miss an inch."

"What about the wheelbarrow?"

There was silence on the line. Then, "What do you mean?"

"I mean the wheelbarrow that you almost fell over," Clarke almost whispered. "The one that didn't tip because it was weighed down with topsoil. Did you search through the topsoil?" Clarke closed his eyes in silent prayer.

"Oh my God."

Yes!

"Minna planted herself in front of that garage," Clarke went on, picking up speed. "You said she was like a statue, a big, ugly statue making damn sure we'd steer clear of her. And steering clear of her, we'd have to steer clear of the garage, as well. As the night progressed and we found nothing we knew she'd become more and more angry. Another reason not to go near her. Kevin, she was making damn certain we wouldn't go back into that garage and look around again. Jesus! How could I be such an idiot! I let an angry old lady dissuade me from a proper search. We've got to get over there fast. Before she empties that wheelbarrow, if she hasn't already. Let's just hope she feels smug enough about fooling us to wait a bit before disposing of the breasts. Meet me there in ten minutes. And bring a flashlight!"

Clarke slammed the phone down and looked again at the IN basket. He lifted the case file, grabbed a bunch of pencils, kissed them, and tossed them to his desk as he ran from the room.

⤜ 41 ⤛

Nikki circled the block and waited in the shadows for the groups of neighbors to disperse and go home. When the last police car slipped away, she stepped out of the darkness, then hesitated. Better wait and be sure everybody's gone she thought, and she stepped once again into the shadows.

About fifteen minutes later she walked down the block and stopped at the corner of Bordentown and Augusta. She hesitated again, uncertain if she had the strength to do what lay ahead of her. It would be so much easier to just head downtown and latch on to some lecherous barfly with a few bucks on him. She almost turned to go when she thought of Mrs. Gorman. How would she feel if Nikki chose that road? The lady lost her husband, lost her tenant and then got her back. How would she cope if she lost her again? Man, Nikki thought, I can't even afford toilet paper and I'm worrying about the psychological welfare of my landlady. Crazy. She shook her head, crossed Augusta Street, and stood before Minna's Corner.

She walked around to the driveway and gasped at the degree of devastation. Even in the semi-darkness, the nearest streetlight being three houses away, Nikki was stunned by what she saw. There was barely a square foot of undisturbed lawn. What had not been dug up by the backhoe had been torn to pieces with the treads. Small piles of earth, flung seemingly at random, peppered the yard. Each flowerbed had been obliterated. In their place were shallow pits about three feet in depth, like the graves of little children. Pieces of bushes, stems, stalks, and leaves of various plants littered the scene. The house was dark, but Nikki knew Minna was not asleep. She couldn't be, not after what the police did to her yard. What they did to her.

Nikki slowly walked into the devastation, turned her head and peered into the darkness about her.

"What do you want, whore?"

She almost dropped to her knees in fright. The voice was ahead of her, a bit off to the left, behind the garage.

"I assumed you'd be either blind drunk or on your back paying for your last round." It came from the shadows. From the darkness beneath the roof of the gazebo, the one small space spared in the ruination.

Nikki walked toward the structure. As she got near, she saw a form sitting in the chair there. "That almost happened. If it wasn't for Mrs. Gorman, it would have."

"Rose," Minna's voice sneered. "Rescuing a stray, how so like her. Once Carl got the cure, she felt like she was God. She could fix anyone."

"That's not right. She supported Mr. Gorman, that's all. He had to do it himself. She forgave him and was there for him, he did the rest."

The voice made a noise of disgust. "Leave. If you know what's good for you, you'll drag your tramp ass out of here."

"No."

"You'd better listen to me, whore." The voice held menace.

Nikki trembled, but stayed put. "No," she said, with more assurance than she felt. "You owe me an apology. I won't leave until you tell me you're sorry for what you said earlier today."

"You want me to apologize to *you?* You, someone passed from man to man for the price of a few drinks? Someone who preys on men's weaknesses and ruins marriages? A piece of garbage this town, this world, would be better off without? You must be drunk now, to be demanding that."

"That's not–"

"You want me to apologize for thinking badly of you, for calling you names, you little slut?"

"No! That's not why. You can think whatever you want, call me anything you want, I don't care. I've probably thought and called myself worse."

"I doubt that."

"What you can't do," Nikki continued, shaking, "you can't say that Donald is better off dead than with me. It's not true. It's a lie. I know I messed up and I'm far from perfect–"

"Miles and miles and miles," said the voice from the gazebo.

"But I loved him and I know damn well for a long time, he loved me too. I may have screwed up at the end, but I was good for him and anyone who says differently is a liar."

"You, judging someone else, surely you're joking. How many men have you had? Any idea at all? Can't count that high? How many men have had you when you were passed out or just too drunk to care? How many?" the voice demanded. "How many wives wondering where their husbands have been? How many marriages on the brink of collapse because of you and whores like you? You harlot, you're not even human, you're a disease, a disease that kills what's good and healthy and natural!" The voice was strident. "You should–"

"Don't you tell me what I should or shouldn't!" Nikki screamed. Her voice echoed off the sides of houses in the still night. "I know all that! *I know!* I don't need some bloated relic from another generation passing antiquated judgment on me. Yeah, I'm everything you said! But I'm also someone who made

Donald happy. I bet I was a better girlfriend to Donald than you ever were a wife to your husband."

There was silence from the darkness. Then, a guttural, "How dare you? How dare your filthy, disease-ridden mouth mention my husband. You aren't worthy of thinking of him much less speaking of him."

There was a creak as Minna rose from the chair in the gazebo. She stepped forward and the muted light from the street told the toll the night had taken on her. The housedress she wore was stained with the mud and manure from her flowerbeds. Her knees were black from kneeling, trying to salvage any shreds from the destruction. The shoes on her feet were no more than huge clumps of earth. They looked like dark ponderous blocks. Her hair, usually carefully coiffed and neatly pinned, hung like gray tendrils around her haggard face. She appeared to have aged a decade in the several hours since she'd verbally eviscerated Nikki. Her left hand was wrapped around a shovel she leaned on like a walking staff. The upright blade was caked with dirt and the handle smeared with handprints.

Nikki was shocked by what she saw. This couldn't be the woman that had vilified her that afternoon. This woman appeared ready for the grave...yet not. There was something, something in Minna's eyes that caused Nikki to stumble over her words.

"Mrs. Cooper, you...you need to apologize to me for what you said. I don't care what you think of me, but you need to apologize. Do it, and I'll leave, I won't though, until you do."

Minna stepped down from the gazebo and walked slowly toward Nikki.

Nikki tensed, trying to stop her knees shaking. She was afraid she would wet herself.

Minna neared her, using the shovel for support. Nikki almost recoiled as the old woman slowly brushed by and said, "Follow me. I want to show you something."

Nikki watched in silence as Minna determinedly plowed through the damaged yard in the direction of the garage. The old woman didn't vary her pace, and never looked back.

As Minna reached the corner of the garage, Nikki did follow. It was dark inside. With the exception of a dim moonlit shadow coming through the window and another near the entrance, it was completely dark. Minna didn't hesitate in the darkness. As Nikki reached the mouth of the garage she saw Minna swallowed up, and if not for the sound of her dirt laden shoes on the hard-packed earthen floor, she would not have known she wasn't alone.

"Can't see, can you?" came the voice from the dark. "We can't have that."

There was a click followed instantly by a wild beam of light careening off the walls and floor of the structure. After a second's disorientation, Nikki saw an overhead light, shielded by a metal cone dangling by a thick electrical cord from the rafters. The low wattage bulb cast little more than a roving beam in the gloom. A beaded metal pull cord hung several inches below the cone. Tied to that was about three feet of fishing line with a weighted red and white bobber at the end, extending the length of the cord to within easy reach.

"I can't remember the last time I used the light," Minna said. "I know my way so well it's really unnecessary. In fact, when Arnie wired it in I told him it was just a waste of energy. But he said, 'You never know. Things can happen, can't have you falling over the mower, Min. There may be a time when this light is the difference between life and death.'" She smiled a ghastly smile. "My Arnie was like that, he loved me so much."

Minna beckoned Nikki into the garage. "Come in, come in."

Nikki took a tentative step and stood just inside the doorway. In the fluttering light Minna looked absolutely deranged.

Leaning on the shovel, Minna surveyed Nikki from head to foot. She shook her head. "You're not much to look at are you?"

"Mrs. Cooper, just apologize for earlier and I'll get out of here. I'm sure neither one of us wants each other's company."

A slow smile crept across Minna's face again. "You're wrong. Right now, there's no one I would rather be with." Jesus, she's freaking nuts, thought Nikki.

The old woman moved out of the light and Nikki could barely see her form for a moment. There was a clunk and the vague figure lowered a bit, then straightened again to full height and Nikki heard a soft grunt and creaking. Minna entered the cone of light, grasping the handles of an old, dented wheelbarrow. The shovel was lying across the top, lightly rocking back and forth as Minna bent her knees and set the wheelbarrow to rest.

"Always lift with your legs, never with your back, use your knees. But surely you know that, spending so much time on them."

"Look, Mrs. Cooper–"

"It's important to keep a strong back," Minna went on, "You never know when you may need to really exert yourself. With a weak back, you're useless."

Terrific, Nikki thought, fitness tips from a lunatic.

Minna again dragged her eyes over Nikki's body.

Nikki was a veteran of leers, gropes, and a multitude of perverts, but she'd never felt as vulnerable and violated as she did then. She crossed her arms over her chest.

Minna erupted in laughter. "Oh, my goodness," she cackled, "The lady is offended." The laughter continued, "What…just what do you think you're covering up? You look like a twelve-year-old boy!"

Nikki waited until the laughter began to subside. "I know what I look like. Why are–"

"Take that shirt off."

Nikki could not have heard correctly. "Are you–"

"Oh, stop it! I'm sure the majority of the men in town have seen your pitiful excuse for a chest, so don't waste my time with your false modesty."

"I don't know what kind of perv you are lady–"

"Whore, shut your mouth."

The words were spoken quietly, but they stopped Nikki cold. "Ah," said Minna, "so what you're called *does* matter."

Nikki was silent, hating this woman even more than that bubble-blonde, Stella.

"You want me to apologize. Remove that filthy shirt and I will. Show yourself to me and then I'll show you something of mine. Don't look like that, you tramp! I have no intention of disrobing in front of you! I won't disgust you with my tired, old, used-up body. No, there's something else you must see."

"Why the hell would you think, even for a second, I would do that?"

"My, such an impressive show of dignity! Why do I think you'll do what I want? Because it is what you know. You're the type of woman, when you want something, you barter for it with your body. It's as natural to you as breathing. Think about it, you want me to apologize for the nasty things I said to you. I will. I swear," said Minna, raising a grubby hand as if in court. "All you have to do is take off that sweat-stained rag and show me what's underneath."

Nikki glared at her, breathing heavily.

"Really, when you think about it, what is this in comparison to what you're accustomed to doing? This is nothing! Who will ever know? Nobody here but us girls." Minna grinned.

Nikki saw a chunk of dirt sticking to one of her incisors.

"Jesus," she muttered under her breath.

"That's it, you've decided to do it for old Aunt Minna, haven't you? Of course you have. After all, what is it to a woman like… you?"

"Shut up, Minna. Yeah, I'll do it, but you owe me something, right? We have a deal?"

"Oh, absolutely."

Nikki waited a second more, then in one swift motion pulled the shirt over her head. It hung from her hand at her side. Her virtually non-existent breasts looked almost pastel in the half-light of the garage. Two pale pink buds resting above prominent ribs, an almost hollow stomach and jutting pelvic bones.

Minna smiled at her and said, "I guess it's really true. Once a whore, always a whore."

Nikki felt herself flush in anger and said, "Now it's your turn. Apologize for what you said about me and Donald."

"Now, don't rush me," she shook her head. "Remember, I said I have something to show you. Trust me," she smiled. "You're going to love this."

⤐ 42 ⤏

"I don't give a damn what you may have. I don't want to see it. What I want is to hear–"

Minna picked up the handles of the wheelbarrow and rolled it a bit closer until it was almost directly under the gently swaying light. The shovel lying across it rattled back and forth.

"Shhhhhh," said Minna. "First you have to see this. It's something you can certainly appreciate," she said, looking at Nikki's chest.

What the hell is going on? Nikki asked herself. She looked into the barrow. Minna's shadow partially blocked the light, but there didn't seem to be much in the wheelbarrow. Nothing but a bunch of dirt, a lot of it loose with several clods.

Minna pulled the shovel off the wheelbarrow. It made a sharp scraping sound as it dragged over the metal. Minna used it once more for support.

"There," Minna said. "My own garden. A real woman's garden, don't you think? I'll nurture them and make sure they have plenty of food and water and provide nourishment for my little children as they sprout and bloom and add much needed beauty to this terrible world."

She's gone. Totally, freaking gone, thought Nikki.

"Here, look. It's so pretty. I know you wish it could be yours." Still using the shovel for support, Minna reached into the mass of dirt and gently lifted a clod about the size of a child's cupped hand. She held it in her palm, extending it toward Nikki.

Nikki felt a bead of sweat slide from the nape of her neck, slowly between her shoulder blades and down her back.

"Mrs. Cooper, I don't know what you're–"

"Here," said Minna, smiling, nodding her head toward Nikki. "Take it. Don't worry, I have others." She laughed. "You don't think I'd give you all I had, do you?"

The atmosphere in the garage became closer, heavier. Nikki longed to leave and return to the relatively fresh air outside. Yet…she couldn't.

She slowly reached out her hands for the clump of dirt. Minna gently placed it in her cupped hands. It was less solid than Nikki thought it would be. There was a certain give to it, especially on the bottom, the part resting against her palms. Most of the surface area was caked in dirt and grime, but there appeared to be areas of smoothness. In the poor lighting of the garage, the color seemed to be a uniform brownish-gray.

Nikki looked from her hands to Minna and shrugged.

"You stupid girl, this is what you've dreamt of, I know it is. Who knows how many nights you laid in bed wishing to possess what you now hold. Stupid, stupid." Minna shook her head and shuffled off in the darkness toward the workbench. "Maybe this will help."

Nikki lifted her hands until they were within inches of her face. She examined the object from various angles. Still, she had no idea what it was.

Minna emerged from the gloom, her right arm grasping the shovel for support and her left hand holding an old galvanized steel watering can.

"A little water should do the trick. We'll give it a nice shower and make it sparkle, all clean and fresh and pure. Don't you wish water could do the same for you? Wouldn't it be so much better?

No, I'm afraid you're well beyond what a light cleansing can do. Your sins won't wash away so easily. There are few options when it comes to atonement for you, my dear. Very few."

Nikki raised her eyes from her hands and glared silently at Minna.

"Hold out your hands," the older woman ordered.

Nikki extended her arms until her cupped palms were over the wheelbarrow and its contents.

Minna wrapped her arm around the shovel and used both hands to slowly pour the water from the can. It showered over Nikki's hands, warm as bathwater, beads ran down her forearms to her elbows and dripped to her sandaled feet.

Bits of dirt and grit flowed off the object in her hands through her fingers. Mud that had been caked on slowly shrank and vanished between her fingers.

Minna hummed tunelessly as she lifted the watering can higher to drain the water from its lower half.

Nikki saw the soiled object in her hands become smooth. In the half-light it still appeared mostly gray, but perhaps it was a shade closer to tan. At the base of Nikki's hands, where her palms met her wrists, was a small area about the size of a Kennedy half-dollar that appeared darker than the rest.

The flow of water ceased and Nikki brought her hands closer to her face. She heard the clang of the empty watering can set on the hard floor of the garage.

No, she thought, no, this isn't what it looks like. It can't be. Her face filled with horror as she heard Minna's voice say, "If that one doesn't appeal to you, I have a larger size. I know how important breasts can be to someone without."

Nikki looked from the severed breast she held in her hands to the wheelbarrow below. The cascading water had puddled in the soil there and washed most of the dirt from the three breasts which sat, like pastries on a tray, in the surrounding earth.

One matched in size the one she held in her hands. Two others, larger and lighter in color, lay amid flecks of grit and earth, rivulets of water running between them. Three tragic, isolated isles in a dark sea.

Nikki stood frozen, her hands still cupped around what once had rested against the heart of Rosaria Donez. She gaped at the contents of the wheelbarrow, still unable to comprehend what she was seeing. The air seemed to rush out of the stifling garage. She stood, solitary, a small, half-naked girl amid the horror created by a lunatic's longing. Part of her mind knew Minna was near, and she was in danger, but her body was immobile. The three, sad, dirt encrusted mounds held her.

From miles away she heard a voice say, "You won't be much of an addition to my collection, but I'll always know they're there and every spring when I watch my blooms open I'll remember how I made the world a better place by ridding it of your filth."

Nikki raised her eyes from the wheelbarrow and in doing so seemed to finally realize what exactly it was she held, cupped gently in her palms. She screamed and yanked her hands apart, dropping Rosaria's breast into the mud of the wheelbarrow, joining its mate. It made a damp plop as it landed, sending a small splash onto Nikki's bare legs. She instinctively pulled back, and in doing so she saw, in the murk, a dull flash as the blade of the shovel swung toward her head.

Minna roared in victory and anger as she swung the heavy blade of the shovel around her. Her arms, shoulders, and back, strengthened by years of work in her yard, accelerated the weight of the shovel's blade as it traveled from behind her body, around to make contact with the horrified face of the whore. Minna curled her lips back over her teeth in a snarl. Another piece of filth eradicated. Another destroyer of marriages and families sent straight to hell. Another pair of breasts, though barely more than nipples, for her garden.

As a flash of light exploded in Nikki's head, just before she lost consciousness, the sound of a squeal reached her ears, and what felt like a swarm of bees stung her legs.

At that same instant, the light in the garage lurched wildly from one side to the other, the metal cone jerked this way and that. A tolling bell of light gone berserk. It created a crazed picture, a dimly lit strobe reflecting on a scene of terror.

The police car's tires squealed as the vehicle jumped the curb and flew up the short gravel driveway. The car lurched to a stop just outside the garage entry, its headlights adding a harsh, piercing brilliance, tires sending bits of gravel flying at the garage and its occupants. Clarke slammed open the car door with his shoulder almost before the vehicle's forward motion had stopped. As he jumped from the car his mind tried to make sense of what was before him, just feet away.

Minna Cooper stood, screaming in rage, grasping the filthy handle of a long shovel. The shovel's dirt-caked blade was tangled in a piece of fishing line hanging suspended from the light, which danced erratically above her head. The weighted bobber had tangled the line around the shovel as it swung, snaring it, refusing to let it go. Minna's screams mixed with tears of frustration as she wrenched the handle, back, forth, up, down, trying to loosen it from the fishing line's near invisible grasp.

"NO, NO, NO! AAAGGHH!" Her shrieks became gasps as she pulled at the handle, propelling the frenzied beams of muted light off the floor and walls of the garage.

"AAAARNIE! NOOOO!"

Clarke halted at the garage threshold, nearly tripping over the body sprawled there. In the near darkness, a boy lay face down in the dirt, wearing a pair of cut off jeans and sandals. He was very thin, blood was pulsing from the left side of his head. His face, as well as his left shoulder and upper torso, were covered in blood.

Clarke quickly stepped over the body, grabbed Minna by her left wrist and twisted it behind her back. He pulled his cuffs from his belt and fastened them on her wrists behind her back before pushing her to her knees and then to the ground.

He turned to the body. The boy was moving, thank God. Perhaps his injuries weren't as horrific as they looked. Clarke pulled a not too clean handkerchief from his pocket and pressed it to the boy's wounded head.

"It's alright son, don't try to move. She's not going to hurt you." A hand gripped his arm like iron as the victim tried to speak. "Don't talk. I'll–"

Just then MacDougall's car skidded into the driveway nearly rear-ending Clarke's own.

That'd be hell to explain to the town council, thought Clarke crazily.

"Kevin! Radio for an ambulance! There's an injured boy here, head wound! I have Minna cuffed in the garage." As if to punctuate his words, Minna let out a snarl as she rocked on her side, trying, failing, to get upright.

"I'm...," the injured boy muttered, struggling to get on all fours.

"Hey, hey there, fella," Clarke said, holding the injured boy's head against his shoulder. "Don't go trying to be a hero, just stay put." The boy dropped on his back and Clarke caught him, cradling him against his body. Clarke looked down at the small figure. His chin the only part of the face not completely covered in blood. It was smeared with dirt, as were the kid's arms and much of the rest of him. His legs were bleeding, too. The flying gravel from the driveway had cut him up badly.

Man, this kid weighs next to nothing, he thought. Jesus, look as those ribs, it's like he hasn't eaten in a month. The belly, if you could call it that, rose and fell as he tried to speak.

"Shhh, quiet." Clarke tried to calm the victim. "You are one brave little guy. I don't know what you know about her, but this lady has hurt several women in town. She probably would have hurt you, as well." Clarke's mind raced, not knowing what to say, but knowing he had to comfort the injured boy. "You did a very dangerous thing tonight, helping us catch her."

The body tried again to speak, "I'm...I'm...," The ribcage rose and fell.

"You've lost some blood, son. You really don't want to exert yourself. Try to relax until the ambulance arrives." Clarke cradled the body, unconsciously, gently rocking back and forth on his knees. He continued speaking as much to calm himself as the injured boy.

"You know, I bet the mayor will want to meet you. Wouldn't that be something? Getting your picture taken with the mayor? Say, are you a scout? You in your Boy Scout uniform getting your picture taken shaking hands with Mayor Shultz. I bet your folks would be really proud."

Clarke felt the body begin to shake slightly in his arms. Oh, Jesus, he thought, what'd I say?

"Hey, little guy, don't cry. You're going to be fine. You don't have to have your picture taken if you don't want to. You're a hero, you can do whatever you want."

The shaking increased and Clarke feared it might be the onset of a seizure or something. Then he realized it wasn't sobbing he felt coming from this victim, it was spasms of laughter.

The blood-caked lips moved again and Clarke leaned over, trying to hear. "What is it, son?" He heard quick pants of breath and then, of all things, giggles. Rather high pitched giggles.

Kid hasn't hit puberty yet, he thought.

"I'm...I'm...,"

"Yes, yes, you're safe, it's alright, go ahead," he encouraged, his ear to the lips.

"I'm a girl," Nikki gasped, dissolving into a fit of laughter.

Clarke's eyes widened as he looked down at the body he held in his arms. No, there's no way, he thought. I mean…look, there's nothing there. Yet, as his gaze moved southward to the hips, he wasn't so sure. He continued down to the dirty bleeding legs and then back to the bare, jutting pelvic bones. Oh, shit.

"Kevin!" he yelled.

"Yeah, Captain," MacDougall said, running from his car. "Ambulance is on the way. Five minutes."

"Great. Get the blanket out of the trunk of my car. Fast."

"You're not cold are you, Captain? It's about a hundred degrees in this garage."

"Just do it!"

"Oh, Jeez, did he…is he…gone?" MacDougall nodded toward the body in Clarke's arms.

"No! He's…she's…get the goddamn blanket!"

MacDougall did an about face and ran to the rear of Clarke's car.

"Miss, I'm sorry. I didn't mean to insult you. I'm not sure why I…oh, God." He realized his arms were wrapped around her bare torso. "Would you rather I lay you down? I don't want you to feel uncomfortable. I don't usually–"

"No," Nikki choked out. The laughter subsided. "It feels safe."

"Okay," said Clarke, not knowing what else to say. He tried not looking down at the body in his arms. He strained his neck to see what the hell was keeping MacDougall.

"Officer?"

"Yes, miss?" Clarke willed his eyes to look only at her face. He saw tears flooding her eyes.

"She killed somebody, didn't she?"

Clarke wondered how he should answer and then thought of the scene that must have occurred just before he arrived. The young woman deserved the truth.

"Yes, she did. Two young women, we think. Maybe more."

"Definitely two, anyway," Nikki whispered through her tears.

Clarke looked down at her and opened his mouth to speak. How did she–

MacDougall came running with a khaki colored army blanket. "Sorry it took so long, it was wadded up under the spare. Where do you want it, Captain?"

"Where the hell do you think?" he growled. "Help me cover this young lady."

"What? But you said he's a–"

"Blanket!"

"Right." MacDougall opened the blanket and draped it over Nikki's dirty, bloody body, still in the embrace of Captain Clarke.

They heard the ambulance arrive at the bottom of the driveway and MacDougall ran to meet it.

"Why did you say, 'definitely two?' How would you know that?"

Tears ran from the corners of Nikki's eyes leaving trails in blood and dirt on her temples. "Those poor, poor women," she whispered. "What she did to them."

Clarke, drenched in sweat from the close proximity of her body under the blanket, leaned even closer. "How do you know what she did? Please, tell me," he whispered back, like two lovers, sharing a secret.

It took a few seconds for Nikki's trembling lips to form the word, but she finally was able. "Wheelbarrow."

Clarke looked down at the wounded body in his arms and nodded. Then he hugged her even closer as she sobbed for two women she'd never known.

⤜ 43 ⤝

The sight of the four severed breasts resting in the mud and soil was one that neither man would ever forget. Three sat as though placed there, soft flesh and nipples visible, the fourth, the one dropped by Nikki, lay apart from the others. The torn tissue once joined to Rosaria Donez's chest, facing upward. Signs of detached veins and hacked off muscle. God. All the while, in the background, Minna screamed and swore at her captors from where she lay. Kicking her plump legs at the men, denouncing them and all the whores of the world.

Clarke looked away from the wheelbarrow and toward Minna. He took a step toward her and stopped himself.

"Kevin, throw that bitch in the squad car. I don't trust myself near her."

"Um…um."

Clarke looked at his junior officer. MacDougall's normally red face was now a shocking pale. Eyes glued to the contents of the wheelbarrow, his Adam's apple was rising and falling quickly as he fought against being sick.

"Officer MacDougall!" Clarke yelled. MacDougall started and blinked a few times. "Put the suspect in the squad car!"

"Yessir!" MacDougall moved toward Minna.

The ambulance had just departed with Nikki. The attendants told the officers they couldn't be certain, but there didn't appear to be severe damage. Apparently the blow from the shovel had been a glancing one. She had surely been saved by the fact the shovel tangled in the fishing line.

They would admit her to the hospital and check for a concussion. There was a strong likelihood the police would be allowed to question her the following afternoon. Walking alongside the stretcher to the ambulance, Clarke held Nikki's hand and promised, at her insistence, to call Mrs. Gorman and let her know that Nikki was fine.

"The poor woman," Nikki said. "She's such a worrier, please call her right away."

Before she was slid into the rear of the vehicle, Nikki said, "Thank you...," she looked at Clarke's uniform insignia and said, "Captain?"

He nodded.

"You saved my life by being here. And you held me. Thank you so much." Tears again puddled in her eyes.

"It was nothing. I meant what I said before, you're very strong and brave. I'll be at the hospital tomorrow to see you."

The rear door slammed and Clarke lost sight of the tiny, dirty hand, slightly raised, waving goodbye.

What an amazing girl, he thought. This town, hell, this world, needs more like her.

MacDougall slammed the door closed behind Minna. There were tears in his eyes as he approached Clarke. He looked like he'd aged ten years since he arrived.

"Can you get her to the station and in a cell on your own?" asked Clarke.

MacDougall nodded. "I'll radio Sully just to be sure. I won't let her out of the car until he gets there."

"Good idea." He looked back at the garage and nodded in that direction. Get the state police out here. "They're going to want to take a look at the scene, as well as taking Minna off our hands. I'm going to…to place the remains of the two women in a safer place."

MacDougall looked back toward the wheelbarrow and his Adam's apple jumped again. "Right," he said, and headed to the squad car to radio for Sully.

Clarke slowly walked back into the garage. He looked again at the sad remains of Nora Wilson and Rosaria Donez. He needed to get the breasts to someplace cooler. Right away. They'd probably been buried in the topsoil and that had kept them reasonably cool, but now that they were exposed, decomposition would accelerate.

There was a small cardboard box, about the size of a large lunch pail on the workbench. He looked inside and saw it was almost empty save for a container of lime for the garden. He tossed the lime on the bench and returned to the wheelbarrow with the box. He looked around the murk for some tool to use to get the breasts into the box. The shovel still dangled from the fishing line hanging off the lamp, but the blade looked too large for the job. Searching the ground, he saw a trowel near the lawnmower. Clarke picked it up and approached his grisly task. He shoveled several spadefuls of dirt into the box as a base for the breasts. Then, sweat pouring down his face, he gently slid the trowel under one of the smaller breasts and tenderly lifted. He placed it and its mate into the box. He had trouble with the remaining pair. Being slightly larger, they would not stay on the blade of the trowel. After twice dropping one into the mud of the barrow he stepped back and sank to his knees. He burst into tears and pounded the trowel against the metal edge of the wheelbarrow, sending sparks and sharp clanks ringing into the night. A neighborhood dog began barking.

"You poor women," he whispered through his tears.

Clarke finally pushed himself to his feet and staggered back to the work bench. After a moment he found what he was looking for, a pair of heavy, canvas gloves. With the help of the gardening gloves, he was able to lift Nora's breasts with the trowel beneath and a hand on the side for support, from the mud to the box.

He closed the lid and gently placed the box on the passenger seat of the car. Upon arriving at the station he carried it to the small refrigerator in the back room and respectfully slid it on a shelf.

Minna left no doubt as to what had happened to the young women. In her hate-filled ramblings she informed the police of how she'd followed Rosaria to the waterworks that fateful night and crushed her skull. She'd been disgusted by Rosaria's brazen displays as she walked by Minna's house. It had been building for some time, and something, maybe the tenor of the times... something had snapped in the old woman and she took matters to hand. "Just like before," she said. Clarke figured that with more searching, perhaps under that gazebo of hers that went up about the time of Angela Castille's disappearance, they might find some remains of the missing woman. Even if not, there was more than enough evidence against Minna for the murders of Rosaria and Nora to be sure that she never spent another day of her life outside an institution.

When asked what she used to cut off the breasts of her victims, Minna smiled and asked, "What do *you* use for carving meat, Captain?"

They searched the kitchen of her house and found a carving knife still bloody with bits if tissue that were sure to belong to Nora Wilson. Minna had been sliding deeper and deeper into insanity, no longer taking the time to clean up after her crimes. It would have been only a matter of time before she was discovered, but how many other women she deemed "unworthy" of living would she have disposed of?

Their theory about Nora Wilson had been correct. While getting her hair cut she told Minna about her affair. She'd mentioned nothing about being pregnant, but Minna said she knew.

"You could tell. The way she held herself, fondled her belly, the whore. Imagine, being happy about something like that. Becoming pregnant by another woman's husband. What's wrong with these people?" she asked Clarke through the bars of her cell, genuinely puzzled.

They called in a doctor and had her sedated. A nurse sat just outside the cell to ensure nothing happened to her while she slept. Clarke stood in the doorway, just outside the hall. He saw the nurse reach into her handbag and pull out a battered copy of TIME magazine. Probably a relic from a hospital waiting room. "Is God Dead?" was the cover story. He wondered.

Spread over the table before Clarke and MacDougall was the detritus of the entire case, only five days old, but feeling like five months.

Vern Wilson had been transferred to the VA hospital. What they would do with him was anybody's guess. Without Nora, there was no way he'd be able to function in the world. In all likelihood, he'd be committed, medicated, and under observation somewhere until the day he died. Not much of a life for a war veteran, yet not much different from so many others returning from the conflict.

Marcus Rodriguez had decisions to make. None of them life or death, or needing to be made immediately, but someone like him was an oddity, especially in Pendale, especially in the Puerto Rican community. Or maybe not, thought Clarke. In this crazy new world, what the hell did he know about what was odd and what wasn't?

Clarke couldn't care less about who the guy shared his bed with, but knew Marcus would probably be better off elsewhere, rather than a small place like Pendale. How long would it be until one of the town's solid citizens found out his "secret" and hunted him down? Just to ensure the safety of their town's youngsters, of course.

Father Ryan was going to be under Clarke's microscope for as long as he remained in the area and it had nothing to do with the fact he'd been keeping company with Marcus. The man was just too self-assured, believing he simply could never be at fault, while the police invariably were. Condescending prick.

God knows what was in store for the McConnell family. Will certainly would never have to spend a full day in jail, but his troubles were far from over. Clarke doubted Lynn was forgiving enough to let his indiscretions pass. The handkerchief she'd found was a match for several they found in Nora Wilson's bureau. Why Will had shoved one in his pocket was anyone's guess. Clarke would be surprised if in the very near future Lynn and Eddie didn't move down to Millville, leaving Will to fend for himself. There was a strong possibility that in addition to being alone he might soon be unemployed. Tough shit for him, Clarke thought. Let's hope Lynn and little Eddie make it through this okay. He made a mental note to be sure and check up on them, after everything died down.

He looked across the table at MacDougall. These few days had significantly changed the young officer. Would he ever be able to look at the faces of the people in this town, the faces that he'd known his entire life, without wondering what truly lurked beneath the surface? In the space of a few hours he'd seen horror Clarke hadn't witnessed in an entire career. It would certainly have an effect.

Clarke had to wonder. Two terrible mutilations and murders, three if Angela Castille's corpse showed up. Clarke ordered the ground under Minna's gazebo excavated to search for remains. He should have done that last night he thought, maybe it would have saved that poor young girl, Nikki, her harrowing experience. At any rate, if the remains were there, they'd keep another day or so. They had for about fifteen years already.

Clarke's eyes scanned the file in front of him. Will McConnell screwing around on his wife and family, Marcus Rodriguez and Father Ryan doing…whatever…. Crazy Vern Wilson, and maybe most troubling of all, the way almost the entire town seemed to dismiss Rosaria Donez's awful death as insignificant. What the hell was happening? This callous disregard for morals, community, life itself, was it unique to Pendale? Did they live in an isolated pocket of bigotry and hate? Clarke feared for his town, but more than that, feared they had become the rule, rather than the exception. The entire country, maybe the world, was a much colder, uncaring place than he could ever remember it being. He sighed.

"How about a little music to greet this lovely Wednesday morning?" He gave MacDougall a tired smile and walked into his office. He unplugged the radio and brought it into the coffee room.

"Is it the same or worse?" MacDougall asked.

"Hmm?" Clarke grunted as he bent over to plug into an outlet.

"It's the same as I remember as a kid…. What people used to think of others that are somehow different. What *I* used to think about them. It's awful. And even though it's the same, it feels worse now. So much worse."

Clarke placed the radio on the table between them, and turned the knob. He slumped in his chair and thought before answering.

"I think it feels worse because we can see now how bad it's been. At least we can recognize the fact there's a problem. I guess it means we're making progress. I hope we're getting better anyway. We can't control what's going on in the world. We can only do our best to ensure there's some civility here…in our town, our home. It's not just about law enforcement anymore, now it's modeling proper behavior, values. You're a good man, Kevin," he said, looking into the eyes of the young man. "If folks use you as a model, the world will be a better place. So, let's hope it doesn't get worse. Let's hope there's a change for the better."

The static cleared and the voice of the newscaster intoned, "At twelve-fifteen Pacific time this morning, Senator Robert Kennedy was shot minutes after claiming victory in the California Democratic Primary…"

As the voice droned on the men looked to each other and then away, each lost in his own thoughts.

⤜ 44 ⤛

That afternoon, Nikki opened her eyes and saw the face of Rose Gorman above her.

"Hey, Mrs. G.," she said with a weak smile. She saw the rosary in the woman's hands. "Don't tell me you're on your way to church again."

"No, Nikki, not without you. You have a lot to give thanks for."

"More church?" she said, eyes closing. "You're one tough cookie, Mrs. G." Eyes closed, her smile widened, "Sure…why the hell not?"

"Language, Nikki," said a smiling Mrs. Gorman. "Not today, but soon."

"Yeah," Nikki whispered, "why not?"

Made in the USA
Monee, IL
05 June 2021